# STEPSISTER

## JENNIFER DONNELLY

Scholastic Inc.

To everyone who's ever felt
that they're not enough

Copyright © 2019 by Jennifer Donnelly

This book was originally published in hardcover by Scholastic Press in 2019.

All rights reserved. Published by Scholastic Inc., *Publishers since 1920.* SCHOLASTIC and associated logos are trademarks and/or registered trademarks of Scholastic Inc.

The publisher does not have any control over and does not assume any responsibility for author or third-party websites or their content.

No part of this publication may be reproduced, stored in a retrieval system, or transmitted in any form or by any means, electronic, mechanical, photocopying, recording, or otherwise, without written permission of the publisher. For information regarding permission, write to Scholastic Inc., Attention: Permissions Department, 557 Broadway, New York, NY 10012.

This book is a work of fiction. Names, characters, places, and incidents are either the product of the author's imagination or are used fictitiously, and any resemblance to actual persons, living or dead, business establishments, events, or locales is entirely coincidental.

ISBN 978-1-338-26847-8

10 9 8 7 6 5 4 3 2 1       20 21 22 23 24

Printed in the U.S.A. 23
This edition first printing 2020

Book design by Maeve Norton

This is a dark tale. A grim tale.

It's a tale from another time, a time when wolves waited for girls in the forest, beasts paced the halls of cursed castles, and witches lurked in gingerbread houses with sugar-kissed roofs.

That time is long gone.

But the wolves are still here and twice as clever. The beasts remain. And death still hides in a dusting of white.

It's grim for any girl who loses her way.

Grimmer still for a girl who loses herself.

Know that it's dangerous to stray from the path.

But it's far more dangerous not to.

# PROLOGUE

Once upon always and never again, in an ancient city by the sea, three sisters worked by candlelight.

The first was a maiden. Her hair, long and loose, was the color of the morning sun. She wore a gown of white and a necklace of pearls. In her slender hands, she held a golden scissors, which she used to cut lengths of the finest parchment.

The second, a mother, ample and strong, wore a gown of crimson. Rubies circled her neck. Her red hair, as fiery as a summer sunset, was gathered into a braid. She held a silver compass.

The third was a crone, crookbacked and shrewd. Her gown was black; her only adornment was a ring of obsidian, incised with a skull. She wore her snow-white hair in a coil. Her gnarled, ink-stained fingers held a quill.

The crone's eyes, like those of her sisters, were a forbidding gray, as cold and pitiless as the sea.

At a sudden clap of thunder, she raised her gaze from the long wooden worktable at which she sat to the open doors of her balcony. A storm howled down upon the city. Rain scoured the rooftops of its grand palazzos. Lightning split the night. From every church tower, bells tolled a warning.

"The water is rising," she said. "The city will flood."

"We are high above the water. It cannot touch us. It cannot stop us," said the mother.

1

"Nothing can stop us," said the maiden.

The crone's eyes narrowed. "*He* can."

"The servants are watchful," said the mother. "He will not get in."

"Perhaps he already has," said the crone.

At this, the mother and the maiden looked up. Their wary eyes darted around the cavernous room, but they saw no intruder, only their cloaked and hooded servants going about their tasks. Relieved, they returned to their work, but the crone remained watchful.

Mapmaking was the sisters' trade, but no one ever came to buy their maps, for they could not be had at any price.

Each was exquisitely drawn, using feathers from a black swan.

Each was sumptuously colored with inks mixed from indigo, gold, ground pearl, and other things—things far more difficult to procure.

Each used time as its unit of measure, not distance, for each map charted the course of a human life.

"Roses, rum, and ruin," the crone muttered, sniffing the air. "Can you not smell them? Smell *him*?"

"It's only the wind," soothed the mother. "It carries the scents of the city."

Still muttering, the crone dipped her quill into an inkpot. Tapers flickered in silver candelabra as she drew the landscape of a life. A raven, coal black and bright-eyed, roosted on the mantel. A tall clock in an ebony case stood against one wall. Its pendulum, a human skull, swung slowly back and forth, ticking away seconds, hours, years, lives.

The room was shaped like a spider. The sisters' workspace, in the center, was the creature's body. Long rows of towering shelves led off the center like a spider's many legs. Glass doors that led out to the balcony were at one end of the room; a pair of carved wooden doors loomed at the other.

The crone finished her map. She held a stick of red sealing wax in a candle flame, dripped it onto the bottom of the document, then pressed her ring into it. When the seal had hardened, she rolled the map, tied it with a black ribbon, and handed it to a servant. He disappeared down one of the rows to shelve the map, carrying a candle to light his way.

That's when it happened.

Another servant, his head down, walked between the crone and the open balcony doors behind her. As he did, a gust of wind blew over him, filling the room with the rich scent of smoke and spices. The crone's nostrils flared. She whirled around.

"You there!" she cried, lunging at him. Her clawlike hand caught hold of his hood. It fell from his head, revealing a young man with amber eyes, dark skin, and long black braids. "Seize him!" she hissed.

A dozen servants rushed at the man, but as they closed in, another gust blew out the candles. By the time they had slammed the doors shut and relit the candles, all that remained of the man was his cloak, cast off and puddled on the floor.

The crone paced back and forth, shouting at the servants. They poured down the dusky rows, their cloaks flying behind them, trying to flush the intruder out. A moment later, he burst out from behind one of the shelves, skidding to a stop a few feet from the crone. He darted to the wooden doors and frantically tried the handle, but it was locked. Swearing under his breath, he turned to the three sisters, flashed a quicksilver smile, and swept them a bow.

He was dressed in a sky-blue frock coat, leather britches, and tall boots. A gold ring dangled from one ear; a cutlass hung from his hip. His face was as beautiful as daybreak, his smile as bewitching as midnight. His eyes promised the world, and everything in it.

But the sisters were unmoved by his beauty. One by one, they spoke.

3

"Luck," hissed the maiden.

"Risk," the mother spat.

"Hazard," snarled the crone.

"I prefer Chance. It has a nicer ring," the man said, with a wink.

"It's been a long time since you paid us a visit," said the crone.

"I should drop by more often," said Chance. "It's always a pleasure to visit the Fates. You're so spontaneous, so wild and unpredictable. It's always a party, this place. A regular bacchanal. It's so. Much. *Fun.*"

A handful of servants spilled out from between the shelves, red-faced and winded. Chance pulled his cutlass from its scabbard. The blade glinted in the candlelight. The servants stepped back.

"Whose map have you stolen this time?" the crone asked. "What empress or general has begged your favor?"

Still holding his cutlass in one hand, Chance drew a map from his coat with the other. He tugged the ribbon off with his teeth, then gave the parchment a shake. It unrolled, and he held it up. As the three women stared at it, their expressions changed from anger to confusion.

"I see a house, the Maison Douleur, in the village of Saint-Michel," the crone said.

"It's the home of—" said the matron.

"A girl. Isabelle de la Paumé," the crone finished.

"*Who?*" asked the maiden.

"All this trouble for a mere girl?" asked the crone, regarding Chance closely. "She's nothing, a nobody. She possesses neither beauty nor wit. She's selfish. Mean. Why her?"

"Because I can't resist a challenge," Chance replied. He rerolled the map with one hand, steadying it against his chest, then tucked it back inside his coat. "And what girl wouldn't choose what I offer?" He gestured at himself, as if even he couldn't believe how irresistible he was. "I'll give her the chance to change the path she is on. The chance to make her *own* path."

"Fool," said the crone. "You understand nothing of mortals. We Fates map out their lives because they wish it. Mortals do not like uncertainty. They do not like change. Change is frightening. Change is painful."

"Change is a kiss in the dark. A rose in the snow. A wild road on a windy night," Chance countered.

"Monsters live in the dark. Roses die in the snow. Girls get lost on wild roads," the crone shot back.

But Chance would not be discouraged. He sheathed his cutlass and held out his hand. As if by magic, a gold coin appeared in his fingers. "I'll make you a bet," he said.

"You push me too far," the crone growled, fury gathering like a storm in her eyes.

Chance flipped the coin at the crone. She snatched it from the air and slammed it down on the table.

The storm broke.

"Do you think a *coin* can pay for what you've set loose?" she raged. "A warlord rampages across France. Death reaps a harvest of bones. A kingdom totters. All because of *you*!"

Chance's smile slipped. For a few seconds, his fiery bravado dimmed. "I'll fix it. I swear it."

"With *that* girl's map?"

"She was brave once. She was good."

"Your head is even emptier than your promises," the crone said. "Open the map again. Read it this time. See what becomes of her."

Chance did so. His eyes followed the girl's path across the parchment. The breath went out of him as he saw its end . . . the blotches and hatches, the violent lines. His eyes sought the crone's. "This ending . . . It's not . . . It *can't* be—"

"Do you still think you can fix this?" the crone mocked.

Chance took a step toward her, his chin raised. "I offer you high stakes. If I lose this wager, I will never come to the palazzo again."

"And if *I* lose?"

"You allow me to keep this map. Allow the girl to direct her own steps forevermore."

"I do not like those stakes," the crone said. She waved her hand, and her servants, who had been slowly edging closer to Chance, charged at him. Some were bearing cutlasses of their own now. Chance was trapped. Or so it seemed.

"There's no hope of escape. Give me back the map," said the crone, holding out her hand.

"There's always hope," Chance said, tucking the map back into his coat. He took a few running steps, launched himself into a flip, and flew over the heads of the servants. He landed on the worktable with the grace of a panther and ran down its length. When he reached the end, he jumped to the floor, then sped to the balcony.

"You are caught now, rogue!" the crone shouted after him. "We are three stories high! What can you do? Leap across the canal? Even *you* are not that lucky!"

Chance wrenched open the balcony's doors and leapt up onto its railing. The rain had stopped, but the marble was still wet and slippery. His body pitched back and forth. His arms windmilled. Just as it looked as if he would surely fall, he managed to steady himself, balancing gingerly on his toes.

"The map. *Now*," the crone demanded. She had walked out onto the balcony and was only a few feet away from him. Her sisters joined her.

Chance glanced back at the Fates; then he somersaulted into the air. The crone gasped. She rushed to the railing, her sisters right behind her, expecting to see him drowning in the swirling waters below.

But he was not. He was lying on his back, cradled in the canopy of a gondola. The boat was rocking violently from side to side, but Chance was fine.

"Row, my fine fellow!" he called to the gondolier. The man obliged. The boat moved off.

Chance sat up, eyeing the Fates with a diamond-bright intensity. "You *must* accept my stakes now! You have no choice!" he shouted.

The gondola grew smaller and smaller as it made its way down the canal. A moment later, it rounded a bend and disappeared.

"This is a bad state of affairs," the crone said darkly. "We cannot have mortals making their own choices. When they do, disaster follows."

The maiden and the mother stepped back into the room. The crone trailed them. "Pack a trunk," she barked at a servant. "I'll need quills and inks . . ." Her hand hovered over the bottles upon the table. She selected a deep ebony. "*Fear*, yes. *Jealousy* will be useful, too," she said, reaching for a poisonous green.

"Where are you going?" the maiden asked.

"To the village of Saint-Michel," the crone replied.

"You will stop Chance from taking hold of the girl?" asked the mother.

The crone smiled grimly. "No, I cannot. But I will do what we Fates have always done. I will stop the girl from taking hold of a chance."

## ONE

In the kitchen of a grand mansion, a girl sat clutching a knife.

Her name was Isabelle. She was not pretty.

She held the knife's blade over the flames of a fire burning in the hearth. Behind her, sprawled half-conscious in another chair, was her sister, Octavia.

Octavia's face was deathly pale. Her eyes were closed. The once-white stocking covering her right foot was crimson with blood. Adélie, the sisters' old nursemaid, peeled it off and gasped. Octavia's heel was gone. Blood dripped from the ugly wound where it used to be and pooled on the floor. Though she tried to hold it in, a moan of pain escaped her.

"Hush, Tavi!" Maman scolded. "The prince will hear you! Just because your chances are ruined doesn't mean your sister's must be."

Maman was the girls' mother. She was standing by the sink, rinsing blood out of a glass slipper.

The prince had come searching for the one who'd worn it. He'd danced all night with a beautiful girl at a masquerade ball three days ago and had fallen in love with her, but at the stroke of midnight, the girl had run away, leaving only a glass slipper behind. He would marry the girl who'd worn it, he'd vowed. Her and no other.

Maman was determined that one of her daughters would be that girl. She'd greeted the royal party in the foyer and requested that Isabelle and Octavia be allowed to try the slipper on in privacy, in deference to their maidenly modesty. The prince had agreed. The grand duke had held out a velvet pillow. Maman had carefully lifted the slipper off it and carried it into the kitchen. Her daughters had followed her.

"We should've heated the blade for Tavi," Maman fretted now. "Why didn't I think of it? Heat sears the vessels. It stops the bleeding. Ah, well. It will go better for you, Isabelle."

Isabelle swallowed. "But, Maman, how will I walk?" she asked in a small voice.

"Silly girl! You will *ride*. In a golden carriage. Servants will lift you in and out."

Flames licked the silver blade. It grew red. Isabelle's eyes grew large with fear. She thought of a stallion, lost to her now, that she had once loved.

"But, Maman, how will I gallop through the forest?"

"The time has come to put childish pursuits aside," Maman said, drying the slipper. "I've bankrupted myself trying to attract suitors for you and your sister. Pretty gowns and fine jewels cost a fortune. A girl's only hope in life is to make a good marriage, and there's no finer match than the prince of France."

"I can't do it," Isabelle whispered. "I *can't*."

Maman put the glass slipper down. She walked to the hearth and took Isabelle's face in her hands. "Listen to me, child, and listen well. Love is pain. Love is sacrifice. The sooner you learn that, the better."

Isabelle squeezed her eyes shut. She shook her head.

Maman released her. She was silent for a bit. When she finally spoke again, her voice was cold, but her words were scalding.

"You are ugly, Isabelle. Dull. Lumpy as a dumpling. I could not even convince the schoolmaster's knock-kneed clod of a son to marry you. Now a prince waits on the other side of the door—a *prince*, Isabelle— and all you have to do to make him yours is cut off a few toes. Just a few useless little toes . . ."

Maman wielded shame like an assassin wields a dagger, driving it straight into her victim's heart. She would win; she always won. Isabelle knew that. How many times had she cut away parts of herself at her

10

mother's demand? The part that laughed too loudly. That rode too fast and jumped too high. The part that wished for a second helping, more gravy, a bigger slice of cake.

*If I marry the prince, I will be a princess*, Isabelle thought. *And one day, a queen. And no one will dare call me ugly ever again.*

She opened her eyes.

"Good girl. Be brave. Be quick," Maman said. "Cut at the joint."

Isabelle pulled the blade from the flames.

And tried to forget the rest.

## – TWO –

The little toe was the hardest.

Which didn't come as a surprise. It's often the small things that hurt the most—a cold glance, a cutting word, laughter that stops when you enter the room.

"Keep going," Maman urged. "Think of what we will gain—a prince for you, perhaps a duke for Tavi, a home for us all in the palace!"

Isabelle heard the desperation in her mother's voice. She knew that the dressmaker had cut off their credit and that the butcher had sent a boy to the house with an overdue bill. She tightened her grip on the knife and finished what she'd started.

The blinding pain, the smell of seared flesh, and the sight of her own toes lying on the hearth were so horrible that for a few seconds Isabelle was certain she would faint, but then Adélie was at her side with gentle hands and soothing words.

A wad of soft cotton was brought. A fresh white stocking. Brandy. And the glass slipper.

Maman handed it to her. "Put it on. Hurry," she said.

11

Isabelle took it. It was heavy in her hands and cold to the touch. As she slid her foot into it, pain bit into her, sharp-toothed and savage. It moved up her leg and through her body until she felt as if she were being eaten alive. The blood drained from her face. She closed her eyes and gripped the arms of her chair.

And yet, when Maman demanded that she get up, Isabelle did. She opened her eyes, took a deep breath, and stood.

Isabelle could do this impossible thing because she had a gift—a gift far more valuable than a pretty face or dainty feet.

Isabelle had a strong will.

She did not know that this was a good thing for a girl to have, because everyone had always told her it was a terrible thing. Everyone said a girl with a strong will would come to a bad end. Everyone said a girl's will must be bent to the wishes of those who know what's best for her.

Isabelle was young, only sixteen; she had not yet learned that everyone is a fool.

## - THREE -

Each step was agony.

Halfway down the hallway that led from the kitchen to the foyer, Isabelle faltered. She heard a thin, rising wail. Had it come from her?

"It's Ella," Maman said darkly. "Hurry, Isabelle. We must finish this business. What if the prince hears her?"

Just before the prince had arrived, Isabelle had locked Ella in the attic. Ella had wept. She'd begged Isabelle to let her out. She wanted to see the prince. She wanted to try the glass slipper.

"Don't be ridiculous," Isabelle had told her. "You didn't even go to the ball. You'd only embarrass us in your ragged dress."

It was a cruel thing to have done. She'd known it even as she'd turned the key in the lock, but it hadn't stopped her. Nothing stopped her anymore. *God in Heaven, what have I become?* she wondered, as she heard another wail.

Maman eyed her closely, so closely that Isabelle felt she could see inside her.

"Let her out, Isabelle. Do," she said. "The prince will take one look at her and fall head over heels in love, like every other man who sees her. Do you want to be kind or do you want the prince?"

Isabelle tried but could not find an answer. The choices Maman gave her fit no better than the slipper did. An image flashed into her mind, a memory from long ago. She, Tavi, and Ella had been playing under the ancient linden tree that shaded the mansion.

A carriage had pulled into the yard. Two men, associates of Ella's father—Isabelle and Tavi's stepfather—had gotten out. Being genial, well-mannered men, they'd stopped to chat with the girls, but what happened next had changed everything.

Isabelle wished she could go back in time. She wished she could stop what had been put in motion that day, but she didn't know how.

And now it was too late.

*Who set us against each other, Ella?* she wondered. *Was it those men? Was it Maman? Or was it the whole heartless world?*

## - FOUR -

"Keep your weight on your heel. That will help with the pain," Maman advised. "Come now. Hurry."

She pinched color into Isabelle's bloodless cheeks, and together they continued down the hallway.

The prince, the grand duke, and the soldiers who'd accompanied them were all in the foyer, waiting for her. Isabelle knew she must not fail as her sister had.

Tavi had fooled everyone at first, but as she'd walked out of the house to the prince's carriage, her heel had bled so much that she'd left carmine footprints on the ground.

No one had noticed the bloody tracks in all the excitement, but as Tavi had neared the carriage, a white dove had flown out of the linden tree. The bird had landed on the prince's shoulder and had begun to sing.

*Blood on the ground! Blood on the shoe!*
*This false, heartless girl is lying to you!*

The prince had paled at the sight of so much blood. The grand duke, a rangy, wolfish-looking man, had become furious when he'd learned that his sovereign had been tricked. He'd demanded that Maman return the glass slipper, but Maman had refused. She'd insisted that Isabelle had a right to try the slipper, too, for the prince had decreed that every maiden in the kingdom could do so.

"Are you ready?" Maman whispered to Isabelle now, as they approached the foyer.

Isabelle nodded, then walked out to greet the prince. She'd glimpsed him at the ball, but only from a distance, and when he'd arrived at the mansion, Maman had quickly ushered her into the kitchen.

Now, standing only a few feet away from him, she could see that his eyes were the blue of a summer sky, and that his blond hair—worn long and loose and tumbling over his shoulders—was shot through

14

with streaks of pure gold. He was tall and broad-shouldered. His color was high.

Gazing at him, Isabelle forgot her wound, her pain, her own name. She was stunned speechless. He was that handsome.

The prince was silent, too. He was staring at Isabelle intently, his eyes taking in every plane and angle of her face.

"Ah, do you see that? He recognizes his own true love!" Maman purred.

Isabelle shrank at her mother's lie. Everyone at the ball had worn masks that covered the tops of their faces. She knew what the prince was doing—he was searching the curve of her lips, the line of her jaw, and the tilt of her chin for traces of the girl he'd fallen in love with.

But that girl wasn't there.

## - FIVE -

Isabelle and the prince continued to stare at each other. Awkwardly. Silently. Until Maman took charge.

"Your Grace," she said, pulling Isabelle down into a curtsy with her. "My younger daughter is the one you are seeking. The glass slipper fits her perfectly."

"I hope you are certain of this, madame," the grand duke cautioned. "The prince will not look kindly on a second attempt to deceive him."

Maman bowed her head. "Please forgive Octavia," she said to the prince. "She is not a dishonest girl. Her only fault is that she was overwhelmed by love for you. What girl wouldn't be?"

The prince blushed at that. The grand duke did not. "May we see the slipper?" he asked impatiently.

Isabelle and Maman rose. Dread knotted Isabelle's stomach as she lifted the hem of her dress. All eyes went to her foot. To her immense relief, there was no blood. The stocking was as white as snow, and the

15

cotton Adélie had stuffed into it filled out the toe. The glass slipper itself sparkled with blue light.

"It fits," said the prince dully.

The grand duke and the soldiers—every single one—bowed to Isabelle.

"Long live the princess!" a captain shouted.

"Long live the princess!" the rest of the company echoed.

Hats were tossed up into the air. Cheers rose, too. Isabelle turned in a slow circle, astonished. For once, the admiration was for her, not Ella. For once, she felt proud, powerful, wanted. Only moments ago, she hadn't been good enough for the schoolmaster's son; now she was going to be a princess.

"We must travel to the palace, mademoiselle," the prince said to her, with a stiff smile. "There are many arrangements to make for the wedding."

He bowed curtly, then headed for the door, and Isabelle saw that his strong shoulders sagged and that the light was gone from his beautiful eyes.

*The prince loves someone else; he longs for her,* Isabelle thought. *If I go through with this, I won't be gaining a husband, I'll be taking a prisoner.*

She felt sick, poisoned by a thing she thought she wanted. Just like the time when she was little and Adélie had made a batch of tiny cherry cakes and left them to cool and she'd eaten every single one.

She turned to her mother, ready to say, "This is wrong," but as she did, she saw that Maman was beaming at her. For a few precious seconds, Isabelle basked in the warmth of her mother's smile. She so rarely saw it.

"I'm proud of you, child," Maman said. "You've saved us from ruin. I shall sell this gloomy house, pay off our debts, and never look back."

Isabelle's protests died in her throat. It was a terrible thing to break the prince's heart, but it was a worse thing to break her mother's. She did not, for even a second, consider what her own heart wanted, for a girl's desires were of no consequence.

Maman took Isabelle's arm and walked her out to the stone steps that swept from the mansion's front door down to its graveled drive. Isabelle could see a golden carriage drawn by eight white horses. The prince and the grand duke stood by it, waiting for her, deep in conversation.

Furrows marred the prince's brow. Worry clouded his eyes. Isabelle knew, as did everyone else, that his father was gravely ill and that a foreign duke, Volkmar von Bruch, had scented the old king's death and had brutally attacked villages along his realm's northern border.

Maman embraced Isabelle, promising that she and Tavi would follow her to the palace as soon as they could. And then, in a daze, Isabelle started for the carriage, but stepping down required that she put her full weight on her damaged foot. Halfway down the steps, the seared veins opened. She could feel blood, wet and warm, seeping into her stocking. By the time she reached the bottom step, it was soaked.

High above her, in the branches of the linden tree, the leaves began to rustle.

- SIX -

The carriage was only ten steps away. Then seven. Then five.

A soldier opened the door for her. Isabelle kept her gaze trained straight ahead. The prince and the grand duke, still deep in conversation, weren't even looking at her. She would make it. She was almost there. Just a few steps. Three more ... two ... one ...

That's when she heard it—the flapping of wings.

A white dove swooped down out of the linden tree and circled her.

17

Maman, who'd been watching from the doorway, ran down and frantically tried to swat it away, but the wary bird kept itself above her reach. As it flew around Isabelle, it began to sing.

*Blood on the ground! Blood in the shoe!*
*This is a girl neither honest nor true!*

The prince stopped talking. He looked at the dove, then at Isabelle. His eyes traveled to the hem of her dress, which was stained with blood, then to the dark tracks she'd left in the dirt.

Isabelle slid her foot out of the glass slipper and took a step back from it. It toppled over, spilling more blood on the ground. The front of her stocking was bright red. Shame flooded through her.

"You cut off your own toes," the prince said, shaking his head in disbelief.

Isabelle nodded, frightened now as well as ashamed. She'd deceived him. God only knew what he would do to her. She'd heard grisly stories about palace dungeons and heads stuck on pikes. Was that to be her fate?

But the prince didn't order his soldiers to seize her. There was no anger on his face, only sadness. And something else, something Isabelle had not expected to see—kindness.

"How did you stand the pain?" he asked.

Isabelle looked at the ground. Maman's words, spoken earlier in the kitchen, came back to her.

*Ugly ... dull ... lumpy as a dumpling ...*

"I've had a lot of practice," she replied.

The prince frowned. "I don't understand."

Isabelle lifted her head. She looked at his heartbreakingly handsome face. "No," she said. "You don't."

The grand duke joined them, fury sparking in his eyes. "I know battle-hardened soldiers who could not do what you did, mademoiselle," he said to Isabelle. Then he turned to the prince. "A girl capable of such an act is capable of anything, sire. She is unnatural. Unhinged. Dangerous." He motioned at a pair of soldiers. "Seize her."

Isabelle's heart lurched with terror as the two men started toward her, but the prince stopped them.

"Leave her," he ordered, waving them away.

"But, Your Grace, surely you will not allow a second deception to go unpunished," said the grand duke. "One is bad enough, but two—"

"I said *leave her*. She has injured herself grievously. What more could I do to her?"

The grand duke gave him a clipped nod. Then he addressed Maman. "I don't suppose you have any other daughters eager to cut off bits of themselves in order to marry the prince?"

"No," Maman said bitterly. "I have no other daughters."

"Then we shall be going," said the grand duke. "Good day, madame."

A fountain burbled in the center of the drive. As the prince climbed into the carriage, the grand duke, who was still holding the velvet cushion, ordered a soldier to rinse the glass slipper off in the water. The soldier did, then placed it back on the cushion. Maman stood watching them, rigid with anger.

Isabelle, light-headed from her ordeal, sat down on a bench under the linden tree. She closed her eyes, trying to make her head stop spinning. She was dimly aware of the horses stamping, impatient to be off. Of bugs whirring in the afternoon heat. Of the dove, now cooing high above her in the branches.

But then a new sound rose above these others—urgent and piercing. "Wait! Don't go! Please, please, wait!"

It was a girl's voice. It was coming from the mansion. She was shouting. Pleading.

Isabelle opened her eyes.

The girl was running down the steps. Her hair was wild. Her dress was little more than rags. Her face and hands were streaked with soot. Her feet were bare.

But even so, she was astonishingly, achingly, breathtakingly beautiful.

It was Ella.

Isabelle's stepsister.

## – SEVEN –

The grand duke gave Maman a deadly look.

"Is this another of your tricks, madame? Sending out a filthy serving wench to try the slipper?" he asked indignantly.

Maman's eyes narrowed as she regarded her stepdaughter. "Ella, how dare you!" she shouted. "Go back inside this instant!"

But Ella didn't even hear her. Her eyes were on the prince, and the prince's eyes were on her. He was already out of the carriage, hurrying toward her.

Watching them, Isabelle saw something she had never seen before. Not between her mother and stepfather, or her mother and father. It was raw and overwhelming. Powerful, deep, and true. It was love.

As Isabelle saw this love, intangible yet so real, she realized that Ella was the one the prince had danced with at the ball, that she was the one he longed for.

Envy's fine, sharp teeth sank deep into Isabelle's heart. Maman had done everything in her power to prevent Ella from going to the ball, yet Ella had found a way. Somehow, this girl, who had nothing, had procured a coach and horses, a sparkling gown, and a pair of glass slippers. *How?* Isabelle wondered.

The prince and Ella stopped inches from each other. Gently, the prince touched Ella's face. His fingers traced the line of her jaw.

"It's you," he said. "I finally found you. Why did you run away?"

"Because I feared that once you discovered who I really was—just a common girl from the country—you would no longer love me," Ella replied.

"There's nothing common about you, Ella," the prince said, taking her hands in his. He turned to the grand duke. "Bring the glass slipper," he commanded.

But to Isabelle's surprise—and everyone else's—the grand duke didn't budge. His lips were set in a hard line. Contempt darkened his flinty eyes.

"Your Grace, this girl is a *servant*," he said. "She wasn't at the ball. The guards would *never* let anyone dressed in rags into the palace. Why, the very idea—"

The prince cut him off. "The slipper. *Now.*"

The grand duke bowed stiffly. He walked toward the prince and Ella, holding the velvet cushion out in front of him. When he was only a few yards away from them, the toe of his shiny black boot caught on something—a rock, he would later say—and he stumbled.

The glass slipper slid off the velvet cushion. It hit the ground.

And smashed into a thousand glittering pieces.

- EIGHT -

The prince cried out in anguish.

The grand duke apologized, hand to his heart.

21

The soldiers shifted nervously, their swords clanking at their hips.

Maman laughed. Isabelle gasped. Only Ella was calm. It soon became clear why.

"It's all right. I have the other one right here," she said, smiling.

As everyone watched, she pulled a second glass slipper from her skirt pocket. She placed it on the ground and lifted her hem. As she slid her small foot inside it, the blue light flared, and the slipper sparkled as if it were made of diamonds.

It fit perfectly.

The prince laughed joyously. He swept Ella into his arms and kissed her, not caring who saw. The soldiers cheered once more. The grand duke wiped sweat from his brow. Maman turned away, hands clenched, and walked into the house.

Isabelle took it all in, wishing as she had a million times before that she was beautiful. That she was valued. That she mattered.

"Ella won," said a voice from behind her.

It was Tavi. She'd limped out of the mansion and was leaning on the back of the bench, holding her injured foot off the ground. She walked around to the front and sat down.

"Pretty always wins," said Isabelle bitterly.

As the two sisters were talking, a third person joined them—Ella.

Tavi gave her an acid smile. "How perfect," she said. "Here we are again. All three of us. Under the linden tree."

Ella barely heard her. She was staring at Isabelle's and Tavi's feet with a look of such deep sadness, it almost seemed like grief. "What have you done?" she asked, tears welling in her eyes.

"Don't you dare cry for us, Ella," Tavi said vehemently. "Don't you *dare*. You don't get to. You got what you deserved and so did we."

Ella raised her eyes to Tavi's. "Did we? Did I deserve your cruelty? Did you deserve these injuries? Is that what we deserved?"

Tavi looked away. Then, with difficulty, she stood. "Go, Ella. Leave this place. Don't come back."

Ella, her tears spilling over, watched as Tavi limped toward the mansion. Then she turned to her other stepsister. "Do you hate me so much, Isabelle? Still?"

Isabelle couldn't answer her; it felt as if her mouth were filled with salt. The memory she'd pushed down earlier surfaced now. She was nine years old again. Ella and Tavi were ten. Maman had been married to Ella's father for a year.

They were all together, under the linden tree.

Sisters.

Stepsisters.

Friends.

## - NINE -

It was a summer afternoon.

The sky was blue; the sun was bright.

Roses tumbled over the stone walls surrounding the mansion. Birds sang in the spreading branches of the linden tree, and under them the three girls played. Ella fashioned daisy chains and made up stories about Tanaquill, the fairy queen, who lived in the hollow of the tree. Tavi did equations on a slate with a piece of chalk. And Isabelle fenced with an old mop handle, pretending to defend her sisters from Blackbeard.

"Time to die, pirate scum! *En garde!*" she shouted, advancing on Bertrand the rooster, who'd wandered close to the tree. She much preferred Felix, the groom's son, as a dueling partner, but he was busy with a new foal.

The rooster pulled himself up to his full height. He flapped his wings, crowed loudly, and attacked. He chased Isabelle around the tree, then she chased him, and on and on they went, until an exasperated Tavi shouted, "For goodness' sake, Izzy! Can't you *ever* be quiet?"

Unable to shake the rooster, Isabelle climbed up into the linden tree, hoping he would lose interest. Just as she'd seated herself on a branch, a carriage pulled into the drive. The rooster took one look at it and ran off. Two men got out of it. One was gray-haired and stooped. He carried a walking stick and a pink silk box with flowers painted on it. The younger had a leather satchel. Isabelle didn't recognize them, but that was not unusual. Men often traveled from Paris to see her stepfather. Most were merchants, like he was, and came to discuss business.

The men didn't see Isabelle, or Ella, who was well in under the canopy of branches, only Tavi, who was sitting on the bench.

"What are you doing there, little girl? Practicing your letters?" asked the older gentleman.

"Trying to prove Euclid's fifth postulate," Octavia replied, her brow furrowed. She did not look up from her slate.

The old man chuckled. He elbowed his companion. "My word, it appears we have a scholar here!" he said. Then he addressed Tavi again. "Now, listen to me, my little duck, you mustn't trouble yourself with algebra."

"It's geometry, actually."

The old man scowled at being corrected. "Yes, well, whatever it is, the feminine mind was not made for it," he cautioned. "You'll tax your brain. Give yourself headaches. And headaches cause wrinkles, you know."

Tavi looked up. "Is that how it works? Then how did you get your wrinkles? I can't imagine you tax *your* brain very much."

"Well, I never ... Not in all my days ... What a rude girl!" the old man spluttered, shaking his walking stick at her.

That was when Ella stepped forward. "Tavi didn't mean to be rude, sir . . ."

"Yes, I did," said Tavi, under her breath.

". . . it's just that Euclid vexes her," Ella finished.

The old man stopped spluttering. He smiled. Ella had that effect on people.

"What a pretty girl you are. So sweet and pleasant," he said. "I shall ask your papa to marry you to my grandson. Then you'll have a wealthy husband and live in a fine house and wear lovely dresses. Would you like that?"

Ella hesitated, then said, "Might I have a little dog instead?"

The two men burst into laughter. The younger chucked Ella under the chin. The elder patted her blond curls, called her a *pretty rose*, and gave her a bonbon from the pink box he'd brought for Maman. Ella smiled and thanked him and eagerly ate the sweet.

Isabelle, still up in the tree, watched the exchange longingly. She dearly loved bonbons. Mop handle in hand, she jumped down, startling the old man. He yelped, stumbled backward, and fell.

"What the devil are you doing with that stick?" he shouted at her, red-faced.

"Fighting Blackbeard," Isabelle replied as the younger man helped him up.

"You almost killed me!"

Isabelle gave him a skeptical look. "I fall all the time. Out of trees. Off horses. Even out of the hayloft once. And it hasn't killed *me*," she said. "Might I please have a bonbon, too?"

"Certainly not!" the old man said, brushing himself off. "Why would I give such a nice treat to such a nasty little monkey with grubby hands and leaves in her hair?"

25

He picked up the pink box and his walking stick, and headed for the mansion, muttering to his companion the whole way. His voice was low, but Isabelle—who still had hopes of a bonbon—followed them and could hear him.

"The one is a charming little beauty and will make a splendid wife one day, but the other two . . ." He shook his head ominously. "Well, I suppose they can always become nuns or governesses or whatever it is that ugly girls do."

Isabelle stopped dead. Her hand came up to her chest. There was a pain in her heart, new and strange. Only moments ago, she'd been happily slaying pirates, completely unaware that she was lacking. That she was less than. That she was a *nasty little monkey*, not a *pretty rose*.

For the first time, she understood that Ella was pretty and she was not.

Isabelle was strong. She was brave. She beat Felix at sword fights. She jumped her stallion, Nero, over fences everyone else was afraid of. She'd chased a wolf away from the henhouse once with only a stick.

*These things are good, too*, she'd thought as she stood there, bewildered and bereft. *They are, aren't they? I am, aren't I?*

That was the day everything changed between the three girls.

They were only children. Ella had been given a sweet and had preened under all the attention. Isabelle was jealous; she couldn't help it. She wanted a sweet, too. She wanted kind words and admiring glances.

Sometimes it's easier to say that you hate what you can't have rather than admit how badly you want it. And so Isabelle, still standing under the linden tree, said she hated Ella.

And Ella said she hated her back.

And Tavi said she hated everyone.

And Maman stood on the terrace listening, a dangerous new light in her hard, watchful eyes.

26

"Isabelle, I'm leaving now. I—I don't know if I'll ever see you again."

Ella's voice pulled Isabelle back from her memories. She leaned down and kissed Isabelle's forehead, her lips like a hot brand against Isabelle's skin.

"Don't hate me anymore, stepsister," she whispered. "For your own sake, not mine."

And then she was gone and Isabelle was alone on the bench.

She thought about the person she once was, and the person she'd become. She thought about all the things she'd been told to want, the things she'd maimed herself to get, the important things. Ella had them now and Isabelle had nothing. Jealousy burned in her, as it had for years.

Isabelle looked to her left and saw Tavi struggle up the steps to the mansion, limp across the threshold, and close the door. She looked to her right and saw the prince help Ella up into the carriage. He climbed in behind her, and then he, too, closed the door.

The grand duke swung himself up next to the driver. He shouted a command at the soldiers ahead of him, all atop their horses now, and they started off. The driver cracked his whip, and the eight white stallions lurched forward in their harnesses.

Isabelle watched the carriage as it rolled out of the long drive, headed down the narrow country road, and crested a hill. A moment later, it was gone.

She remained where she was for quite some time, until the day grew cool and the sun began to set. Until birds flew to their roosts and a green-eyed fox loped off to the woods to hunt. Then she rose and whispered to the lengthening shadows, "It's not you I hate, Ella. It never was. It's me."

## ELEVEN

"Hand over the eyeball, Nelson. *Now*."

A lively little black monkey, his face ruffed with white, scampered across the ship's deck. In one paw he clutched a glass eye.

"Nelson, I'm *warning* you . . ."

The man speaking—tall, well-dressed, his amber eyes flashing—cut a commanding figure, but the monkey paid him no attention. Instead of surrendering his treasure, he climbed up the foremast and jumped into the rigging.

The ship's bosun—one hand covering an empty eye socket—lumbered after the creature, bellowing for his pistol.

"No firearms, please!" cried a woman in a red silk gown. "You must *coax* him down. He responds best to opera."

"I'll coax him down, all right," growled the bosun. "With a bullet!"

Horrified, the diva pressed a hand to her ample bosom, then launched into "Lascia ch'io pianga," a heroine's aria of sorrow and defiance. The monkey cocked his head. He blinked his eyes. But he did not budge.

The diva's gorgeous voice, flowing over the ship's deck down to the docks, drew dozens of onlookers. The ship, a clipper named *Adventure*, had made the port of Marseille only moments ago after three weeks at sea.

As the diva continued to sing, another member of the amber-eyed man's entourage—a fortune-teller—hastily consulted her tarot cards. One by one, she slapped them down on the deck. When she finished, her face was as white as the sails.

"Nelson, come down!" she shouted. "This does not end well!"

A magician conjured a banana, tossed the peel over her shoulder, and waved the fruit in the air. An actress called to the monkey beseechingly. And then a cabin boy ran up from belowdecks, brandishing the bosun's pistol. The diva saw it; her voice shot up three octaves.

As the bosun took his gun and cocked it, a group of acrobats, all in spangly costumes, cartwheeled across the deck and launched themselves into the rigging. The monkey raced up the mast to the crow's nest. The bosun aimed, but as he did, a fire-breather spewed flames in his direction. The bosun stumbled backward, stepped on the banana peel, and lost his balance. He fell, hit his head on the deck, and knocked himself out. The gun went off. The shot went wide. And so did the flames.

Their orange tongues licked the lower edge of the rigging, igniting it with a whoosh, then rapidly climbed upward, devouring the tarry ropes. Terrified, the monkey flung himself from the crow's nest to the fore-mast. The acrobats leapt after him one by one like shooting stars.

As the last acrobat landed, a flaming drop of tar fell onto the fuse of a cannon that had been primed and at the ready in case of a pirate attack. The fuse caught; the cannon fired. The heavy iron ball whistled across the harbor and blasted a hole in a fishing boat. Shouting and swearing, the fishermen jumped into the water and swam madly for the shore.

Certain the *Adventure* was under attack, six musicians in lavender frock-coats and powdered wigs took their instruments from their cases and began to play a dirge. They were nearly drowned out a moment later by the city's fire brigade, clanging down the street in a horse-drawn wagon.

The diva, at the end of her aria now, hit a high note. The fire brigade, pumping madly from the dock, shot fountains of water into the rigging, putting out the flames and dousing her and everyone else on deck. And still the diva sang, arms outstretched, chin raised, holding her note. The crowd on the dock erupted into thunderous applause. Hats were tossed high into the air. Men wept. Women fainted. And in the captain's cabin, every window shattered.

The diva finished. Sopping wet, she walked to the ship's railing and curtsied. Choruses of *Brava!* rang out.

The monkey scrambled down the foremast and jumped into the arms of his master. The amber-eyed man extricated the eyeball from the creature's grasp, polished it on his lapel, then gingerly put it back where it belonged. He had no idea whether it was right side up or upside down and the bosun, still unconscious, couldn't tell him.

The captain emerged from his cabin, brushing glass off his sleeves. He stood on the deck, clasped his hands behind his back, and surveyed the scene before him.

"Mr. Fleming!" he barked at the first mate.

"Sir!" the first mate barked back, snapping a salute.

"Who is responsible for this? Please do not tell me that it's—"

"The Marquis de la Chance, sir," the first mate said. "Who else?"

## - TWELVE -

Captain Duval was furious.

And Chance was doing his best to look sorry. It was something he was quite good at, for he'd had a lot of practice.

"What about the rigging you burned, the windows you broke, and the fishing boat you destroyed?" the captain thundered. "It will cost a fortune to replace it all!"

"Then it will be a fortune well spent!" Chance said, flashing his most charming smile. "I don't believe I've ever heard a more exquisite rendition of 'Lascia ch'io pianga' in my entire life."

"That is not the point, sir!"

"Pleasure is always the point, sir!" Chance countered. "It's not burned rigging and broken windows you'll remember on your deathbed, but the sight of a drenched diva, her gown clinging to every large and luscious

30

curve, her magnificent voice soaring as the cannon fires and the flames climb. Let the bean counters count their beans, sir. You and I shall count moments of wonderment, moments of joy!"

The captain, having endured many such speeches during the voyage, pinched the bridge of his nose. "Tell me, Marquis. How did the monkey come to have the eye in the first place?"

"A bet was made on a hand of cards. I wagered the bosun five ducats against his glass eye. The foolish man took the eye out and placed it atop the coins. I ask you, Captain, have you ever met a monkey who could resist a glass eyeball?"

The captain gestured at Nelson, sitting atop Chance's shoulder. "Perhaps I should ask the monkey to pay for the damages?"

Chance reached into his satchel, lying on the deck by his feet, and pulled out a fat leather purse. "Will this cover it?" he asked, dropping it into the captain's hand.

The captain opened the purse, counted the coins inside it, and nodded. "The gangplank will be lowered shortly," he said. "The next time you decide to take a sea voyage, Marquis, please take it on someone else's ship."

But Chance wasn't listening. He'd already turned away to check that all the members of his retinue were above decks. Each and every person was needed. He was bound for the country. There were no opera houses there. No grand theaters or concert halls. Why, there were hardly any coffee houses, and very few patisseries, bookshops, or restaurants. He would not survive five minutes without his musicians, his acrobats and actors, his diva, ballerinas, magician, fortune-teller, fire-breather, sword-swallower, scientist, and cook.

"Wait! The cook is missing!" Chance exclaimed as he completed his head count. He looked at Nelson. "Where is he?"

The monkey pressed his paws over his mouth and puffed out his cheeks.

31

"Not again," Chance muttered.

A moment later, a short, bald man in a long black leather coat with a red kerchief tied around his neck staggered up from the aft deck. He was rumpled and bleary-eyed. His face was as gray as week-old porridge.

"Seasickness," he said, as he joined Chance.

"Seasickness, eh? Is that how one says 'I drank too much gin last night' in French?" Chance asked, arching an eyebrow.

The cook winced. "Do you have to be so loud?" He leaned his head on the gunwale. "Why the devil are they taking so long with the gangplank? Where are we going anyway? Tell me it's Paris."

"I'm afraid not. Saint-Michel."

"Never heard of it."

"It's in the country."

"I hate the country. Why are we going there?"

Chance's hands tightened on the gunwale. He thought of the girl's map. Isabelle, her name was. He pictured the end of her path. The splotches of red. The violent lines etched into the parchment, as if a madman had made them.

And then he remembered that a madman had.

"It can be changed, her path," he whispered. "I can change it. I *will* change it."

"What path?" the cook asked. "What are you talking about? Why are you . . ."

His words trailed off. Something down below them had caught his attention. Chance saw it, too.

A swift black carriage was making its way up the bustling street that ran alongside the docks. A face was framed in its window—a woman's face, pale and wizened. She must've sensed that she was being watched, for she suddenly looked up. Her gray eyes found Chance's and held them. In her merciless gaze, he saw that no quarter would be asked in this fight and none given.

The cook took a deep breath, then blew it out again. "She's the reason we're here, isn't she?" he asked.

Chance nodded.

"That is *not* good. She's the worst of the three, and that's saying something. Why has she come? Why have we? Are you ever going to tell me?"

"To do battle," Chance replied.

"For what this time? Gold? Glory? Your pride?" There was a cutting tone to his voice.

Chance watched Fate's carriage round a corner and disappear, and then he replied, "For a soul. A girl's soul."

The cook nodded. "You should have said so. That's a thing worth fighting for."

The bleary look had left the cook's face; a determined one had taken its place. He put his forefingers in his mouth and blew an earsplitting whistle. Then he strode off, bellowing at a hapless sailor, demanding that the man get the blasted gangplank down. The magician, the acrobats, and the rest of Chance's entourage, all milling about on deck, gathered their things and hurried after him.

Chance picked up his satchel, slung it over his shoulder, and followed his cook. If he had any hope of winning this fight, he needed to stay one step ahead of Fate, and already he was ten steps behind her.

- THIRTEEN -

Isabelle, sweaty, dirty, and bruised, leaned forward in her saddle and addressed her horse.

"Maman tried to sell you, Martin. Did you know that? To the slaughter-house, where they'd boil your bones down for glue. I'm the one who stopped her. Maybe you should think about that."

Old, slow, and bad-tempered, Martin was also swaybacked, splay-toed, and nippy, but he was all Isabelle had.

"Come *on*," she urged him. She pressed her heels into his flanks, try-ing to get him to trot around the barnyard. But Martin had other ideas. He heaved himself into a sulky canter, then stopped short—sending her tumbling out of her saddle. She hit the ground hard, rolled onto her back, and lay in the dirt groaning.

It was the third time Martin had thrown her that morning. Isabelle was a skilled rider, but everything was different now. She couldn't get her weight right in her stirrups. There was no purchase where the toes of her right foot should've gripped the tread. Unable to balance prop-erly, she had difficulty correcting when Martin reared, bucked, or simply stopped dead.

The falls didn't discourage her, though. She didn't care about the dirt in her face, the bruises, the pain. They kept her from remembering that Ella was gone. That Ella had won. That Ella had everything now and she had nothing.

She was still lying on the ground, staring up at the clouds scudding across the sky, when a face leaned over her, blocking them out.

"How many times have you fallen today?" Tavi asked. She didn't wait for an answer. "You'll kill yourself."

"If I'm lucky."

"Stop this. You can't ride anymore."

Fear pooled in Isabelle's belly at the very thought. It wasn't true. She wouldn't let it be true. Riding was all she had left. It was the only thing that had kept her going as her foot healed. As she got used to hobbling

34

instead of walking. As the servants left. As Maman closed the shutters and locked the doors. As the weeds grew over the stone walls.

"Why are you here?" she asked Tavi. Her sister preferred to stay inside with her books and equations.

"To tell you that we have to go to the market. We can't put it off any longer."

Isabelle blinked at her. "That's not a good idea."

Word had spread. About the glass slipper and what they'd done to themselves to fit into it. About Ella and how they'd treated her. Children threw mud at their house. A man had pitched a rock through one of their windows. Isabelle knew they would only be inviting more trouble if they went to the village.

"Do you have a better one?" asked Tavi. "We need cheese. Ham. Butter. We haven't tasted bread in weeks."

Isabelle sighed. She stood up and brushed herself off. "We'll have to take the cart," she said. "We can't walk. Not with our—"

"Fine. Hitch up Martin. I'll gather some baskets," Tavi said brusquely, starting for the kitchen. She didn't like talking about their injuries. Ella. Any of it.

"Fine," Isabelle said, limping over to her horse.

She hadn't gotten used to her slow, lurching gait. Tavi's injury was not as severe. After it had healed, her stride had returned to normal. Isabelle doubted hers ever would.

"And, Izzy . . ."

Isabelle turned around. Tavi was frowning.

"What?"

"Behave. In the village. Do you think you can?"

Isabelle waved Tavi's question away and picked up Martin's reins. But the truth was, she had no idea if she could. She'd tried to behave. For years. In drawing rooms and ballrooms, at garden parties and dinners. With her hands knotted and her jaw clenched, she'd tried to be all the things Maman told her to be: pleasant, sweet, considerate, kind, demure, gentle, patient, agreeable, and self-effacing.

Occasionally it worked. For a day or two. But then something always happened.

Like the time, at a fancy dinner Maman had hosted, a cadet back from his first year at the military academy said that the Second Punic War ended after Scipio defeated Hannibal at the Battle of Cannae, when any fool knew it was the Battle of Zama. Isabelle had corrected him, and he'd laughed, saying she didn't know what she was talking about. After she got her favorite book—*An Illustrated History of the World's Greatest Military Commanders*—from her library and proved that she did, in fact, know what she was talking about, he'd called her an unpleasant name. Under his breath. Furious, she'd called him one back. Not under her breath.

Maman hadn't spoken to her for a week.

And then there was the time she'd attended a ball at a baroness's château, gotten bored with the dancing, and decided to take a walk. She never meant to get into a duel with the baron, but he'd found her admiring a pair of sabers mounted on a wall in the foyer and offered to show her his moves. She'd shown him hers, too, slicing several buttons off his jacket and nicking his chin in the process.

That time, Maman had given her the silent treatment for a month.

Her mother had said her behavior was atrocious, but Isabelle didn't think cutting off a baron's buttons was all that bad. She knew she was capable of worse. Much worse.

Just a few months ago, she'd been searching in her wardrobe for the pink parasol Maman insisted that she carry—*Pink enhances the complexion, Isabelle!*—and a pair of horrible silk slippers—*Too bad if they pinch, they make your feet look small!*—and had found a book on Alexander the Great that she'd hidden to keep Maman from taking it away.

She'd sat down on the floor of her bedchamber, rumpling her fussy dress, and had eagerly opened the book. It was a relic from a happier time, a time before she'd been made to understand that warriors and generals were men, and that showing an interest in swords and war-horses and battlefield strategies was unbecoming in a girl. As Isabelle had turned the book's pages, she'd found herself once again fighting alongside Alexander as he battled his way through Egypt. Tears of longing had welled in her eyes as she'd read.

Just as she'd been wiping them away, Ella had walked into the room, carrying a silver tray. On it she'd placed a cup of hot chocolate and a plate of madeleines.

"I heard Maman shouting at you about the parasol and the slippers. I thought this might help," she'd said, setting the tray down next to Isabelle.

It had been a kind thing to do. But Ella's kindnesses only ever made Isabelle angry.

She'd looked at her stepsister, who had no need of parasols and pinchy shoes. Who looked like a goddess in a patched dress and an old pair of boots. She looked down at herself, awkward and gauche in the ridiculous gown, and then she'd picked up the cup of hot chocolate and hurled it at the wall. The madeleines had followed it. The silver tray, too.

"Clean it up," she'd ordered, a nasty glint in her eyes.

"Isabelle, why are you so upset?" Ella had asked, wounded.

Seething, her hands clenched, Isabelle said, "Stop, Ella. Stop being nice to me. Just *stop!*"

"I'm sorry," Ella had said meekly as she'd bent down to pick up the broken pieces.

That meekness should have mollified Isabelle, but it had only fueled her anger.

"You're pathetic!" she'd shouted. "Why don't you ever stick up for yourself? You let Maman bully you! You're kind to me and Tavi even though we're horrible to you! *Why*, Ella?"

Ella had carefully put the shards of porcelain on the tray. "To try to undo all of this. To make things better," she'd replied softly.

"You *can't* make things better. Not unless you can change me into you!"

Ella had looked up, stricken. "Don't say that. Don't ever change into me. *Ever*."

Isabelle had stopped shouting, struck silent for a moment by the vehemence of Ella's words. And then Maman's footsteps had been heard in the hallway, and it had been all Isabelle could do to hide her book and grab her parasol before her mother was in the room, shouting at her to hurry up. They'd left for a garden party minutes later, one so mind-numbingly dull that Isabelle had forgotten her intention to press Ella for an answer. And now it was too late.

Martin, tired of standing still, nipped Isabelle's arm sharply, dispelling her painful memories.

"You're not much good at behaving, either, are you, old man?" she said to him.

She led the horse into the cool stone stables and removed his tack. She didn't need to tie him. Martin was a horse of few ambitions and running off was not one of them. Before putting his harness on, she gave him a quick brushing. It wasn't necessary; he hadn't been worked very hard, but Isabelle craved the feel of him under her hands, the velvet of his nose against her cheek, his gusty, grassy breath.

When she finished, she led him to the cart. As they walked through the stables, Isabelle glanced at the empty stalls. The pair of graceful Arabians that had pulled the carriage, and the huge Percherons who'd worked the fields, were gone, sold off after the groom left.

Though she tried not to, Isabelle couldn't help looking at the very last stall. It brought memories, too. The horse that had lived in it had also been sold. Years ago. Nero. A black stallion seventeen hands high, with onyx eyes and a mane like rippling silk. Riding him was like riding a storm. She could still feel his strength as he stamped and danced underneath her, impatient to be off.

She could feel Felix, too. He was sitting behind her, his arms around her waist, his lips by her ear, his eyes on the stone wall ahead of them. He was laughing, and in his laugh was a dare.

"Don't, Isabelle!" Ella had called out. "It's too dangerous!"

But Isabelle hadn't listened. She'd touched her heels to Nero's sides, and an instant later, they were galloping straight at the wall. Ella had covered her eyes with her hands. Isabelle had leaned forward in her saddle, her chest over Nero's neck, her hands high up in his mane, Felix leaning with her. She'd felt every muscle in the stallion's body tense, and then she'd felt what it was like to fly. She and Felix had whooped as they landed, then they'd streaked across the meadow and into the Wildwood, leaving Ella behind.

As quickly as they'd come, the images faded and all that was left was an empty stall with cobwebs in the corners.

Nero was gone. Felix, too. Taken away by Maman like so many other things—her leather britches, her pirate's hat, the shiny rocks and animal skulls and bird nests she'd collected. Her wooden sword. Her books. One by one they'd all disappeared, each loss like the swipe of a carver's knife. Whittling her down. Smoothing her edges. Making her more like the girl Maman wanted her to be.

Isabelle had cut off her toes, but sometimes she could still feel them.

Maman had cut out her heart.

Sometimes, she could still feel that, too.

## – FOURTEEN –

"Six sous," the baker's wife said, her meaty arms crossed over her huge, freckled bosom.

"Six?" Isabelle echoed, confused. "But the sign says three." She pointed to a slate on the baker's stall with a price marked on it in chalk.

The woman spat on her palm, rubbed the 3 away and wrote 6 in its place. "For you, six," she said insolently.

"But that's double the price. It's not fair!" Isabelle protested.

"Neither is treating your stepsister like a slave," said the woman. "Don't deny it. You were cruel to a defenseless girl. Got your comeuppance, though, didn't you? Ella is queen now and more beautiful than ever. And you? You're nothing more than her ugly stepsister."

Isabelle lowered her head, her cheeks flaming. She and Tavi had only just arrived at the market and already the taunts were starting.

Taking a deep, steadying breath, she remembered her sister's directive: *Behave.* She counted out coins from her pocket and handed them over. The baker's wife gave her an undersized loaf, burned on the bottom, and a sneering smile to go with it.

"Serves her right," said a woman standing in line.

"Burned bread's too good for her," sniffed another.

The women stood there, nodding and pointing and making remarks, basting themselves in righteousness like geese on a spit, when just yesterday the first had slapped her small daughter so hard for spilling milk that the child's cheek still bore a welt, and the second had kissed her sister's husband behind the tavern.

No one jeers louder at a hanging than the cutthroat who got away.

"I hope you choke on it," said the baker's wife as Isabelle fumbled the loaf into her basket.

Isabelle felt anger kindle inside her. Harsh words rose in her throat, but she bit them back.

"I hope your ugly sister chokes, too."

At the mention of her sister—Tavi, who'd grown thin since Ella had left, who rarely smiled and barely ate—Isabelle's smoldering temper ignited.

The centerpiece of the baker's display was a carefully constructed pyramid of shiny brown rolls. Isabelle cocked her arm back and smacked the top off. A dozen rolls tumbled off the table and landed in the muddy street.

"Choke on *that*," she said to the spluttering baker's wife and her squawking customers.

The look on the woman's face, her shriek of outrage, her dismay—they all felt good, for a moment. *I won*, Isabelle thought. But as she limped away from the stall, she realized, with a sick, sinking feeling, that she hadn't won. Her anger had. Once again.

*Ella would not have done that*, she thought. *Ella would have disarmed them all with a sweet smile and soft words.*

Ella was never angry. Not when she'd had to cook and clean for them. Or eat her meals alone in the kitchen. Not even when Maman wouldn't let her go to the ball.

Ella had had a cold room in the attic and a hard bed; Isabelle and Tavi had blazing fires in their bedchambers, and feather mattresses. Ella had had only a tattered dress to wear, while Isabelle and Tavi had dozens of pretty gowns. Yet day after day, it was Ella who sang, Ella who smiled. Not Isabelle. Not Tavi.

"Why?" Isabelle asked herself, desperate for an answer, certain that if she could get it, she could learn to be good and kind, too. But no answer came, only a pain, deep and gnawing, on the left side of her chest.

Had Isabelle asked the old wives of Saint-Michel, all sitting by the fountain in the village square, they could have told her what caused it. For the old wives have a saying: *Never is a wolf more dangerous than when he's in a cage.*

At the edge of Saint-Michel is the Wildwood. The wolves who live there come out at night. They prowl fields and farms, hungry for hens and tender young lambs. But there is another sort of wolf, one that's far more treacherous. This is the wolf the old ones speak of.

"Run if you see him," they tell their granddaughters. "His tongue is silver, but his teeth are sharp. If he gets hold of you, he'll eat you alive."

Most of the village girls do what they're told, but occasionally one does not. She stands her ground, looks the wolf in the eye, and falls in love with him.

People see her run to the woods at night. They see her the next morning with leaves in her hair and blood on her lips. *This is not proper*, they say. *A girl should not love a wolf.*

So they decide to intervene. They come after the wolf with guns and swords. They hunt him down in the Wildwood. But the girl is with him and sees them coming.

The people raise their rifles and take aim. The girl opens her mouth to scream, and as she does, the wolf jumps inside it. Quickly the girl swallows him whole, teeth and claws and fur. He curls up under her heart.

The villagers lower their weapons and go home. The girl heaves a sigh of relief. She believes this arrangement will work. She thinks she can be satisfied with memories of the wolf's golden eyes. She thinks the wolf will be happy with a warm place to sleep.

But the girl soon realizes she's made a terrible mistake, for the wolf is a wild thing and wild things cannot be caged. He wants to get out, but the girl is all darkness inside and he cannot find his way.

So he howls in her blood. He tears at her bones.

And when that doesn't work, he eats her heart.

The howling and gnawing—it drives the girl mad.

She tries to cut him out, slicing lines in her flesh with a razor.

She tries to burn him out, holding a candle flame to her skin.

She tries to starve him out, refusing to eat until she's nothing but skin over bone.

Before long, the grave takes them both.

A wolf lives in Isabelle. She tries hard to keep him down, but his hunger grows. He cracks her spine and devours her heart.

Run home. Slam the door. Throw the bolt. It won't help.

The wolves in the woods have sharp teeth and long claws, but it's the wolf inside who will tear you apart.

## - FIFTEEN -

Isabelle managed to finish her marketing without further incident. There was a cutting glance from the cheesemonger and a few harsh words from the butcher, but she ignored them.

Now she was walking toward the village square. She and Tavi had decided to split up in order to finish their shopping faster, then meet back at their cart. Isabelle was headed there now, but the streets were unfamiliar to her and she hoped she was going the right way. Maman rarely allowed them to go to Saint-Michel. *Only common girls traipse through the village*, she said.

Isabelle was eager to get home. The rutted cobbles made for difficult walking and her foot was aching. Scents of the things she'd bought—slices of salty ham, tiny pickled cucumbers, a pungent blue-veined Roquefort—wafted up from her basket. Her stomach twisted with hunger. It had been weeks since she'd enjoyed such treats.

Isabelle made sure to keep her head down as she entered the square, hoping to go unnoticed. Though she couldn't see much looking at the ground, she could hear a great deal.

Villagers stood together outside shop fronts and taverns swapping rumors in tense voices. Volkmar von Bruch had raided another village. He was moving west. No, he was moving south. Refugees were everywhere. Good Queen Ella, God bless her, was trying to help. She had ordered noble families to open their manors and castles to children orphaned by the raids.

As Isabelle hurried on, she heard the sound of hooves on cobblestones. She turned and saw a group of soldiers approaching the square. Leading them was a tall man astride a beautiful white horse. Isabelle hobbled out of their way, joining the crowd at the fountain. No one bothered her; the people only had eyes for the soldiers. A loud cheer rose as they crossed the square.

"Bless you, Colonel Cafard!" a woman shouted.

"God save the king!" another bellowed.

The colonel sat tall and straight-backed in his saddle, eyes ahead. His dark blue coat and white britches were spotless, his boots polished to a high shine.

"At least Saint-Michel is safe," a man said as the soldiers passed by. Others agreed. Hadn't the king sent his finest regiments? Hadn't the good colonel set them up right outside the village in Levesque's pasture? Why, there were over two thousand soldiers in that camp. There was nothing to fear.

Though she was not cold, Isabelle felt a deep chill move through her. *Someone's just walked over your grave*, Adélie used to say when that happened.

She had no idea that the bloodthirsty Volkmar had advanced so far into France. Neither she, Tavi, nor Maman had left their home in over a month. The last bit of news they'd heard—that the old king had died, that the prince had been crowned king and Ella queen—had come from the servants before they'd departed.

Distracted by the villagers' talk, Isabelle did not see the pothole in front of her until she stepped down in it hard. A searing pain shot up her leg. She stifled a cry, limped to a lamppost, and leaned on it to take the weight off her throbbing foot. In agony, she glanced up the street, hoping to see her cart, but there was no sign of it.

She did, however, see Odette, the innkeeper's daughter, walking toward her, tapping her cane over the cobblestones. Odette was blind and used the cane to navigate the village's winding streets.

Then Isabelle saw something else.

Cecile, the mayor's daughter, and her gaggle of friends were walking behind Odette. Cecile's eyes were crossed; her tongue was hanging out. She was waving her parasol in front of her as if it were a cane, mocking Odette. Her friends were giggling.

Dread gripped Isabelle. She knew she should go to Odette and defend her. But her foot hurt and she had no heart for another confrontation. She told herself that Odette didn't know what was happening. After all, she couldn't see Cecile, but she, Isabelle, could and knew she would be the girl's next victim. She looked around anxiously for a place to hide, but it was too late. Cecile had spotted her.

"Isabelle de la Paumé, is that *you*?" she drawled, forgetting about Odette.

As Cecile spoke, Isabelle's eyes fell on the entrance to an alley. She didn't bother to reply but rushed down the narrow passage, heedless of the pain she was in. The alley was damp and smelled like a sewer. A rat darted out in front of her and someone nearly emptied a chamber pot on her head, but she managed to avoid Cecile and emerge on the very street where she'd left her cart.

Relief flooded through her. Tavi wasn't there yet, but Isabelle was certain she'd come soon. In the meantime, she could sit down. Her foot felt like it was on fire now. As she hobbled toward the cart, though, guilt pricked her conscience. She thought about Odette. Had Cecile left her alone? Or had she been so frustrated she couldn't taunt Isabelle that she'd tormented the blind girl twice as hard?

History books say that kings and dukes and generals start wars. Don't believe it. We start them, you and I. Every time we turn away, keep quiet, stay out of it, behave ourselves.

The wrong thing, the cowardly thing, the easy thing. You do it fast. You put it behind you. It's over, you tell yourself as you hurry off. You're finished with it.

But it may not be finished with you.

Isabelle had been in such a hurry to escape that she'd started for the cart without looking up and down the street.

"Isabelle, darling! *There* you are!" a voice called out.

Isabelle's stomach tightened. Slowly, she turned around.

Standing behind her, smiling like a viper, was Cecile.

## − SIXTEEN −

Cecile, blond and haughty, strolled up to Isabelle. She was wearing a yellow dress, carrying a matching parasol, and trailing a dozen lesser girls in her wake.

"It's been *such* a long time, Isabelle," she trilled. "I *heard* about Ella and the prince. Tell us, what was the royal wedding like?"

There were snickers. Whispers. Pointed glances. Everyone knew that Isabelle, Octavia, and Maman had not been invited to Ella's wedding.

"Do you have your own room in the palace?" asked one of the girls.

"Has Ella found you a duke to marry?" drawled another.

"Who's marrying a duke? I wish I could!" said a third, smiling excitedly. She had just caught up with the group. Her name was Berthe. She was small and plump with prominent front teeth.

Cecile turned to her. "A *duke*? What would a duke want with *you*, Berthe? We'll find you a hunter to marry. *They* like fat little rabbits."

Berthe's smile slipped. Her cheeks flushed a bright, blotchy red. The other girls burst into laughter. They had no choice. Cecile would remember any girl who didn't laugh. She would take it as a challenge and make that girl her next victim.

Under Cecile's pretty dress, under her silk corset and linen chemise, was a heart like a rotten log. Turn it over and the things living under it would scuttle from the light. Things like envy, fear, anger, and shame. Isabelle knew this because her own heart had become just like it, but unlike Cecile, she knew that cruelty never came from a place of strength; it came from the darkest, dankest, weakest place inside you.

Something in the street caught Cecile's eyes. It was a small rotten cabbage. She kicked it toward Berthe.

"Do it," Cecile commanded. "She deserves it. She's ugly. An ugly stepsister."

Berthe looked at the cabbage uncertainly.

Cecile's eyes narrowed. "Are you scared? *Do it.*"

Her challenge emboldened the other girls. Like a pack of hyenas, they egged Berthe on. Reluctantly, Berthe picked the cabbage up and threw it. It hit the cobblestones in front of Isabelle, splattering her skirts. The jeering grew louder.

Fear ran a sharp fingernail down the back of Isabelle's neck. She knew Cecile was only getting started. From deep inside her a voice spoke. *I am not afraid of an army of lions led by a sheep. I am afraid of an army of sheep led by a lion.*

In times of trouble, Isabelle heard generals in her head; she had ever since she was old enough to read about them. It was Alexander the Great who spoke to her now, and she realized he was right: Cecile's lackeys, desperate for her approval, would do anything she commanded.

Isabelle knew she could fight one girl off, even with a bad foot, but not a dozen. She would have to find another way out of this.

"That's enough, Cecile," she said. Though she was in agony, she hobbled off, back toward the market, figuring that Cecile would tire of the game if she refused to play it.

But Cecile had no intention of letting her quit. She bent down and picked up a chunk of a broken cobblestone. "Stay where you are, Isabelle. Or I'll throw this at your horse."

Isabelle stopped in her tracks. She turned around. "You wouldn't," she said. This was a step too far, even for Cecile.

"I would." Cecile gestured to the others. "They all would." As if to prove her point, she handed the cobblestone to Berthe. "Throw it. I dare you."

Berthe stared at it; her eyes grew round. "Cecile, no. It's a *rock*," she said.

"Fraidy-cat."

"I'm *not*," Berthe protested, a quaver in her voice.

"Then do it."

Isabelle stepped in front of Martin's head, shielding him. Berthe threw the rock, but she hit the cart.

"You missed on purpose," Cecile accused.

"I didn't!" Berthe cried.

Cecile picked up another chunk of cobble and dropped it into her hand. "Go closer," she said, giving her a push.

Berthe took a few halting steps toward Isabelle, gripping the stone so hard, her knuckles turned white. As she raised her arm again, her eyes met Isabelle's. They were brimming with tears. Isabelle felt as if she were looking into a mirror. She saw the girl's anguish and recognized it; it was her own.

"It's good that you still cry," Isabelle whispered to her. "It's when you stop crying that you're lost."

"Shut up. I'm not crying. I'm *not*," Berthe said, cocking her arm back.

Isabelle knew that being hit by a rock would hurt. It could kill her. If that was her fate, so be it. She refused to abandon Martin. Eyes closed, fists clenched, she waited for the pain.

But it didn't come. Seconds slowly passed. She opened her eyes. The girls were gone, scattered like sparrows. Standing where Cecile had stood only a moment ago was an elderly woman dressed entirely in black.

- SEVENTEEN -

The woman was gazing down the street, watching the girls hurry away.

Her face was etched with lines. Her snow-white hair was braided and coiled at the nape of her neck. A black ring graced one clawlike hand. She seemed to Isabelle to be the picture of frail old age, as brittle and breakable as a twig under ice.

49

Until she turned and bent her gaze upon Isabelle, and Isabelle felt as if she were drowning in the gray depths of those ancient eyes, pulled under by a will far stronger than her own.

"The one in the yellow dress, the ringleader, she'll come to a bad end," the woman said knowingly. "I guarantee it."

Isabelle shook her head, trying to clear it. She felt buffeted and unsteady, as if she were walking out of a heavy, roiling sea. "You . . . you chased them away?" she asked.

The woman laughed. "*Chased?* Child, these old legs couldn't chase a snail. I was coming to speak with you. The girls scurried off as soon as they saw me." She paused, then said, "You're one of the ugly stepsisters, no? I thought I heard them call you that."

Isabelle winced, bracing for a torrent of abuse, but none came. The woman merely clucked her tongue and said, "You are foolish to go out in public. Hard words cannot kill you, but hard rocks can. You must stay home where it's safe."

"Even ugly girls have to eat," Isabelle said, shame coloring her cheeks.

The woman shook her head dolefully. "People will not forget. Or forgive. An ugly girl is too great an offense. Trust me, I am old and have seen much. Why, I've seen a dishonest girl who stole a king's ransom of jewels be forgiven because of her pretty smile. And a violent girl who robbed coaches at gunpoint walk out of jail because of her long black lashes. Why, I even knew a murderous girl who escaped the gallows because she had full lips and dimples and the judge fell head over heels for her. But an ugly girl? Ah, child, the world is made for men. An ugly girl can never be forgiven."

The woman's words were like a knife between Isabelle's ribs. They pierced her so deeply, she found herself blinking back tears. "When I was small, I thought the world was made for me," she said.

"Children always do," the woman said sympathetically. "And lunatics. I'm sure you know better now, though. Do be careful. I doubt those girls will trouble you again but others may."

"Thank you, madame," Isabelle said. "I'm in your debt."

"You may be able to repay it," the woman said. She gestured at Isabelle's cart. "Might I trouble you for a ride? We arrived at the village inn last night, my maidservant and I, and have been trying since early this morning to get to my relatives' farm but can't find anyone to take us."

"Of course, I will take you, Madame . . . er, Madame . . ." Isabelle realized she did not know the woman's name.

"Madame Sévèrine. I'm the great-aunt of poor Monsieur LeBenêt, who passed away a few months ago, God rest him. Tante Sévèrine, he called me when he was a boy. Tantine for short. And you must, too, dear girl. I wish to go to the LeBenêts'."

Isabelle brightened. "Nothing could be easier, madame. The LeBenêts are our neighbors. What a coincidence!" she exclaimed, happy that she could help this woman who'd been kind enough to help her.

"Yes, what a coincidence," said the old woman. A smile curved the corners of her mouth; it did not touch her eyes.

Isabelle explained that she had to wait for her sister, but as soon as she arrived, they would go to the inn and collect Madame's trunk and her servant.

"Tantine," the old woman corrected.

"Tantine," Isabelle repeated. "Would you like to sit while we wait?" she asked.

"I would. These old bones tire easily."

Isabelle helped her step up into the cart and settle herself on the wooden seat. She had warmed to this kindly old woman.

"Thank you, my child," said Tantine. "I think we shall be good friends, you and I."

"We're lucky our paths crossed," Isabelle said, smiling.

The old woman nodded. She patted her hand. "Some might call it luck. Myself? I'd call it fate."

## – EIGHTEEN –

It was just before noon when Isabelle and Tavi headed out of the village with Tantine seated between them. The sun was high and the August day was scorchingly hot.

Losca, Tantine's servant, a slight girl with a hooked nose, bright eyes, and ebony hair worn in a long braid, sat in the back of the cart on top of Tantine's trunk. She said nothing as she rode; she just watched the scenery go by, tilting her head and blinking.

Martin plodded up the road as slowly as possible, which gave Tantine plenty of time to tell the girls why she had come to Saint-Michel.

"It's this Volkmar business," she said darkly. "I live in Paris, you see, and he intends to take it. The king has fortified the city, but people are still leaving in droves. I plan to stay here with my relatives for the foreseeable future. It's the safest course. One must always follow the safest course."

"The LeBenêts will be so relieved to have you safe and sound with them, Tantine," Tavi said. "They must be worried about you."

"The LeBenêts have no idea that I'm coming," said Tantine. "We are not close. In fact, I've never met Madame LeBenêt. It was my husband who was related to Monsieur LeBenêt. My late husband, I should say. He passed away recently, too."

Isabelle and Tavi expressed their condolences. Tantine thanked them.

"In his will, my husband left a sum of money to Monsieur LeBenêt," she added. "Now I am wondering what to do with it. I'm told there is a son, Hugo, but I know nothing of the boy. I would like to see if he is the sort who will bring honor to the family name before I bestow the inheritance on him."

*I wish you luck with that*, Isabelle thought. She'd known Hugo since they were children. He'd played pirates and musketeers with her and Felix a few times, always scowling behind his thick eyeglasses. In all the years she'd known him, he'd barely grunted three words to her. She doubted he'd grunt even one to Tantine.

As the sun rose higher, and Martin continued to grudgingly pull the cart past meadows, wheat fields, and orchards, the old woman continued to talk. She was just telling the girls about her elegant town house in Paris, when a scream, ragged and high, tore through the air.

Isabelle sat up straight. Tavi jumped. They traded wide-eyed glances, then quickly looked around for its source. Losca leaned over the side of the cart, craning her neck.

"There," Tantine said, pointing straight ahead.

A military wagon, pulled by two burly workhorses, had crested a hill and was rolling toward them. Even from a distance, Isabelle could see that the driver's uniform was blotched with red. As the wagon drew near, and she saw what it contained, she uttered a choked cry.

In the back, unprotected from the merciless sun, were at least thirty men, all badly injured. Bandages soaked with blood were tied around heads and torsos. Limbs were missing. One man lay stretched across a wooden seat, his legs mangled. He was the one who'd screamed. A wheel hit a rut, jostling the wagon, and he cried out again.

By the time the wagon passed by, Tavi was clutching her seat, and Isabelle's hands were trembling so badly she had to squeeze Martin's reins hard to steady them. Tantine's mouth was set in a grim line. No one spoke.

Isabelle remembered her book, *An Illustrated History of the World's Greatest Military Commanders.* She and Felix had pored over it when they were little, looking at the hand-colored plates depicting famous battles. The pictures made them look glorious and exciting and the soldiers who'd fought them dashing and brave. But the suffering she'd just witnessed didn't seem glorious at all. It left her stunned and sickened. She tried to picture the man responsible for it. Volkmar. He was a duke, she'd been told. Did he wear medals on his uniform? A sash across his chest? Did he ride a horse? Carry a sword?

For a moment, Isabelle's vision narrowed. She no longer saw the road ahead of her, the stone walls that lined it, the roses that tumbled over them. In her mind's eye, a figure, tall and powerful, strode toward her across a battlefield. White smoke swirled around him, obscuring his face, but she could see the sword he held in his hand, its blade razor-sharp. A shiver ran through her, just as it had in the marketplace.

Tavi spoke and the image faded. "Where are they going?" she asked.

"To an army camp on the other side of Saint-Michel. I heard villagers talking about it," Isabelle replied, shaking off the strange vision and the sense of dread it left behind.

"I've seen many such wagons on my way from Paris," said Tantine. "Ah, girls, I fear this war will not go well for us. Our king is young and untested, and Volkmar is ruthless and wily. His troops are fewer, yet they defeat the king's at every turn."

The three fell silent again. The only sounds were of Martin's plodding hooves, the creaking of the cart, and the droning of insects. Before long, they reached the turnoff to the LeBenêt farm. A dusty drive led to an old stone farmhouse. Threadbare white curtains hung in its windows;

sagging shutters framed them. Chickens scratched around the weathered blue door.

The cow barn and dairy house, also built of stone, were connected to the farmhouse. Behind them, cattle grazed in a fenced pasture, and fields bearing cabbages, potatoes, turnips, and onions stretched all the way to the edge of the Wildwood.

Losca was out of the cart before it stopped. As Isabelle helped Tantine down, and Tavi opened the back of the cart to get her trunk, Madame LeBenêt, threadbare and weathered herself, came out to greet them, if one could call it a greeting.

"What do you want?" she barked, the look on her face sour enough to curdle milk.

"We've brought your great-aunt, madame," Isabelle said, nodding at Tantine. "She has come all the way from Paris with her maidservant."

Madame LeBenêt's eyes narrowed; her scowl deepened. "I have no great-aunt," she said.

"I am Madame Sévèrine, your late husband's great-aunt," Tantine explained.

"My husband never mentioned you."

"I'm not surprised. There was a family feud, so much bad blood—"

Madame LeBenêt rudely cut her off. "Do you take me for a fool? Every day now, strangers fleeing Paris come to Saint-Michel pretending to be someone's long-lost this-or-that to get themselves food and shelter. No, madame, I'm sorry. You cannot stay here. You and your maid will eat us out of house and home."

*Eat them out of house and home?* Isabelle thought. *This little old lady? Her scrawny maid?* She ducked her head and fiddled with a buckle on Martin's harness. She didn't dare look up lest Madame caught her rolling her eyes.

The whole village knew Avara LeBenêt was a miser. Not only did she

55

have bountiful fields, she had two dozen laying hens, ten milk cows, berry bushes, apple trees, and a large kitchen garden. She made a small fortune at the market every Saturday, yet all she ever did was complain about how poor she was.

"Ah, I am sorry to hear you have no place for me," Tantine said, with a crestfallen sigh. "I fear I shall have to settle the inheritance on another member of the family."

Madame LeBenêt snapped to attention like a pointer that had spotted a nice fat duck. "Inheritance? What inheritance?" she asked sharply.

"The inheritance my late husband instructed me to bestow upon your late husband. I thought to possibly give it to your son, but now . . ."

Madame LeBenêt slapped her forehead. "Tante *Séverine*!" she exclaimed. "Of *course*! My husband often spoke of you! And with *such* fondness. You must be exhausted from your travels. Let me fix you a cup of tea."

"She should be on the stage," Tavi said to Isabelle.

Madame LeBenêt heard her. "What are you two waiting for?" she snapped. "Fetch her trunk!"

With great difficulty, Isabelle and Tavi managed to slide the trunk off the cart and carry it into the house. Isabelle hoped Losca might help them, but the girl was peering intently at a grasshopper on the scraggly rosebush near Madame LeBenêt's door, completely absorbed by it. Madame directed Isabelle and Tavi to place the trunk in a small bedroom, then hurried into the house to start the tea. When the girls returned to their cart, they saw that Tantine was still standing by it.

Tavi climbed back up into the cart and sat down, but Isabelle hesitated. "Will you be all right here?" she asked.

"I'll be fine," Tantine assured her. "I can handle Avara. Thank you again for the ride."

"It was nothing. Thank you for saving me from certain death at the hands of Cecile," Isabelle said wryly.

She turned to leave, but as she did, Tantine caught hold of her hand. Isabelle was surprised by the strength in those gnarled fingers.

They stood there for a moment, staring into each other's eyes, perfectly still. Fate, a creature with no heart and no soul, who walked with the dust of Alexandria on her shoes, the ashes of Pompeii on her hem, the red clay of Xi'an on her sleeves. As old as time. Without beginning or end.

And a human girl. So poorly made. Just tender flesh and bitten nails and a battered heart beating in a fragile cage of bone.

Isabelle had no idea whose fathomless eyes she was gazing into. She had no idea that Fate meant to win the wager she'd made, no matter the cost.

"We must be going, Tantine," she finally said. "Are you sure you'll be all right?"

Fate nodded. She gave Isabelle's hand one last squeeze. "Yes, and I hope you will, too. Be careful of those fleeing Paris, child," she warned. "Not all refugees are harmless old biddies like me. Some are scoundrels, just looking to lead young girls astray. Be wary. Close your shutters. Bolt your doors. And above all, trust nothing—*nothing*—to chance."

## - NINETEEN -

Many hours later, on a blue damask picnic cloth, in a field well south of Saint-Michel, a diva, a magician, and an actress sat under an oak tree eating fruit and sweets.

Around them, musicians played. A juggler tossed flaming torches into the air. A sword-swallower gulped down a saber. And three noisy capuchins leapt to and fro in the branches of the oak while the fourth sat on the picnic cloth, eyeing the diva's pearls.

"Watch out. The little robber is planning his next theft," the magician warned.

"Nelson," the diva cautioned, wagging a finger at the monkey. "Don't even think—"

Her words were cut off by a loud bellow. *"Now?"*

*"No!"* came the shouted reply.

The three women turned toward the source of the racket. Chance, hands on his hips, was standing by a large, painted carriage. He'd flung off his coat. His white ruffled shirt was open at the neck, his long braids gathered up and tied with someone's shoelace. Sweat beaded on his brow.

Standing on top of the carriage, and on top of one another's shoulders, were four acrobats. The bottommost had rooted his strong legs to the roof; the topmost held a telescope to her eye.

"Go," Chance commanded a fifth, gesturing to the carriage. "Tell me what you see."

A moment later, a wiry boy was climbing to the top of the human tower.

"Anything?" Chance shouted as the boy took the telescope from the acrobat under him. "You're looking for a village called Saint-Michel. It has a church with a statue of the archangel on it . . ."

"I can't see it!"

Chance swore. "You're next!" he said, to a second wiry boy.

*"Another* one?" the diva said, turning away. "I can't look."

Chance and his friends were lost. The driver had been navigating on instinct and had taken a wrong turn. He'd had no road map to consult; Chance didn't like them. They spoiled the fun, he said. Now evening was coming down, the village of Saint-Michel was nowhere in sight, and Chance was hoping his acrobats could spot it.

The diva helped herself to a macaron from a pretty paper box in the center of the picnic cloth and bit into the sweet. Its brittle meringue shattered; crumbs fell into her cleavage. The monkey scampered over and fished them out.

"Nelson, you fresh thing!" she cried, swatting him. Nelson threw his furry arms around her neck, kissed her, and shot off. Had she not been so annoyed by his antics, she might've noticed that he was trailing something through the grass.

"The crone's already there. I feel it," the magician fretted, threading a silver coin in and out of her long, nimble fingers.

"If she finds the girl before Chance does, she'll poison her with doubt and fear," said the diva.

"But this Isabelle, she's strong, no?" the actress asked.

"So I've heard," said the magician. "But is she strong enough?"

"He thinks so," the diva said, nodding at Chance. "But who can say? You know what it takes to break free of the crone. It's a battle, as we who have waged it well know. And battles inflict wounds."

She pushed up her sleeve. An ugly scar ran from her wrist to her elbow. "From my father. He came after me with a knife when I told him I would not enter a convent as he wished but would go to Vienna instead to study opera."

The magician pulled the neck of her jacket open to show her scar, livid and shiny, just under her collarbone. "From a rock. Thrown by a priest who called me a devil. Because the townspeople liked my miracles better than his."

The actress's hand went to a gold locket pinned on her jacket, over her heart. She opened it and showed the others painted miniatures of a girl and a boy.

"No scar, but a wound that will never heal," she said, tears shimmering in her eyes. "My children. Taken from me by a judge and given to my drunken husband. Because only an immoral woman would exhibit herself upon a stage."

The magician pulled the actress close. She kissed her cheek and wiped her tears away with a handkerchief. Then she balled the handkerchief up and pressed it between her palms. When she opened her hands again, it was gone and a butterfly was sitting in its place.

As the three women watched, the butterfly took wing, carried aloft by the breeze.

It flew past a little monkey playing with a rope of pearls. Past a violinist and a trumpeter, a cook, a scientist, and three ballerinas, all with scars of their own.

Past a man with amber eyes, raging at the falling dusk. Swearing at the treacherous roads. Building his teetering human tower taller and taller.

A smile, small but defiant, curved the magician's full red lips. "That's what we do with our pain," she said, watching the butterfly rise. "We make it into something beautiful."

"We make it into something meaningful," said the diva.

"We make it matter," whispered the actress.

## - TWENTY -

As night came down, Fate sipped a cup of chamomile tea with Madame LeBenêt, Chance tried to find his way to Saint-Michel, and Isabelle, standing in her kitchen, cast a worried glance at her sister.

Tavi was doing what she always did in the evening: sitting by the hearth, a book open in her lap. But the furrows in her forehead looked deeper tonight, the shadows under her eyes darker.

Always bookish and inward, she'd become even more so since Ella had left. Sometimes Isabelle felt as if she were watching her sister fade like cooling embers, and that one day soon she would turn to ash and blow away.

The two sisters were a year apart in age and looked very much alike. They both had auburn hair, high foreheads, a smattering of freckles across their noses, and eyes the color of strong coffee. Tavi was taller, with a lean figure; Isabelle was curvier. But it was their personalities more than anything else that set them apart. Tavi was cool and contained; Isabelle was anything but.

As Isabelle arranged slices of ham, apple, bread, and cheese on a plate to take upstairs to her mother, she wondered how to draw her sister out. "What are you reading, Tav?" she asked.

"*The Compendious Book on Calculation by Completion and Balancing* by the Persian scholar Al-Khwarizmi," Tavi replied, without looking up.

"Sounds like a page-turner," Isabelle teased. "Who's Al-Khwarizmi?"

"The father of algebra," Tavi replied, looking up. "Though many believe the Greek mathematician Diophantus can also lay claim to the title."

"That's a funny word, *algebra*. Don't you think?" Isabelle asked, eager to keep her talking.

Tavi smiled. "It comes from Arabic. From *al-jabr*, which means 'the reunion of broken parts.' Al-Khwarizmi believed that what's broken can be made whole again if you just apply the right equation." Her smile dimmed a little. "If only there were an equation that could do the same for people."

She was about to say more, but a voice, shrilling from the doorway, cut her off.

"Isabelle! Octavia! Why aren't you dressed? We're going to be late for the ball!"

Maman stepped into the kitchen, her lips set in an icy frown. She was wearing a satin gown the color of a winter sky and a plume of white ostrich feathers in her badly pinned-up hair. Her face was pale; her eyes were feverishly bright. Her hands fluttered around her body like doves, patting her hair one minute, twining in her pearls the next.

Isabelle's heart sank at the sight of her; she had not been right since Ella left. Sometimes she was her competent, imperious self. At other times, like tonight, she was confused. Lost in the past. Convinced that they were going to a dinner, a ball, or the palace.

"Maman, you have the date wrong," she said now, giving her a soothing smile.

"Don't be silly. I have the invitation right here." Maman showed Isabelle the printed card she was holding, its ivory surface smudged, its edges bent.

Isabelle recognized it; it had arrived months ago. "Yes, you do," she said cheerily. "But you see, Maman, that ball has already taken place."

Maman stared at the engraved words. "I—I can't seem to read the date . . ." she said, her words trailing off.

"Come. I'll help you undress. You can put on a nice comfortable night-dress and lie down."

"Are you quite certain about the date, Isabelle?" Maman asked, her tyrannical tone giving way to a bewildered one.

"Yes. Go back to your room now. I'll bring you your supper," Isabelle coaxed, taking her mother's arm.

But Maman, suddenly vexed again, shook her off. "Octavia, put that book down!" she demanded. "You'll ruin your eyes with all those numbers." She strode across the room and snatched the book from Tavi's hands. "Honestly! What man ever thinks, *Oh, how I'd love to meet a girl who can solve for x*? Go get *dressed*. We cannot keep the countess waiting!"

"For God's sake, Maman, stop this!" Tavi snapped. "That ball was ages ago and even if it wasn't, the countess doesn't want us anymore. Nobody does!"

Maman stood very still. She said nothing for quite some time. When she spoke again, her voice was little more than a whisper. "Of course the countess wants us. Why wouldn't she?"

"Because she *knows*," Tavi said. "About Ella and how we treated her. She hates us. The whole village hates us. The whole *country* does. We're outcasts!"

Maman pressed her palm to her forehead. She closed her eyes. When she opened them again, the febrile brightness had receded and clarity had returned. But something else was there, too—a cold, menacing anger.

"You think yourself very clever, Octavia, but you are not," she said. "Before the prince came for Ella, I had five offers of marriage for her. *Five.* Even though I turned her into a kitchen girl. Do you know how many I've had for you? Zero. Solve *that* equation, my dear."

Tavi, stung, looked away.

"What, exactly, do you expect to do with all your studying?" Maman asked, waving the book in the air. "Become a professor? A scientist? Such things are only for men. If I cannot find a husband for you, who will keep you when I'm no longer here? What will you do? Become a governess to another woman's children, living in some cold attic room, eating leftovers from her table? Work as a seamstress, stitching day and night until you go blind?" Maman shook her head disgustedly. "Even in rags,

Ella outshined you. She was pretty and pleasing, and you? You make yourself ugly with your numbers, your formulas, your ridiculous equations. It must stop. It *will* stop."

She walked to the hearth and threw the book into the fire.

*"No!"* Tavi cried. She leapt out of her chair, grabbed a poker, and tried to rescue it, but the flames were already blackening the pages.

"Finish dressing, both of you!" Maman ordered, striding out of the room. "Jacques! Bring the carriage!"

"Tavi, did you have to upset her?" Isabelle asked angrily. "Maman!" she called, running after her mother. "Where are you?"

She found her trying to open the front door, still calling for the carriage. It took Isabelle ages to get her back upstairs. Once she had her in her bedroom, she helped her undress and gave her a glass of brandy to calm her. She tried to get her to eat, but Maman refused. Eventually, Isabelle managed to get her into bed, but as she was pulling the covers over her, Maman sat up and grabbed her arm. "What will become of you and your sister? Tell me?" she asked, her eyes fearful.

"We'll be fine. We'll manage. Stepfather left us money, didn't he?"

Maman laughed. It was a tired, hopeless sound. "Your stepfather left us nothing but debts. I've sold the Rembrandt. Most of the silver. Several of my jewels . . ."

Isabelle was exhausted. Her head hurt. "Hush, Maman," she said. "Go to sleep now. We'll talk about it tomorrow."

When she returned to the kitchen, she found Tavi kneeling by the hearth, staring into the fire. Isabelle took the poker from her hand and tried to pull the book out of the grate, but it was too late.

"Stop, Iz. Leave it. It's gone," said Tavi, with a hitch in her voice.

Isabelle's heart ached for her. Steady, logical Tavi never cried. "I'm sorry. I just wanted to help," she said, putting the poker down.

"Do you? Dress my hair, then," Tavi said brokenly. "Rouge my cheeks. Make me pretty. Can you do that?"

Isabelle didn't reply. If only she could make Tavi pretty. And herself. How different their lives would be.

"I didn't think so," said Tavi, staring at the ashes of her beloved book. "I could solve all the Diophantine equations, extend Newton's work on infinite series, complete Euler's analysis of prime numbers, and it wouldn't matter." She looked at Isabelle. "Ella is the beauty. You and I are the ugly stepsisters. And so the world reduces us, all three of us, to our lowest common denominator."

## – TWENTY-ONE –

Deep within the Maison Douleur, a tall grandfather clock, its pendulum sweeping back and forth like a scythe, ticked the minutes away.

Maman and Tavi were both in bed, but Isabelle couldn't sleep. She knew she'd only toss and turn if she tried, so she stayed in the kitchen and sat by the hearth, picking at the supper she'd fixed for Maman.

Once, she welcomed the night. She would climb down the thick vine that grew outside her bedroom window and meet Felix. They would gaze at the night sky and count shooting stars, and sometimes, if they were as still as stones and lucky, they would see an owl swoop down on her prey or a stag walk out of the Wildwood, his antlers rising over his noble head like a crown.

Now the darkness haunted Isabelle. She saw ghosts everywhere. In mirrors and windows. In the reflection of a copper pot. She heard them in the creak of a door. Felt them fluttering in the curtains. It wasn't the darkness that was haunted, though; it was Isabelle herself. Ghosts are not the dead, come back from the grave to torment the living; ghosts are already here. They live inside us, keening in the ashes of our sorrows, mired in the thick, clutching mud of our regrets.

As Isabelle stared into the fireplace at the dying coals, the ghosts crowded in upon her.

She saw Ella, Tavi, Maman, and herself riding in their carriage. Maman was complimenting Ella luxuriantly. "How pretty you look today!" she purred. "Did you see the admiring glance the mayor's son gave you?"

Other images flickered to life. Maman frowning at Tavi's needlework, telling her she should practice until she could sew as nicely as Ella. Maman wincing at Isabelle's singing, then asking Ella for a song.

Envy, resentment, shame—Maman had rubbed these things against Isabelle's heart, and Tavi's, until they were raw. Maman was subtle; she was clever. She'd started early. She'd started small. She knew that even tiny wounds, left untended, can fester and swell and turn a heart black.

More ghosts came. The ghost of a black stallion. The ghost of a boy. But Isabelle couldn't bear these, so she stood up to carry her plate to the sink.

The clock struck twelve as she did, its chimes echoing ominously throughout the house. Isabelle told herself it was time for bed, then remembered that she hadn't locked the door to the stables or closed the chickens in their coop. With all the upset Maman had caused, she'd forgotten.

As she hobbled back to the fireplace to bank the coals, a darting movement caught her eye. A mouse had ventured onto the hearth and was digging in a crack between the stones. As she scrabbled furiously, two tiny mouselings scurried to her side. An instant later, the mouse stood up on her hind legs, squeaking in triumph. Clutched in her paw was a small green lentil. She bit it in two and handed the halves to her children, who nibbled it greedily.

Guilt's thin, cold fingers gripped Isabelle as she remembered how that lentil got there.

Ella had overheard Maman telling Isabelle and Tavi that the prince was holding a ball and that all the maidens in the realm were invited. She'd asked if she could go, and in response, Maman had picked up a bowl of lentils and thrown them into the fireplace.

"There were a thousand lentils in that bowl. Pick them all out of the ashes and you can go," she'd said, a cruel smile quirking her lips.

It had been an impossible task, yet Ella had managed it. Isabelle had just discovered how: the mice had helped her. When she had presented the full bowl, Maman had snatched it out of her hands, dumped it out on the kitchen table and counted the lentils. Then she'd triumphantly announced that one was missing and that Ella could not go to the ball.

*What was it like for Ella to be so alone, to have no friends except for mice?* Isabelle wondered. Then, with a sharp stab of pain, she realized she didn't have to wonder—she knew.

The mouselings finished their meal, then looked at their mother, but she had nothing more for them. She'd eaten nothing herself.

"Wait!" Isabelle said to the mice. "Wait there!" She hurried back to the supper tray but moved so clumsily that she scared the creatures. They scampered away.

"No! Don't go!" Isabelle cried, heartbroken. She snatched a piece of cheese off the tray, then limped back to the hearth, but the mice were nowhere to be seen.

"Come back," she begged, looking for them. *"Please."*

Kneeling by the fireplace, she placed the cheese on a hearthstone. Then she sat back down in her chair. Waiting. Hoping. But the mice did not return. They thought she meant to hurt them. Why wouldn't they? That's what she did.

Unbidden, voices from the market echoed in Isabelle's head. Tantine telling her that people wouldn't forget or forgive. Cecile calling her ugly. Worst of all, the words of the baker's wife: *You were cruel to a defenseless girl.*

Remorse curled around Isabelle's heart like a snake and squeezed. Tears spilled down her cheeks. Her head bowed, she did not see the shadow fill the kitchen window. Or the hand, pale as moonlight, press against it.

By the time Isabelle lifted her head again, the shadow was gone. Wiping her eyes, she stood. The barn and the chicken coop were still waiting for her. She shuffled to the door, lit the lantern that was resting on a hook next to it, and walked out into the night, sorrow hanging off her like a shroud.

Had Isabelle waited just a few more seconds, she would have seen the mother mouse creep out of the shadows and back to the hearth. She would have seen the hungry creature pick up the cheese. She would have seen her, whiskers quivering, blink up at the window where the shadow had passed.

Then shudder. And run.

## - TWENTY-TWO -

Isabelle was glad of her lantern.

The moon was full tonight but had disappeared behind clouds. Once, she could navigate the grounds of the Maison Douleur in the dark, but it had been a long time since she'd ventured outside after midnight.

The outbuildings were located to the west of the mansion. Isabelle followed the path of flat white stones that led over the lawns, around the linden, through a gate in a wooden fence, and down a gentle hill.

Bertrand the rooster opened one suspicious eye as Isabelle shined the lantern into the chicken coop. After a quick head count, she latched the door and continued to the stables. Martin was dozing in his stall. He woke briefly as she checked on him, snorted with irritation, then settled back into sleep. Isabelle secured the stable door and started back for the mansion.

It was as she was closing the gate that it happened.

Out of nowhere, the gentle night breeze stiffened into a vicious wind. It ripped her hair loose, slammed the gate shut, and snuffed out her lantern. And then it was gone.

Isabelle pressed a hand to her chest, startled. Luckily, the wind had also scattered the clouds. Moonlight now illuminated the white stones snaking across the grass, making it possible for her to find her way. As the path carried her past the linden, the tree's leafy branches swayed in the breeze, beckoning to her.

Isabelle walked closer to the linden, thinking of the dove who had warned the prince of her deception. Was it roosting in those branches now? Watching her? The thought made her shiver.

She put her lantern down and stared up at the tree, remembering the days she'd spent climbing in those branches, pretending she was scaling the mast of a pirate ship or the walls of an enemy's fortress, going higher and higher.

The ghosts she'd tried to banish earlier crowded in on her again. She saw herself as a child, fearlessly threading her way through the tree limbs. She saw Tavi with her slate and her equations, and Ella with her daisy chains. They had been so innocent then, the three of them. So happy together. Good, and good enough.

The remorse that had squeezed her heart now crushed it.

"I'm sorry. I'm so, so sorry," she whispered to the three little girls, aching with longing and loss. "I wish things were different. I wish *I* were different."

The leaves murmured and sighed. She almost felt as if the tree was speaking to her. Shaking her head at her own foolishness, she went on her way.

She'd only taken a few steps when she saw it . . . a movement in the darkness.

Isabelle froze. Her heart stuttered with fear.

She wasn't alone.

Someone was standing in the shadow of the linden tree.

Watching her.

## – TWENTY-THREE –

The figure stepped out of the darkness.

Isabelle, her heart still battering against her ribs, saw that it was a woman—tall, lithe, pale as bone. Long auburn hair floated around her shoulders. She wore a high crown of twining blackbriar. Living forester moths, their blue-green wings shimmering, adorned it. A yellow-eyed hawk sat perched on her shoulder. Her own eyes were emerald green, her lips black. The gown she wore was the color of moss.

The woman was clutching a struggling rabbit by the scruff of its neck. As Isabelle watched, she lifted the animal to her face, breathed its scent, and licked her lips. Her sharp teeth glinted in the moonlight.

Isabelle had never seen her before, yet she recognized her.

When Ella was small, she'd woven fanciful tales about a magical creature who lived in the hollow at the base of the linden tree. She was a woman sometimes, and sometimes a fox. She was a wild thing, majestic and beautiful, but sly and fierce, too. Isabelle had always thought Ella's stories were just that—stories.

Until now.

The woman gave her a smile, the same smile she'd given the rabbit right before she snatched it from a patch of clover. Then she started toward her, step by slow step.

Everything inside Isabelle told her to run, but she couldn't, she was mesmerized. This was no gossamer-winged creature sipping dew from flower petals. Nor was she a plump, cozy old godmother, all smiles and rhymes. This was a being both dark and dangerous.

This was Tanaquill, the fairy queen.

## - TWENTY-FOUR -

"You summoned me," the fairy queen said, stopping a foot away from Isabelle.

"I—I didn't. No. I don't think. D-Did I?" Isabelle stammered, saucer-eyed.

Tanaquill's eyes glittered darkly. Her teeth looked sharper up close. She had long black talons at the end of her fingers. "Your *heart* summoned me." She laughed dryly. "What's left of it."

She pressed a pale hand to Isabelle's chest and cocked her head, listening. Isabelle felt the fairy queen's talons curve into the fabric of her dress. She heard the beat of her heart amplified under Tanaquill's palm. It grew louder and louder. For a moment, she feared that Tanaquill would rip it, red and beating, right out of her chest.

Finally, Tanaquill lowered her hand. "Cut away piece by piece by piece," she said. "Ella's heart was not."

*How would she know that?* Isabelle wondered, and then, with a jolt, it

71

came to her: "It was *you*," she whispered in amazement. "You're the one who helped Ella get to the ball!"

She and Tavi had tried to puzzle out how their stepsister had acquired a coach, horses, footmen, a gown, and glass slippers. And how she'd escaped from her room after Isabelle had locked her in it when the prince had come to call. Now she knew.

"A pumpkin transformed into a coach, some mice into horses, a lizard or two for footmen . . . child's play," Tanaquill sniffed. She regarded her rabbit again.

Isabelle's pulse quickened. *If the fairy queen can make a coach out of a pumpkin, what else can she do?* she wondered. For a moment she forgot to be scared. Hope kindled inside her.

"Please, Your Grace," she said, "would you help me, too?"

Tanaquill tore her gaze from the rabbit. "It was easy to help Ella, but I cannot help a girl such as you. You are too full of bitterness. It fills the place where your heart used to be," she said, turning away.

Isabelle lurched after her. "No! Wait! Please wait!"

The fairy queen whirled around, her lips curled in a snarl. "For what, girl? Ella knew her heart's deepest wish. Do you?"

Isabelle faltered, frightened, but desire made her bold. A dozen wishes welled up inside her, all born from her happiest memories. In her mind's eye, she saw swords and books, horses, the Wildwood. Summer days. Daisy chains. She remembered a promise and a kiss.

Isabelle opened her mouth to ask for these things, but just as the words were about to leave her tongue, she bit them back.

All her life, everything she'd wanted, everything she'd loved . . . they were always the wrong things. They got her into trouble. They broke her heart. They weren't for her; the world had said so. So why ask for them? They'd only bring more heartache.

There was one thing, though, that could fix everything. It could make people stop hating her. It could make her what Maman wanted her to be, what the baker's wife and Cecile and the villagers and the old merchant and all the suitors who came to the house and the whole entire world demanded that she be.

Isabelle looked Tanaquill in the eye and said, "I wish to be pretty."

Tanaquill growled low in her throat and Isabelle felt as if she'd given the wrong answer, but the fairy queen didn't refuse her. Instead, she said, "Wishes are never simply granted. They must be earned."

"I'll do anything," Isabelle said fervently.

"That is what all mortals say," said Tanaquill with a scornful laugh. "They'll do *anything*. Anything but that which must be done. Only one thing can rid you of the bitterness inside. Do it, and perhaps I will help you."

"I'll do it. I *swear*," Isabelle said, clasping her hands together. "What is it?"

"Find the lost pieces of your heart."

## - TWENTY-FIVE -

Isabelle blinked. "Find the pieces of my heart?" she repeated, as if she hadn't heard the fairy queen correctly. "I—I don't understand. How do I find pieces of a *heart*? How did Ella?"

"Ella did not have to."

Isabelle scowled. "Of course not. I bet all *she* had to do was smile."

Her words, prompted by resentment, were tart and disrespectful. Tanaquill's emerald eyes hardened; she turned away.

Panic exploded inside of Isabelle like a dropped glass. Why could she *never* control herself? "I'm sorry. Tell me what the pieces are. Tell me how to find them. *Please*," she begged, running after her.

Tanaquill relented. "You know what they are."

"But I don't!" Isabelle protested. "I have no idea!"

"And you must find your own way to them."

"How? Show me," Isabelle implored, growing desperate. "Help me."

Still clutching the struggling rabbit, Tanaquill bent down by the base of the linden tree and, with her free hand, raked through the small bones scattered in the grass around it. She picked up a small, slender jawbone that had belonged to a darting, wily animal—a weasel or marten—and the empty half shell of a walnut, and gave them to Isabelle. Next, she reached into the thick blackbriar climbing the linden's trunk, drew a prickly seedpod from between its sharp thorns, and handed that to her, too.

"These gifts will help you attain your heart's desire," Tanaquill said.

Isabelle looked down at the things she was holding, and as she did, the emotions she'd tried to hold down spiked like a fever, weakening everything strong and sure inside her. Her blood felt thin, her guts watery, her bones as crumbly as old mortar. The apology she'd made only moments ago was forgotten. Angry, jealous words burst from her lips.

"Gifts? *These* things?" she cried, staring at the bone, the nutshell, and the seedpod. "You gave Ella a beautiful gown and glass slippers! A carriage and horses. *Those* are gifts. You've given *me* a handful of *garbage!*"

She looked up, but Tanaquill had turned away again. As Isabelle watched, the fairy queen disappeared into the hollow in a swirl of red hair and green skirts. Isabelle hobbled after her, but as she did, a thin, high-pitched scream rose and was abruptly cut off—the rabbit's death cry. She took a wary step back.

Her gaze returned to the objects in her hand. The fairy queen was mocking her with them, she was certain of it, and that certainty was painful to her.

74

"Ugly," she said as her fingers touched the jawbone. "Useless," she said as they brushed the nutshell. "Hurtful," she said as the seedpod pricked them. "Just like me."

She would toss the objects into the hearth in the morning. They could at least help kindle a fire. She shoved them into her skirt pocket, then walked the rest of the way to her house, convinced that there was no help for her, no hope. There was only despair, heavy and hard, weighing on what was left of her cutaway heart.

Most people will fight when there is some hope of winning, no matter how slim. They are called brave. Only a few will keep fighting when all hope is gone. They are called warriors.

Isabelle was a warrior once, though she has forgotten it.

Will she remember? It does not look good. Then again, few things do in the dead of night. The small dark hours are the undoing of many. Candlelight throws shadows on the walls of our souls, shadows that turn a mouse into a monster, a downturn into disaster.

Should you ever decide, in those small dark hours, to hang yourself, well, that is your choice.

But don't hunt for the rope until morning.

By then you'll find a much better use for it.

## - TWENTY-SIX -

As Isabelle made her way upstairs to her bed, Fate made her way through the Wildwood.

Spotting a fallen tree, she stopped, plucked a centipede from the rotted wood, and bit off its head. "Perfect," she said, licking droplets of black from her lips. "Bitter blood makes bitter ink."

As she dropped the still-writhing body into the basket she was carrying, she looked up into the high branches above her and said, "I need wolfsbane. Keep an eye out for it. A sprig of belladonna would be helpful, too."

A raven, perched on a pine bough, flew off and Fate resumed her stroll. A plump brown spider went into the basket, a mossy bat skull, white Queen of the Night flowers, speckled toadstools—all ingredients for the inks she was making.

Fate was prodding the bleached rib cage of a long-dead deer, hoping to scare some beetles out of it, when her raven flew down and landed beside her. A moment later, a girl stood where the bird had been, bright-eyed and blinking, wearing a black dress. She dropped a purple bloom into Fate's basket.

"Ah! You found the belladonna. Well done, Losca. Its berries give a nice luster to the darker inks, like *Doubt* and *Denial*. Of course, I must get the girl's map back before I can make changes to it. Chance thinks *he* can redraw it, but that may prove more difficult than he anticipates. Have you seen any sign of him yet?"

Losca shook her head.

"He'll come. I've never known Chance to back out of a wager. I shall win this game, but not without a fight. He often gains the upper hand, however briefly, through sheer unpredictability. Mortals lose their heads around him. They start to put stock in their hopes and dreams, the poor fools. He *actually* makes them believe they can do anything." She clucked her tongue. "And he has the cheek to call *me* cruel."

Fate walked on, poking and digging, glad to be out of dour Madame LeBenêt's uncomfortable house for a few hours. Losca followed her. Absorbed in the hunt for ingredients, they didn't realize they'd reached the edge of the Wildwood until they heard voices.

"What's this?" Fate muttered, peering between the branches of a bushy tree. She soon saw that a shallow, grassy hill sloped away from where she was standing and flattened into a broad pasture. Stretching across it, as far as the eye could see, were neat rows of white canvas tents. Here and there, fires flickered. A horse whinnied. Someone played a sad, sweet tune on a violin.

Fate drew the hood of her black cloak up over her head. She was curious to see Colonel Cafard's encampment up close.

"Take this," she said, handing Losca the basket. As she did, she noticed that the tail of a small snake was hanging from the girl's mouth. Fate glared at her. "What have I told you about eating the ingredients?" she scolded.

Shamefaced, Losca sucked the tail into her mouth and swallowed it, like a child with a string of spaghetti.

"Stay close and don't make any noise," Fate cautioned. Losca nodded.

The two hugged the edge of the camp to avoid being seen. Though it was late, men were huddled around the fires, unable to sleep. They talked of Volkmar and what they would do to him once they got hold of him. Fate heard bravado in their voices but saw fear in their eyes. A grizzled sergeant sat among them, trying to raise their spirits by regaling them with tales of battlefield glories—until a scream, ragged and raw, rang out, abruptly ending his tale.

Fate heard the flapping of wings, then felt a weight descend on her shoulder. The basket Losca had been carrying lay on the ground.

"Now, now, child. There's nothing to be afraid of," she murmured, stroking the bird's back.

She picked up the basket, then sought out the source of the scream. Her search led her to the far side of the camp, where its hospital was located. There, men lay on cots, writhing and moaning, some mortally wounded, others delirious with pain and fever. A surgeon and his assistant moved among them, cutting and stitching, administering morphine, mopping drenched brows.

A woman moved among them, too.

Graceful and slender, she wore a gown the color of night with flowing sleeves and a high neck. Her long dark hair hung down to her waist. She was out of place among all the soldiers, impossible to miss, yet no one seemed to notice her.

A man cried out. He called for his sweetheart, then begged to die. The woman went to him. She knelt by his cot and took his hand. At her touch, his head rolled back, his eyes opened to the sky, his tortured body stilled.

The woman rose, and Fate saw what the soldier had seen—not a face, but a skull—its eyes yawning black pits, its mouth a wide, mirthless smile. She nodded at Fate, then moved off to another soldier, a boy of sixteen, crying for his mother.

"Death is busy tonight," Fate said somberly, "and has no time for pleasantries."

Fate had seen enough; she turned away and headed back to the enveloping darkness of the Wildwood. When she reached the trees, she cast a last glance over the camp and the sleeping village beyond it.

"Volkmar's out there. I feel him," she said. "Hiding in the hills and hollows. Coming closer every day. What will be unleashed upon these poor, innocent people?"

The raven shook out her feathers. She clicked her beak.

"Who is responsible? Ah, Losca, must you ask?" Fate said heavily. "This is *his* fault, of course. All his. Will that reckless amber-eyed fool ever learn?"

## - TWENTY-SEVEN -

Isabelle, still bleary-eyed from sleep, her hair in a messy braid, pulled a clean dress over her head and buttoned it.

She'd slept badly, kept awake all night by images of Tanaquill. By the time the sun had risen, she'd convinced herself she'd only dreamt the fairy queen. Such creatures did not exist.

But as she picked up yesterday's dress off the floor, meaning to put it in her clothes hamper, something fell out of one of its pockets. Isabelle bent down to retrieve it. It was roughly two inches long, black, and covered with small thorns.

It was a seedpod.

She thrust her hand into the pocket and fished out two more objects—a walnut shell and a jawbone. A shiver moved through her as she remembered how she got these things. The dark creature she'd met by the linden tree was no dream.

*I wish to be pretty*, she'd said to the fairy queen. And the fairy queen had told her to find the lost pieces of her heart.

Isabelle examined the three gifts one by one. Tanaquill said they would help her, but how? It was no clearer to her now than it had been last night. *Maybe they're meant to turn into something*, she reasoned. Hadn't Tanaquill said that she'd transformed a pumpkin and mice for Ella?

She turned the nutshell over in her hand. *This could become a pretty hat*, she thought. Running a finger over the jawbone's tiny teeth, she imagined that it might turn into a lovely hair comb. Next she regarded the seedpod but couldn't imagine how the knobby, spiky thing could ever turn into anything pretty.

Frustrated, Isabelle shoved the three objects into her pocket, then tossed her dirty dress into the hamper. She put her boots on and made her way downstairs. She'd had enough of the fairy queen's mysteriousness for the moment. There were chores to do.

As she walked across the foyer to the kitchen, a rich, bitter scent wafted toward her. *Tavi's up and she made a pot of coffee*, she thought. *I hope she's scrambled some eggs, too.*

Gone were the days when she would come downstairs to a full

breakfast set out by the servants. Whatever she and Tavi wanted now, they had to make themselves.

Finding enough to eat in the summer wasn't difficult. The hens were laying, the fruit trees were heavily laden, and good things were growing in the garden. But what would happen come winter? A few days ago, Isabelle had decided to try her hand at pickling vegetables and Tavi had promised to help. Today seemed like a good day to start. The garden was full of cucumbers and they'd bought salt during their trip to the market. If her efforts were successful, she would put the pickles in the cellar for the cold months. She pushed open the kitchen door now, eager to see what her sister had made for breakfast.

As it turned out, nothing.

Except a breathtaking mess.

## – TWENTY-EIGHT –

Tavi was sitting at the long wooden table, peering through a magnifying glass.

The tabletop was littered with plates and bowls, all containing food, but everything was rotten. A slice of bread was furry with mold. A bowl of milk had curdled. A plum had shriveled in its skin.

"What are you *doing*, Tavi? This is disgusting!" Isabelle exclaimed. Her sister often conducted experiments, but they usually involved levers, ramps, and pulleys, not mold.

Tavi lowered her magnifying glass. "I'm hunting for very small, possibly single-celled, organisms," she said excitedly. "I set all of this out on a high shelf in the pantry a few days ago. I selected a high shelf because warm air rises, of course, and speeds the organisms' growth. Just look how they've progressed!"

Isabelle wrinkled her nose. "But *why*?"

Tavi grinned. "I'm glad you asked," she said. "The dominant theory of disease proposes that sickness occurs when miasma, or bad air, rises from rotting matter and is breathed in. But *I* think it occurs when some kind of organism, one invisible to the human eye, is passed from a sick person to a healthy one." She gestured at the stack of books on the table. "Why, just read Thucydides on the Plague of Athens. Or Girolamo Fracastoro in *De contagione et contagiosis morbis*."

"I'll rephrase my question. Why hunt for organisms *now*? We're supposed to be pickling cucumbers today. You promised to help me."

"That's exactly why I'm conducting my research," Tavi replied. "When you mentioned preserving food, I began to wonder about the processes involved—mechanical, chemical, biological."

"Of course you did," said Isabelle, suppressing a smile. Her happiness at seeing color in Tavi's cheeks and fire in her eyes far outweighed her irritation over the mess. Only one thing could pull Tavi away from math and that was science.

Looking at her sister, Isabelle wondered how anyone could ever call her ugly. She longed to tell Tavi that the intensity in her eyes and the passion in her voice made her catch her breath. The same way a falcon in flight did. A still lake at dawn. Or a high winter moon. But the sudden lump in her throat wouldn't let her.

"Take jam, for example," Tavi continued. "Heat is applied to fruit and sugar is added, correct?"

Isabelle swallowed. She nodded.

"Is that why jam doesn't spoil? Does the heat kill organisms? Does the sugar play any role? And what about pickling? Does vinegar inhibit organisms' growth? Depending on the type of organism you have, and what it colonizes—milk, cabbage, dough, or a human body—you could end up with cheese, sauerkraut, bread, or the Black Death!" Tavi said gleefully. "But what *is* that organism, Iz? That's what I'm dying to know. Aren't you?"

"No. I'm dying to know when you plan to stop theorizing about pickles and help me make some."

"Soon, soon!" Tavi said, picking up her magnifying glass again. "I made coffee. Help yourself," she added.

Isabelle shook her head. "No, thanks. I've lost my appetite. I'm going to feed Martin and let the chickens out."

Isabelle walked to the kitchen door, but halfway there, she turned and looked back at her sister, who was still peering through her magnifying glass, and thought, *Tavi is so smart. Maybe she can help me figure out what I'm supposed to be searching for.*

Isabelle's hand went to her pocket, she started to hobble back to the table, but then she stopped. Tavi was so logical, so skeptical, she probably wouldn't believe in Tanaquill. And if she told her about the fairy queen, she'd also have to tell her what she'd wished for and she was ashamed to admit that she'd asked to be pretty. Tavi would scoff. She'd mock.

As if sensing that Isabelle was still there, Tavi looked up from her work. "All right," she huffed impatiently. "I'll go."

"Go where?" Isabelle asked, puzzled.

"To the stables. The chicken coop. That's what you're about to ask me to do, isn't it? Abandon my scientific investigations to do the oh-so-important work of shoveling horse manure?"

"Don't rush," Isabelle said, glad she'd decided against telling her about Tanaquill. *Sarcasm is the weapon of the wounded*, she thought, *and Tavi wields it lethally.*

As Tavi scribbled figures in a notebook, Isabelle took the egg basket from its hook. Then she grabbed a clasp knife from a shelf, dropped it into her pocket, and left the kitchen. A minute later, she was making her way down the hill to the coop. As she neared the bottom, a fox—green-eyed, her coat a deep russet—darted in front of her. She paused, watching the creature lope across the grass.

In the stories Ella had spun, Tanaquill had sometimes taken the form of a fox. *Is that her?* Isabelle wondered. *Is she watching me? Waiting to see if I carry out her task?*

She didn't have long to wonder. Just as the fox disappeared into some brush, a shriek, high and bloodcurdling, ripped through the air.

There was only one creature who could make such a terrible sound.

"Bertrand the rooster," Isabelle whispered as she set off running.

## – TWENTY-NINE –

The shriek came again.

*That fox is no fairy queen*, Isabelle thought. *It's a chicken thief. And it sounds like another one is still in the coop.*

She, Tavi, and Maman depended on their hens for eggs. Losing even one would be disastrous.

Isabelle kept running, as fast as she could, heedless of the pain her bad foot caused her.

"Hang on, Bertrand!" she cried. "I'm coming!"

The rooster was a fierce creature with sharp, curved spurs on his legs. He'd chased Isabelle up a tree many times. But he was no match for a fox.

*Or a wolf*, she thought. Her blood ran cold at the very idea. She'd been so frightened for Bertrand and the hens, she'd hurried to the coop without grabbing so much as a stick to defend the henhouse, or herself.

As she ran past the stables now, flushed and panting, her eyes fell on the coop. She saw that the door was open and hanging off its hinges.

She also saw that it was no fox that was stealing her chickens, no wolf. It was a man—dirty, thin, and desperate.

## – THIRTY –

The man was holding a cloth sack. It was moving and clucking. On the ground near the coop lay Bertrand, his neck broken.

Anger shoved Isabelle's fear aside. "What have you done to my rooster?" she shouted. "Put those chickens down!"

"Ah, forgive me, mademoiselle!" the man said with an oily smile. "The house is shuttered. I had no idea anyone lived here."

"Now you do. So leave," Isabelle demanded, gesturing to the road.

The man chuckled. He stepped out of the coop. His eyes swept up and down Isabelle, lingering on her hips, her breasts.

*The opportunity of defeating the enemy is provided by the enemy himself.*

This time, the words in Isabelle's head were not Alexander the Great's, as they had been when she faced down Cecile, but Sun Tzu's—a Chinese general who'd lived over two thousand years ago.

She put the words to good use. While the man ogled her, she eyed him back and determined that he was unarmed. No sword hung from his waist, no dagger protruded from his boot. She also saw that she'd left a pitchfork leaning against a tree, a few yards behind him. All she had to do was get to it.

His gaze shifted from her to her house. "Why are you out here all alone? Where's your father? Your brothers?"

Isabelle knew better than to answer that question. "Those chickens are all my family has. If you take them, we'll starve," she said, trying to appeal to his better nature.

"And if I don't, *I'll* starve. I haven't eaten a proper meal in weeks.

84

I'm a soldier in the king's army and I'm hungry," the man said righteously.

"What kind of soldier leaves his barracks to steal chickens?"

"Are you calling me a liar, girl?" the man asked, taking a menacing step toward her.

"And a deserter," said Isabelle, holding her ground.

The man's eyes narrowed. "And if I am, what of it? We are led to battle like lambs to the slaughter. Volkmar knows the king's every move before the king himself knows it. The others can die if they wish. Not me."

"You can take a few eggs if you're hungry," Isabelle said, adamant. "Put the sack down."

The man laughed. He nodded at the pitchfork behind him. "Or what? Or you'll come after me with that rusty tool you've been eyeing? Have you even held a tool before tonight?" He took another step toward her and with a leer said, "How'd you like to hold mine?"

"Go. *Now*. Or you'll be sorry," Isabelle said, ignoring his ugly joke.

"I'm taking four chickens. That's how it will be," he said.

Fury flared in Isabelle. Her mother and sister were not going to go hungry so this thief could gorge himself. But what could she do? He was standing directly in front of the pitchfork now, blocking her access to it.

*I need a weapon*, she thought, looking around desperately. *A rake, a shovel, anything.*

Remembering her clasp knife, she dropped the egg basket she was still holding and plunged her hand into her pocket. A pain, sharp and startling, nipped at her fingers. She gave a small cry, but the deserter, who'd gone back into the coop, didn't hear her.

She pulled her hand out of her pocket and saw that her pointer and middle fingers were sliced across the tips and bleeding. Stretching her pocket wide, she peered inside it, thinking that the knife must have came open, but no. An object, white, slender, and smeared with her blood, jutted up at her. She realized it was the jawbone Tanaquill had given her. She pulled it out of her pocket and saw that its tiny teeth were what had cut her. With a screech, the angled portion of the jaw suddenly straightened in her hand, making her gasp. The end that had hinged to the animal's skull fattened into a hilt. The other end lengthened into a blade, its edge serrated with the razor-like teeth.

To her astonishment, Isabelle found that she was holding a sword, one that was finely balanced and lethal. As she was marveling at the weapon, the man reemerged from the chicken coop. Immediately she advanced on him. "You're going to put my hens down and leave. *That's* how it's going to be," she said.

He looked up, laughing, but his laughter died when he saw the fearsome sword in her hand. "Where did you get that?" he asked.

But Isabelle was in no mood for questions. She struck at him, and the blade bit, opening a gash in his arm. He yelped and dropped the sack.

"That was for Bertrand," Isabelle said. Her blood was no longer running cold. She felt like she had fire in her veins.

The man pressed his palm to the wound. When he pulled it away, it was crimson. He raised his eyes to Isabelle's. "You're going to pay for that," he snarled.

"Isabelle? What's going on? Is that . . . is that *Bertrand*? What happened to him?"

"Stay back, Tavi," Isabelle warned. Her sister had picked the wrong moment to appear.

"Get out of here. *Go*," she said to the man, keeping her sword trained on him. When he didn't move, she charged at him again. He stepped back just in time. Slowly, he raised his hands. "All right," he said. "You win."

*He's leaving*, Isabelle thought. *Thank goodness.*

Which was exactly what he wanted her to think.

Isabelle had been so outraged to discover a man raiding the coop, she hadn't noticed the satchel in the grass a few feet away or the sword lying next to it. The man lunged for his sword, pulled it free of its scabbard, and turned to face her, his weapon drawn.

Fear sluiced down Isabelle's spine like cold rain through a gutter. Her nerve almost gave way. He had been a soldier in the king's army, trained in the use of a sword. She had dueled with Felix. As a child. With a mop handle.

"I'm going to slice you to bits. When I'm finished with you, the vultures will carry you off, piece by piece. What do you say to that, you stupid little bitch?"

Isabelle swallowed hard. Deep inside her, the wolf, asleep under her heart for so long, opened his eyes.

She hefted her sword and stared the man down. "I say, *en garde.*"

## – THIRTY-ONE –

There are those who believe that fear is an enemy, one that must be avoided at all costs.

They run at its first stirrings. They seek shelter from the storm inside the house only to get crushed when the roof falls in.

Fear is the most misunderstood of creatures. It only wants the best for you. It will help you if you let it. Isabelle understood this. She listened to her fear and let it guide her.

*He's faster than you!* it shouted as the chicken thief rushed her. So she retreated under low-hanging tree branches, which scratched his face and poked his eyes, slowing him.

*He's stronger than you!* her fear howled. So she led him over the tree's knobby roots and made him trip.

She parried every thrust and jab the deserter made and managed to land another blow herself, swiping a bloody stripe across his thigh. Cursing, he scuttled back, away from the tree, pressing on his wound. Out of the corner of her eye, Isabelle saw Tavi trying to get around them, to get to the pitchfork.

*No, Tavi, no!* she silently shouted.

But it was too late. The man saw her, too, and went after her.

"Run, Tavi!" Isabelle screamed, breaking from the cover of the tree to chase after him.

He heard her and pivoted. Now he had her out in the open. With a roar, he ran at her, swinging for her head.

"No!" Tavi screamed.

Isabelle caught his blade with her own. The crash of steel sent shock waves down her arms.

Using all her strength, she managed to turn his blade, stumble away from him, and open a few feet of distance between them. The man wiped sweat from his face, then charged her again. He feinted left, then lunged right. Isabelle jumped back but caught her heel on a jutting rock and fell. Instinctively, she rolled to her right as she hit the ground. Sparks flew as her attacker's sword struck the rock.

As Isabelle staggered to her feet, the man raised his sword once more. Winded, the muscles in her arms screaming with exertion, Isabelle lifted her weapon high to block him again, but he was stronger and sure-footed, and she knew that this time, the force of the blow would knock her sword right out of her hands. She would be defenseless when that happened, completely at his mercy. She braced herself for the worst.

But just as the man swung at her, a gunshot ripped through the air. Isabelle dropped into a crouch, her heart hammering. The blade whooshed over her head harmlessly; the sword fell to the ground.

*Where did the shot come from?* she wondered wildly.

She looked up at her assailant. He was holding his sword hand up. Blood was running down his palm. Two of his fingers were gone. He wasn't looking at Isabelle, but at something, or someone, behind her. His eyes were huge.

"I'm leaving. I—I swear," he stammered. "Please . . . let me take my things." He raised his wounded hand in surrender and picked up his sword with his other one. Backing away step-by-step, he scooped up his belongings and ran.

Isabelle put her weapon down and her hands up. A sword was no match for a gun. Chest heaving, she stood, then slowly turned around, certain that another deserter had come up behind her and was pointing the pistol straight at her head.

Or maybe a burglar. A brigand. A cold-blooded highwayman.

Never, for a second, did she expect to see a monkey wearing pearls.

- THIRTY-TWO -

It took Isabelle a full minute to believe what her eyes were telling her.

A small black monkey with a ruff of white around his face was sitting a yard away from her. A rope of pearls circled his neck. He was brandishing a small silver pistol.

As she stared at him, he hammered the pistol on the ground, peered down the barrel, then scampered off around the side of the stables, still holding the firearm.

Isabelle pressed a hand to her chest, trying to calm her pounding heart.

"Tavi!" she called out. "Be careful!" She took a hesitant step forward. "There's a monkey ... he—he has a gun ..."

"I see him!" Tavi called out, rushing to Isabelle's side. She'd gotten hold of the pitchfork and was clutching it for dear life.

Isabelle's foot was throbbing, but she limped after the monkey nonetheless, worried that he might shoot himself with the pistol, or Tavi, or her.

"Monkey? Little monkey, are you there?" she called out, following the creature's path.

The monkey ran out screeching from a water trough, bolted across the drive, and made a beeline for a birch tree. A woman, her hair swept up with jeweled combs, her bosom rising up out of her sprigged gown like brioche, was standing at the base of the tree, looking up into its branches. She turned as she heard the monkey's screech.

"*There* you are, Nelson! Give me the pistol! You'll kill someone!" she scolded. The monkey darted around her and climbed up the trunk. Three more monkeys were already in the tree. The four made a game out of tossing the pistol back and forth while the woman stood below, shaking her fist at them.

Isabelle blinked. *I'm hallucinating. I must be*, she told herself. She squeezed her eyes closed and opened them again. The woman was still there.

"Are you seeing this, too?" she asked her sister.

Tavi nodded, speechless.

Isabelle approached the woman carefully, hoping she wasn't here to steal chickens, too. She didn't think she had another sword fight in her.

"Madame, pardon me, but what are you doing in our stable yard? With a monkey?" she asked. "How did you get here?"

"How do you think?" the woman called over her shoulder, hooking her thumb behind her. "How else does one convey oneself to a godforsaken backwater in the middle of nowhere?"

90

Isabelle's eyes followed the direction of her gesture. Her mouth dropped open. There, standing a little way down the drive, but with a clear view of the chicken coop, was the most magnificent carriage she had ever seen.

## - THIRTY-THREE -

In front of the enormous, painted coach, four dapple gray horses stood, tossing their heads and stamping their hooves.

Up high in the driver's seat sat a man wearing a jade-green jacket and pink trousers. A teardrop-shaped pearl dangled from one ear. He nodded at Isabelle and Tavi.

Goggle-eyed, they nodded back. Behind the driver, a dozen trunks were lashed to the carriage's roof. On top of them sat a troop of acrobats, one of whom was juggling knives blindfolded. Next to her a fire-breather blew lazy smoke rings; a magician caught them and turned them into coins. Musicians held their instruments as if at a concert hall awaiting their conductor. Isabelle was spellbound.

The carriage door opened, and a man stepped out. Isabelle glimpsed a pair of mesmerizing amber eyes, a sweep of black braids, the flash of a gold earring. The man started to clap. The others joined him. The applause was thunderous. Then the man waved his hand and it stopped.

"That was quite the duel, mademoiselle!" he said to Isabelle. "We saw you from the road and pulled in to help, but before I could even get my door open, Nelson took matters into his own hands. Paws, I should say. Though I shouldn't have left my pistol lying on the seat. Have you ever met a monkey who could resist a silver pistol?" He suddenly snapped his fingers. "Forgive me, I haven't introduced myself."

He took off his hat, bowed, then straightened again, and with a smile—one so beguiling that in a single day in Marseille it had inspired three sea captains to set sail for Cape Horn, a duchess to run off with her gardener, and two brothers named Montgolfier to invent the hot-air balloon—said, "The Marquis de la Chance, at your service."

As the words left his lips, the musicians shot to their feet atop the carriage and played a rousing fanfare.

The marquis winced. Turning to them, he said, "A bit much for the country, don't you think?"

The music stopped. The French horns looked down at their shoes. The trumpeter polished an imaginary speck off his instrument.

Isabelle, who'd dipped a curtsy, and pulled a stunned Tavi down with her, now rose. "Isabelle de la Paumé, Your Grace. And this is my sister Octavia. We are . . ." *What?* she wondered. *Shocked? Stunned? Utterly astonished?* ". . . *pleased* to make your acquaintance."

"I wonder if you could tell me how to get to the Château Rigolade," the marquis said. "I'm under the impression that it's somewhere around here, but we're a bit lost. I won it."

"You *won* it?" Tavi echoed, clearly baffled.

"Yes, in a game of cards. I needed somewhere to go. I and my household." He gestured to the carriage. "Paris is chaos at the moment, with that beast Volkmar on the rampage. And I require peace and quiet. I'm writing a play, you see."

"You're a playwright, sir?" Isabelle asked.

"Not one bit," the marquis said. "Never even put pen to paper before. But I'm always doing things I can't do. Otherwise, I'd never get to do them."

As Isabelle tried to follow that logic, the marquis said, "Now, about the château . . ."

Isabelle quickly gave him directions. "It's not far. Turn left at the end of our drive. Follow the road for a mile. When you come to a fork in the road . . ."

The marquis's eyes lit up. "A fork in the road! How wonderful! I *love* forks in the road! They lead to opportunity!"

"Change!" shouted an acrobat.

"Adventure!" trilled a musician.

"Excitement!" crowed the fire-breather.

Isabelle looked between the marquis and his friends uncertainly. "Yes, well . . . when you come to *this* fork, make a right. Keep on for another half mile or so, and you'll see the drive. The château itself sits on a rise. You can't miss it."

"We are forever in your debt," said the marquis. "But before we leave, I would like to offer you a bit of advice . . ."

The marquis walked up to Isabelle and took her hands in his. She caught her breath. His touch felt as though lightning had just ripped through the air. Like she'd stolen a bag of diamonds. Found a trunk full of gold.

But as they stood close, Isabelle saw that the merriment that lit his eyes, the ebullience that animated his every movement, the teasing challenge that sparkled in his voice, were all gone, replaced by a sudden, unnerving ferocity.

"You are good with a sword, but not good enough," he said to her. "Practice. Become faster. Better. There are worse creatures afoot in France than chicken thieves. Far worse. Promise me, young Isabelle. *Promise me.*"

It seemed very important to him that she learn to protect herself. She had no idea why, but he was clearly not going to let go of her until she agreed to his demand. "I—I promise, Your Grace," she said.

"Good," the marquis said, releasing her. "Now, if you ladies will excuse me—"

*Ka-blam!*

Another bullet whistled through the air. It hit the weather vane on top of the barn and sent it spinning. It sent Tavi running for cover.

It also spooked the horses.

Whinnying and wild-eyed, they lurched forward in their harnesses, wrenching the carriage around the circular drive so violently that it went up on two wheels and teetered there for a few heart-stopping seconds. The driver threw himself across his seat. Everyone on the roof leaned over. The marquis ran for the carriage, caught hold of the open door, and hung his full weight on it. Finally, the wheels slammed back down. The carriage careened under the birch tree, and as it did, the monkeys dropped out of the branches onto its roof. The marquis, safely inside now, stretched across the magician and the cook and leaned out of the window.

"Thank you!" he shouted. "Good-bye!"

"Good-bye, Your Grace!" Isabelle and Tavi called back.

They stood by the stables waving until the carriage sped down the drive, turned into the road, and disappeared.

In all the commotion, they never saw the monkey unhook the pearls from his neck, stretch a furry arm out over the carriage's roof, and drop them into the grass.

## – THIRTY-FOUR –

After the excitement of the morning, the rest of the day passed slowly for Isabelle, full of chores outside of the mansion, and inside it, too.

Nightfall found her sitting at her kitchen table. Tavi had made them a delicious omelet with tarragon in it. Isabelle had cleaned her plate and was now staring at the sword the fairy queen had given her, lost in thought.

She'd hung the sword on a hook by the door. Tavi had asked her where she'd gotten it. Isabelle had fibbed and said she'd found it in a trunk in the stables some time ago, and had grabbed it as soon as she'd seen the chicken thief.

Tanaquill's voice drifted through her mind. *Cut away piece by piece by piece . . .* She'd said the word *piece* three times. *Is that a clue?* Isabelle wondered. *Are there three pieces that I'm supposed to find?* "We should wash the dishes, Iz," Tavi said now.

"Yes, we should," Isabelle agreed, but she made no move to do so.

Tavi followed her gaze. "You've been frowning at that sword all through supper. Why?"

Isabelle's frown deepened. "I've been wondering, Tav . . . what is a heart, exactly?"

"What a strange question. Why are you asking?"

"I just . . ." Isabelle shrugged. "Want to know."

"A heart is a four-chambered, pump-like organ that circulates blood throughout the body via rhythmic contractions."

"I meant *besides* that. In poems and songs, the heart is the place where goodness comes from."

Tavi gave her a long look. "Are you writing poetry now?"

"Yes! Ha. Yes, I am. How did you guess?" Isabelle said brightly. It was another fib, and she felt bad about telling it, but it *was* the perfect cover for asking what she wanted to know without mentioning why she wanted to know it. "In my poem, the main character—"

"Do poems have main characters?"

"This one does, and she's lost her heart. Or rather, pieces of it. I need to find them. In the poem, I mean. For my main character. What would you say pieces of a heart could be?"

Tavi sat back in her chair, an expression of grave concern on her face.

Then she picked up a candleholder that was standing on the table and moved the flame past Isabelle's eyes.

"What on earth are you doing?" Isabelle asked, shrinking away from it.

"Seeing if your pupils dilate and contract properly. I'm worried you've taken too many falls off Martin. Hit your head once too often."

Isabelle rolled her eyes. "I *haven't* lost my wits, if that's what you're suggesting. Answer my question, Tavi. Theoretically."

"Well, let's say—theoretically—that it was you we were talking about. I'd say that sword you've been staring at is a piece of your heart."

Isabelle stubbornly shook her head. "I don't think so. No."

"Why not? You used to love swords. You loved fencing and . . . and Felix. Why, the two of you—"

"Yes, I did," Isabelle said, brusquely cutting her off. Tavi's words were salt in a deep wound that had never healed. "And what did it get me? Felix made a promise and then he broke it. And me along with it."

"We're not talking theoretically anymore, are we?"

Isabelle inspected her hands. "No," she admitted.

"I'm sorry. I shouldn't have mentioned him."

Isabelle waved her apology away. "Whatever the pieces of my heart are, they don't include him. Or swords."

"Then what do they include? And how are you going to find them?" Tavi asked.

"I don't know," Isabelle replied. She thought hard, then said, "Since a heart is where goodness comes from, maybe I could do some good deeds."

Tavi burst out laughing. "Do good deeds? *You?*"

Isabelle glowered, offended. "Yes, *me.* What's so funny about that?"

"You've never done any!"

"Yes, I have!" Isabelle insisted. "I gave Tantine a ride to the LeBenêts' the other day. That's a start."

"Oh, Izzy," Tavi said softly. She reached across the table for her hand and squeezed it. "It's too late for good deeds. People shout at us. They throw rocks at our windows. Mean is all we have left. And all we can do is get better at it. Good deeds won't change anything."

Isabelle squeezed back. "Maybe they'll change *me*, Tav."

Tavi rose to wash the dishes then, and Isabelle, seeing how dark it was getting, said she'd help her right after she locked up the animals.

"Take the sword with you," Tavi cautioned. "Just in case."

Isabelle did. As she lifted it off its hook, she wondered again how the fairy queen's gift would help her attain her heart's desire. She was glad to have had it, for it had helped save her life today, but pretty girls twirled parasols and fluttered fans. They didn't swing swords.

And yet, when Isabelle got outside and felt how the sword's hilt fit so perfectly in her hand, how the blade was so finely weighted, she couldn't help but take a swipe at a rosebush, then smile as several pink flowers fell to the ground. She decapitated two lilies as she walked, then whacked a blowsy blue hydrangea off its stalk.

"The marquis told me to practice," she said aloud, almost guiltily, as if some unseen person had accused her of enjoying herself.

Dangerous characters were afoot. She was making sure she could defend herself, that's all.

It was magical, the sword. Incredible. Breathtaking. She couldn't deny it.

But it wasn't her heart.

And it never would be.

She wouldn't let it.

## THIRTY-FIVE

As Isabelle fenced in the darkness, Chance, comfortably installed in the Château Rigolade, peered down at the flask of silvery liquid he'd concocted.

All around him, his retinue busied themselves. Only the magician was nowhere to be seen.

His attention focused on the flask, Chance was barely aware of the people around him. The silver liquid was simmering on a burner in the center of a diabolically complex distilling system. Its color was shimmering and rich, but Chance was not satisfied.

His scientist had set up the apparatus on the enormous table in the center of the château's dining room just after they'd arrived. It was surrounded by brass scales, presses and expellers, a mortar and pestle, and apothecary jars containing all manner of ingredients.

Chance reached for one of the jars now. He removed its stopper, extracted a piece of yellowed lace, and dropped it into the flask. A spoonful of dried violets was added next, followed by a cobweb, a scrap of sheet music, a crumbled madeleine, and numbers pried off a clock face.

The liquid bubbled and swirled after each addition, but Chance was still not happy. He combed through the jars, searching for one last ingredient. With a triumphant *Aha!* he found it—a pair of shimmering moth wings. As he dropped them into the flask, the liquid transformed into a beautiful faded mauve.

"Perfect!" he declared. With a pair of tongs, he carefully lifted the flask off the flames and set it on a marble slab to cool.

"I need a name for this ink," he said to the scientist, who was working across from him. "A name for the feeling you get when you see someone again. After many years. Someone lost to you. Or so you thought. And you remember them a certain way. In your mind, they never age. But then suddenly, there they are. Older. Changed by time. Different, but exactly the same."

The scientist looked up from his work. He peered at Chance over the top of his glasses.

"This person meant something to you?" he asked.

"Could have. Might have. Almost did. Would have," Chance said. "If the timing had been right. If you'd been wiser. Bolder. Better."

The scientist, spare and rigorous, not a man given to flights of fancy, put a hand over his heart. He closed his eyes. A wistful smile played across his lips.

"Wonderfulness," he said. "That's the name."

Chance smiled. He wrote *Wonderfulness* on a paper label, stuck it on the bottle, and carried it to the far end of the table. The map of Isabelle de la Paumé's life lay rolled up there. One never knew when a reunion might be called for. It was important to be prepared for any contingency.

Other inks he'd created were scattered around the map. There was *Defiance*, a swirling red-orange ink made from ground lion's teeth mixed with bull's blood. *Inspiration* was pale gold, made from black tea mixed with cocoa, a pinch of dirt from a poet's grave, and four drops of a lunatic's tears left to ferment in the light of a full moon. And *Stealth*, the color of midnight, was composed of owl's breath, hawk feathers, and the powdered finger bones of a pickpocket.

*Are the pigments bold enough, the formulas strong enough, to draw new paths?* he wondered as he set the bottle of *Wonderfulness* down. He'd tried to make ink before, many times, but had never been able to devise tints powerful enough to undo the crone's work.

Dread jabbered at the edges of his mind now. He poured himself a generous glass of cognac from a crystal decanter to silence it. After draining it in one gulp, he sat down in front of the map. As he unrolled it, smoothing it flat, he couldn't help but marvel at the beauty of the Fates' work. Their parchment was the finest he'd ever seen, their inks exquisite, the quality of their drawing unparalleled.

Isabelle's full name was at the top of the map, hand-lettered in Greek, the Fates' native tongue. Covering the rest of the parchment was the richly colored landscape of her life. Chance saw her birthplace, other towns she'd lived in, Saint-Michel. He saw the peaks and valleys, the sunny plains and the dark woods through which she had crossed. He saw her path, a thick black line, and the dotted, dashed, and hatched lines of lives that intersected hers.

But it was what Chance could not see that so unnerved him.

## – THIRTY-SIX –

"Are they ready?" he called out impatiently.

The scientist, polishing a pair of wire-framed eyeglasses with a soft cloth, nodded. He brought them to Chance.

"They're powerful?" asked Chance, taking them.

"Very. I ground the lenses myself. The left gives you hindsight; the right, foresight."

Chance held them up to the light. "Pink?" he said as he looked through the lenses. It was not his favorite color.

"*Rose*," William corrected. "It's hard to look at mortal life any other way. View it through clear lenses and it breaks your heart."

Chance put the eyeglasses on, hooking the curved ends behind his ears. As he gazed at the map through them, he caught his breath. The entire parchment looked like the pages of the clever little books paper cutters made for children in which everything popped up.

No one, certainly no mortal and not even Chance himself, possessed the Fates' sharpness of vision. They drew with such painstaking detail that most of their art was impossible to see with the naked eye. Chance had stolen many maps from the three sisters, but never before had he been able to view their work so clearly.

All along Isabelle's path, the moments of her life stood out in vibrant three-dimensional scenes. He saw her as a child, fencing with a boy. He saw her standing in front of a mirror in a fancy dress with tears in her eyes. And he saw her at the village market, just a few days ago, arguing with the baker's wife.

"You're a genius," he whispered.

The scientist smiled, pleased.

But Chance did not return the smile. His pleasure in the power of his new eyeglasses to show Isabelle's past so clearly was tempered by the knowledge that they would also reveal the details of her future. He already knew what lay at the end of her path, for he'd seen it when he was in the Fates' palazzo, but he didn't know exactly when it would occur.

He might have weeks to prevent it, even months. Then again, he might have only days.

His eyes darted to the bottom of the map, seeking the answer to his question. The legend was there. It explained that an inch equaled a year and gave Isabelle's birth date.

The Fates' seal was there, too. The crone put one on every mortal's map when she completed it by dripping melted red wax onto the bottom of the parchment and pressing her skull ring into it. The resulting impression was a death date, for the closer a mortal came to the end of her path, the darker the skull turned, deepening from bloodred to black.

The skull on Isabelle's map was a somber burgundy, streaked with gray.

"She has only weeks left. *Weeks*," Chance said. He pressed a shaky hand to his head. "How the devil am I going to undo this?" he muttered.

He snatched his quill off the table, dipped it in *Defiance*, and started to draw Isabelle a new path, one that led away from her terrible fate. The ink shimmered brightly on the parchment.

"Ha! *Defiance*, indeed!" he crowed, encouraged.

But an instant later, the ink started to fade and then disappeared completely; the parchment had sucked it in like desert sands absorbing rain.

Chance took another tack. He dipped the quill into *Defiance* again and tried to cross out what lay at the end of Isabelle's path, but no matter how much ink he scribbled, stippled, hatched, and dripped onto the parchment, Isabelle's fate still showed through, like a corpse bobbing to the surface of a lake.

Swearing, Chance threw the quill down. He took his glasses off and put them on the table. This was a disaster. His inks weren't strong enough to draw so much as a detour, never mind counter the violent reds and slashing blacks that had been put there not by the Fates but by one whose power to change paths was growing stronger by the day.

The scientist looked up from his work. "What's wrong?" he asked.

Chance was about to reply when a loud, insistent pounding at the door stopped him. It echoed through the château, shaking the furniture and rattling the windows.

The cook, who had just walked into the dining room from the kitchens, set down the silver tray of pretty cakes he was carrying. He hurried out of the dining room, through the château's grand foyer, to a window at the side of the door. "Destiny calls," he shouted back to the others, glancing out of it.

The sword-swallower held up his hands. "Everyone stop talking!" he whisper-shouted. "Maybe she'll go away!"

"Don't be ridiculous. She knows we're here," said the diva. "The whole village does. We don't exactly blend in."

The knock came again. Chance groaned with frustration. A visit from the crone was the last thing he needed.

"Open the door," he finally said. "Let her in. But keep an eye on the map, all of you."

## – THIRTY-SEVEN –

"My dear marquis," said Fate as she walked into the hall, a raven on her shoulder. "What a handsome home. And what . . ." She paused, walked over to the table, and examined the distilling apparatus. ". . . *interesting* furnishings. Making gin, perhaps? Perfume?" She tapped a finger to her chin. "Or, possibly, ink?"

Chance gave her a curt bow. "My dear madame," he said. "To what do I owe the pleasure of your visit?"

"Why, neighborliness, of course," Fate replied. "We are dwelling in the same village, are we not? We must keep relations cordial."

She slowly strolled around the enormous hall, taking it in. As she did, the members of Chance's entourage stopped what they were doing and eyed her, intrigued.

"This *is* a magnificent château," she said enviously. "I wish my accommodations were half as nice."

"Are you not staying at the village inn?" Chance asked.

"I was, but now I'm staying with . . ." She smiled, inclining her head. "Some long-lost relatives."

As she continued her stroll, her eyes fell on Isabelle's map.

"Don't even think about it," Chance said. "You won't make it to the door."

Fate clucked her tongue. "I hope you haven't made a mess of my work," she said, running her gnarled fingers over Isabelle's path.

As her hand neared the end of the path, it stopped short, as if it had hit an obstacle. Fate's mouth twitched. Her gaze sharpened. And then, as if remembering that eyes were upon her, she quickly rearranged her expression back to one of bemused coolness.

*Did I imagine it?* Chance wondered. The cook was standing on the other side of Fate. He gave Chance a quick, barely perceptible nod. *He saw it, too*, Chance thought. *What does it mean?*

"Why do you even bother?" Fate asked airily, turning to Chance. "You've brewed up a new batch of inks, but I doubt they're any match for mine. What I draw cannot be changed. Not by you."

"But *they* can change it," Chance said. "With a bit of luck, mortals can do incredible things."

Fate gave him a patronizing smile. "And some do. But one needs determination to change one's fate. Courage. Strength. Things most mortals grievously lack. One needs to be exceptional, and the girl Isabelle, most assuredly, is not."

"She has courage and strength. A tremendous will, too," Chance countered. "She just needs to find them again."

Fate's smile turned brittle. "As usual, you are meddling where you should not. Let the girl enjoy what little time she has left. You will break her heart by encouraging her to want things she has no business wanting. Girls die of broken hearts."

Chance snorted. "Here are the things girls die of: hunger, disease, accidents, childbirth, and violence. It takes more than heartache to kill a girl. Girls are tough as rocks."

Fate paused, as a cat does before sinking its teeth into a mouse, then said, "But Volkmar is tougher."

Guilt bled into Chance's eyes. He turned away, trying to hide it, but Fate had glimpsed it and she circled him for the kill.

"Volkmar certainly changed *his* fate, didn't he?" she said. "But he *is* an exceptional mortal. Exceptionally ruthless. Exceptionally cruel." She nodded at the map. "It's his work, that ugly scrawl at the end of Isabelle's path, as you well know."

The scientist squinted in confusion. "I don't understand . . . *Volkmar* redrew the girl's map?"

"Not with quills and inks as I do, but with the sheer force of his will," Fate replied. "He is so bold, so strong, that he is able to change his fate. And by so doing, he changes the fates of thousands more."

"So his actions have compelled your inks to redraw his map," the scientist reasoned. "And the maps of those whose lives he touches."

"Precisely," said Fate. "Volkmar wishes to rule the world and begins his cruel campaign in France. One by one, villages and towns will fall to him as he tightens his noose around Paris. Saint-Michel will fall, too, and with such savagery that the young king will have no choice but to surrender. Volkmar will slaughter Isabelle in cold blood. Her sister. Her mother. Their neighbors. Every last person in this poor, forsaken place."

A gasp rose from several people in the room. The diva uttered a cry.

Fate turned to her, affecting an innocent expression. "Did you not know? Did he not tell you?"

The diva, tears welling, shook her head.

"That is *enough*, crone," Chance growled.

But Fate, her gaze still on the diva, ignored him. "Why, my dear, don't you see?"

"I said *stop*."

But Fate did not. Eyes shining with spite, she walked to the diva and took her hands. "*That* is why your marquis is so desperate to change Isabelle's fate. Because he himself brought it about!"

## THIRTY-EIGHT

It was utterly silent in the grand hall.

Chance stood still, fists clenched, heart seared by shame and regret. No one else moved, either. No one spoke.

Until Fate, circling back to him, said, "I have come, however unwillingly. I accept your stakes. We will play our old game. You know the rules . . . neither can force the girl's choice. Or buy it. She may take what is offered or not."

Chance nodded stiffly. As Fate looked at him, something like sadness darkened her eyes.

"If you loved these mortals, you would leave them—"

"To your tender mercies?" he spat.

"—alone."

"It's because I love them that I won't. They deserve a chance. Some of them never get one. This girl will."

"But will she take it?" Fate asked.

"Thank you for your visit, but I must get back to work," Chance said brusquely.

Fate laughed, shaking her head. "She *won't.* Humans are what they are—dreamers, madmen, but most of all, fools."

She let herself out of the Château Rigolade and disappeared into the night, but her laughter, harsh and mocking, lingered in Chance's ears. He slammed the door shut after her and leaned his forehead against it. After a moment, he faced his friends and attempted to explain.

"There was a party . . ."

The cook shook his head. "There always is."

". . . in a castle in the Black Forest. There was a sumptuous dinner. I drank a good deal of champagne. After dinner, there was a card game. The stakes were high."

"How high?" the cook asked.

Chance grimaced. "One million gold ducats."

The cook swore. "You never learn, do you?"

"I didn't know then who he was . . . *what* he was. I didn't know what he was planning. I never dreamt—" He closed his eyes against the crushing pain he felt. "Once he had the money, he used it to dark advantage. He built up his army, marched on France. Everything he's done is *my* fault. I created him."

Chance lowered his head into his hands. The diva hurried to his side; she squeezed his arm.

"Volkmar created himself," she said. "He had a choice. He could've used his fortune for good, not ill."

Chance groaned in despair. He felt so weary. His bones ached. His heart hurt. Everything seemed pointless. All his energy seemed to have drained out of him. "The crone is right," he said, sagging into a chair. "Mortals are fools. I should walk away. Leave them to their own devices. I mean to help, but too often I wreck things. And people."

"But you always tell us that one person can make a difference," the diva countered. "Isabelle might be such a person. If Volkmar can change his fate, and the fates of thousands more, why can't this girl do the same?"

Chance gave a joyless laugh. "Isabelle can barely *walk*."

The diva sat down heavily. Everyone looked leaden and defeated. No one spoke.

Until the magician strode in from the night through a pair of glass doors that opened onto the terrace. She was wearing riding boots, britches, and a close-cut jacket, all in black. Her lips were rouged. Her color was high. She was holding a dark flower in one hand.

"It took me a while, but I found the night orchid you wanted. For *Courage*."

Chance shook his head. "I won't be needing it anymore. My inks don't work."

The magician looked from Chance to the others. "What happened? Did somebody die? Why are you all sitting around like mushrooms?" She made a face. "It *stinks* in here. Like surrender. Failure. And rot." Her eyes narrowed. "It's the *crone*. She's been here, hasn't she? Who let her in?"

The cook sheepishly raised his hand.

"Never, *ever* do it again," the magician scolded, opening the rest of the terrace doors. "She's like sulfurous gas from a fumarole. Bad air from an old mine. She poisoned you. Made you think you have to accept things rather than fight to change them."

She pushed the cakes off the silver tray, opened the neck of Chance's shirt, and fanned him with it. Then she strode over to the cook and slapped his cheeks.

"Snap out of it!" she ordered. "If the inks don't work, then we'll find something that does."

A breeze blew through the open doors, freshening the room. Chance blinked, then looked around as if he were waking from a deep sleep. A little spirit trickled back into him.

"There *was* something on the map. Something—" he started to say.

The cook snapped his fingers. "Something that bothered the crone. I caught that, too. If it's not good for her, it's very good for us."

Chance was back at the table in a flash with the cook right behind him. He put his glasses back on, then trailed his finger over Isabelle's path, searching for whatever it was that had rattled Fate.

He moved past the day Isabelle cut her toes off, past Ella leaving, to where Volkmar's brutal line started, and beyond, to where it finished, and then he went back and retraced the line, but he didn't see anything he hadn't seen before. Even with the glasses, he couldn't see as clearly as the Fates.

And then he did see something.

It was faintly etched. But it was *there*. A detour. Newly made. "Yes!" he shouted, clapping his hands together.

"What is it? *Speak*, man!" the cook said.

Chance ripped his spectacles off and handed them to him. The cook put them on, squinted at the map, then grinned. "Ha!" he cried. "No wonder the crone's face looked like a bucket of spoiled milk! That path—"

"Isn't Fate's work, or Volkmar's . . . it's *hers*. Isabelle's. Her actions redrew her path," Chance finished, his eyes dancing. "I was right. She *can* change. She *will* change. We're going to win this game. We're going to beat the Fates."

"Easy. It's only a start. Let's not get cocky," the cook cautioned.

"It's *more* than a start," Chance insisted. "Did you see where it led?"

The cook peered at the map again. "It looks like a tree . . . an old linden . . ." He took the glasses off. "Bloody hell," he said, turning back to Chance. "Do you know who that is?"

"Tanaquill," Chance said.

"The fairy queen?" the magician asked, joining the two men. "Chance, she's—"

"Very, very powerful," Chance cut in.

"Actually, I was thinking *murderous*," said the magician.

"Did Isabelle summon her?" the cook wondered aloud. "For what purpose?"

"I doubt it was to invite her to tea," said the magician, with a shiver.

"I can't quite make that out. The glasses aren't powerful enough, but I think Isabelle asked her for help," said Chance. He ran his hands through his braids, then pointed at the cook. "I'll need a gift. I can't go empty-handed. Are there any rabbits in the larder?"

"I used the last ones for the stew we had tonight. I have pheasants, though," he replied, heading for the kitchen.

"I'll take them," said Chance.

"You're going to look for Tanaquill *now*?" the magician asked. "It's nearly midnight!"

"I don't have a choice," Chance said. "Fate saw that detour, too. She's hunting for the fairy queen as we speak, I'm sure of it. I've got to find her first." He sped off after his cook.

The scientist, his face etched with worry, picked up the rose-tinted glasses and polished them. "She'll eat him alive," he said.

The magician stared after Chance, a worried look on her face. "You're right," she said. She patted her hip, making sure her dagger was there, then added, "I'm going with him."

## - THIRTY-NINE -

The fairy queen was standing in a clearing in the Wildwood, an enormous yellow-eyed owl perched on her forearm.

It was well after midnight, but the darkness only set off her vivid presence. Her russet hair was braided and coiled. A circlet of antlers adorned her head. She wore a dress that shimmered like a minnow, and over it a cape of gray feathers held together at the neck by a pair of large iridescent beetles, their powerful pincers clasped.

Chance had found her by following her magic. It left traces, silver drops that gleamed on the forest floor, then slowly faded. As he and the magician watched, hidden in a copse of birch trees, Tanaquill stroked the owl and whispered to him, heedless of the sharp, curved beak that could crack bone and rip out hearts, of the curved talons that could flay hide.

"Ready?" Chance whispered. The magician nodded, and they both stepped out into the clearing.

"Hail mighty Tanaquill!" Chance called out. "My search is at last rewarded. It's an honor to be in your presence."

Tanaquill laughed. It was the sound of the autumn wind swirling dead leaves around. "You've been in my presence for a good half hour, cowering behind the birch trees. I smelled you. And your pheasants."

Chance approached her, with the magician close behind him. "Please accept them, Your Grace, as a small token of my esteem," he said with a bow, holding the birds out.

With a sneer, Tanaquill refused them. "Leave them for the vultures," she said. "They like dead things. I prefer my tribute living. The heart beating, the blood surging."

She put a hand on Chance's chest. Leaning in close to his neck, she breathed in his scent, licked her lips. Chance was enthralled by her beguiling green eyes, like a mouse transfixed by a snake. He'd let her come too close.

The magician saved him. She pulled him away, then stood in front of him, her hand on the hilt of her dagger. Tanaquill snarled like a fox who'd lost a nice fat squirrel.

"Why are you here? What do you want of me?" she asked.

"Your help. I want to save a girl. Her name is Isabelle. You know her. I have her map. Drawn by the Fates. It shows that you spoke with her."

"And just how did you come to possess the map?" Tanaquill asked. "The Fates guard their work closely."

Chance explained. As he finished, Tanaquill made a noise of disgust. "I want nothing to do with your foolish games," she said, walking away. "I do not serve you or Fate. I serve only the heart."

Chance took a desperate step after her. He couldn't let her slip away.

He was certain something important had passed between her and Isabelle. Something he could use to help the girl.

"Volkmar comes closer to Saint-Michel with each passing day," he said.

"What of it?" said Tanaquill with a backhanded wave.

"He has rewritten Isabelle's fate. In blood. But she can change it. If she can change herself."

Tanaquill's laughter rang out through the Wildwood. "*That* selfish, bitter girl? You think *she* can best a warlord?"

"It is not only the village, and the mortals who live in it, that will fall. Volkmar plunders and burns everything in his path. The Wildwood and all that dwell in it . . . they will not survive him, either."

Tanaquill stopped. She turned around. Sorrow and anger warred in the depths of her fierce eyes. Chance saw her distress. And pushed his advantage.

"Please, I beg you. What did Isabelle say to you?"

"She asked for my help," Tanaquill said at length. "She wishes to be *pretty*." The fairy queen spat the word.

"And did you grant her wish?"

"I told her I would help her," Tanaquill replied in such a way that Chance had the distinct feeling she was evading his question.

The fairy queen continued. "I also told her that she would have to earn my help by finding the lost pieces of her heart."

"Those pieces . . . what are they?" asked Chance.

"Why should I tell you? So you can find them and drop them into her lap?"

"So I can give her a *chance*. That's all I ask. A chance at redemption."

Tanaquill smirked. "Redemption? Would that be for the girl? Or for you?"

Her words cut Chance. He flinched, but his gaze did not falter. His smile was no longer golden but naked and vulnerable. "Both, if I'm lucky," he said.

Tanaquill's eyes held his. Her gaze was piercing. Then she said, "Nero, a horse. Felix, a boy. Ella, a stepsister."

As soon as the words had left the fairy queen's lips, Chance shot the magician a look. She nodded, then melted away into the woods.

"Thank you, Your Grace," Chance said fervently. He took her cool, pale hand in his, lifted it to his lips, and kissed it.

Tanaquill growled, but there was little threat in it. "What happens next is up to the girl. Not you. Not Fate," she warned as Chance released her.

As if on cue, Fate walked into the clearing. "Ah, Tanaquill! Well met by moonlight!" she said. She gave Chance a smug smile. "Taking the night air, Marquis? A bit stuffy in the château?"

Chance's stomach sank to his boots. *How much of our conversation has she overheard?* he wondered anxiously.

Fate had a basket on her arm and a raven on her shoulder. "Are you hunting mushrooms, too?" she asked the fairy queen.

"I know why you've come," the fairy queen said, ignoring her question. "But I'm afraid your adversary here"—she nodded at Chance—"has beaten you to the draw."

Fate's smile soured. Chance let out a shallow breath of relief. Perhaps she had not overheard them.

"Leave the girl alone, Tanaquill," Fate said. "This is not your fight, and she is not worth your efforts. Stick to the woods. Go hunting."

The fairy queen whirled on her, snarling with fury. Fate stumbled back. Her raven squawked.

"Do *not* patronize me, crone. I have been summoned by a human heart and am not so easily put back in my box," Tanaquill warned.

"You could no more contain me than you could contain a hurricane. I am older than you. Older than Chance. Older than time itself."

She waved her hand. There was a high-pitched shriek, a blur in the air. The raven never saw the yellow-eyed hunter coming. The owl tore the bird off Fate's shoulder and drove it to the ground. Then it lifted its wings over its prey and screeched at Fate, daring her to take it.

Fate did not. She stood still; her body was tense. Her eyes—back on Tanaquill—were calculating, like those of a lioness who wishes to attack a rival but is not certain of a win.

Tanaquill saw her wish. "I would not if I were you. Have you forgotten what I am? I am the heart's first beat and its last. I am the newborn lamb and the wolf that rips out its throat. I am the bloodsong, crone." She tossed a glance at the struggling raven and smiled. "So much for your box."

And then she was gone, vanished into the darkness, and her owl with her. And where the raven had been a girl sat, her chest hitching, her trembling fingers hovering over the gouges on her neck.

"Up, Losca," Fate ordered. "Go back to my room. Wait for me there."

Losca stood. She stumbled out of the clearing on unsteady legs.

"That owl could've killed the poor girl. Why don't you pack up, before someone else gets hurt?" Chance said gloatingly. "I've as good as won this wager."

Fate regarded him coolly. "Go back to your château, Marquis. Get some rest. You'll need it. I believe you have a horse to find. A boy. And a stepsister, no?" she said, walking away.

Chance swore, furious. The crone *had* overheard his conversation with Tanaquill.

Fate stopped at the edge of the clearing, turned back to him, and, with a poisonous smile, added, "Unless *I* find them first."

## FORTY

Tavi stood by the kitchen door, cradling a bowl of fresh-picked plums, her white apron and the skirts of her blue dress fluttering in the morning breeze. She cast a skeptical eye over the contents of the large basket Isabelle had placed in the back of their wooden cart.

"But what if the orphans don't *want* eggs?" she asked.

"Of course they will," Isabelle said, adjusting a buckle on Martin's harness. "Orphans don't have much. They'll be happy to get them."

Tavi raised an eyebrow. "Do you even know where the orphanage is?"

Isabelle shot Tavi a look. She didn't reply.

"Do you have your sword with you?"

"I don't need it," Isabelle said.

The truth was that she didn't have it. She'd woken up this morning, two days since she'd used the sword to fight off the deserter, and had discovered that it had turned back into a bone, as if it had sensed that the danger has passed. She'd put it back in her pocket with Tanaquill's other gifts.

"And exactly why are you giving away our much-needed eggs?" Tavi pressed.

"Because it's a nice thing to do. A good deed."

"Still trying to find the pieces of your heart?"

"Yes," Isabelle said as she climbed into the cart and settled herself on the seat.

"Have you figured out what they are?"

Isabelle nodded. She'd been thinking about it nonstop. "Goodness, kindness, and charitableness," she replied confidently. "I'm working on the charitableness piece today."

Tanaquill said that Ella hadn't had to search for the pieces of her heart. *Because she never lost them*, Isabelle thought, as she lay in bed last night. *Ella was always good, kind, and charitable. Maybe Tanaquill wants me to be those things, too.*

"Izzy, I was serious when I said not to ride anymore. Have you been?"

Isabelle, who was leaning forward gathering Martin's reins, sat up and looked at her sister. "You *still* think this is all because I hit my head?"

"I think this is all very strange," Tavi said, carrying her plums into the kitchen.

Isabelle watched her go. "I haven't lost my mind. Things will get easier, you'll see," she said quietly. "Things are always easier for pretty girls. People hold doors for you. Children pick flowers for you. Butchers hand you a free slice of salami, just for the pleasure of watching you eat it."

And then she snapped Martin's reins and set off.

## – FORTY-ONE –

Isabelle found the orphanage, tucked down a narrow road behind the church, without any trouble.

It was run by nuns and housed in their convent. An iron fence enclosed the building and its grounds, but the gate wasn't locked. Isabelle pushed it open and walked inside, carrying her egg basket.

Children dressed in rough gray clothing were playing games in a grassy courtyard. A sweet-faced boy approached her. A few of his friends followed him.

"Here, little boy," Isabelle said. "I brought some eggs for you."

The boy took a few hesitant steps toward her. "My name's Henri," he said, giving her a close look. "And yours is Isabelle."

"How did you guess?" Isabelle asked, kneeling down and smiling.

116

"I didn't. Sister Bernadette pointed at you when she took us to the market. She said we mustn't ever be like you. You're one of the queen's ugly stepsisters. You're awful and mean."

Isabelle's smile curdled. Two of the little girls who'd trailed the boy stepped forward. They started to sing.

> *Stepsister, stepsister!*
> *Ugly as an old blister!*
> *Make her drink some turpentine!*
> *Then hang her with a melon vine!*

Before Isabelle even knew what was happening, the children had all joined hands and were dancing around her like imps, singing:

> *Stepsister, stepsister,*
> *Mother says the devil kissed her!*
> *Make her swallow five peach pits,*
> *Then cut her up in little bits!*

They let go of one another's hands when they finished their song and backed away giggling.

Isabelle decided to leave before they were inspired to sing another verse. "Here, take them," she said, thrusting the basket out to Henri. "They're nice fresh eggs."

"I don't want them. Not from *you*," said Henri.

Isabelle felt a current of anger move through her, but she clamped down on it.

"I'm going to leave the basket here," she said. "Maybe one of you can take it inside."

Henri gave her a sullen shrug. He looked at the basket of eggs, then turned to his friend. "Do it, Sébastien," he said.

"You do it, Henri," said Sébastien. Henri turned to a little girl. "Émilie, *you* do it."

Isabelle gave up. They could argue about who was going to carry the basket inside without her.

But that's not what the children were arguing about.

Isabelle had only taken a few steps when she felt a pain, sudden and shocking, right between her shoulder blades. The force of the blow sent her stumbling forward. She caught herself and spun around.

The children were laughing gleefully. Isabelle reached behind over her shoulder and touched the back of her dress. Her palm came away covered in yellow slime.

"Which one of you threw the egg?" she demanded.

No one answered her, but Henri sauntered up to the basket, picked up another egg and, before Isabelle could stop him, launched it straight at her head. His aim was excellent. It hit her right between the eyes.

Isabelle gasped. "Why, you . . . you little *troll*!" she shouted as egg ran down her face.

That was all the others needed to hear. They converged on the basket, grabbed eggs, and pelted her with them as hard as they could.

Isabelle should have run straight out of the courtyard and back to her cart. But Isabelle was not one to turn tail. She lunged for the basket, grabbed an egg, and threw it at Henri. Her aim was not as good as his, for she was still blinking egg out of her eyes. The egg went wide and hit little Sébastien instead, right in the back of his head. He tripped, fell down in the grass, and started to howl.

Isabelle threw another egg and pegged Henri in the shoulder. As she grabbed a third from the basket, three more hit her—one in the face.

She lobbed the one she was holding just to get rid of it, so she could wipe her eyes again. Though she couldn't see where it landed, she heard it hit with a loud, wet splat.

"Great God in Heaven, what is going *on* here?" a voice shrilled.

Isabelle blinked; she opened her eyes all the way and discovered that it was not a child that her egg had hit, but an old woman who was dressed all in white and wearing a rosary around her neck.

Isabelle watched in horror as eggshell slid down the front of her spotless habit, then fell to the ground. Globs of yolk dripped onto the toes of her shoes. The old woman looked at the mess on her clothing. She looked at the children around her, at Henri, rubbing his shoulder, at Émilie, staring at her stained pinafore and sobbing piteously, at little Sébastien, sitting up in the grass now, wailing, "Isabelle, the ugly stepsister . . . she a-a-*attacked* us!"

Then the old woman looked at Isabelle. Her eyes, set deep in her wrinkled face, blazed. Her nostrils flared.

"Oh, dear," Isabelle whispered, pressing her hands to her cheeks. "Oh *no*."

It was Sister Claire, the head of the convent, the ancient and venerable mother superior, and she was *furious*.

## - FORTY-TWO -

The iron gate slammed shut behind Isabelle with a loud, ringing clang.

Shamefaced, she looked back through the iron bars. "I'm so sorry," she said miserably.

"Never, *ever* let me see you anywhere near this orphanage again!" Sister Bernadette shrilled, wagging a finger at Isabelle from the other side of the gate. "The mother superior's fifty-year vow of silence broken . . . *fifty years*! All because of you!"

The nun turned on her heel and stalked off, leaving Isabelle by herself. Still cringing, she hobbled to her cart and climbed up to the seat. Martin looked back at her over his shoulder.

"Don't even ask," Isabelle said to him.

She wanted to get home desperately, but she was so overcome with regret for what she'd done that she leaned over, put her head in her hands, and groaned. Her mind replayed every dreadful second of what had happened after she'd hit the mother superior in the chest with an egg.

"You should be *ashamed* of yourself!" the old woman had shrieked. "Throwing eggs at *children*! Making poor orphans *cry*! Wasting desperately needed food while a war rages! Never, in all my days, have I witnessed such egregious behavior. I didn't want to believe what I'd heard—I closed my ears to the gossip—but you, Isabelle de la Paumé, are every bit as awful as everyone says you are!"

As she had been shouting at Isabelle, two nuns that had followed her into the courtyard had been frantically gesturing at her. One had held a trembling finger to her lips. The other had shook her head, saucer-eyed. "Sister, your *vow*!" she'd said.

To show her piety and devotion, Sister Claire had made a solemn oath of silence five decades ago. Through superhuman effort, she had kept the vow, never uttering a word, communicating with the other nuns through writing only. When she'd realized what she'd done, the old woman had clapped a hand over her mouth and fainted on the spot.

"I—I think she's *dead*!" Sister Bernadette had cried.

The minute they heard that, the children—every single one of them—had started wailing in earnest. Alarmed by their noise, a dozen nuns had come running. One had had the presence of mind to sit Sister Claire up and chafe her wrists. A moment later, the old woman had come to. That's when Sister Bernadette had ushered Isabelle out.

"Oh, Martin," Isabelle said, now sitting up. "I threw eggs at *children*. Ten-year-olds. Eight-year-olds. I think one was *five*."

She thrust her hand into her skirt pocket, feeling for the bone, the nutshell, and the seedpod. They were still there but felt more like curses now than gifts. Throwing eggs at orphans was no way to earn the fairy queen's help. She fervently hoped that Tanaquill would not find out about it.

Isabelle made her way home as quickly as she could. Luckily, she met no one else on the road. As soon as she pulled up to the stables, she untacked Martin, brushed him, and left him loose outside to graze. Then she held her head under the pump at the water trough to rinse the egg off.

A few minutes later, she strode into the kitchen, her hair sopping wet, her face red from the cold water, her clothing a filthy mess.

Tavi was stirring a bubbling pot of plum jam. Her eyebrows shot up when she saw her sister. "Looks like charitable pursuits aren't all they're cracked up to be," she said.

Isabelle held up a hand. "Don't."

"Where's our basket? Did someone poach it?"

"Just . . ."

"Now I'll have to scramble to find another one."

". . . *stop!*" Isabelle yelled, covering her ears. She hurried out of the kitchen and went upstairs to change her clothing.

It was a relief to step out of her dress, which was as stiff as meringue. She poured water from the pitcher on her bureau into a basin, wet a cloth, and removed the last traces of egg from her neck. A few minutes later, she was standing in the hallway, doing up the top buttons on a clean dress. As she walked toward the stairs, a voice from behind her said, "Where have you been, Isabelle?"

Isabelle's heart sank. *Not now, Maman,* she thought. She still had Martin to deal with and the day's long list of chores. She did not have time to persuade her mother that there was no ball, dinner, or garden party to ready themselves for.

Tavi had just come up the stairs carrying a tray with a cup of tea on it for their mother. "She went walking," she said, taking Maman by the arm and leading her back to her room.

"Really, Octavia?" Maman trilled, pressing a hand to her chest. "With whom? A chevalier? A viscount?"

"No, the Duke of Egg-ceter!" Tavi said, winking at Isabelle over her shoulder.

Isabelle scowled, but she was grateful to Tavi for distracting Maman. It allowed her to slip down the stairs and out of the house without any further questions.

Martin needed to be put in the pasture. She made her way back to the stables, got his halter, and walked over to him.

"Well, Martin, I'm clean. You're brushed. That's something," she said. "Perhaps the rest of the day will be peaceful and quiet." She gave him a wry smile. "After the morning's disaster, what else could possibly go wrong?"

The horse was standing in front of the stables in the shade of a tall birch tree, his head down. As Isabelle walked over to him, she noticed that he was intent upon something in the grass. He nosed at it, then raked his hoof over it.

"What have you got there, old man? Some chamomile?"

She knew he loved to eat the tiny white-and-yellow flowers that grew around the stables, but as the horse raised his head, Isabelle saw it was not chamomile flowers that had captured his interest.

Dangling from Martin's mouth was a priceless pearl necklace.

## FORTY-THREE

Isabelle and Martin cantered up the winding, tree-lined drive of the Château Rigolade.

After she'd gotten over the shock of seeing her horse about to swallow the valuable pearls, Isabelle had grabbed the necklace out of his mouth, wiped the spit off, and put it in her pocket. The necklace belonged to the marquis or one of his friends, she was certain of it. The little monkey—Nelson—had been wearing it when he shot the chicken thief.

*Whoever owns it must be worried sick*, Isabelle thought. Each pearl was as big as a hazelnut.

As Isabelle reached the top of the drive, she looked for the stables, thinking she could hand Martin to a groom and then ask to see the marquis, but the drive led straight to the château itself, with its burbling fountains, its rosebushes, oak trees, and manicured lawns.

Isabelle could see no one—not a maid or footman or gardener, not the marquis nor any of his friends. She felt awkward sitting on her horse in the middle of a nobleman's drive, so she decided to knock on the château's front door, but as she got down out of her saddle, she heard music coming from behind the château. It came to a slow, disorderly stop, as if one of the players had made a mistake, then it started again.

Isabelle followed the sound, leading Martin around the side of the building, to the back. The lawns there sloped down to a clearing framed by towering oak trees. At the very end of the clearing, a good distance away, was a partially constructed stage. Isabelle could just make out a man up on a ladder, his back to her, hammering boards into place.

Closer by, on the château's shaded terrace, members of the marquis's retinue appeared to be rehearsing a play. The musicians sat in chairs on one side of the terrace, wincing as their conductor angrily upbraided them. Actors roamed the other side. Some held scripts, others brandished fake swords and shields. Trunks, open and spilling costumes, stood nearby. Four monkeys chased one another in and out of them, skirmishing over glass beads and foil crowns.

Isabelle limped toward the terrace, nervously twisting Martin's reins. Several women looked up as she approached. They were older and sumptuously dressed, and she felt dull and drab in comparison. She recognized the diva, elegant and imperious; the magician, who was biting into a peach and somehow making it look mysterious; an acrobat spinning a plate on her finger; and an actress wearing a red wig and holding a scepter.

The magician was the first one to speak to her. "Isabelle, isn't it? You're the one who gave us directions, no?" Her eyes flashed with mischief. "I've been asking around about you. I hear you're one of the queen's ugly stepsisters."

Isabelle shrank at her words. These splendid women knew who she was; they wouldn't want anything to do with her.

The magician saw her discomfort. "Now, now, child. Ugly's not such a bad thing to be called. Not at all!" she said, tossing the peach pit. "We've all been called it at one time or another, and it hasn't killed any of us," she added, wiping juice off her chin with her palm.

"In fact, we've been called far worse," said the actress.

The others chimed in. *Difficult. Obstinate. Stubborn. Shrewish. Willful. Contrary. Unnatural. Abominable. Intractable. Immoral. Ambitious. Shocking. Wayward.*

"*Ugly*'s nothing," said the diva. "*Pretty* . . . now *that's* a dangerous word."

"Pretty hooks you fast and kills you slowly," said the acrobat.

"Call a girl pretty once, and all she wants, forevermore, is to hear it again," the magician added.

She drew a long silk cord from inside her jacket, tossed one end over a high tree branch overhanging the terrace, and secured it on a lower one. Then she jumped up onto a chair under the tree and knotted a loop in the other end of the cord.

"Pretty's a noose you put around your own neck," she said, doing just that. "Any fool can tighten it on you and kick away your footing. And then . . ." She lost her balance and teetered back and forth on the chair. Arms windmilling, she fell. The cord caught with a sickening twang. Her body spun in circles. Her legs kicked wildly.

Isabelle screamed, certain the woman just killed herself, but the magician slipped out of the noose, landed on her feet with a whump, and burst into laughter.

"That's a *horrible* trick," the diva scolded, as Isabelle pressed a hand to her chest. "You've frightened the poor girl to death."

"What a dreadful welcome," said the actress, scowling at the magician. She turned to Isabelle. "Can I get you a cup of tea, my dear? A slice of cake?"

"N-No. No, thank you," Isabelle said, trying to calm her thumping heart. "I must get back. I came because I found something, or rather my horse did, that belongs to you, I think." She pulled the necklace from her pocket and handed it to the diva. "It was lying in the grass near our stables."

The diva gasped. "I thought it was gone forever!" she exclaimed, hugging Isabelle. "Thank you!" She fastened the pearls around her neck, then patted them. "The marquis himself gave these to me. I'm sure he'd like to thank you, too. Go to him, won't you? I believe he's down in the clearing with the carpenter."

Isabelle's gaze swept over the lawn, down the hill, to the stage. It looked like a long walk and her foot was aching. "Would it be all right if I rode him across the clearing?" she asked, nodding at Martin.

"Of course!" said the diva. "And, Isabelle?"

Isabelle hoisted herself into the saddle, then turned around. "Yes?"

"You'll come back, won't you? To see our play when it's done?"

"I would love to," Isabelle said shyly.

"Splendid! We'll send you an invitation. Good-bye!" said the diva, waving her off.

"Good-bye," Isabelle said. She clucked her tongue at Martin and headed across the lawn.

The diva watched Isabelle go, her smile fading. She was joined by the magician and the actress. The three stood in silence, brows furrowed. Nelson lowered himself from a tree branch to the diva's shoulder.

"Are you *certain* you found the right one?" the diva finally said.

The magician nodded. "I'm positive. It took me three days to track him. Over hill and dale. Through four other villages. Turned out he was right under my nose the whole time."

"Boy hunting. Your favorite sport," the actress said tartly.

The magician's full lips curved into a wicked smile. "They *do* smell delicious."

"Fate knows what we know," the diva said. "Chance has to stay one move ahead of her. This better work."

"Yes. It better," Chance said, coming up behind them. "I just looked at her map . . ."

The magician turned to him, worry flashing in her eyes. "Her death date . . ." she said.

"The skull . . ." said diva at the same time.

Chance nodded grimly. "It just turned two shades darker."

## – FORTY-FOUR –

Martin plodded his way across the clearing, pausing now and again to rip up a mouthful of grass or take a bite out of a shrub.

"Can you *behave*?" Isabelle scolded, tugging on his reins. "Just for once?"

As they drew closer to the theater, Isabelle looked at the framing. She could see that it was going to be a small but gracefully built structure, complete with apron, wings, and an arch.

The carpenter, she noticed, was still up on his ladder, hammering away. He was slender and tall and wore his thick brown hair tied back. His white shirt was soaked with sweat; his blue trousers flecked with wood shavings. Eager to find the marquis, she glanced around the theater, at the piles of lumber in front of it, the worktable littered with saws and drills, but she didn't see him.

*He's not here; he can't be*, she reasoned. *He's too colorful, too boisterous, to overlook.*

Her gaze drifted back to the carpenter. There was something familiar about the slope of his shoulders and the easy way he stood on the ladder, lost in his work, careless of the danger. For a moment, she was certain she knew him, but then she shook her head at the very notion. Maman had never allowed her to speak to workmen.

She decided to speak to this one, though, in case he knew where the marquis was.

She had just leaned forward to call out to him when disaster struck. An enormous raven swooped down out of a tree and struck at Martin, beating its wings in his face, raking its sharp talons across his nose.

Martin shied, terrified, but the bird kept at him. He gave a shrill whinny, spun around and bucked, trying to kick the bird away. Isabelle lost her balance and pitched headfirst out of the saddle. Her boot caught in the stirrup as she fell and was pulled off, ripping her stocking and opening her wound. She landed facedown on the ground with a bone-jarring thud. Martin trotted off toward the trees, still kicking at the bird.

For a few seconds, everything went white. But then her senses came back and, with them, the pain. It was exquisite, but she was glad of it. She knew that it was only when you couldn't feel anything, like your legs, that you were in trouble.

Groaning, she rolled over onto her back. A moment later, she opened her eyes and was startled to see a face peering down at her. Though it was blurry and distorted, it looked like a boy's face.

*Or maybe,* she thought, *I'm dead and it's a saint's face. Like the ones in the village church with their high, carved cheekbones and sad, painted eyes. Or maybe it's an angel's face. Yes, that's it. An angel's face, tragic and kind.*

"Am I dead, angel?" she asked, closing her eyes again.

"No. And I'm not an angel."

"Saint?"

"No."

"Boy?"

"Yes.

There was a pause, and then the boy said, "People lose toes all the time, you know. Arms and legs. Eyes and ears. It's no reason to kill yourself. That's what you're doing, isn't it? Trying to kill yourself?"

*Who are you, boy?* Isabelle wondered. But he didn't give her the chance to ask.

"You're lucky your foot came free of the stirrup," he continued. "You could've been dragged. Broken a leg. Or your neck. Martin's a horrible animal. Why aren't you riding Nero? He would have chomped that bird in two."

How did the boy know Martin? And Nero?

Isabelle forced her eyes open. Slowly they focused on the boy's face. Now she knew why his eyes had looked familiar. Why she wondered if she'd seen him before. She had. Every day of her childhood. Climbing trees. Dueling with mops. Playing pirates.

She still saw him every night in her dreams.

"Blackbeard," she whispered.

"Anne Bonny," the boy said with a bow. And the softest, saddest of smiles.

## — FORTY-FIVE —

"It's been a long time, Pirate Queen."

Isabelle didn't trust herself to speak. She wasn't sure what would come out of her mouth. She just nodded as best she could, given that she was lying flat on her back.

*He's older*, she thought. *Taller. He has cheekbones now and stubble on his jaw. His voice is deeper, but his eyes are exactly the same, that faded indigo blue. Artist's eyes. Dreamer's eyes.*

She longed to reach up and touch the face she knew so well, to run her fingers over the edge of his jaw, his lips. To ask how he got the tiny scar above his right cheekbone.

"Felix," she said, sitting up.

"Isabelle."

"It's so . . . um . . ." She cast about for a word. ". . . *wonderful* to see you again."

Felix gave her a worried look. "Maybe you shouldn't get up. I saw the fall. You hit your head. Can you see straight?"

"I'm fine," Isabelle said, standing up. Then she yelped. Pain, sharp and hot, shot up her leg as she put her weight on her bad foot.

"I think you should sit," Felix said, his eyes on her foot.

Isabelle followed his gaze. Her white stocking had a bloom of red on

129

it. The pain from the fall had been so intense, she hadn't even realized she was bleeding. Felix took her hand and the warmth of his touch, the feeling of his skin against hers, made her feel woozy all over again.

He led her to a stone bench under a tree. She sat, glancing around for Martin. He was munching grass in the shade, his reins looped over his neck.

"He has a few scratches on his nose. Nothing terrible," Felix said.

"Thanks. I'm fine now. I won't keep you," Isabelle said, forcing a smile. "You have a stage to build."

"I do. And the marquis wants it done quickly. He's paying us—my master and me—well for it."

"Your master?"

"Master Jourdan. The carpenter in Saint-Michel. He hired me a month ago."

Isabelle digested this. Felix was back in Saint-Michel. She didn't know if she should be happy about that, excited, furious, or all of the above.

"So you're a carpenter now," she said, trying to sound nonchalant. Instead, she sounded ridiculous. *He's sawing boards and hammering them together, for God's sake!* she chided herself. *What else would he be?*

Felix nodded. "I learned the trade working for other carpenters. In other villages."

"You were always carving, I remember that. You wanted to be a sculptor. Like Michelangelo."

"I wanted a lot of things," Felix said quietly, looking down at his scarred, work-roughened hands.

An uncomfortable silence descended. Isabelle longed to break it. She longed to shout at him, to tell him she wanted things, too. To ask him why he lied to her. But pride prevented it.

130

Felix looked up. His eyes met hers. They drifted down to her blood-stained stocking.

"I heard about it," he said. "All of it. The prince. Ella. The glass slipper."

Isabelle looked up. The bird that had spooked Martin was perched on a branch above them. "You know, I've never seen a raven that big," she said, trying to change the subject.

Felix glanced at the bird; then his gaze settled on her again. "Why did you do it? Why did you hack off half of your foot?"

Isabelle blanched. "Ever hear of something called small talk, Felix?"

"I never made small talk with you. I'm not going to start now. Why did you do it?"

Isabelle didn't want to talk about it. Not with him. But Felix was not going to let it go.

"Isabelle, I asked you—"

"I *heard* you," Isabelle snapped. She felt cornered.

"Then *why*?"

*Because you left. And took everything with you*, she thought. *My dreams. My hopes. My happiness.*

But she couldn't admit that to him; she could barely admit it to herself. "To get something—*someone*—I was supposed to want," she finally said.

Felix winced. "You did that to yourself for someone you were *supposed* to want?"

"You know what Maman is like. I couldn't fight anymore. Not after I'd lost all the things I lov—" She bit the word off. "Not after I'd lost all the things that were important to me. Not after I became an ugly stepsister."

"Ugly? Where did that come from? I never thought you were ugly," said Felix. "I liked your laugh. And your eyes. I liked your hair, too. I still do. It's russet. Like a red squirrel."

"I have hair like a squirrel?" Isabelle said in disbelief. "Is that your idea of a compliment?"

"I love squirrels," Felix said with a shrug. "They're scrappy. And smart. And beautiful."

With that, he put his bag down again and knelt by Isabelle. Then he lifted the hem of her skirt and pulled her stocking off.

"Hey!" she cried. "What are you doing?"

Felix held her heel in his hand. "My God," he said, his voice catching.

Isabelle was horrified. The scar was livid and raw; part of it was split open and dripping blood. She tried to pull free of his grip, but he was too strong.

"Let go!" she cried, trying to cover her foot with her skirt.

"It's bleeding. I have bandages and medicine. I'm always cutting myself."

"I don't care!"

"Let me fix it."

"No!"

"Why?"

"Because . . . because it's mortifying!"

Felix sat back on his haunches. "I've seen your feet before, Isabelle," he said gently. "We used to wade in the stream together. Remember?"

Isabelle clenched her fists. It wasn't embarrassment over her bare feet that was bothering her. It was that Felix saw more than her feet; he saw inside of her. He'd always been able to do that. And she felt scaldingly vulnerable under his gaze.

"Just let *go*!"

"No. You got dirt in the wound," Felix said, setting her heel down. "If we don't do something, it'll get infected. And then you'll have to cut off your entire leg. I don't think even *you* could manage that."

Isabelle slumped down, defeated. She'd forgotten how stubborn he could be. Felix walked to a nearby tree and picked up the leather satchel and canteen of water that were lying at the base of it, then carried them back to Isabelle.

He opened the canteen and doused the wound. Then he unbuckled his satchel and dumped out its contents. Chisels came spilling out. Pencils. Carving knives. A rasp. Rulers.

And a tiny soldier, about two inches high.

Isabelle picked it up. "Did you make this?" she asked, glad to have something to talk about other than the mess she'd made of her foot. And her life.

"I carve them in my room at night," Felix said. "I've made a small army complete with rifle companies, fusiliers, grenadiers, their commanders . . . It's almost complete. I just have a few officers to carve."

"What are you going to do with them all?" Isabelle asked.

"Sell them. To a nobleman for his sons to play with. A wealthy banker or merchant. Whoever can pay my price."

Isabelle regarded the little soldier closely. "He's incredible, Felix," she marveled. Beautifully carved and intricately painted, he was so lifelike that she could see the buttons on his coat, the trigger on his rifle, and the determination in his eyes.

"It makes a change from building coffins," Felix said ruefully. "I sometimes think we'll need to cut down every tree in France to make enough to bury all the dead."

Isabelle put the soldier down. "Is it that bad?" she asked quietly.

Felix nodded.

"What's going to happen to us?"

"I don't know, Isabelle."

Some boys would have told her a happy story about how the king's forces would win, of course they would, so as not to upset her feminine sensibilities. Not Felix. He had never sugarcoated things. She'd always loved that about him.

*At least that hasn't changed between us*, she thought wistfully. *Even if everything else has.*

He continued to sift through his things until he finally found what he was after—a folded wad of clean linen strips and a small glass vial. He tipped a few drops of the vial's contents onto Isabelle's wound. It burned. She howled. He paid her no attention and carefully bandaged the wound.

"You're welcome," he said when he'd finished. Then he pulled the boot and stocking off her other foot.

*"Felix,"* Isabelle said. "You can't just go around peeling girls' stockings off. It's inappropriate."

Felix snorted. "Feet don't do much for me. Especially sweaty ones. And anyway, I *don't* go around peeling girls' stockings off. Only yours."

He pulled her legs straight and placed her feet together, side by side, heels on the ground.

"What are you *doing*?"

"Maybe something, maybe nothing," he said, taking measurements, then jotting them down on a scrap of paper with a nub of pencil.

When he was done, he put her stockings and boots back on. Then he stood and said that the marquis was a kind employer but an impatient one, and that he'd better get back to work. Isabelle stood, too, and convinced him that she was fine to ride home. Together they walked over to Martin.

"Hello, you old bastard. Miss me?" Felix said to the horse.

Martin lifted his head. Pricked up his ears. And bit him. Felix laughed. "I'll take that as a yes," he said, patting the horse's neck.

Isabelle noticed that his eyes had become shiny. *Old horses still make him cry. That hasn't changed, either,* she thought. *Or made it any easier to hate him.*

She climbed into her saddle once again and took up Martin's reins. "Thank you, Felix. For fixing me up," she said.

Felix, scratching Martin's ears now, didn't respond right away. *"Loved,"* he said at length.

"What?" Isabelle asked, sliding her feet into her stirrups.

"Earlier, you said, *Not after I'd lost all the things that were important to me.* But you were going to say, *Not after I'd lost all the things I loved.*"

"What if I did?" Isabelle asked warily. "What does it matter?"

"It matters because once I thought . . ." His eyes found hers. "That I was one of those things."

And suddenly, Isabelle lost the small amount of composure she'd been struggling so hard to hold on to. How *dare* he, after what he'd done.

"And people say *I'm* heartless? You're cruel, Felix!" she shouted, her voice cracking with anger.

*"Me?"* Felix said. "But I didn't—"

"No, you didn't. And that's where the trouble started. Good-bye, Felix. Yet again."

Isabelle turned Martin around and touched her heels to his side. Martin must've sensed her upset, for he obeyed her command immediately and launched into a canter. They were across the clearing in no time.

Isabelle rode away without once looking back.

Just as Felix had.

## FORTY-SIX

In the Wildwood, Fate bent down to a patch of mushrooms, slender-stalked and ghostly in the pale light of a crescent moon.

She plucked a plump one. "*Amanita virosa*, the destroying angel. Horribly poisonous, Losca," she said, handing it to her servant. "And essential when making any ink with a greenish hue such as *Jealousy*, *Envy*, or *Spite*."

Fate had brought some inks with her from her palazzo, and she'd been making more, but she needed to get Isabelle's map back in her clutches before she could use them. *Getting Isabelle in my clutches would be helpful, too*, she thought. *How can I convince her of the folly of struggling against her fate when I never even see her?* Chance had contrived to meet the girl twice already. Fate knew she needed to pull Isabelle firmly into her orbit, but how?

"Making ink tonight? Even though you don't have a map?" said a voice from the darkness.

Losca squawked with fright. Fate, not so easily startled, turned around. "Chance?" she called, peering into the shadows.

There was a whoosh, and then a brilliant, blazing light. Three flaming torches illuminated Chance, his magician, and his cook.

"How uncharacteristically optimistic of you," Chance said baitingly.

Fate gave a contemptuous laugh. "How does the skull look? The one on Isabelle's map? Has it grown any lighter?"

Chance glowered.

"I didn't think so."

"I'm winning," Chance said, jutting his chin. "I've given her one piece of her heart back. The boy loves her and she loves him. Love has altered the course of many lives."

"I hear that meeting didn't go quite to plan," said Fate, with a coiled smile. "I hear they didn't exactly fall back into each other's arms."

"Next time I see that raven, I'm going to shoot it," Chance growled, casting a menacing glance at Losca.

"You've won a battle, not the war," said Fate dismissively. "It's easy to love the lovable. Can Isabelle love when it hurts? When its costs? When the price of love may be her life?"

"Mortals aren't born strong, they become strong. Isabelle will, too."

"You are many things," said Fate, shaking her head. "Most of all, you are ruthless."

"And you are dreary, madame," Chance said hotly. "So dreary, you'd have everyone in bed at eight with a cup of hot milk and a plate of madeleines. Can't you see that the courage to risk, to dare, to toss that gold coin up in the air over and over again, win or lose, is what makes humans human? They are fragile, doomed creatures, blinder than worms yet braver than the gods."

"Challenging the Fates is hard. Eating madeleines is easy. Most mortals choose the madeleines. Isabelle will, too," Fate said.

As she spoke, the moon disappeared behind a cloud.

"It's getting late. Past midnight already," Fate said. "There are dangerous creatures afoot in the woods at this hour, and I and my maid must return to the safety of Madame LeBenêt's farm."

Fate's shawl had settled in the crooks of her arms; she drew it up around her shoulders. Her gray eyes came to rest on the three burning flames held aloft by Chance and his friends. Suddenly, she smiled.

"It's so dark without the moon. So hard to find one's way. Might I beg a torch from you?" she asked.

Chance hesitated.

"Come, now," Fate chided. "Surely you wouldn't deny an old woman the means to light her way home?"

Chance nodded and the magician handed her torch to Fate.

"Good night, Marquis," Fate said. "And thank you."

Chance watched her as she started off, her torch held out in front of her, her maid scurrying behind her. He could not see her face, nor hear her voice as she walked away. Had he, he might've realized how foolish he'd been.

"Yes, there *are* dangerous creatures afoot tonight, Losca," Fate said to her servant. "And none more dangerous than I."

## – FORTY-SEVEN –

The drunken man swayed back and forth as violently as if he'd been standing aboard a small boat in rough seas.

The bottle of wine he'd guzzled, the one that had made him feel so happy only an hour ago, now sloshed around like bilge inside him.

It was *somebody's* fault, what had happened to him. It had to be. He wasn't quite sure whose, but he would find out and then that somebody would pay.

He'd lost his job that day. For stealing from his employer. And then he'd gotten drunk on borrowed coins and had staggered home. His wife had thrown him out of the house after he'd told her there was no money left to feed their children. "Go to hell!" she shouted at him. And now here he was, stumbling down a lonely road in the dead of night, halfway there already.

But wait . . . what was this? People? They were jeering, yelling. They were throwing handfuls of mud. At what?

The drunken man hurried closer on his unsteady legs and saw that it was a house—no, a mansion. The moon had come out from behind a cloud, and the drunken man could see that it was shuttered and dark.

"What are you doing?" he asked a boy, short and loutish, with small eyes and bad teeth.

"The ugly stepsisters live here," the boy replied, as if that was the only explanation needed. Then he picked up a rock and lobbed it at the front door.

The ugly stepsisters! The drunken man had heard of them. He knew their story. *What nerve they have*, he thought. *Being mean when girls are supposed to be pleasant. Being ugly when girls are supposed to be pretty.* It was an insult. To him! To the village! To all of France!

"Avenge it," whispered a voice from behind him.

He whirled around, lost his balance, and fell on his face. It took him a few tries to get up, but when he was finally on his feet again, he saw who'd spoken—a kindly old woman, dressed in black, with a basket over her arm and a raven on her shoulder. She was holding a torch.

"What did you say, grandmother?" he asked her.

"Here you are out on the street, penniless and alone. And there they are in a big, comfortable mansion. Each one a shrew, just like your wife. How they shame you, these women. You should avenge their insolence."

The drunken man turned her words over in his head. A light, dull but dangerous, filled his bloodshot eyes. "Yes. Yes, I will. This instant!" he said, thrusting a finger into the air. But then the finger sank down again, little by little, until it hung limply at his side. "But how?"

"You look like a clever fellow," the old woman said.

"Oh, I am, grandmother, I am," he agreed. "You won't find any man more cleverer than me."

139

The old woman smiled. "I know you'll find a way," she said.

And handed him the torch.

## – FORTY-EIGHT –

Isabelle, legs tucked underneath her in a window seat in her bedroom, was blinking up at a silvery crescent moon that was playing peekaboo behind filmy, drifting clouds.

She was so tired, but she couldn't go to bed. She hadn't even undressed.

People had come again tonight, to shout and jeer and throw things at the house. They would stop after a while, when they saw that no one was coming to the door, when they finally grew bored, but until then, she would not sleep. Until then, she would remain wakeful and watchful, peering out between the slats of her shutters every so often to make sure the crowd did not drift too far into the yard, or go down the hill toward their animals.

Isabelle hoped the noise wouldn't wake Maman and upset her. Tavi would be fine. Unlike Isabelle's window, which faced the front yard and the drive, hers overlooked the back gardens. She wouldn't hear a thing.

Isabelle yawned. Her body craved sleep. She'd worked from the moment she'd arrived home from the Château Rigolade to sundown, only stopping for a bit to eat at midday.

She'd scrubbed the kitchen floor. Beat the dust out of rugs. Washed windows. Swept steps. Weeded the garden. Pruned the roses. Did anything and everything to keep from thinking about Felix, to keep from remembering his kind eyes and lopsided smile. His gentle hands. The way tendrils of his hair, worked loose from his ponytail, curled down the back of his neck. The stubble-covered line of his jaw. The freckle above his top lip.

*Stop it*, she told herself. *Right now.*

It was treason, this wanting. How could you long for the very person who'd hurt you worse than you'd ever been hurt in your entire life? It was like longing to drink a glass of poison, pick up a cobra, hold a loaded gun to your head.

She forced herself to think about something else, but soon regretted it, for only memories of the day's other disaster came to her. The taunts of the children at the orphanage rang in her ears. So did the outraged shriek of the mother superior.

She was no closer to finding a piece of her heart, and Tanaquill's gifts weighed heavily in her pocket, reminding her of her failure.

She still had hope, no matter how fragile, of becoming pretty. She just had to find another way of earning the fairy queen's help.

*Tavi made jam,* she thought now. *I could bring some to an elderly shut-in . . . if only I knew one. I could knit socks to bring to Colonel Cafard's soldiers . . . but I never learned how to knit. I could make some soup and bring it to a sick person, or a refugee, or a poor family with lots of children . . . but I'm not a very good cook.*

Still looking out of the window, Isabelle heaved a deep sigh. "How'd you do it, Ella? How did you always manage to be so good? Even to me?" She leaned her weary head against the wall. Shouts and laughter and ugly words drifted up to her from outside. She knew she mustn't sleep, but she didn't think there would be any harm in closing her eyes. Just for a minute.

Isabelle was out instantly. As she drowsed, she dreamt of many things. Of Tanaquill. The marquis. The magician dangling from her silk noose. A monkey in pearls. Felix.

And Ella.

She was here again, in the Maison Douleur. She was standing at the hearth, wearing a threadbare dress. Her face and hands were smudged

141

with cinders. Isabelle was so happy to see her, but Ella wasn't happy. She was pacing back and forth fearfully.

"Wake up, Isabelle," she said urgently. "You need to leave."

A fire was burning in the hearth, and as she spoke, it grew. Its flames curled around the sides of the hearth and up to the mantel. Isabelle coughed. It hurt to breathe. Her eyes stung. Smoke, thick and choking, billowed through the air. Tongues of flame licked the walls and ceiling. The room began to blacken and curled at its edges, as if it were not a real room at all, only a picture.

"Isabelle, wake up!"

"I *am* awake, Ella!" Isabelle cried, turning in frantic circles. The flames were devouring everything in their path. An oil lamp exploded. Windowpanes shattered. The curtains ignited with a thunderous whoosh.

"Go, Isabelle! *Hurry!*" Ella shouted. "Save them!"

And then Isabelle watched, horrified, as the flames engulfed her stepsister, too.

"Ella, no!" she screamed, so loudly that she woke herself up. Her heart slammed against her ribs. She could still feel the heat of the fire, hear wooden tables and chairs crackling in the flames. It was hard to see; her vision was blurry from sleep. She rubbed her eyes with the heels of her hands, trying to clear them.

"It was so *real*," she whispered.

She stood. The floor was hot beneath her bare feet. Her eyes were stinging. With a sickening jolt of fear, she realized it wasn't sleep that had blurred her vision; it was smoke.

The fire . . . it wasn't a dream. It was real. Dear God, it was *real*.

Terror sent her flying across the room. "Maman! Tavi!" she screamed, wrenching open her door. "Get up! Run! *Run!* The house is on fire!"

## FORTY-NINE

"Isabelle?" Tavi murmured. "What is it? What's—" She didn't get to finish her sentence.

"Fire!" Isabelle shouted, pulling her bodily out of her bed. "Get out! Go!"

She ran out of Tavi's room and down the long hallway that led to her mother's chamber.

"Maman! MAMAN!" she called, bursting through her doors.

Maman was not asleep. She was seated at her vanity table, trying on a necklace.

"Stop shouting, Isabelle. It's unladylike," she scolded.

"The house is burning. We have to go," Isabelle said, grabbing her mother's hand.

Maman wrenched it free. "I can't go out like this. I'm not dressed properly."

Isabelle took her mother by the wrist and half cajoled, half dragged her down the hallway. At the top of the stairs, they met Tavi. Her arms were full of books. She was gazing down the stairwell at the conflagration below, paralyzed by fear.

"It's all right, we can make it," Isabelle said. "Look at the door, Tavi. Not the flames."

Tavi nodded woodenly, then followed Isabelle as she started down the steps. Windows shattered in the heat. Air ran into the house through the broken panes, feeding the fire, bellowing flames into the foyer. The three women had to cross it to get to the front door, and safety.

"We can do it. Stay close," Isabelle said.

"I don't want to go outside!" Maman protested. "My hair's a fright!"

"It'll look far worse burnt to a crisp!" Isabelle shot back, tightening her grip.

Isabelle continued down the curving staircase, pulling Maman behind her, forcing Tavi to keep up. By the time they got to the foyer, the flames were halfway across it.

"What do we do?" Tavi shouted.

"We run," Isabelle replied. "Go, Tavi. You first."

Head down, Tavi bolted across the floor. Isabelle heaved a sigh of relief as she watched her disappear through the front door. Now it was her turn. She tightened her grip on her mother's wrist and took a few steps across the floor.

As she did, a gust of wind blowing through a shattered window billowed a burning drapery panel at them. Isabelle instinctively raised her hands to protect herself against it, letting go of her mother.

Maman saw her chance. With an animal cry, she shot back up the stairs.

"Maman, *no!*" Isabelle shouted, darting after her.

She found her back in her room, frantically brushing her hair. Isabelle tore the brush away from her. "Look at me!" she said, taking her mother's hands in her own, forcing Maman to meet her eyes. "The fire is destroying the mansion. You *must* come with me."

Maman stood. She raked her hands through her hair. "What will I wear? What, Isabelle? Tell me!" She picked up a gown off the floor, and a pair of shoes, and clutched them to her chest. Then she lifted her heavy mirror off its hook on the wall. The gown and shoes fell to the floor as she did. "No!" she cried, snatching at them. She lost her grip on the mirror. It toppled forward, pinning her to the floor.

"Stop this!" Isabelle pleaded, pushing the mirror off her.

But Maman would not. She abandoned her finery but took hold of the mirror once more and carried it out of her room. She made it to the landing before dropping it again. It fell to the floor with a loud, echoing boom. Weeping, she sat down next to it.

Isabelle glanced over the railing. Her stomach clutched with fear as she saw that the fire was climbing the walls to the first floor. It was licking the staircase, too.

"Maman, we cannot take the mirror," Isabelle said, her panic rising.

But her mother only stared at the glass sorrowfully. "I can't leave it. I'm nothing without it. It tells me who I am."

Isabelle's heart was battering her ribs. Everything inside her was telling her to run. But she did not. Instead, she sat down next to her mother.

"Maman, if you don't leave the mirror, you will die."

Her mother stubbornly shook her head.

"Maman," Isabelle said, her voice breaking, "if you don't leave the mirror, *I* will die."

Would it matter to her mother if she did? Isabelle didn't know. She was nothing but a disappointment. Was there ever a time she'd pleased Maman instead of making her angry?

Maman looked at Isabelle. In the icy depths of her eyes, something was shifting and cracking. Isabelle saw it and saw that her mother was helpless to stop it. "You are strong. So strong," Maman said. "I saw that in you when you were a tiny baby. It has always frightened me, your strength. I would rock you in my arms and wonder, *Where is there a place in the world for such a strong girl?*"

Below them, a giant wooden ceiling beam gave way. It crashed down to the foyer, bringing much of the second floor with it. The noise was deafening. The dust and smoke it threw into the air were blinding. Isabelle covered her head with her arms and screamed. When the dust cleared, she peered over the railing again and saw a jagged, gaping hole

145

in the foyer floor, next to the stairwell. In the darkness, with fire raging all around it, the hole looked like the gateway to hell.

"Maman . . . *please*," she begged.

But her mother, still gazing at the mirror, didn't seem to hear her.

Isabelle's stomach squeezed with terror. But another emotion rose inside her, pushing the terror down—hatred.

How many times had her mother summoned her to her room, stood her in front of that very mirror, and looked over her shoulder? Frowning sourly at the way her dress bunched here or puckered there? Disapproving of her freckles, her crooked smile, her wayward hair?

How many times had Isabelle lifted her eyes to her own reflection only to see a miserable, awkward girl looking back at her?

That mirror, and all the others in her house, had stolen her confidence, her happiness, her strength and courage, over and over again. It had stolen her soul; now it wanted her life.

From deep within the house, another window exploded. The sound of breaking glass told Isabelle exactly what she had to do. She stood, tore the mirror from her mother's hands, and, with a wild yell, threw it over the banister. It hit the stone floor below and shattered into a million glittering pieces.

"No!" Maman screamed, reaching through the balusters. She stared into the flames for a few long seconds, then looked at Isabelle helplessly.

"Get up, Maman," Isabelle ordered, taking her hand. "We're leaving."

Together they started down the stairs once more. When they got to the bottom, they saw that most of the foyer floor was gone. Only a narrow strip remained, running along one wall and supported by burning joists. One misstep, and they would fall to a fiery death.

Isabelle led Maman along what remained of the floor, hugging the wall the whole time. When they got close to the door, they had to jump across a two-foot gap where the floor was gone completely, and then they were outside, and a sobbing Tavi was running to them.

Isabelle quickly pulled her mother and sister away from the inferno to the sheltering safety of the linden tree. From under its branches, their clothing singed, faces stained with soot, their arms around each other, the three women watched as the fire raged, collapsing the Maison Douleur's walls, bringing its heavy slate roof down, destroying everything that they owned, their past and their present.

"And, with any luck," whispered an old woman dressed all in black and watching from the shadows, "their future."

## – FIFTY –

As the sun rose the next morning, Isabelle stood under the linden tree, gazing at the smoldering heap that had been her home.

Her dress was soaked. Tendrils of wet hair stuck to her skin. A heavy morning rain had doused the fire, but not before a strong wind had swept glowing embers across the yard, to the chicken coop and the open window of the hayloft.

Tavi had wrenched the door of the coop open and had chased the birds out of the yard to safety. They were gone now, vanished into the woods. Isabelle had gotten Martin out before fire took the stables. He stood under the linden tree with them, shaking raindrops out of his mane. Tavi and Maman sat huddled against the linden's trunk, asleep under some horse blankets Isabelle had managed to save from the stables.

Everything in the mansion had been destroyed. Clothing. Furniture.

147

Food. Any paper money Maman had had was ashes; any coins or jewelry had likely melted or were hopelessly buried under piles of hot stone and smoking beams.

Not one neighbor had come to help them. To see if they were hurt. To offer food or shelter. They were utterly alone. Destitute. Friendless. That terrified Isabelle even more than the fire had.

Chilled from the rain, numb inside, Isabelle did not know how they would eat that day or find shelter that night. She did not know how to take the next step. She could not see a way forward.

She stood, cupping her elbows, mutely watching wisps of smoke spiral up into the air for over an hour. Until she heard the sound of hooves and the creak of wagon wheels, and stepped out from under the tree to see who it was.

"Isabelle, is that you?" a voice called. "My goodness, child! What happened here?"

Isabelle saw an old horse and an even older farm wagon, piled high with cabbages, creaking toward her. Holding the reins was Avara LeBenêt. Seated next to her, her face creased with concern, her dark eyes as bright and busy as a vulture's, was Tantine.

## — FIFTY-ONE —

"It was a fire," Isabelle said dully. "It took everything."

Tantine pressed a wrinkled hand to her chest. "That's terrible. Just terrible, child!"

"What goes around comes around," sniffed Madame LeBenêt.

"How did it start?" Tantine asked.

"I don't know," Isabelle said, pressing a hand to her forehead. "I woke up, and the downstairs was in flames."

"It must've been a spark from the fireplace. Or an ember that rolled out of the grate," Tantine said. "Where is your mother? Your sister?"

"They're under there, asleep," Isabelle replied, pointing to the linden.

"This is dreadful. You're soaking wet. Cold, too, from the looks of you. Have you nowhere to go?"

Isabelle shook her head but then had a thought. "Perhaps the marquis could help us. His château is so big. All we would need is a room in the attic. We could—"

Tantine paled. She shot to her feet, startling Madame LeBenêt and Isabelle. "Absolutely not!" she declared. "I won't hear of it. The marquis is a man of loose morals, my dear. He lives with several women, not one of whom is his wife. I will not stand by and see two young women corrupted by that scoundrel!"

"But he seems so very—" *Nice*, Isabelle was going to say.

But Tantine held up a hand, silencing her. She turned to Madame LeBenêt. "They must stay with us, Avara. We are their closest neighbors."

Avara LeBenêt nearly choked. "*Three* more mouths to feed, Tantine? With a war going on and food so scarce?"

Isabelle thought of the rows of cabbages in the LeBenêts' fields. The plump chickens in their coop. The branches of their plum trees bent to the ground with heavy fruit. She did not relish the idea of accepting charity from this harsh, stingy woman, but she knew she had no choice. *Please, Tantine*, she begged silently. *Please convince her.*

"It's a burden, yes," Tantine allowed. "But you are an unselfish woman, Avara. A woman who always puts others first."

Madame LeBenêt nodded vigorously, as one does when accepting praise, or anything else, that does not belong to one. "You're right. I *am* far too kind. It's my undoing."

"Look at what you will gain from the arrangement: three desperately

149

needed farmhands," Tantine said. "All yours have joined the army. Only Hugo remains because of his poor eyesight. Your cabbages will rot in the fields if you can't get them to market."

Avara looked Isabelle up and down. Squinted. Worked a piece of food from her teeth with her thumbnail. "All right," she finally said. "You and your family may come to the farm and I will feed you, if"—she held up a finger—"*if* you promise to work hard."

Isabelle nearly wept with relief. They could dry themselves off. Warm themselves by the farmhouse's hearth. Maybe there would even be a bowl of hot soup for them.

"We will work *very* hard, madame. I promise," she said. "Me, Tavi, Maman, Martin . . . all of us."

Madame LeBenêt shook her head. "No, absolutely not. The offer does not include your horse."

Isabelle looked from Madame LeBenêt to Tantine pleadingly. "But I can't leave him here," she said. "He's old. He needs his oats. And a dry stall to sleep in."

"You see, Tantine? I'm being taken advantage of already," Madame LeBenêt said, flipping a hand at Isabelle.

"I doubt the animal will eat much," Tantine assured her. "And you can use him, too."

Madame relented. "I suppose that's true," she said. She gestured at her own cart horse. "Louis here is on his last legs."

*Because you worked him to death*, Isabelle thought, looking at the poor bony creature. *And you'll do the same to us.* The realization sat heavily on her.

"It's settled, then," Tantine declared with a satisfied smile.

"Get yourselves to the farm," Madame LeBenêt said. "Find Hugo. He's cutting cabbages. He'll show you what to do." She snapped her reins

150

against Louis's haunches. "Tantine and I must take this load to market."

"Thank you, madame," Isabelle said as the wagon rolled off. "Thank you for making room in your house for us."

Madame LeBenêt snorted. *"House?"* she called over her shoulder. "Who said anything about the house? You three will sleep in the hayloft and be glad of it!"

## – FIFTY-TWO –

Fate stared at the stingy portion of weak coffee in a cracked mug on the table in front of her. And the hard heel of bread to dip into it. There was a small pitcher of cream next to the mug. No sugar. No biscuits. No warm, pillowy brioche.

"Perhaps I was too liberal with my use of *Smallsoul* on Avara LeBenêt's map," she said to herself, drumming her fingers on the table.

*Smallsoul*—a dusty, dry black ink—was versatile. It could prompt miserliness, or, if applied properly, shrink the soul. It was also useful in curbing the artistic impulse, but one had to be careful; a little went a long way.

Fate closed her eyes and imagined a delicate porcelain cup of steaming espresso brewed from dark, oily beans. A plate of buttery anise biscuits. A velvet-covered chair for her old bones to sink into.

Ah well, it wouldn't be too much longer before she left Saint-Michel for good. Progress was being made. A drunken fool had burned the Maison Douleur down for her, and Isabelle and her family were now destitute. They were stuck here on the LeBenêts' farm, which meant Fate could control the girl. Chance no longer had the upper hand.

She rose now, moved to the old stone sink, and dumped the coffee down the drain. She rinsed the cup, dried it, then walked outside. Avara and Hugo were already in the fields; Isabelle, Tavi, and their mother, too.

As Fate bent to admire the late-summer blooms on a straggly rose-bush struggling up the wall of the house, Losca landed above her on the roof.

The crone smiled, delighted to see the sly creature. "Where have you been? Impaling field mice with that sharp beak? Snatching hatchlings from their nests? Pecking the eyes out of dead things?"

Losca shook out her feathers. With barely contained excitement, she started to chatter. The crone listened, rapt.

"Two hundred miles west of here? Volkmar's moving quickly; that's good. The sooner this is behind us, the better."

Losca bobbed her head. Then chattered again.

Fate laughed. "That's *two* pieces of good news! The horse is with a widow, you say? And the stables are crumbling?" The crone nodded. "She probably doesn't have much money. A few coins should do the trick. I can't do the deed myself—too much blood—but I know a man who can. Well done, my girl! Chance found the first piece of Isabelle's heart and put the boy right in her path, but the horse is one piece he won't find. And without all three, she won't gain Tanaquill's help."

She reached into her skirt pocket. "Here we are!" she said, pulling out a gangly spider. She tossed it to Losca, who greedily snapped it out of the air.

Fate started for the barn. She would ask Hugo to hitch up a cart so she could go to the village and set her plan for the horse in motion. She was pleased, certain that it would only be a matter of days, a fortnight at the most, before she was ready to leave.

Volkmar was coming closer.

And she wanted to be long gone when he arrived.

## FIFTY-THREE

Isabelle straightened—her face to the sun—and stretched, trying to ease her aching back.

Her callused hands were as filthy as her boots. The sun had bronzed her arms and added freckles to her nose and cheeks, despite the old straw bonnet she wore. Her skirts were hitched up and knotted above her knees to keep them from dragging in the dirt.

"Isabelle, Octavia, does my hair look all right? What if a countess or duchess should pay us a visit?" Maman asked anxiously.

"Oh, I'm sure one will, Maman. After all, cabbage patches are a favorite destination of the nobility," Tavi said.

"Your hair looks lovely, Maman. Pick up your knife now and cut some cabbages," Isabelle said, shooting her sister a dirty look.

As she did, she noticed that Tavi, who was one row over but well behind her, was bent over a cabbage, peering at it intently.

*No vegetable can be that interesting*, Isabelle thought. "Tavi, what are you doing over there?" she asked, jumping over her row to her sister's.

"Nothing!" Tavi replied quickly. "Just cutting a stem!"

But she wasn't. She'd pressed a large outer leaf flat and was using a sharp stone to scratch equations across it.

"No wonder you're behind!" Isabelle scolded.

Tavi hung her head. "I'm sorry, Iz," she said. "I can't help it. I'm so bored I could cry."

"Bored is better than dead, which is what you'll be if we don't eat, *again*, because we haven't filled the wagon," Isabelle scolded.

Madame LeBenêt had decreed that the three women must load the farm's large wooden wagon with cabbages every day or there would be no supper for them.

"I'm sorry," Tavi said again.

She looked so miserable that Isabelle softened. "You and I can go without a meal or two, but not Maman. She's getting worse."

Both girls cast worried glances in their mother's direction. Maman, sitting on the ground, was patting her hair, smoothing her tattered dress—the same silk gown she'd been wearing the night of the fire—and talking animatedly to the cabbage heads. The hollows in her cheeks had deepened. Her eyes were lackluster. There seemed to be more gray in her hair every day.

Since their arrival at the farm, she'd only slid deeper into the past. The few moments of clarity she'd had on the stairs of the Maison Douleur as it had gone up in flames had not come again. Isabelle blamed it on the trauma of losing their home and all their possessions, and on the hard life they now lived. But she knew there was more to it, too; Maman felt she had failed at a mother's most important task—seeing that her daughters made good marriages—and the failure had unhinged her.

Isabelle had startled awake their first night of sleeping in the hayloft, certain that a mouse had run across her cheek, but it was Maman. She'd been sitting in the hay beside her, smoothing the hair off her face.

"What will become of you?" she whispered. "My poor, poor daughters. Your lives are over before they've even begun. You are farmhands with dirty faces and ragged dresses. Who will have you now?"

"Go to sleep, Maman," Isabelle had said, frightened.

Her fearsome mother was fading before her very eyes. It had often been hard living with Maman. Hard coming up against her constant disapproval. Her anger. Her rigid rules. But no matter what, Maman had seen to it that the bills were paid. Widowed twice, she'd still managed to keep a roof over their heads and food on the table. Now, for the first time, Isabelle had to do it. Sometimes with Tavi's help, often without it. That was hard, too.

They had arrived at the LeBenêts' a week ago, after salvaging what they could from the barn—horse blankets, two wooden chairs, two saddles and bridles. Miraculously, their wooden cart had not burned, but it had taken them hours to extricate it because part of the barn's roof had fallen on it. After loading it with their things, they hitched up Martin and rode to the LeBenêts'. By the time they arrived, Madame and Tantine had returned from the market. Madame had put them straight to work.

They'd learned how to cut cabbages, dig potatoes and carrots, slop pigs, and milk cows.

Tavi had proven herself even less capable around animals than she was around cabbages, so Madame had given her the cheese making tasks. It was her responsibility to tend the milk in the wooden vats in the dairy house as it soured and curdled, stirring the curds gently with a long wooden paddle, then setting them in molds to ripen into cheese. It was the one job Tavi did with enthusiasm, as the transformation milk underwent to become cheese fascinated her.

Their days were long and hard. Meals were meager, comforts nonexistent. Beds were horse blankets spread over hay. Baths were taken once a week.

With a wry smile, Isabelle remembered asking Madame if she could bathe at the end of her first day on the farm.

"Certainly," Madame said. "The duck pond's all yours."

Isabelle had thought she was joking. "The *duck pond*?" she'd repeated.

"You were expecting a copper tub and a Turkish towel?" Madame had said with a smirk.

Isabelle had walked to the pond. Her hands were blistered. Dirt had worked itself under her nails. Her muscles were aching. She stank of smoke, sweat, and sour milk. Her dress was so filthy it was stiff.

The banks of the pond afforded no privacy and Isabelle was too modest to strip off her clothing in plain view of others, so she'd simply removed her boots and stockings, placed the bone, nutshell, and seed-pod in one of her boots, then waded in fully dressed. She would take off her dress in the hayloft and let it dry overnight. Her chemise would dry as she slept in it. The one dress was all she had. The gowns in her ward-robe, the silks and satins Maman had carefully chosen to impress suitors, were nothing but ash now.

The pond was spring-fed, and the water was so cold it had made Isabelle catch her breath, but it also numbed her torn hands and sore body. She'd undone the dirty ribbon that cinched her braid, ducked her head under the water, and scrubbed her scalp. When she'd surfaced, Madame had been walking by.

"The tables have turned, haven't they?" she mocked, looking a sodden Isabelle up and down. "If only your stepsister could see you now. How she would laugh."

"No, I don't think so," Isabelle had said, wringing the water out of her hair.

"Of course she would!"

Isabelle shook her head. "I would have. But Ella? Never. That was her strength. And my weakness."

She ducked under again. When she came back up, Madame was gone.

She'd watched the swallows swoop through the air, and listened to the frogs and crickets. She thought about Tanaquill and the possibility of help she'd offered, and it seemed as far away as the stars. How could she find the pieces of her heart when all she did, day after day, was cut cabbages? She thought about the people who had burned down her house, who would never let her forget that she was nothing but an ugly stepsister.

*Maybe there is no help for me,* she'd thought. *Maybe I have to find a way to live with that.*

That's certainly what Tantine counseled. *Ah, child,* she'd said the night after the fire. *Our fates are often hard, but we must learn to accept them. We have no choice.*

Maybe the old woman was right. A feeling of hopelessness had descended on Isabelle ever since she'd arrived at the LeBenêts' farm. Her life was cows and cabbages now and it seemed like that was all it would ever be.

"It's noon already and you don't even have half the wagon filled," said a voice a few rows over, pulling Isabelle out of her thoughts.

Isabelle's spirits, already heavy, sank even lower. Here was someone who made Tantine look like a devil-may-care optimist.

It was Hugo, Madame LeBenêt's son.

## – FIFTY-FOUR –

Isabelle's shoulders rose up around her ears. "I *know* we haven't filled the wagon, Hugo. Thank you," she said tartly.

Hugo blinked at her through his thick eyeglasses. "I'm just saying."

"Yes, you are."

There were many unpleasant things about their new lives. Hunger. Exhaustion. Sleeping in the hot hayloft. Mucking out cow stalls. Raw, blistered hands that cracked and wept. Nothing, though, was more unpleasant than the hulking, surly Hugo. He didn't like Isabelle or Tavi and took every chance he could to make that clear.

"You don't get that wagon filled, you won't get any soup tonight," he said.

"You could help us. It would go faster. We'd get done that way," Tavi said.

Hugo shook his head. "Can't. Have to sharpen the plow. And then—"

157

"Hugo! Hey, Hugo!" a voice called, cutting him off.

Hugo, Isabelle, and Tavi all turned to see a wagon trundling down the drive. Two young men were riding in it. Isabelle knew them. They were soldiers under Colonel Cafard's command. They worked in the camp's kitchen and came every day to pick up vegetables.

"You've got to help Claude and Remy now," Hugo said. "Both of you. My mother said so. That'll take a good hour. You're going hungry again tonight."

Hugo said this without malice or glee, just dull resignation. Like an old man predicting rain.

"You could give us some of your supper. You could sneak it up to the hayloft after dark," Tavi suggested.

"It's soup. How am I supposed to sneak soup?"

"Bread, then. Sneak us some bread. Wrap it up in your napkin when no one's looking and put it in your pocket."

Hugo's face darkened. "I wish you'd never come here. You're always thinking of . . . of *things*," he said. "You shouldn't do that. Girls shouldn't. It's up to the man to think. It's up to *me* to think of sneaking you bread."

"Then think of it! Think of sneaking us cheese. A bit of ham. Think of *something* before we starve to death!" Tavi snapped.

"Hey, Hugo! Where are the potatoes?" Claude called out. "Cook says we're supposed to get potatoes and carrots today. Hey, Isabelle. Hey, Tavi. Hey, Madame de la Paumé."

Maman, still talking to the cabbages, stood. "Your Excellencies," she said with a reverent curtsy. "You see, girls?" she added grandly. "It pays to keep up appearances. The pope has come to visit us. And the king of Spain."

Claude and Remy gave each other puzzled looks.

"Never mind," Isabelle told them.

Hugo nodded in the direction they'd come. "That's quite a cloud you kicked up on the road," he said to the boys. The road was half a mile from where they stood, and a tall hedgerow blocked it from their view, but above it, they could all see a huge mass of dust rising into the air.

"That's not us," Remy said. "It's more wounded."

Hugo took off his glasses and cleaned them on his shirt. Then he put them back on and gazed at the dust cloud again. It rose higher and higher in the sky, swirling like a gathering storm. "Must be a lot of them," he said.

"Wagons for miles," said Remy. "As far as you can see." He looked down at the reins in his hands. "We're losing."

"Come on, Rem. That's only because *we're* not there yet!" Claude boasted, elbowing him. "I'll send Volkmar running back to the border with my sword up his ass!"

Remy mustered a smile, but it was a wan one.

Isabelle knew that both boys were being sent to the front soon. She wondered if she would see them again. Would they, too, be carried back over rutted roads in a rattling wagon missing pieces of themselves? Or would they end up in hastily dug graves, never to see their homes again?

They'd talked a little over the last few days, she, Remy, and Claude, as she'd helped load their wagon. She'd learned that Claude, olive-skinned and dark-eyed, came from the south, from a family of fishermen. Remy, fair and blond, was from the west, a printer's son who had hopes of not only printing books but writing them one day. They had no more wanted to be soldiers than Isabelle had wanted to marry the prince. But the choice to fight was not theirs to make, no more than the decision to cut off her toes had been hers.

Leaving Maman with the cabbages, Isabelle and Tavi helped the boys. Hugo decided to pitch in, too. When the last potato sack had been hoisted in, Remy and Claude climbed back into their seats.

"See you tomorrow," Hugo said, squinting up at them.

Claude shook his head. "Someone new will come tomorrow. We're heading out, me and Rem."

It was quiet for a moment; then Hugo said, "Then we'll see you when you get back."

Remy swallowed hard. Then he reached inside his shirt and pulled a silver chain over his head. A cross was dangling from it. "If I don't . . . if I don't return, could you get this to my mother?" he asked Isabelle, handing it to her. He told her his surname and the town where he was from. He looked very scared and very young as he asked, and Isabelle said it wouldn't be necessary and tried to hand the cross back, but he wouldn't take it. Instead, he thanked her.

"It's nothing. I . . . I wish I could do more to help you, to help all the soldiers," she said.

Remy smiled at her. "What could you do? You're a girl," he teased.

"I'm good with a sword. As good as you are. Maybe better. I've been practicing."

"Girls don't fight. Stay here and cut cabbages for us, all right? Soldiers need to eat."

Isabelle forced a smile and waved them off. They trundled out of the farmyard and down the drive. She was back in the cabbage rows by the time they turned onto the road.

For several long minutes, she watched them go, holding her harvesting knife as if she were gripping the hilt of Tanaquill's sword. A terrible longing took hold of her as she did, a yearning buried so deep inside her, she couldn't even name it anymore. It was a hunger deeper and more ferocious than the need for mere food, a hunger that sang in her blood and echoed in her bones.

Isabelle turned away and, with a heavy sigh, bent her back to the cabbages. She, Tavi, and Maman had many more to cut if they were going to eat tonight.

As she worked, she worried about empty wagons and empty bellies.

She needn't have, though. The stomach is easily satisfied.

It's the hunger in our hearts that kills us.

## - FIFTY-FIVE -

It was dusk, Isabelle's favorite time of day.

And she was spending it in her favorite place, the Wildwood.

Isabelle had ridden Martin across the LeBenêts' land and dismounted as soon as they'd reached the woods in order to give the old horse a rest. As they made their way through the trees, Isabelle took a deep breath of the clear forest air. It had been years since she'd set foot in the Wildwood. She'd forgotten how intoxicating the scent of the forest was—a mixture of damp, rotting leaves; resiny pine needles; and the dark, mineralish waters of the rocky streams they crossed. She took note of all the familiar markers as she walked—the giant white boulder, the tree felled by lightning, a stand of silver birches—though she could have found her way blindfolded.

Finally, she reached her destination—a hidden bower far within the woods. Everything was just as she remembered it—the leafy canopy, the shaggy berry bushes, even the little heart. It was still there, on a mossy bank, shaped of stones and walnut shells. Some were missing, but most remained, bleached by rain and snow.

Isabelle sat down on the soft moss and touched one of the stones. She had tried her best to not think of Felix since her visit to the marquis's, but now everything came rushing back. She could see him, and herself, right here, just as they were the day they'd made the heart.

They'd been best friends. Soul mates. Since the day her mother had married Ella's father and had brought her and Tavi to live at the Maison Douleur. He was the groom's son and had loved horses every bit as much as she did. They'd ridden over hill and dale together, through streams and meadows, deep into the Wildwood.

From the start, Maman had disapproved. Two years ago, when Isabelle had turned fourteen and Felix sixteen, she'd declared that Isabelle was too old to be acting like a hoyden. It was time to give up riding and learn to sing and dance and do all the things that made one a proper lady, but Isabelle wanted no part of that. She'd escaped with Felix every chance she got. She'd adored him. Loved him. And then, one day, she'd discovered she was in love with him.

They'd ridden into the Wildwood and had stopped at the top of the Devil's Hollow, a wooded canyon. As much as they liked to explore, they knew better than to venture into the Hollow, for it was haunted. Instead, they'd flung themselves down on the mossy bank and had eaten the cherries and chocolate cake that Isabelle had filched from the kitchen.

As they were finishing, and Felix was wiping cherry juice off Isabelle's chin with his sleeve, they'd heard a twig snap behind them.

Slowly, they'd turned around. A red deer had ventured near to them. She was only a few yards away and with her were twin fawns, still wobbly on their spindly legs. Their blunt black noses were shiny and wet, their soft coats dappled white, their dark eyes huge and trusting. As the doe grazed and the fawns stared at the pair of strange animals sitting on the bank, Isabelle had felt as if her heart would burst with joy. Never had she seen anything so beautiful. Instinctively, she'd reached for Felix's

162

hand. He'd taken it and held it and hadn't let go even after the deer had gone.

She'd looked down at their hands and then up at him questioningly, and he'd answered her. With a kiss. She'd caught her breath and laughed; then she'd kissed him back.

He'd smelled like all the things she loved—horses, leather, lavender, and hay.

He'd tasted like cherries and chocolate and boy.

He'd felt safely familiar and dangerously new.

Before they'd left, they'd made the heart together. Isabelle could still see them, side by side, placing the stones and shells . . .

"What a pretty picture," said a voice at Isabelle's side.

Isabelle jumped; she gasped. The images were swept away like rose petals in the wind.

Tanaquill laughed. "Ah, mortal happiness," she said. "As fleeting as the dawn, as fragile as a dragonfly's wing. You poor creatures have it, you lose it, and then you spend the rest of your lives torturing yourselves with memories until old age carries you off in some slow, bloodless death." She wiped a crimson smudge from the corner of her mouth with her thumb and licked it. "Better a quick and bloody one, if you ask me."

"You . . . you could see what I saw?" Isabelle said, her heart still jumping from her scare.

"Of course. The heart leaves echoes. They linger like ghosts."

Tanaquill was dressed in a gown of shimmering blue butterfly wings, their edges traced in black. A wreath of black roses adorned her head; several live butterflies had lighted upon it, their gossamer wings slowly opening and closing.

"Have you found the pieces of your heart yet, Isabelle?" the fairy queen asked.

"I—I need a little more time," Isabelle replied, hoping Tanaquill

163

wouldn't ask why. She did not want to tell her how badly wrong her trip to the orphanage had gone. "I think I know what they are now, at least. Goodness, kindness, and charitableness."

Isabelle hoped Tanaquill would be delighted that she had at least figured out what the pieces were, even if she hadn't found them yet, but the fairy queen was not.

"I instructed you to find the pieces of *your* heart. Not someone else's," she said coldly.

"I'm trying. I really am! I—"

"By throwing eggs at orphans?"

Isabelle looked at her boots, her cheeks flaming. "You heard about that," she said.

"And your wish . . . is it still to be pretty?"

"Yes," said Isabelle resolutely, looking up again.

Tanaquill turned away, growling, then she rounded back on Isabelle. "I watched you as a child. Did you know that?" she said, pointing a taloned finger at her. "I watched you duel, swing out of trees, play at being generals . . . Scipio, Hannibal, Alexander the Great. None of *them* wished to be pretty."

Frustration sparked in Isabelle. "Alexander didn't have to be pretty," she retorted. "*His* mother didn't make him wear ridiculous dresses or dance minuets. Alexander was an emperor with vast armies at his command and a magnificent warhorse named Bucephalus. I'm a girl who can hardly walk. And that's *my* magnificent warhorse." She nodded at Martin, who, in his greed, had pushed himself so far into a blackberry thicket, all that was visible of him was his bony rear end. "He and I won't be invading Persia anytime soon."

Tanaquill looked as if she would speak again, but instead she froze. She scented the air, then listened as an animal does, not only with her ears, but with her flesh, her bones.

Isabelle heard it, too. A twig snapping. Footsteps kicking through the leaves.

The fairy queen turned back to her. "Try harder, girl," she said. "Time is not on your side."

And then she was gone, and Isabelle was alone with whoever was coming. Few people ventured this far into the Wildwood at dusk. Isabelle remembered the deserter who'd tried to steal her chickens. He'd tried to kill her. He'd try again, she was certain.

Cursing herself for being stupid enough to ride so far from safety with no sword, no dagger, not even a clasp knife, Isabelle looked around frantically for a weapon—a tree limb, a heavy rock, *anything*. Then she remembered Tanaquill's gifts. She dug in her pocket, hoping that one of them would transform into something she could use to defend herself, but they remained a bone, a shell, and a seedpod.

Isabelle knew she was in trouble. She was about to run for Martin, to try to ride out of the woods fast, when a figure emerged from the dusk, and her traitor heart lurched.

This was no chicken thief making his way toward her, but he was still a deserter.

"The very worst kind," Isabelle whispered.

## - FIFTY-SIX -

Felix didn't see her at first.

He was too busy looking up, squinting into the dusk. At what, Isabelle couldn't guess.

He tripped over a tree root, righted himself, then did a double take as he saw her. After the initial shock of surprise wore off, a wide grin spread across his face. His beautiful blue eyes lit up.

*Don't be happy to see me. Don't smile. You don't get to*, Isabelle said silently.

"Isabelle, is that you?" he called out. "What are you doing here?"

"Talking to fairies," Isabelle replied curtly. "What are *you* doing here?"

"Looking for a downed walnut tree or at least a nice, thick limb."

"Why?"

"I need walnut to carve my commanders. For my army of wooden soldiers. Usually, I can find scraps from furniture we make in the shop." The light in his eyes dimmed a little. "Only we don't have any orders for desks or cabinets right now. Just coffins. We use pine for those."

He shrugged his satchel off his shoulder and put it on the moss bank. Then he sat down next to Isabelle.

"I heard about your house. I'm sorry."

Isabelle thanked him. He asked how living at the LeBenêts' was going. Isabelle told him it was better than starving. Their conversation might have continued in terse questions and answers had the bushes nearby not shaken violently.

Felix started at the sound

"It's only Martin," Isabelle said.

"Let me guess . . . blackberries," he said, laughing. "Do you remember when he ate the entire bucketful we'd picked for Adélie?" He leaned back as he spoke, and his hand came down on one of the stones in the heart.

He turned around, lifted his hand. "It's still there . . ." he said, looking down at it.

His eyes sought Isabelle's, just for an instant, and what she saw in their depths made her catch her breath—pain, as deep and raw as her own.

She hadn't expected that. She hadn't expected him to remember the heart and wondered if he'd remembered other things that had happened here. If he did, he wasn't sharing his memories. His eyes were

166

elsewhere now, their depths hidden from her. He'd opened his satchel and was digging through it furiously.

"I have something for you," he said. Quickly. As if he were trying to change a subject that no one had brought up.

He pulled out the same tools of his trade Isabelle had seen when he'd emptied his bag at the marquis's, but he was taking out other things, too. Strange things. A human hand. Half a face. A set of teeth. Two eyeballs.

Isabelle's own eyes widened in horror.

Felix noticed. He laughed. "They're not *real*," he said, picking up the hand and offering it to her.

Isabelle took it, half expecting it to feel warm. The painted skin was so lifelike. "Why do you have them?" she asked.

"I made them. I make a lot of body parts now, what with all the wounded men in the army camp. There's such a demand for them that Colonel Cafard won't let me enlist. I tried, but he said I'm more valuable to the army working for Master Jourdan than I would be working for him."

*Plus, you can't shoot straight*, Isabelle thought, remembering the time they'd been allowed to fire her stepfather's pistols. He'd hit everything but the target.

Felix continued to dig in his satchel, then finally he pulled out an object and put it in Isabelle's lap. "There. That one's for you."

Isabelle put the hand down and looked at what he'd given her. It was a leather slipper, thin and finely stitched, with a gusset and laces above the arch. She picked it up. It was heavy.

"What is it?" she asked.

Felix didn't reply. Instead, he took the slipper from her, opened the laces, and pulled out whatever it was that had made it heavy. As he put the object into Isabelle's hands, she saw that it was a block of wood, carved in the shape of toes. Each was well delineated, separate from its fellows, sanded to smoothness.

"Toes . . ." she said wonderingly.

"*Your* toes," Felix said, taking them back from her.

"That is an unusual gift. Most girls get candy. Or flowers."

"You were never most girls. Are you now?" he asked, an edge to his voice. He put the wooden toes back inside the slipper, then wadded a bit of lambs wool he had in his satchel in after them. "Try it," he said, handing the slipper back to her.

Isabelle hitched up her skirt and took her boot off. She put the slipper on, then started to tie the laces.

"That's not tight enough," Felix said. "It has to fit like a glove." He leaned over her, pulled the laces tighter, and knotted them. "Stand up," he said when he'd finished.

Isabelle did. The slipper fit better than a glove; it fit like her own skin. She put her boot back on.

"Take a step. But be careful. Don't forget that you reopened your scar when you fell off Martin," Felix said, shoveling body parts back into his satchel.

Isabelle clenched her fists. He was making her want something badly. Yet again. What if the slipper didn't work? What if it hurt? What if it only made things worse? He had a talent for making things worse.

"Come on, Isabelle. You're braver than this. Take a step."

His voice was challenging, goading, and Isabelle bridled at it. He saw the fear in her, and she didn't want him to. Gingerly, she put her foot down, holding her breath. It didn't hurt. She exhaled. Took a step. And then another. The weight of the carved toes was perfectly balanced. The tight fit kept the toes snug up against the rest of her foot. Nothing slipped or rubbed. She'd never expected to walk without a limp again, and now she was. Her gait was smooth and easy.

Happiness flooded through her. She walked briskly back and forth.

"Take it slow," Felix cautioned.

She ran back and forth.

*"Isabelle."*

She jumped up on the mossy bank and jumped down again. Balanced on her new foot. Twirled. Lunged. Laughed out loud. Giddy and excited, she forgot herself. Forgot to be awkward. Forgot to be angry.

"Thank you, Felix. Thank you!" she said, and then she impulsively threw her arms around him.

She didn't see Felix's eyes fill with longing as she hugged him. She didn't know that just for an instant, he pressed his cheek against her head. She felt his arms stiffen at his sides, though. She felt him pull away from her.

Hurt, she took a step back.

"Isabelle, I can't—" Felix started to say.

"Can't what? Get too close?" Isabelle asked, her voice raw. "No, you shouldn't. I'm broken. And broken things draw blood."

"Either I back away or I wrap my arms around you. And then what?"

Isabelle couldn't believe what she'd just heard. "Is that some kind of rotten joke, Felix?" she asked angrily. "You should leave. Go. As far as you can."

"I already tried that," Felix said.

And then he reached across the space between them and cupped her cheek. Isabelle grasped his wrist, meaning to push it away. Instead, her fingers curled around it. She leaned into his palm, his nearness, his warmth, melting her defenses.

"Don't," she said. "It's not fair."

"No, it isn't."

"You said you loved me, but you didn't. It was a lie. How could you do that? How could you lie to me, Felix?"

Felix kissed her then, his lips sweet and sad and bitter, and Isabelle kissed him back, clutching handfuls of his shirt, pulling him to her. He broke the kiss, and she looked up at him, her eyes searching his, confused.

"That's how much I didn't love you," he said, his voice husky. "How much I still don't."

And then he picked up his satchel and walked away, leaving Isabelle alone in the gathering gloom.

"You're walking away?" she called after him. "Again?"

"What should I do? Let you break my heart a second time?"

"Me?" she sputtered. "*Me?*"

Isabelle paced back and forth, furious. Then she picked up a walnut that had fallen from the tree, round and green in its husk, and threw it at his back.

She missed him by a mile.

## – FIFTY-SEVEN –

"I would like to book a carriage," Fate said to the girl behind the desk. "To Marseille. In a week's time. I was told I could make the arrangements here."

She was standing in the bustling lobby of the village inn. Travelers were coming and going. A cat in a wicker cage was yowling. The child holding the cage was crying. Her harried mother was trying to quiet them.

"Yes, madame," said the girl. "How many passengers?"

"Just myself, my servant, and our trunk. My name is Madame Sévèrine. I'm staying with the LeBenêts."

"Very good, madame," the girl said with a nod. "I shall make the arrangements and send a boy to the farm to confirm them." She folded her hands on the desktop.

Fate frowned. She did not want her request forgotten or bungled. "Is that all? Shouldn't you write it down in a ledger?"

The girl smiled. She touched the side of her head. "This is my ledger. I cannot write. Do not worry, madame. I will see to the carriage."

Fate had been so distracted by all the noise, she hadn't noticed that the girl's pale blue eyes gazed straight ahead, unseeing.

*Ah, yes, the innkeeper's daughter ... Odette*, she mused. She tried to recall the details of the girl's map and vaguely remembered an unhappy life. *Denied her true love, was it?* she wondered. Well, whatever fate she'd drawn for her, Volkmar had undoubtedly altered it. The girl would end up a casualty of war, like the rest of the villagers.

Fate thanked her and turned to go, eager to leave the rackety inn. How good it felt to know she'd soon say good-bye to Saint-Michel and the unpleasant business that had brought her here. Things were about to get more unpleasant. Markedly so.

"Leaving so soon?" said a voice at her elbow. "You must be feeling very confident. I can't imagine why."

Fate's good mood turned rancid. "Marquis," she said, regarding him. "Always a pleasure."

Chance was elegant in a black hat, butter-yellow jacket, and buff britches. He offered Fate his arm, and together they left the inn.

"Where is your coach? I'll escort you to it," Chance said.

Fate pointed down the street at Losca, who was sitting in the driver's seat of a wooden cart, holding Martin's reins. "There it is. It's every bit as comfortable as it is stylish."

Chance laughed, and they set off. He inclined his head toward hers as they walked. "Just because you burned down Isabelle's house," he said in a low voice, "doesn't mean you win the wager. We established rules, remember? Neither of us can force the girl's choice."

Fate affected an innocent expression. "Surely you don't think that *I* had a hand in that?"

"Two hands, actually," said Chance. "Clever move, inviting them to the LeBenêts' farm. But I can invite them to live with me, too. And I will."

"You can, but they won't come. I've told them that you're a man of dubious morals."

"I shall go to them, then," Chance countered.

Fate smiled smugly. "No, I don't think so. I hear there's a lovely young baroness who lives in the next village . . ."

"Is there?" Chance said lightly, brushing invisible lint off his jacket.

"She's very fond of card games. And likes to bet kisses instead of coins—a proclivity her husband strenuously frowns upon."

"You can hardly blame *me* for what happened," Chance said, aggrieved. "She never so much as *mentioned* a husband!"

"The baron is a good shot, I'm told."

"Very," Chance said ruefully. "He put a hole through my favorite hat."

"Word got to Madame LeBenêt. And the girls' mother. I made sure of it. They're scandalized. I wouldn't set foot on the farm if I were you," Fate said. She changed the subject. "What were you doing at the inn anyway?"

"Sending a man to Paris to fetch me some decent champagne," Chance replied. "Plus a wheel of Stilton. Good strong tea. And the broadsheets." His warm eyes found Fate's chilly ones. "The country is beastly. We must at least agree on that."

"Indeed," Fate said heavily. "I recently sent to Paris myself for a few little luxuries to brighten the dreariness of life with Madame LeBenêt."

"Is it that bad?"

"The woman is so stingy, she uses the same coffee grounds ten times. I would sell my soul for a good pot of coffee." She chuckled. "If I had one, that is. Ah, Marquis, if these mortals only knew, if they had the merest understanding of the grave, and of the eternity they will spend lying in it, they would eat chocolate for breakfast, caviar for lunch, and sing arias as they slopped the pigs. The worst day above ground is better than any day under it. Ah, well. We'll soon be away from this place. At least *I* will."

They arrived at the cart. Chance tipped his hat to Losca. "I wouldn't be so sure," he said. "My magician was in the Wildwood last night and witnessed a rather romantic interlude. That's one piece of her heart found, two to go."

Fate regarded him and with an acid smile said, "Finding pieces of a heart takes time. How is the skull looking? You know the one I mean, don't you? At the bottom of young Isabelle's map? How much time does she have left? Is it weeks? Days?"

Chance pressed his lips together. The muscles in his jaw tensed.

"*Days*, yes. I thought so," Fate purred. She patted his arm. "Do enjoy your champagne."

## – FIFTY-EIGHT –

Bette, chewing her cud, blinked her patient brown eyes.

"Good girl, Bette," Isabelle said, patting the cow's rump.

She sat down on a low wooden stool, leaned her cheek into the cow's soft warm side, and started to milk her. Bette's slow breathing, the rhythmic sound of the milk squirting into the wooden bucket, made a tired Isabelle feel even sleepier. She'd barely closed her eyes during the night. Images of Felix had crowded her brain. His angry words had echoed in her head.

How could he accuse her of breaking his heart, when he had broken hers?

Isabelle's memories dragged her back in time to a place she did not want to go. After their kiss in the Wildwood, when they first realized they were in love, she and Felix had decided to run away. They both knew Maman would never allow them to be together, so they'd made a plan: They would take Nero and Martin and ride to Italy. Felix would find work in Rome as an apprentice in the studio of a sculptor. Isabelle would spend her days giving riding lessons, and in the evenings, she and Felix would visit the city's ancient ruins, walking where the Caesars had walked, treading the same roads their armies had marched down.

And when Felix was a sculptor himself, famous and very wealthy, they would travel to Mongolia and race horses with chieftains. Watch eagles hunt in the Russian steppes. Ride camels with the Bedouin. Discover the whole wide wonderful world.

But Maman had found out about their plans. Enraged, she'd fired Felix's father and sent his family packing. Before they'd left, though, Felix had climbed up the vine to Isabelle's bedroom window and had sworn that he would come back for her. They would meet in the Wildwood. He needed a few days to help his family find a place to live, he said, and then he would leave a note in the hollow of the linden tree telling her when.

Isabelle had packed a bag and hidden it under her bed. Every night, after Maman had gone to sleep, she'd climbed down the vine and dashed across the yard to the linden tree, hoping to find Felix's note. But it never came.

Summer gave way to autumn and then winter. Icy winds and deep snow prevented her from stealing out of her room at night, but by then it didn't matter; she'd given up. Felix had meant the world to her, but she'd meant nothing to him.

How many nights had she cried herself to sleep, with Tavi rocking her? Ella had somehow found out, too. She'd been nicer than ever to Isabelle, but Isabelle, heartsore and miserable, had been nothing but mean in return.

And now Felix was back. Making a slipper for her. Making her think he still cared for her. Holding her and kissing her in the Wildwood, and then behaving as if she were to blame for what had happened. Or hadn't.

And here she was, distraught and losing sleep over someone who, no matter what he did, or said, still didn't care enough to tell her why he'd walked away. It was foolish; *she* was foolish. She had more important things to worry about. She lived in a hayloft. She owned one dress. Her mother regularly mistook a cabbage for the Duke of Burgundy.

Bette lowed impatiently. Isabelle hadn't realized it, but she'd milked the cow dry. With effort, she pushed all thoughts of Felix out of her head and picked up the milk bucket. Bette was the last cow that needed to be milked that evening and Isabelle was glad. The day's chores felt endless, and she was eager to finish.

She picked up the milk bucket and hurried to the dairy house. Lost in her thoughts, she didn't hear the angry voices arguing inside until she walked through the doorway.

"You're an idiot!"

"No, *you're* an idiot!"

Hugo and Tavi were standing only a foot away from each other, shouting. Isabelle banged her pail down and got between them.

Through the barrage of rude remarks and gestures, she was able to ascertain that Tavi had added things to one of the cheeses as she set it into its mold last night. Honey from the farm's hives. Sediment from an empty wine cask. A dash of vinegar.

"But that's not the way it's done!" Hugo thundered. "Did you see it? It's ugly. It doesn't look like the others. It has spots. And a strange smell. It's different!"

"Is it so bad to try something new?" Tavi thundered back. "All I want to do is see if and how the substances affect the flavor. Honey, wine dregs, vinegar—they all contain different microorganisms—"

"What are you talking about?"

"Microorganisms?" Tavi repeated. "Single-celled life-forms? You know . . . Leeuwenhoek? The father of microbiology?"

Hugo gave her a blank look.

"Microorganisms acidify the milk," Tavi explained. "They curdle it. Cheese becomes cheese through the process of fermentation."

Hugo stuck out his chest. "Cheese becomes cheese through cheesification," he said truculently.

Tavi blinked at him. Then she held up her hands. "Fine, Hugo," she said. "My point is, that if we alter just one factor of the . . . *cheesification* process, even slightly, we vary the result."

"So?"

"So we might very well come up with something other than bland, boring white cheese. Wouldn't that be exciting?"

"I wish you had never come here."

"That makes two of us."

"You're changing things. Why do you have to do that?"

"I wonder if anyone said that to Da Vinci or Newton or Copernicus." Tavi put her hands on her hips and affected a put-upon voice. "Oh my *God*, Nicolaus. Did you *have* to make the earth orbit the sun? We liked it so much better the other way!"

"They were men. You're a girl," Hugo said, glowering. "Girls don't

176

change things. They bake things. And sew things. They wipe things, too. Like tables. And noses."

Tavi picked up a cloth and scrubbed Hugo's face with it. "And asses," she said, stalking off.

Hugo swore. He kicked at a floorboard.

"She likes to do experiments," Isabelle said, hoping to mollify him.

"I saw the cheese. It's ruined," Hugo said. "My mother will throw a fit."

"Maybe Tavi's right. Maybe it'll turn into something amazing," Isabelle said. She picked up her pail and poured the milk into a vat. "It'll be fine. You'll see."

But Hugo's thoughts were not on the cheeses anymore.

"She'll never get married," he said. "No man wants a woman who won't do what she's told."

Isabelle bristled. "Tavi doesn't want a man. She wants math," she said, defending her sister.

"Math won't get the two of you out of here. A man would, though. And I'm going to see if my mother or Tantine can find one," Hugo said, stalking off. Isabelle rolled her eyes. "Good luck. If Maman couldn't manage it, I doubt they will."

Alone now in the dairy house, Isabelle ventured to the back, to see the cheese that had caused all the upset. It was on a rack on the left side of the room. She spotted it immediately.

Hugo had called it ugly, but Isabelle found it interesting. Its odd green spots, its lopsidedness, the pungent smell it gave off—they all set it apart from the other cheeses, which seemed dull and smug to her in their sameness.

"You might do something with yourself," she said to the cheese. But her hopes were not high. Being different was not something that was tolerated in cheeses.

Or girls.

## FIFTY-NINE

The evening was warm and clear. The setting sun was painting the sky in brilliant shades of orange and pink; the scent of roses hung in the air.

It was calm. It was peaceful. Isabelle prayed it would last.

Tavi and Hugo were sitting side by side on a wooden bench, in the shade of the barn. Working silently. Neither had spoken to the other since their fight in the dairy house yesterday.

*At least they're not yelling anymore*, Isabelle thought.

She and Maman were sitting on the grass across from them. They were all shelling beans into a wide bowl for a soup Madame planned to make. Isabelle glanced up at Tavi and Hugo every now and again. She was eager to keep the peace. She knew that their being here was Tantine's doing, not Madame's, and definitely not Hugo's. Staying here depended on working hard and not making themselves objectionable. She would remind Tavi of that tonight when they went to bed.

She and Tavi slept next to each other now in the hayloft. They talked before they fell asleep, much more than they had when each had had her own bedchamber in the Maison Douleur. Last night, Isabelle had told her sister about meeting Felix in the Wildwood and had showed her the slipper.

"I *thought* you were walking better," she'd said. "*And?*" she'd added expectantly.

"*And* nothing. There is no *and*." Isabelle had decided to keep the argument, and the kiss, to herself.

"That's too bad. I always liked Felix." Tavi had gone silent for a bit; then she'd said, "Just wondering . . ."

"Wondering what?"

"If you were still searching for the pieces of your heart. Because I'd say that he's definitely—"

"Not one," Isabelle had said firmly, turning on her side.

"The bowl is full," Hugo said now, dispelling Isabelle's thoughts.

She stood and stretched. "I'll take it inside to Madame and get—"

*Another one*, she was going to say, but her words were cut off by a hair-raising scream.

She and Tavi looked at each other, alarmed. Maman dropped the bean pod she was holding.

The shriek came again. It was coming from the dairy house and was followed by a single shouted word: "Huuuuuuuuuuuugo!"

Hugo leaned back against the barn wall and groaned. "It used to be quiet here. It used to be nice," he said. "Well, maybe not nice but definitely quiet. Whatever my mother is screeching about, it's because of you two. I just know it."

Another shriek was heard. "Hugo, come on!" Isabelle said, tugging at his hand. "It sounds like she's hurt!"

She started running toward the dairy house; the others were right behind her. When they arrived, they saw that Tantine was already there.

"I was in the kitchen . . . I heard screaming. Is someone hurt?" she asked, a hand pressed to her chest.

Before anyone could answer her, Hugo pushed the door to the dairy house open and stepped inside. The others followed. As Isabelle entered the room, an eye-watering stench hit her.

"What *is* that?" she cried.

"It's a monster!" Madame LeBenêt shrilled. "It's an abomination!"

She was standing at the back of the room among the ripening cheeses, pointing at one. Isabelle ventured closer and gasped as she saw the offender. It *was* a monster—wrinkled, misshapen, furry with mold.

"God in Heaven, the *smell*!" Tantine said, pressing a handkerchief to her nose.

"Like dirty feet."

"Rotten eggs."

"Like a sewer."

"Like a dead dog," said Hugo.

"A dead dog that's been rotting in the sun for a week," Isabelle added.

"And sweating," Hugo said.

"Technically, dogs don't sweat," Tavi pointed out. "At least, not in the way human beings do. Dogs especially don't sweat when they're dead."

"This dog does," Hugo stated. "Look at it!"

In the short time that they'd all been standing there, beads of clear yellow fluid had erupted from the cheese. They were rolling down its sides and dripping onto the floor.

"That does it. I want you three out. Tonight!" Madame shouted.

A grin lit up Hugo's face.

Isabelle's heart lurched. "No, madame, please!" she begged. "We have nowhere else to go!"

"Your sister should've thought of that before she ruined my cheese!"

"Now, Avara," Tantine soothed, taking her by the arm. "Let's not be hasty. The girl made a mistake, that's all."

"It was an experiment, actually, not a mistake," Tavi corrected, peering closely at the cheese. "I'll need to modify my hypothesis."

"Out!" Madame sputtered. "Tonight!" She turned to her son. "Hugo, take that—that sweaty dead dog out of here this instant before it contaminates the other cheeses. Throw it into the woods or toss it into a pit!"

Tantine ushered Madame to the door. As Madame stepped outside, Tantine turned to Isabelle. "Help Hugo clean up this mess, child. I'll set things to rights." She patted Isabelle's cheek, then hurried after Madame.

Isabelle pressed the heels of her hands to her forehead, trying to think. This was a disaster. What if Tantine couldn't bring Madame around? What if she still insisted that they leave?

"Happy now?" Tavi asked a still-grinning Hugo. "You got rid of us. Be sure to throw some dirt over our bones after we starve to death in a ditch."

"I . . . I didn't think you'd *starve*," Hugo said, his grin fading.

"What *did* you think we'd do?" Tavi asked.

"Don't blame this on me! It's not *my* fault. You're the one who makes things hard!"

"For whom?"

"Can't you make yourself likable? Can't you even try?"

Something shifted in Tavi then. She was always so flippant, trailing sarcasm behind her like a duchess trailing furs. But not this time. Hugo had pierced her armor and blood was dripping from the wound.

"Try for whom, Hugo?" she repeated, her voice raw. "For the rich boys who get to go to the Sorbonne even though they're too stupid to solve a simple quadratic equation? For the viscount I was seated next to at a dinner who tried to put his hand up my skirt through all five courses? For the smug society ladies who look me up and down and purse their lips and say no, I won't do for their sons because my chin is too pointed, my nose is too large, I talk too much about numbers?"

"Tavi . . ." Isabelle whispered. She went to her, tried to put an arm around her, but Tavi shook her off.

"I wanted books. I wanted math and science. I wanted an education," Tavi said, her eyes bright with emotion. "I got corsets and gowns and high-heeled slippers instead. It made me sad, Hugo. And then it made me angry. So no, I can't make myself likable. I've tried. Over and over. It doesn't work. If I don't like who I am, why should you?"

And then she was gone. And Hugo and Isabelle were left standing in the dairy house, awkward and silent. Isabelle reached for the mop and bucket, which were kept near the door, to clean up the mess pooling under the sweaty dead dog.

"Well done, Galileo," Hugo muttered under his breath.

But Isabelle heard him. "She could be. She could be Galileo and Da Vinci and Newton all rolled into one if she had the chance, but she never will. That's why she's the way she is." She took a tentative step toward him. "Hugo, don't make us go. Please."

"You don't understand. There's a reason I wanted . . ." He swore. "Never mind."

"What reason? What are you talking about?"

Hugo shook his head. He moved toward the door.

"Where are you going?" Isabelle asked.

"There's an old wooden tea box in the barn. It's lined with lead. Hopefully, it will contain the smell. I'm going to put the dead dog in the box, put the box in the wagon, then drive until I find an old well to throw it down. Maybe I'll throw myself down it, too, while I'm at it."

Isabelle watched him go, a fearful expression on her face. This was terrible. She would go to Tantine. As soon as she and Hugo had this mess cleaned up. If the old woman hadn't succeeded in changing Madame LeBenêt's mind, they would be homeless. Helpless. As good as dead.

- SIXTY -

Just before dawn, in the Wildwood, a fox stalked her meal.

The object of her attention, a red squirrel, was on the forest floor, busily collecting fallen nuts.

Hugging the lingering shadows, the vixen crept close. She tensed, teeth bared, but just as she was ready to spring, a huge, tufted owl landed on a branch above her, shaking the leaves noisily.

With a frightened squeak, the squirrel dropped her nuts and ran for her nest. A second later, the vixen was gone, too. In her place stood an auburn-haired woman in a dusk-gray gown. She spun around violently. Her green eyes flashed.

"That was my *breakfast!*" she shouted at the bird.

Creatures great and small scurried to their dens at the sound of her voice. Deer hid in the brush. Songbirds spread their wings over their young.

But the owl was not bothered. Let the fairy queen rage. He had chosen a nice high branch for his perch. He hooted at her now.

Tanaquill narrowed her eyes. "For *this* you rob me of my meal?"

The owl continued to speak.

"What of it?" Tanaquill growled. "Fate and Chance, Fate and Chance, one moves, the other countermoves. As if living creatures were nothing more than pieces on a game board. Their doings are no concern of mine." She turned her back on the bird and, with a swirl of her skirts, walked away. But the owl called after her, hooting harshly several times.

Tanaquill stopped dead. "A stallion?" she said. Slowly, she turned around. "Fate did this?"

The owl bobbed his great gray head.

Tanaquill paced back and forth, dead leaves rustling under her feet. The owl clicked his beak.

"No, I'm *not* going to tell Chance," she retorted. "He'll buy the horse and gift wrap him for the girl. I'll deal with this myself."

Tanaquill licked her lips. Her sharp teeth glinted in the pale morning light. "Isabelle has regained the first piece of her heart, though she refuses to admit it. Courage will be needed to regain this, the second piece." She snapped her fingers. "Come, owl. Let's see if she still has some."

- S I X T Y - O N E -

The village had almost forgotten about Isabelle.

Saint-Michel was so crowded with weary, bewildered refugees frantic to buy food that the baker's wife, the butcher, and the cheesemonger had better things to do than taunt her.

She had found herself selling vegetables at the market with Hugo this morning because Madame, who usually went with him, was busy tending a sick cow. Tavi was more likely to conduct an experiment with the cabbages than sell them, so the task had fallen to Isabelle. Although she hadn't relished the idea of returning to the village, she undertook the task without complaint. Somehow, Tantine had convinced Madame to let them stay, and a deeply relieved Isabelle was determined not to give her any reason to change her mind.

She and Hugo had been swamped with customers from the moment they'd pulled into the market square. The refugees, all living in tents, or wagons in the surrounding fields, clamored for cabbages and potatoes. Isabelle had no idea where they'd all come from, so she asked them and they told her.

Volkmar had stepped up his attacks on the villages surrounding Paris, they'd explained. They'd seen their farms pillaged, their homes burned. Many had escaped with only their lives. The king fought bravely, but his troops were being decimated. The grand duke had been seen riding throughout the countryside with a train of wagons, calling on citizens who possessed weapons of any sort—guns, swords, axes, *anything*—to donate them to the war effort. The queen traveled with him, searching for orphaned children and spiriting them to safety.

Some of the refugees were thin and sickly. An elderly woman, trailing four grandchildren, begged Isabelle for any leaves that had fallen off the cabbage heads. Isabelle gave her a whole cabbage and didn't charge her. The woman hugged her. Hugo saw the exchange. He frowned but didn't stop her.

Someone else saw her do it, too.

"That doesn't change anything, Isabelle," said Cecile, walking up to the wagon. "You're still ugly."

Isabelle felt herself flushing with shame. The village *hadn't* forgotten about her. It never would, not with Cecile around to remind everyone. She tried to think of something to say, but before she could get a word out, Hugo spoke.

"It changes things for the old woman," he said.

Isabelle glanced at him. She was grateful he'd come to her defense but also surprised. She knew he didn't like her much. From the set of his jaw, the hardness in his eyes, she guessed he liked Cecile even less. She didn't have long to wonder why, because another refugee, an old man, shuffled up to the wagon and asked for a pound of potatoes.

"Don't buy from her!" Cecile said as he handed over a coin. "Don't you know who she is? Isabelle de la Paumé, one of the ugly stepsisters!"

The old man laughed mirthlessly. The laugh turned into a deep, racking cough. When he could speak again, he said, "There's nothing uglier than war, mademoiselle," then shuffled off with his purchase.

Cecile snorted. She looked as if she'd like to say something clever and cutting, but cleverness was not her strong point, so she flounced off instead.

An hour or so after Cecile left, Isabelle and Hugo sold the last cabbage. Isabelle gathered the loose green leaves from the bed of the wagon, handed them to a small, barefoot boy in a threadbare shirt, and told him to take them to his mother to boil for a soup. Then she took off the canvas apron Hugo had given her to wear—its single pocket full of coins—and handed it to him.

But Hugo shook his head. "Hang on to it. Here's mine, too," he said, untying his own apron.

"Why? Where are you going?" Isabelle asked, taking it from him.

"I . . . uh . . . I need to do an errand. Head back without me. I'll catch up." He rubbed the toes of his boots on the back of his trouser legs as he spoke, then spat on his hands and smoothed his unruly hair.

Isabelle thought he was being very mysterious. She carefully folded both aprons so that no coins could drop out and tucked them underneath the wagon's seat.

"And, Isabelle?"

"Yes?"

"If you do get home before me, don't tell my mother about my errand. Say I went to fix a fence in the pasture or something."

Isabelle agreed to his request, more intrigued than ever. Then Hugo tugged on the sides of his jacket, took a deep breath, and went on his way. Isabelle climbed into the driver's seat and snapped the reins. Martin started off. They'd finished early at the market and she was glad. It meant she could get a head start on the rest of the day's work.

She'd only just driven out of the square when she spotted Hugo again. He was helping Odette across the street. She'd taken his arm. Her face was turned toward his. She was wearing a pretty blue dress. Her strawberry-blond hair was pinned up in a soft bun. A pink rose was tucked into the side of it.

*She must be going to a party or a wedding*, Isabelle thought. *I bet she got lost and Hugo is helping her find her way.*

It was a nice thing for him to do. Odette didn't have an easy life. Most of the villagers were good to her, but a few—like Cecile—were not.

*Who knew he had it in him?* Isabelle thought, softening toward Hugo, but only a little.

A few minutes later, she was heading out of the village toward a fork in the road. To the right was the way back to the LeBenêts'. To the left was the river and the various businesses that were not allowed to operate within the village because of the smells they made or the fire risk they posed—the tannery, the blacksmith's, the dye works, the slaughter yard.

Isabelle was so lost in her thoughts—wondering if Tavi managed to get the morning milking done without causing problems, and if Maman was cutting cabbages or conversing with them—that she didn't see the animal sitting directly in the center of the fork, watching and waiting, as if it were expecting her.

By the time she raised her head and realized a fox was blocking her way, it was too late.

- SIXTY-TWO -

The fox ran at Martin, her head down, her teeth bared. She dove under him and wove in and out of his legs, snarling and snapping, nipping at his hooves.

Terrified, Martin bolted to the left, ripping the reins from Isabelle's hands. The wagon lurched violently, throwing her across the seat. She managed to right herself but could not recover the reins.

"Stop, Martin! Stop!" she screamed, but the horse, crazed by fear, kept going. The fox followed, running at his side, snarling. The wagon banged down the rutted road to the river, with Isabelle holding on to the seat for dear life. They sped by buildings and work yards. Men tried to wave Martin down, but no one dared get in front of him. And then the river came into view.

*He's not going to stop!* Isabelle thought. *He's going to gallop straight off the dock. We're both going to drown!*

And then, as quickly as she'd come, the fox was gone and an exhausted Martin slowed, then halted a few yards shy of the water. Isabelle stumbled out of the wagon on legs that were rubbery, her breath coming hard and fast.

"Shh, Martin, easy," she soothed, stroking his neck. "Easy, old man."

Martin's eyes were so round, Isabelle could see the whites. His lips were flecked with foam, his coat with lather. She bent down to check his legs. There was no blood; the fox hadn't bitten him. She found the reins, tangled in the traces, and freed them. Then, taking hold of his bridle, she slowly turned him around. Miraculously, the wagon was intact.

Isabelle's breathing slowed little by little as they walked back up the road. They passed the tannery and then the dye works. Some of the workers asked if she was all right.

"If I were you, that horse would be the next one to come through these gates," a man called to her as they approached the slaughter yard.

Isabelle glanced at him. He was leaning against the fence, smoking. Blood dripped off his leather apron onto his shoes. Isabelle heard a desperate cry coming from a frightened animal on the other side of the fence. She looked away; she didn't want to see the poor hopeless creature.

"That horse is no good," the man said. "He could've killed you."

Isabelle ignored him, but Martin didn't; he looked right at him. His ears pricked up. His nostrils flared. He stopped dead. A smell hit Isabelle then, a rank, low stink of blood and fear and death, moving like a wraith through the iron spikes. Martin smelled it, too. He was trembling. Isabelle was worried he would bolt again.

"Come on, Martin, *please*. We have to go," Isabelle said, pulling on his noseband.

But Martin refused to budge. He planted all four hooves into the dirt, raised his head high, and let out a whinny so loud and piercing, so heart-rending, that Isabelle let go of his bridle.

And that's when she realized that Martin wasn't looking at the man; he was looking past him, at a horse on the other side of the fence. She took a step toward the yard, slowly, as if in a trance, and then another. Martin called out again, and the horse behind the fence answered.

"Don't," the man said. "It's not something a girl should see."

But Isabelle did see. She saw a flash of darkness between the bars. Wild eyes. Lethal hooves. There were four burly men around the animal, but they couldn't subdue him. Even though they had ropes and weapons and he had nothing, they were the ones who were afraid.

Martin had a friend once. He was magnificent. Tall, strong, and fearless. If Martin had been human, he might've hated him for being everything that he, Martin, was not. But Martin was not human and so he loved him.

Horses never forget a friend.

Martin had smelled his friend. And heard him. A horse as black as night and ten times more beautiful.

Martin knew that horse. He loved that horse.

And so did Isabelle.

She wrapped her hands around the iron bars and whispered his name. *"Nero."*

## – SIXTY-THREE –

Isabelle ran.

Along the fence. Past the man, who was yelling at her to stop. Through the gates. And straight into hell.

Two sheep who'd jumped out of their pen were running through the yard, bleating, ducking their pursuers, desperate to escape. Cattle lowed piteously. Fresh carcasses were being hung to bleed out; older ones were being quartered.

And in the center of it all, a black stallion fought for his life.

Death's servants, four burly men, circled him. One of them had managed to get a rope around the horse's neck. Another had caught one of his back legs, throwing him off balance. A third man caught the other back leg. The horse went down. He made a last, valiant attempt to get up, then lay in the mud, his sides heaving, his eyes closed.

The fourth man was leaning on a sledgehammer. He gripped its wooden handle with both hands now and lifted the heavy steel head.

"No!" Isabelle screamed. "Stop!"

But no one heard her, not over the bleating of the sheep and bawling of the cattle.

Isabelle ran faster, shouting, pleading, screaming. She was only a few feet away from the horse, when her foot came down in a puddle. She slipped and went sprawling.

Spitting filth, Isabelle picked up her head in time to see the man lift the sledgehammer off the ground and raise it high, spiraling it around his body, the muscles in his strong arms rippling.

A ragged scream burst up from her heart and out of her throat. She launched herself, half crawling, half stumbling through the mud and blood and threw herself on the horse's neck.

Just as the man swung the sledgehammer.

## - SIXTY-FOUR -

The hole the sledgehammer made was deep.

Isabelle knew this because the man who'd swung the tool forced her to look at it. He grabbed the back of her dress, yanked her off the horse as if she were a rag doll, and dropped her in the mud. She landed on her hands and knees.

"Do you see that sledgehammer? Do you see what it did?" he shouted at her.

Isabelle nodded even though she could only see the handle. The head was buried in the ground.

"That could've been your *skull*!"

The man, a burly giant, was shaking like a kitten. He'd swung the sledgehammer with all his might and then, in the space of a heartbeat, a girl had thrown herself in its path. He'd wrenched his body to the left at the last possible instant, swinging through and hitting the ground instead of the girl.

Isabelle stood up. Her dress was smeared with gore. Her face streaked with it. She didn't care. "Don't kill my horse," she begged. *"Please."*

"He's *my* horse. I bought him. You don't want him. He's too wild."

"I *do* want him."

"Then you can pay me for him. Four livres."

Isabelle thought of the money tucked under the wagon's seat and had to fight down the urge to run and get it. But she was not a thief.

"I don't have any money," she said miserably.

"Then find some, girl, and fast. You've got until tomorrow morning. We open the gates at seven sharp. Be here on time, with the money, or he goes."

Isabelle nodded. She told the man she'd be back. She told herself that she'd think of something. She'd get the money. Somehow.

"Let him up," she said, looking at her horse.

No one moved.

"Let. Him. *Up*." It was not a plea this time, but a command, and the men heard it. They removed the ropes they'd used to restrain him.

As soon as he was free, the horse got to his feet. He blinked at Isabelle, then slowly walked to her. He sniffed her. Snorted in her face. Tossed his proud head and let out a whinny.

Isabelle tried to laugh, but it crumbled into a sob. She leaned her cheek against his, knotted her dirty fingers in his lank, tangled mane. Nero had been sold away. She'd thought she'd never see him again. Now here he was, but he would be gone forever if she couldn't get hold of four livres.

"I will get you out of here. I swear it," she whispered to him.

"You have to leave now. We have work to do," the man with the sledge-hammer said.

Isabelle nodded. She patted Nero's neck, then walked out of the yard.

One of the men who'd roped the horse—a boy, really—closed the gates after her. He lingered there, watching her go. In that moment, he would've done anything she asked of him. Followed anywhere she led. He would have died for her.

He could not know it then, but the image of the girl, straight-backed in her dirty dress, her face streaked with filth, would stay with him for the rest of his life. He looked down at the knife in his hand and hated it.

Behind him, the others talked.

"Was that one of the de la Paumé girls? I thought they were ugly."

"What, you think she's *pretty*? Dirty as an old boot? Bold as a trumpet?"

"No, but—"

"I pity the man she ends up with."

"She has guts, I'll give her that."

"Yes, she does. Imagine if every girl had such strength . . . and learned of it!"

"Better hope they never do. What would our world become, eh?"

"Ha! A living hell!"

"No," the boy whispered. "A paradise."

## - SIXTY-FIVE -

The door to Madame's kitchen was open. Isabelle took a deep breath and walked inside.

The day was bright, but Madame's house was dark. It took a few seconds for Isabelle's eyes to adjust. When they did, she saw that Madame was standing at her kitchen table kneading bread.

"I'm back. I have your money," Isabelle said, placing the aprons on the table.

Madame wiped her hands on a dish towel, eager to count her coins, and caught sight of Isabelle. "What happened to you? You're *filthy!*" she squawked.

Isabelle began to tell her. Madame listened for a few seconds, but the lure of money was too tempting. She unrolled the aprons, dumped out the coins, and counted them. Tantine was sitting nearby in a rocking chair, knitting. Unlike Madame, she listened intently to every word.

When Isabelle finished her account, she said, "I need to buy my horse back. Nero. I need to bring four livres to the slaughter yard tomorrow or they'll kill him."

"Yes, so? What has that to do with me?" Madame asked absently. She had eight columns of coins stacked already and still had half the pile to go.

"Please, madame. It's only four livres. I've worked very hard for you."

Avara stopped counting. She looked at Isabelle aghast. "You're not asking *me* for the money, are you?"

"I will pay you back."

"Absolutely not," Madame said. "It's not just the four livres, you know. You've already put me in the poorhouse feeding that old nag of yours, Martin. Another horse will bankrupt me."

She said more, but Isabelle had stopped listening. She crossed the room and knelt by Tantine.

"Please, Tantine. I beg you," she said.

The old woman put her knitting down. She took Isabelle's dirty hands in hers. "Child, you said this creature was sold to the slaughter yard because he is unmanageable, no? What if he were to throw you? I could never live with the guilt. An unruly stallion is not a suitable animal for a young lady."

Isabelle saw that there would be no help for her here. She rose and started for the door.

Tantine arched an eyebrow. "Where are you going?" she asked.

"To the Château Rigolade. To see the marquis. I thought he might lend me—"

"No. I forbid it," Tantine said sharply.

"But—"

Tantine held up a hand, silencing her. "If you will not consider your

194

own reputation, Isabelle, at least consider my family's. As long as you reside here, you are not to set foot near the Château Rigolade."

"Indeed!" Madame chimed in.

Isabelle lowered her head, devastated. "Yes, Tantine," she said.

"Instead of worrying about horses, worry about cabbages. They are not going to harvest themselves," Madame scolded. "See that the wagon is filled up again for tomorrow."

Isabelle left the house and drove the wagon out to the fields. All the way there, she racked her brain. There had to be a way to get the money. She refused to give up. By the time she'd unhitched Martin and had led him back to the barn, her head was high again. Her eyes were glinting. As she put him in his stall, she gave him an extra helping of oats.

"Eat up, Martin, you'll need your strength. We have a job to do tonight," she told him.

Martin pricked up his ears; he liked a bit of intrigue. Much more than he liked pulling cabbage wagons.

Isabelle had come up with an idea; it was desperate and risky. She would have to get her sister's help to pull it off. Hugo's, too, which would be more difficult. But he owed her; she'd said nothing about his errand.

As she brushed Martin, Tanaquill's words, spoken when they'd met in the Wildwood, came back to her. They rang out so clear, so true, it was as if the fairy queen was standing right next to her. *Find the pieces of your heart. Not someone else's . . .*

Nero was a piece of her heart. She knew this with an unshakable certainty. When she'd ridden him, she'd been braver than she ever thought she could be. It terrified her to admit this, because she knew if she lost him again, it would kill her.

195

"Nero is not going to die. We won't let him," Isabelle said, patting Martin's neck. "Get some rest, old man. We leave after dark."

## – SIXTY-SIX –

"How hot does a fire have to be to melt gold?" Isabelle asked.

"Very," Hugo replied.

"One thousand nine hundred forty-eight degrees Fahrenheit," said Tavi. "One thousand sixty-four Celsius."

"Had that right on the tip of your tongue, didn't you?" Hugo said.

"What should I have on the tip of my tongue? The words to some silly love song? A recipe for meatballs?"

"Yes," Hugo said. "Both of those would be good things for you to know."

Tavi rolled her eyes.

The three were walking down the lonely stretch of road that led from the LeBenêts' farm to the Maison Douleur in the darkness. Isabelle had decided to search the ruins of her old home in the hopes of finding something of value. She knew she could not move charred beams and heavy stones alone and had begged Tavi and Hugo to help her. Tavi had agreed because she knew how much Nero meant to Isabelle. Hugo had because he'd made Isabelle promise that if she found more than one valuable thing, she would use it to find somewhere else to live.

Isabelle had owned a few pieces of jewelry. So had Tavi. Maman had owned many. When the Maison Douleur burned, they'd all assumed that the fire had destroyed them, but they'd never actually looked. Now Isabelle was hoping that she could unearth a necklace, or perhaps a silver serving spoon, a gold coin—*anything* that she could barter for Nero's life.

Martin trailed behind them on a lead. No one was riding him. He would need all his strength for what was to come. Hugo had a heavy coil of rope on one shoulder. He and Tavi were both carrying lanterns.

"Did you ever think about making sauerkraut with your cabbage?" Tavi asked. "That way you could have something to sell at the market in the winter."

"Did you ever think of leaving things just the way they are?"

"No. Never. You can't make wonderful discoveries that way."

Hugo snorted laughter. "Like the sweaty dead dog?"

Tavi shot him a look. "Whatever happened to it, anyway?" she asked.

"It's still in a box in the wagon, under the back seat. I haven't found a good place to chuck it yet. Someplace where it won't kill someone. I'm hoping to find a bubbling lava pit one day. Or a dragon's cave. Or the gates of hell."

Tavi looked at the side of his face. "You're funny, Hugo. Who knew?"

Hugo was silent for a moment; then he said, "Odette. She knows."

"Odette from the village?" Tavi asked.

Hugo nodded.

"How does she know you're funny?" asked Isabelle. She remembered seeing him helping Odette across the street earlier at the market.

"Because we're in love. And we want to get married."

Tavi and Isabelle stopped dead. Martin did, too. But Hugo kept walking, his hands clenched.

"Does your mother know?" Tavi asked, running to keep up with him. Isabelle and Martin trotted after her.

"That I'm funny?" Hugo asked.

"*No*, Hugo," Tavi said. "About Odette."

"Yes. I told her. A year ago."

"Then why haven't you married her yet?" Isabelle asked, catching up.

"My mother won't allow it," Hugo said forlornly.

Isabelle and Tavi exchanged glances of disbelief. Never had Hugo spoken so many words at once, or with such emotion.

"Hugo . . ."

"Don't make fun, Tavi. *Don't*," he warned.

Tavi looked stricken. "I—I wasn't going to."

"Odette practically runs the inn. She keeps all the reservations straight. She makes the best onion soup you've ever tasted. And her apple cake . . . I would fight the devil himself for a piece of it. But my mother says a blind girl can't run a farm. She says she'll be useless, just another mouth to feed. She only sees what Odette isn't, not what she is."

Tavi put a gentle hand on his back.

"This world, the people in it—my mother, Tantine—they sort us. Put us in crates. *You* are an egg. *You* are a potato. *You* are a cabbage. They tell us who we are. What we will do. What we will be."

"Because they're afraid. Afraid of what we *could* be," Tavi said.

"But we let them do it!" Hugo said angrily. "Why?"

Tavi gave him a rueful smile. "Because we're afraid of what we could be, too."

A silence fell over them then, as deep and dark as the moonless night.

Hugo was the first to break it. "What am I going to do? Can one of you tell me?" he asked. "She's everything to me."

"I can't believe you're asking us," Isabelle said. "I thought you hated us."

"I do hate you. But I'm desperate and you're smart."

"Marry her anyway," Tavi suggested.

"Live at her house," Isabelle said.

"There's no room for me there. Her family lives in a little cottage

198

behind the inn. She has so many brothers and sisters it's bursting at the seams."

"There has to be a way. We'll think of something. We *will*," Tavi said.

Hugo nodded. He mustered a smile. But Isabelle could see that he didn't believe her.

They walked on down the road in silence, uncertain and aching. Hugo aching for Odette. Tavi aching for formulas and theorems. Isabelle aching to be pretty. Or so she told herself.

But alongside the ache, perhaps because of it, was a determination, too.

Neither Isabelle, Tavi, nor Hugo knew if any of them would ever be able to show the world what they were, not what they weren't. They didn't know if they'd be able to save their hearts from breaking.

But tonight, maybe, just maybe, they could save a horse. A difficult creature who didn't know how to be anything but what he was.

They hoped for him, deep down inside. All three of them.

Because they didn't dare hope for themselves.

- S I X T Y - S E V E N -

Hugo let out a low whistle. He was standing at the top of the front steps to the Maison Douleur, holding his lantern out in front of him. The steps had survived the fire, but nothing else had.

Isabelle and Tavi were standing next to him.

It was much worse than Isabelle remembered. Parts of the house that had still been standing the morning after the fire had since collapsed. The roof, three of the walls, the floors and ceilings, had all crashed down. Only the back wall remained upright. Stone, mortar, and wooden beams lay tangled in treacherous, teetering piles.

"We're going to have to move slowly or we'll bring rubble down on our heads," Hugo said.

That was not what Isabelle wanted to hear. They'd gotten a late start. Madame and Tantine had stayed up longer than usual; Hugo hadn't been able to sneak out until eleven thirty. Isabelle had to be back at the slaughter yard with something of value by seven, they hadn't even begun to search yet, and now Hugo was saying they'd have to go slow.

Fear chattered at her, telling her that there wasn't enough time. That the rocks were too heavy to move, the beams too large. That even if she dug to the bottom of the ruins, she wouldn't find a thing of value, that the flames had taken it all.

As she stood there, at a loss how to begin, or even where, a loose rock tumbled down off the back wall into a pile of debris with a loud crash. It made her jump. It felt as if the Maison Douleur was warning them off.

Isabelle thought of Nero, standing in the slaughter yard staring into the darkness. She walked back down the stairs, climbed into the remains of her home, and refused to listen.

- SIXTY-EIGHT -

"Hup, Martin! Hup, boy!" Hugo shouted, urging the horse on.

Martin leaned into the rope harness and pulled with all his might.

He was tired. They all were. They'd been searching for hours, crawling over charred debris with their lanterns, moving whatever stones they could by hand, and using Martin to move heavy beams, but they'd found nothing.

"Come on, Martin! Hup!"

Martin dug in, and the beam slid out of the rubble and across the grass. Hugo patted him and unknotted the rope.

"Anything?" he called out.

"No!" Isabelle shouted back.

Sighing, a weary Hugo turned Martin around and together they walked back to the ruins. Isabelle and Tavi were busy digging in what had once been their drawing room. Moving one thing often loosened something else. More than once, they'd had to jump out of the way of falling roof tiles or a chunk of lath.

Although no one knew it, the beam Hugo and Martin had just slid out into the yard had also destabilized debris. It had been supporting the pile of burned timbers Isabelle was picking around. Her back to the pile, she didn't see it shudder, then start to slide.

But Hugo did. "Isabelle! Look out!" he shouted, lunging for her.

He grabbed her arm and yanked her out of the way. She stumbled and fell against him, knocking him off his feet. They both hit the ground. The timbers crashed down near them. The jagged edge of one caught Isabelle's shoulder, slicing an ugly gash into it.

Tavi screamed. She clambered to Isabelle and Hugo and helped them up.

"That's it. We're finished here," she said, her voice quavering. "I'm sorry we didn't find anything. I'm sorry for Nero. But there's nothing here. Oh my God, Isabelle. Look at your shoulder!"

Tavi made her sister leave the ruins and sit down under the linden tree. There, she pressed a handkerchief against her wound.

Isabelle didn't want to sit. "I'm all right," she said, taking the handkerchief from Tavi. "I'm going back. Just one more time . . ."

"No," Tavi said. "You could've been killed. Hugo could've been. We're leaving."

Hugo had joined them. He lay down in the grass, spent. Tavi sat next to him. Isabelle reluctantly joined them.

"Are you all right?" Tavi asked him. He nodded, his eyes closed. "Thank you for saving Isabelle. I couldn't bear it if anything happened to her. To either of you." Her voice caught.

"It's all right," Hugo said. "We're both fine."

"No, it's not all right. I thought you were both dead. Oh, Hugo, I . . . I shouldn't have done it."

"Done what?"

"Called you an idiot. In the dairy house the other day. I'm sorry. Mean is all I've got, you see, so I'm always trying to get better at it."

Hugo gave her a tired smile. "You have more than mean, Tavi. A lot more. I'm sure if you lived a hundred years ago, *you* would've been the one who discovered that circles are round. Not Newton da Vinci."

Had Isabelle's attention not been entirely focused on the ruins, she might've seen that a bit of treasure had already been gleaned from the ashes—Tavi's newfound readiness to apologize for bad behavior, Hugo's willingness to speak sweet words instead of sullen ones. But Isabelle had only one thought in mind—saving Nero, and time was running out.

With a groan, Hugo stood. He picked up his rope, coiled it, and slipped it over his shoulder. "The sky's starting to lighten," he said. "My mother will be getting up soon. I better be in my bed when she comes to wake me."

Tavi stood, too. She turned to Isabelle. "Come on, Iz. Get up. It's time to go."

## – SIXTY-NINE –

Isabelle rose. Her hands were scraped raw, her shoulder was bleeding into the sleeve of her dress.

She looked at her sister and Hugo and Martin as they started down the drive, but instead of following them, she picked up her lantern and walked back into the ruins.

Despair swirled down on her like a thick fog, but she refused to give into it. Or to give up.

As she bent down to move a timber, she felt something tug at her hem. Certain she'd snagged her skirts on a nail, she looked down, ready to yank them free, and saw that it wasn't a nail.

It was a mouse.

The creature's tiny paws were sunk into Isabelle's hem. She was hanging on to it with all her might; her back feet were half off the ground.

"Shoo!" Isabelle said. "I don't want to step on you."

But the mouse would not let go.

*Her claws must be caught,* Isabelle thought, reaching toward her to free her. But as she did, the mouse released the hem. She stood upright on her hind legs and squeaked.

Isabelle recognized the little creature. It was the same mother mouse she'd seen digging for lentils in the cracks between the hearthstones, the one for whom she'd left some cheese.

"Hello," Isabelle said. "I don't have any food for you. I wish I did. I—"

The mother mouse held up a claw, like a parent silencing a prattling child. She squeaked again. And then once more.

There was only a whisper at first. A low rustling, like a breeze whirling through the grass. But then it grew louder, more urgent, pushing in at Isabelle from all sides of the ruins.

Isabelle raised her lantern high and caught her breath, astonished. All around her, standing on stones, crouched on timbers, their whiskers twitching, their black eyes glinting in the light, their tails curled above them like question marks, were mice. Hundreds of them.

At another squeak from the mother mouse, they all disappeared into the ruins. Isabelle heard scrabbling, scritching, squeals, and yelps.

Mystified, she glanced at the mother mouse.

"Where did they go?" she asked. "What are they—"

With a look of annoyance, the mouse held up her paw again. She was listening intently, her large ears quivering.

Isabelle listened, too, but she didn't know what she was listening for. She looked up. The stars were fading. The darkness was thinning. She had little time left.

And then a series of shrill calls rang out from the ruins. The mother mouse squeaked excitedly, hopping from foot to foot. She waved Isabelle close and pointed.

Isabelle put her lantern down and knelt on the ground, the better to see what the mouse was pointing at. As she did, another mouse, brawny and tall, emerged from the ruins. He was wearing something on his head. It looked like a crown.

"Is he your king?" Isabelle asked, completely perplexed now. "You want me to meet your king?"

Other mice reappeared from the ruins. They responded to Isabelle's question with strange little noises that sounded like laughter. The mother beckoned the large mouse over. He eyed Isabelle warily and shook his head. The mother mouse stamped her foot. The large mouse came.

He took off his crown with both paws and held it out to Isabelle. Not sure what else to do, Isabelle took it from him, then held it up to her lantern. A small cry escaped her as she saw that it wasn't a crown, not at all.

It was a gold ring.

- SEVENTY -

Isabelle's heart flooded with gratitude. For a moment, she couldn't speak.

204

She recognized the ring. Maman had given it to her. The band was thin. The stone—an amethyst—was small. Still, it had to be worth four livres. Maybe more.

"Thank you," she finally managed to say.

Two more mice emerged from the ruins dragging something behind them. They presented it to her. It was a bracelet made of small gold links; a little gold heart with a ruby in its center dangled from one of the links. Her father had given it to her. It was covered with soot, but that could be wiped away.

The ring would pay for Nero. The bracelet would buy her freedom. She could sell it and use the money to rent a room in the village for herself and her family. They could be free of Madame, her cows, and her cabbages.

Humbled by the gifts, Isabelle placed her hand on the ground, palm up, in front of the mother mouse. The mouse hesitated, then climbed on. Isabelle lifted her up until they were eye to eye.

"Thank you," she said again. "From the bottom of my heart, *thank you*. You don't know what this means to me. I'll never be able to repay you."

She kissed the mouse on the top of her head and gently set her down. Then she got up, clutching her jewels, and headed out of the ruins.

The sun was peeking over the horizon now. Songbirds were welcoming the dawn. By the time Isabelle reached the road, she was running.

- SEVENTY-ONE -

"You came back," the burly man said as he unlocked the gate. "I didn't think you would. Do you have my money?"

Isabelle, who had reached the gates only a minute before he had, was bent over, her hands on her knees, struggling to catch her breath. She'd run the whole way from the Maison Douleur to the slaughter yard without stopping.

"I have this," she said, straightening. She dug in her pocket, pulled out the ring, and handed it to him.

He handed it back, aggrieved. "I said four livres, not a ring! Do I look like a pawnbroker?"

Panic seized her. Never for a second had she considered that he might not accept it. "But it—it's gold. It's worth more than four livres," she stammered.

The man waved her words away. "I'll have to sell it to the jeweler. He's a tightwad. It's a lot of trouble."

*"Please . . ."* Isabelle begged. Her voice broke.

The man glanced at her, then tried to look away but couldn't. Her face was streaked with soot. Her dress was soaked with sweat. One sleeve was stained with blood.

"Please don't kill my horse," she finished.

The man looked past her, down the street. He swore. Muttered that he was a soft touch, always had been, that it would be his undoing. Then he pocketed the ring.

"Go get him," he said, nodding toward the yard. "But be quick about it. Before I change my mind."

Isabelle didn't give him the chance.

"Nero!" she cried.

The horse was standing at the far end of the yard, tied to a post. His ears pricked up when he heard Isabelle's voice. His dark eyes widened. Isabelle ran through the mud to him and threw her arms around his neck. He whickered, then nudged at her with his nose.

"Yes, you're right. We need to get out of here," Isabelle said. She quickly untied him and led him across the yard.

In her haste to get to him, she had not seen the other horses in the yard. But she did now. There were two of them.

*They must've come in after I left yesterday*, she thought. They were bony, fly-bitten. Their coats were dull, their tails full of burrs. She looked away. There was nothing she could do.

More men had arrived. The burly man was now making coffee over a small black stove in a ramshackle shed. The others stood around, waiting for a cup, but soon they would pick up their sledgehammers and knives and start their work.

Isabelle led Nero past them and out of the gates.

As she was about to lead him away, she glanced back at the horses. No one had fed them or given them water. Why would they? Why waste food on animals that were going to die? They were old, used up. Worthless. Hopeless.

Isabelle squeezed Nero's lead so tightly her hands cramped. The bracelet, the one she was going to use to buy her freedom from Madame, and Tavi's and Maman's, weighed heavy in her pocket. It weighed even heavier on her heart.

Isabelle looked up at the sky. "What am I doing?" she said, as if hoping the clouds might answer her. Then she tied Nero to the fence, took the bracelet from her pocket, and walked back inside the slaughter yard.

"What a fool Isabelle is," many people would say. "What an idiot to throw her bracelet away on a lost cause."

Never listen to such small-souled folk.

The skin-and-bones dog who shows up at your door. The broken-winged bird you nurse back to health. The kitten you find crying at the side of the road.

You think you're saving them, don't you?

Ah, child. Can't you see?

They're saving you.

## – SEVENTY-TWO –

Isabelle, her head down, walked up the road from the slaughter yard, past the outskirts of Saint-Michel, trailing the three horses behind her.

*Madame is going to kill me,* she worried. *She didn't even want Martin, who earns his keep. What will she say when she sees Nero and these two poor wrecks?*

And then a more disturbing thought occurred to her. *What if Madame is so angry, she threatens to throw us out again?*

Isabelle hadn't considered that possibility when she was bargaining for the horses' lives—all she'd cared about then was saving them—but it loomed before her now. Tantine had been able to talk Madame into letting them stay after the sweaty dead dog disaster, but Isabelle doubted she would be able to save them a second time.

"Isabelle? Is that you? What are you doing?"

Isabelle looked up at the sound of the voice. She mustered a broken smile.

"I don't know, Felix. The mice found a ring for me, and a bracelet. And I was going to get us all away from Madame and her blasted cabbages. But I traded it all for Nero and these other two. I couldn't let them die. Oh, God. What have I done?" she said all in a rush.

Felix, who had been sent to the blacksmith's for nails, tilted his head. "Wait . . . that's *Nero*? What mice? Why are you bleeding?" he asked.

Isabelle explained everything.

Felix looked away as she spoke. He swiped at his eyes. Isabelle, nervously kicking at the dirt, never saw the silver shimmer in them.

She was just finishing her story when a noisy group of boys, trouping up from the river, interrupted her.

"Let's see here . . . are there three horses or four?" one called out.

"Three horses and one ugly, horse-faced girl!" another shouted.

They all hooted laughter. Isabelle winced.

"Get out of here before I kick your little asses," Felix threatened, starting toward them.

They scattered.

"Don't pay any attention to them," he told Isabelle. "What they said . . . it isn't true."

"Then why do they say it?" Isabelle asked quietly.

Felix looked at her. At this girl. Who was weary and dirty, bloody and sweat-soaked, but defiant. This girl. Who was leading three helpless creatures that nobody wanted away from the slaughter.

"That's not the question, Isabelle," he said softly. "The question is, why do you believe them?"

## – SEVENTY-THREE –

"Nelson, Bonaparte, Lafayette, Cornwallis!" Chance shouted. "You've been right all along, gentlemen! I shall never ride inside again!"

Chance was standing atop his carriage, legs planted wide apart for balance, as it thundered down the road to Saint-Michel. A card game was starting shortly, in a room above the blacksmith's shop. He didn't want to be late. His four capuchins were with him, chasing one another back and forth, screeching with delight.

"Faster, faster!" he shouted to his driver.

"Any faster and we'll be airborne!" the driver shouted back.

Nelson picked that moment to snatch the scarf Chance had tied pirate-style around his head—his hat had blown off miles back—and ran to the back of the roof with it. Chance gave chase, and as he did, he saw a rider cantering over the fields that bordered the road. She was nearly parallel with his coach.

It was a young woman. Her skirts were billowing behind her. Her hair had come free. She rode astride like a man, not sidesaddle. Her head was low to her horse's neck, her body tensed in a crouch. She jumped a stone wall, fearless, completely at one with her magnificent black horse. With a shock of delight, Chance realized he knew her.

"Mademoiselle! Isabelle!" he called. But she didn't hear him.

"That's Nero, it must be," he said to himself, his pulse leaping with excitement. "She got her horse back!"

He retrieved his scarf from Nelson and waved it, finally getting Isabelle's attention. She did a double take, then laughed. Chance, never able to resist a bet, a contest, or a dare, pointed up ahead. There was a church in the distance, at the top of a hill. He cupped his hands around his mouth. "I'll race you!" he shouted.

Isabelle grinned. Her eyes flashed. She tapped her heels to her horse's side, and he lunged into a gallop. Effortlessly, he jumped a fence, two streams, then streaked across a field. She was leaving Chance in the dust, but as she reached the end of the field, a hedgerow loomed—a tall, thick wall of scrubby trees and brush that separated one farmer's field from another. It was a good five feet tall and at least a yard deep.

"Huzzah, my fine fellows!" Chance declared to the monkeys. "Victory is ours! She can't jump that. She'll have to . . ."

His words died in his throat. *Go around it*, he was going to say. But Isabelle was not going around the hedge. She was headed straight for it.

"No, don't! It's too high! You'll break your neck!" Chance called out. "I can't watch." He covered his eyes, then opened his fingers and peered through the slit.

Isabelle's hands came up the horse's neck, giving him his head. The stallion closed in on the hedge. He pushed off with his powerful back legs, tucked his front hooves under, and flew over it. Chance didn't see them land—the hedge blocked his view—but he heard them. Isabelle let out a loud whoop, the horse whinnied, and then he carried her the rest of the way up the hill.

She was trotting him in circles, cooling him down, as Chance and his driver pulled into the church's driveway.

"Mademoiselle, you are dangerous! A foolhardy daredevil! Completely reckless!" Chance shouted angrily, his hands on his hips. Then he smiled. "We shall be the very best of friends!"

"*I'm* reckless?" Isabelle said, laughing. "Your Grace, you're standing on top of your carriage!"

Chance looked down at his feet. "So I am. I'd quite forgotten." He looked up again. "My monkeys were having all the fun, you see, and I thought, why should they? Tell me, where did you get that stunning horse?"

"I rescued him. He was mine and then he wasn't and then I found him in the slaughter yard. It's a long story."

*Slaughter yard?* Chance thought, outraged. *I bet that miserable crone had something to do with it.*

"What's his name?" he asked nonchalantly.

"Nero."

*Ha!* Chance crowed silently. It was all he could do not to dance a hornpipe on the top of the carriage. *Her horse . . . a second piece of heart returned to her!*

He had been watching Isabelle's map closely and had noticed that two new lines had appeared on it. One veered into the Wildwood and crossed Felix's path. The other careened to the slaughter yard. Chance had not been able to guess why Isabelle had made the second detour. Now he knew.

*The boy, the horse*, Chance thought, *all that's needed now is the stepsister.*

Chance knew that if he was going to help Isabelle find the third piece, he needed to keep her here with him for a bit, to keep her talking and hopefully edge his way around to the topic of Ella. Fate had forbidden Isabelle from going to the Château Rigolade and had banned him from visiting the LeBenêts' farm. This was the first opportunity he'd had to speak with her since Nelson had shot the chicken thief.

He sat down on top of the carriage and dangled his legs over the side. "You ride him as if you raised him," he said, reaching a hand out. Nero walked over and allowed Chance to scratch his nose.

"I did raise him," Isabelle said, patting his neck. "I got him when he was only a colt. For my eleventh birthday. He was a gift from Ella's—I mean, from the *queen's* father—my stepfather. Tavi and I, we're the queen's ug—"

"You're her stepsisters, yes. I know. My magician told me. What an incredible gift. Was Octavia not jealous? What about Ella?"

"Tavi had been given a leather-bound edition of Isaac Newton's *Mathematical Principles of Natural Philosophy* the month before for her birthday. She wouldn't have noticed if our stepfather had given me a herd of elephants. And Ella was never jealous. She was afraid of Nero, though. Afraid I would kill myself on him." Isabelle smiled wistfully, remembering. "She worried every time I galloped off on him. Usually with Felix. Your carpenter. He was one of our grooms . . ."

"Oh, was he?" Chance lightly interjected.

"Ella threw her arms around us every time we returned and kissed us, as if she was afraid that one night we wouldn't come back . . ." Her voice trailed away. "She was always so sweet, so kind."

Chance saw his opportunity. "You miss her," he said.

Isabelle looked down at the reins in her hands. "Every day. It's a hard thing to admit."

"Why?"

Isabelle laughed sadly. "Because she certainly doesn't miss me. She hates me."

"You know this?"

"How could she not?"

"Because you are bold and dashing. Who would not love such a girl?"

Isabelle shook her head. "You are kind, Your Grace, but you don't know me. I was . . . I was not good to her."

"I know cavalry officers who wouldn't jump that hedge. I know a brave soul when I see one."

Isabelle gave him a questioning look. "Are you saying I should—"

"Try to see your stepsister? Try to make amends? Why, child, you read my mind!"

"Do you think she would see me?" asked Isabelle, hesitantly. And hopefully.

Chance leaned forward, his elbows on his knees. "I think we all make mistakes. What matters is that we don't let our mistakes make us."

The church bell began to toll the hour—eight o'clock. Chance grimaced. The card game had likely started. "We must part ways, I'm afraid. I have business in the village. Paris is not far, young Isabelle!"

He jumped down and opened the carriage's door. Once inside it, he lowered the window, leaned out, and slapped the door. The driver turned the horses, heading them back toward the road.

Chance and Isabelle waved good-bye to each other, and then Chance fell back against his seat.

Things were going well. Isabelle was forging some paths of her own. The horse was hers. The boy, too. Or rather, he *would* be if they could stop sparring with each other. And now Isabelle was going to try to see her stepsister.

Chance should have been elated at this thought, but he was troubled. He had Isabelle's map. He looked at it daily, and no matter how much progress she made, the horrible wax skull at the bottom continued to darken. He guessed Isabelle had only a handful of days left before the skull turned black.

Finding Ella and gaining the fairy queen's help . . . these things were her only hope. And his.

Chance leaned out of the window again, searching for Isabelle. He spotted her galloping back over the fields, growing smaller and smaller.

"Go, you splendid girl," he whispered. "Ride hard. Ride fast. Make the road your own. *Hurry*."

## – SEVENTY-FOUR –

Madame LeBenêt slammed the bread dough on the table as if she meant to kill it.

"Twice, Tantine!" she said resentfully. "Not once, but *twice* those girls have taken advantage of my kind nature. First the cheese, now the horses!"

"Isabelle has a soft heart, Avara. Just like you," Tantine said.

Her voice was soothing, her expression placid, but inside she was livid. Things had been coming together so well, and now they were falling apart. That damned stallion was supposed to be dead, not happily grazing in the LeBenêts' pasture. Fate had bought him from a poor widow, then sold him to the slaughter yard, telling them he was too wild to ride, a killer, and must be put down.

And if the very fact that he was alive wasn't bad enough, at the midday meal, which had been the usual thin and tasteless affair, Isabelle had announced that she would be riding to Paris tomorrow to try to see her stepsister. Fate had to pretend to be happy about Isabelle's wish for a reconciliation. Avara hadn't pretended at all, but Isabelle had promised to do the morning milking before she left and to be back in time for the evening one. Plus, it was Sunday, supposedly a day of rest, and so there was little Avara could say about it.

The horse, the boy, now the stepsister—was Isabelle forging the paths to them herself? Or had Chance drawn them on her map? He still had it, of course. What if he'd somehow learned how to make stronger inks? Fate shuddered to think of the chaos that rogue would unleash with such power at his fingertips.

"Three horses she brings here from the slaughter yard. *Three!*" Avara fumed, driving the heels of her hands into the dough so hard the table rattled.

Fate could bear no more of Madame's tirade. "Have you seen Losca?" she asked, rising. "I have some mending for her."

"She's probably in the garden. Seems to be her favorite place," Avara replied. "Now *there's* a girl who causes no trouble. She's quiet, helpful, and she eats like a bird."

Avara said more, but Fate, already outside, didn't hear her. Losca was indeed in the garden. She was sitting in the tomato patch, pulling fat green caterpillars off the plants and stuffing them into her mouth. Her cheeks were flushed. The neckline of her dress was soaked with sweat. She looked exhausted.

"Where have you been?" Fate asked.

Losca, her mouth full, couldn't reply. Instead, she picked up something lying on the ground next to her and handed it to her mistress.

215

Fate's eyes lit up when she saw what it was—Isabelle's map.

"You *wonderful* girl! How did you manage this?" she asked.

Losca swallowed her caterpillars, then explained to Fate, in her high, harsh voice, that she'd flown to the Château Rigolade early that morning before the household was awake. She'd squeezed through an open bedroom window and had silently glided down to the dining room. The map had been lying open on the table there, but Chance had been slumped over it, snoring.

A decanter of cognac stood on the table nearby him. Playing cards and a pile of gold coins were next to it.

Staying in her raven form, in case she had to quickly escape, she'd clasped a corner of the map in her beak, then carefully tugged it out from under Chance, inch by inch, until it was free. Chance had grumbled and twitched in his sleep, but he hadn't woken. After rolling the map with her beak, Losca had grasped it in her talons and had flown back out of the window. Landing in the tomato patch hadn't been her intention but flying for miles with the map had made her so ravenous, she'd felt faint.

"Rest, Losca, and eat your fill," Fate said. "This fine work of yours deserves a special reward. We shall go walking in the woods tonight to see if we can find a dead thing crawling with nice, juicy maggots."

Losca smiled and went back to snatching caterpillars.

Fate hurried to her room and spread the map out on her table. With a bent, shriveled finger, she traced Isabelle's path. Relief washed over her face as she saw that though Isabelle had forged detours, the main path of her life was unchanged and so was its ending. Chance had not managed to alter them. The wax skull was the blue-black of a crow's wing. In four days, five at the most, Fate estimated, it would turn as black as the grave.

Yet Fate knew that now was not the time for complacency. What if the girl actually managed to get an audience with her stepsister? What if Ella forgave her and invited her to live in the palace?

"Perhaps it's time to hurry things along a bit," Fate mused aloud. "Perhaps I can shorten four or five days to one."

She sat down at her table, picked up a quill, and dipped it into an ink bottle. With sure, practiced movements, she hatched in new contours to the existing landscape. When she finished, she highlighted the hills in *Doom*, a murky gray, and shaded the hollows with *Defeat*, a purple as dark and mottled as a bruise.

As she worked on the map, Losca walked into the room. She had recovered from her exertions. Her eyes had regained their bright beadiness, her cheeks their usual pallor.

"Ah, Losca! I'm glad you're here," Fate said.

She explained to her that Isabelle was riding to Paris tomorrow, and that she wanted her to fly out early in the morning and lay a little groundwork for the girl's trip. When she finished speaking, she returned to Isabelle's map, but instead of rolling it up and putting it away, she scowled. Something was still missing.

She reached for another ink, bright red *Destruction*, and stippled it liberally over Isabelle's path.

"Yes," she said with a satisfied smile. "That should get the job done. Perhaps instead of trying to stop the girl from changing her fate, it's time to send her rushing headlong toward it."

## – SEVENTY-FIVE –

The fox ran ahead of Isabelle.

Then she stopped and sat on a tree stump at the side of the road, as Isabelle, riding Nero, caught up to her.

"It was you, wasn't it, Tanaquill?" she said, stopping Nero a few feet from the stump. Unlike Martin, he was not afraid of foxes.

The fox blinked her emerald eyes.

"You chased Martin past the slaughter yard so that he'd see his old friend. You gave Nero back to me. Thank you. He's one of the pieces, I know he is."

The fox lifted her snout and yipped.

Isabelle nodded. "I guess I've been wrong all along. About the pieces being goodness, kindness, and charity. You said my heart had been cut away piece by piece by piece, but things can't be cut away if they weren't there to begin with."

The fox licked her paw.

"I'm on my way to Paris now. To see Ella. I think she's a piece, too," Isabelle ventured, waiting for the fox's reaction. But if the fox agreed, she gave no sign.

"Nero made me a better person. He gave me courage," Isabelle continued. "And Ella? If I was ever good, even a little bit, it's because of her."

The fox flicked her tail.

"Tavi thinks Felix is a piece, too. But he's not. I *know* he's not. Can you tell me what it is? Give me a hint? A nudge? *Anything*, Your Grace?"

The fox turned her head and gazed down the road intently, as if she saw something, or heard something there. Isabelle followed her gaze but could see nothing. When she turned back to the fox, the creature was gone.

"I'm talking to foxes now. That's almost as bad as talking to cabbages," she said, then she and Nero continued on their way. They'd put a good six miles of the twenty-mile trip behind them, and the whole way, Isabelle had been wondering if she was crazy.

Everyone thought that going to see Ella was a terrible idea. Tantine said the guards would never let her through. Tavi said Ella wouldn't want to see her. Madame said she'd probably be robbed and murdered and left in a ditch before she got halfway there.

218

Only Maman thought the trip was a good idea. She'd told Isabelle to find a duke to marry while she was there. And, of course, the marquis wanted her to go.

Her resolve wavered for a moment, but then she pictured the marquis as he'd looked as he stood on top of his speeding carriage, the wind snatching at his braids and billowing his jacket out behind him.

Most would have been screaming in terror; he'd been laughing, his head back, his arms outstretched to the sky.

She remembered his sparkling amber eyes, and how, when he trained them on her, he made her feel as if luck itself was on her side, as if anything was possible.

And then she clucked her tongue and urged Nero on.

They'd been cantering for a mile or so, when they saw a man walking along the side of the road ahead of them. It was a quiet Sunday, and they'd barely seen anyone else, just a few wagons and a carriage.

Isabelle didn't think anything of the man, until they got closer to him and she realized that she knew the slope of his shoulders and his easy, loping gait. She recognized the satchel slung over his back and the battered straw hat on his head.

It was Felix.

Isabelle's stomach knotted. She didn't want to see him. Whenever they were together for more than two minutes, bad things happened. They argued. Shouted. He kissed her, then walked away. He could be incredibly kind, and carelessly cruel.

Isabelle decided to gallop straight past him, pretending she didn't realize who he was, but then he suddenly turned around, having heard a rider come up behind him, and her chance was lost.

"Isabelle," he said flatly, as he realized it was her. It appeared he wasn't eager to see her, either.

"Hello, Felix," she said coolly. "I'm on my way to Paris. I'm afraid I can't stop."

"That's a shame."

The baiting note in his voice irritated Isabelle. She scowled, but Felix didn't see her reaction. He wasn't looking at her anymore; his eyes were on Nero.

The horse's ears pricked up at the sound of Felix's voice. He trotted up to him, sniffed him, then gave a gusty snort.

"Thanks, boy," Felix said, laughing as he wiped horse breath off his face.

His harsh expression had melted. Isabelle knew Felix loved Nero and Nero returned the love. He lowered his head, inviting Felix to scratch his ears. Prickly Nero, who shied from anyone's touch but Isabelle's, who was far more likely to bite or kick than behave.

*Turncoat*, Isabelle said silently.

"Why are you going to Paris?" Felix asked.

"To see Ella."

Felix glanced up at her from under the brim of his hat. "An audience with the queen. That doesn't happen every day. When did she summon you?"

Isabelle hesitated. "She didn't, exactly. Summon me, that is."

"So you're just dropping in on the queen of France?"

The skeptical tone of his voice shook Isabelle's confidence, and irritated her even more. It made her wonder, yet again, if the marquis's idea wasn't, perhaps, a little bit insane. And if she wasn't, too.

"I'm going to *try* to see her," she corrected. "I need to. There's . . . there's something I need to say to her."

"Isabelle?"

"What?"

"Whatever you have to say to Ella . . . *say* it, don't yell it. There are guards in the palace. Lots of them. With swords and rifles. Don't throw things, either. Not eggs. Not walnuts."

"Where are *you* going?" Isabelle asked huffily, keen to change the subject. Obviously, Felix had heard about the orphan incident, too.

"Also to Paris," Felix said, running his hand over Nero's neck and down to his shoulder. "I'm delivering a face," he continued. "Well, half a one."

"Another war injury?" Isabelle asked, her pique forgotten for the moment.

Felix nodded. "Shrapnel took the left cheek of a captain. His eye, too. He can't go out. People stare. They turn away from him. I made a half mask to cover the injury. I hope it helps."

Isabelle was about to say that she was certain it would, but he spoke before she could.

"Nero's sweaty," he said, frowning. "You should get down and walk for a bit. Give him a rest. You've got miles to go before you reach Paris."

"Are you telling me how to take care of my own horse?" Isabelle asked. But she leaned forward and felt Nero's shoulder, too.

"Yes."

Isabelle, simmering, didn't budge.

"Afraid?" Felix asked her, a taunt in his voice.

"Of what?"

"That I'll kiss you again."

Isabelle glared at him, but she jumped down because he was right, damn him; Nero *was* a little sweaty.

"*You're* the one who's afraid," she said testily as she pulled the horse's reins over his head and led him.

"Oh, am I?"

"You must be. Every time you kiss me, you run away."

Felix scoffed at that. Which was a mistake.

The rude noise, the dismissive look on his face—they brought Isabelle's simmering anger to a boil. She stopped dead in the middle of the road, hooked an arm around his neck, and pulled him close. The kiss she gave him was not sweet or soft; it was a hot, hard smash, full of fury and wanting.

She kissed him with everything in her, until she couldn't breathe, and then she let go. Felix stumbled backward. His hat fell off.

"Run. Go," she said, gesturing to the road. "That's what you do."

Pain twisted in his blue eyes. It hurt Isabelle to know that she'd put it there, but she couldn't rein in the anger she felt toward him. It had been pent up for so long.

"Why, Felix? Just tell me why," she demanded. "You owe me that. Did you change your mind? Did you find yourself a better girl? A pretty girl?"

Felix looked as if she'd run a sword through his heart. "No, Isabelle, I didn't," he said. "I waited. Alone in the woods. Night after night. For someone who swore she would come but never did. I waited until it turned cold and I had to leave the Wildwood, and Saint-Michel, to find work. I thought *you'd* changed your mind. Found a rich boy. Some noble-man's son."

Uncertainty skittered over Isabelle's heart like mice in a wall.

"That's not true," she said slowly, shaking her head. "After Maman found out about us and made you and your family leave, you said you'd come back for me. You promised to leave a message in the linden tree, but you didn't."

Felix raked a hand through his hair. He looked up at the sky. "My God," he said. "All this time . . . all this time you thought that I . . ."

"Yes, Felix, I did. I thought you loved me," Isabelle said bitterly.

"But, Isabelle," Felix said. "I *did* leave a note."

## SEVENTY-SIX

Isabelle shook her head.

She felt as if she'd ventured out onto a pond that wasn't frozen solid, and now the ice was cracking under her.

"You *didn't*," she insisted. "I checked. Every night."

"And I waited every night. Right where I'd told you I'd be. Where we saw the deer and her fawns."

"No, it's not true," Isabelle said, but with less conviction.

"It is. I *swear* it."

"What happened to it, then?"

"I—I don't know," Felix said, throwing his hands up. "I don't see how anything *could* have happened to it. I was worried about it blowing away, so I put a stone on top of it to weigh it down."

*It can't be true. He must be lying,* Isabelle thought. *None of this makes any sense.*

And then it did. The ice broke and a freezing shock of truth pulled Isabelle under.

"Maman," she said. "She was so watchful. I bet she saw you hide it. I bet she took it and burned it."

Isabelle felt like she was drowning. The hurt, the sorrow, the bitterness—all the emotions she'd carried for years, emotions that had been so real to her, she now saw were false. But a new one threatened to overwhelm her, to catch her and tangle her, suffocating her in its cold depths—regret.

She saw herself running to the linden night after night, hoping in vain for a note. She saw Felix, waiting for her in the Wildwood. And then both of them giving up. Believing the worst of each other. And of themselves.

"Oh, Felix," she said, her anguished voice barely a whisper. "If only I'd found the note. What would our lives have been like if I had? We'd be in Rome now, and happy."

"Maybe we'd be living by a turquoise sea in Zanzibar. Or high up in a mountain fortress in Tibet." He laughed mirthlessly. "Or maybe we'd be dead. Of starvation. Exposure. Or sheer stupidity. We didn't exactly plan the trip out. I had a few coins saved up. You were going to bring some hard-boiled eggs and ginger cake."

Isabelle desperately wanted to kick free, to surface, to find something hopeful in the dark, roiling water and use it to pull herself out. Could she?

She put a hand on Felix's chest. Over his heart. And then she kissed him.

"Are you going to walk away again?" she asked afterward, leaning her forehead on his chest. "Don't. Promise you won't."

"I can't promise that, Isabelle," he said.

She looked up at him, stricken, and tried to pull away, but he grabbed her hand and held it fast.

"I'm leaving Master Jourdan's. And Saint-Michel. I'm leaving France," he said, all in a rush.

"I—I don't understand . . ."

"I'm going to Rome, Isabelle. To become a sculptor like I always wanted to." He lifted her hand to his lips and kissed it. "Come with me."

## – SEVENTY-SEVEN –

Isabelle and Felix walked down the road in silence, Nero clopping along behind them.

Half an hour had passed since he had asked Isabelle to go with him to Rome.

At first she'd laughed, thinking that he was making an impulsive joke, but she'd soon learned that he was serious.

"I have a place with a master sculptor," he'd explained. "He wrote me a month ago. I'll be doing the worst jobs, the ones no one else wants to do, but it's a start. I've given my notice, bought my passage."

"Felix, when . . . how . . ." Isabelle said, dumbfounded.

"I've been saving money from every job I've had for the past two years," he'd told her. "From all the feet and hands and eyes and teeth I've carved on the side. And from my wooden army. I sold it. A nobleman in Paris bought it. He's already sent the money. I've only three officers left to finish. As soon as I send word, his servant will come to collect it." He paused, then said, "It's enough. To buy you a passage, too. To rent an attic room somewhere. Come with me."

Isabelle wanted to say yes more than she'd ever wanted anything in the entire world, but it was impossible and she knew it.

"I can't go, Felix. Maman has lost her wits and Tavi's head is always in the clouds. If I leave, who will take care of them? We're barely surviving as is. They won't last a week without me."

"I can't get you back just to lose you again," Felix said now, dispelling the silence. "There must be a way. We'll find it."

Isabelle mustered a smile, but she couldn't imagine what that way might be. "I have to go," she said. Felix was spending the night in the city, at the home of the captain for whom he'd made the mask, but she needed to get to Paris, and get back to Saint-Michel by evening.

"Stay with me for one more mile. There's the sign." Felix nodded at a whitewashed post ahead of them. "We're nearly halfway there."

"All right," Isabelle relented. "One more mile."

A moment later, they passed the post. On it, a bright, newly painted sign pointed left to Paris. Another pointed right to Malleval. With barely a glance at it, Isabelle and Felix headed left.

225

Had their emotions not been running so high, had they not been so distracted by talk of Rome, had they not stopped, right in the middle of the road, for another kiss, they might've noticed that the white paint on the signs was not just new, but still wet. And that black block letters ghosted through it—Paris under Malleval, Malleval under Paris.

They might've seen boot prints around the base of the signpost and freshly disturbed dirt a few feet away from it. Had they cared to dig in that dirt, they would've found two empty paint pots and two used brushes—all of it stolen earlier that morning from a nearby farmer's barn.

But they did not see any of these things, and so continued on their way.

As soon as they were out of earshot, the coal-black raven, who'd been perched out of sight on a leafy branch, flapped her wings noisily and flew off.

There was no need to stay. Her mistress had told her so.

The girl, and the boy with her, would not be coming back.

## – SEVENTY-EIGHT –

It was the smoke that first got Isabelle's attention.

A burnt-hay smell. Sharp and out of place on the summer breeze.

Farmers burned their fields to rid them of weeds and stubble in autumn, when the harvest was in. Not in August.

"Do you smell that?" she asked Felix.

"I do," he said, looking around for the source of the smoke.

Nero whinnied uneasily. He pulled at his reins. Isabelle realized nothing around her looked familiar. She had been to Paris before, several times, on shopping trips for dresses with Tavi and Maman, but she did not recall the huge apple orchard on the right side of the road. Or the old, tumbledown stone barn on the left.

"We took the right road, didn't we?" she asked Felix, realizing that she'd barely glanced at the signpost.

"I'm sure we did. I remember seeing the sign for Paris pointing left. That's the way we went."

They walked on. A few minutes later, they spotted another signpost. A man was sitting under it, his back against the wooden post, his head down, clearly taking a rest. He was wearing the rough clothing of a farmer—battered boots, long pants, a red shirt. His straw hat was tilted over his face.

As Isabelle and Felix drew closer, they saw that there was only a single sign on the post, and that it read *Malleval*.

"That *can't* be right," Felix said. "Malleval's in the opposite direction."

Isabelle decided to get an answer. She handed Nero's reins to Felix and approached the resting man. "Excuse me, sir, will this road take us to Paris?"

The man didn't answer her.

"He's sound asleep," Isabelle said.

She hated to wake him, but she needed to know where they were. She didn't have time to waste.

"Sir? Excuse me," she said. But the man slept on. Isabelle bent down and gave his arm a gentle shake. His hat fell off. His head lolled sickeningly to the side. His body toppled over like of sack of meal.

That's when Isabelle realized that he wasn't napping, and he wasn't wearing a red shirt. He was wearing a white shirt that had turned red. His throat had been cut from ear to ear. Blood had cascaded from the wound down the front of his body. Some was still trickling out.

Terror broke lose inside her. "Please, somebody help! In God's name, help!" she screamed.

Felix was at her side in an instant. The blood drained from his face as he saw the murdered man. He grabbed Isabelle's arm and pulled her away. Nero, hearing her screams and smelling blood, grew wild-eyed. Isabelle took him from Felix and tried to calm him. Felix shouted for help again. But nobody answered them. Nobody came.

The breeze picked up and so did the scent of smoke. The bitter smell was like a slap; it brought Isabelle back to her senses. She realized how stupid they'd been.

"Whoever killed this man might still be nearby," she said to Felix. "And we've just let him know we're here."

"If that signpost is correct, Malleval will be close," Felix said. "We'll be safe there. We can tell them what happened. They'll send someone to get this poor man."

Casting a fearful glance around, Isabelle put her foot in the stirrup. Felix boosted her up into her saddle; then she pulled him up behind her.

"Go," he said, closing his arms around her waist.

Isabelle spurred Nero on. He galloped the mile or so down the road toward the village, but as it came into view, he stopped, raised his head, and let out an earsplitting whinny.

Isabelle's eyes widened. One hand came up to her chest.

"No," she whispered. "God in Heaven . . . no."

There would be no help from the villagers of Malleval.

Not now, not ever.

– SEVENTY-NINE –

Isabelle slid out of her saddle, then staggered through the wheat fields at the edge of Malleval like a drunk. Felix followed her.

Nero stood in the road where they'd left him, his reins trailing in the dust.

Lying in the dirt, amid the stubbly stalks of cut wheat, were bodies. Men's. Women's. Children's. They had been shot and stabbed. Many in the back. There was a man with a gaping hole in his side, still clutching his pitchfork. There lay an old woman, a bayonet wound in her chest.

Dark gray smoke swirled over them. The village's homes, its stables and barns, all had thatched roofs, and they were burning.

Isabelle started to shake so hard that she couldn't stop. Her legs gave way. She fell on her backside next to a dead mother and her dead child. A low keening sound moved up from her chest into her throat, then rose into a wild howl of pain. Thick, strangling sobs followed it. She folded in on herself, clutched at the dirt, and wept.

Sometime later—minutes? An hour?—Isabelle heard voices. Men's voices. She picked up her head and looked around. It wasn't Felix; he was carrying an old woman who was bleeding badly through a field, running with her toward one of the only houses that wasn't burning.

And then Isabelle saw the men. They were soldiers. They'd gathered at the far edge of the field. They were talking and laughing. Some held the reins of their horses, others sacks full of plunder.

One of them turned. His gaze fell on Isabelle and an ugly grin spread across his face. He started toward her through the swirling smoke, through the falling ash, like a demon from hell. Two others made as if to follow him, but he waved them back. She was to be his sport, his alone.

She had never seen the man before, but she knew him. From rumors and stories. From a vision she'd had when a wagonload of wounded soldiers had passed by her on the road to Saint-Michel. He held a sword in one hand, a shield in the other. He wore no coat. His leather waistcoat and white shirt were streaked with blood. His black hair, shot through

229

with silver, was pulled back. A scar puckered one cheek. His eyes burned with dark fire. He was Volkmar.

Inside Isabelle, under her heart, the sleeping wolf woke.

## - EIGHTY -

Isabelle was terrified. She was going to die; she knew that. But she would not run; she would face Volkmar down.

She scrambled to her feet, praying that Felix would stay with the old woman inside the house, and searched for a weapon. There had to be *something* she could fight with—a pitchfork, a shovel, a hay rake. She would aim for Volkmar's neck if she could. His thigh. His wrist. She would do her best to make him bleed.

Volkmar closed in. He was only twenty yards away now.

"How did I miss this little rat in the wheat field?" he said, raising his sword.

And still, Isabelle was defenseless. Her heart kicked in her chest. Her blood surged, pounding in her ears. But over it, she heard another noise. It sounded like fabric tearing. She felt a weight, sudden and heavy, pulling at her clothing.

She glanced down and saw that her pocket had torn open. Because the nutshell inside it was growing.

Isabelle quickly pulled it out before it ripped her dress apart. As she did, it flattened and expanded until it was half her size. Leather straps appeared on the side facing her. She realized she was holding a shield. She snaked her arms through the straps and raised it over her head.

In the very nick of time.

A split second later, Volkmar's blade crashed down upon it. Isabelle was strong now, her arms well muscled from endless farm chores, and she managed to hold the shield firm. Without it, the blow would have cleaved her in two.

She thrust her hand into her pocket again, remembering Tanaquill's first gift. Her fingers closed around the bone. She pulled it out, and as she did, it transformed into the same fearsome sword she'd used to fight off the chicken thief.

"Coward!" she spat at Volkmar. "Murderer! They were innocent people!"

The horror and grief had receded. She felt as if she were made of rage now.

Volkmar's grin twisted into a snarl. Her words were an offense to him. A stab through the heart would be too good for her now. He would aim for her neck instead, and send her head flying.

He swung high, just as she'd known he would. She ducked, and his blade passed over her head. Her legs pistoned her back up. The tip of her sword caught his side and ripped a jagged gash up his rib cage. He bellowed in surprise and staggered backward.

Isabelle's heart was pounding like a war drum. Her blood was singing.

Volkmar touched his fingertips to his wound. They came away crimson. "The rat has sharp teeth," he said. Then he charged again.

Isabelle knew she had one chance left. She had to do better than a flesh wound.

She lifted her shield, raised her sword, but before she could use them, a bugle blast was heard. Two men came galloping across the field from her left. A riderless horse trailed them.

"The king's cavalry is coming!" one of the men shouted. "Jump on! Hurry!"

The horsemen swooped close. The riderless horse slowed to a canter. Volkmar threw his weapons down and caught the horse by his bridle. He ran alongside the animal for a few strides, then launched himself into the saddle. And then the three riders were gone, vanished into the smoke.

Isabelle lowered her sword and shield. As she did, they turned back into a jawbone, a walnut shell. She put them in her pocket. Seconds later, forty soldiers on horseback galloped into the village. They surrounded Isabelle and asked her what had happened. She told them, pointing in the direction in which Volkmar had gone and urged them to hurry.

The captain shouted commands at his men and they charged off.

Isabelle watched them go, longing to ride with them and chase down Volkmar. Then, sickened and spent, she looked for Felix. He was ministering to a dying man now, bare-chested, pressing his bunched-up shirt to the man's side, trying to keep the last of his life from leaking into the dirt.

As Isabelle watched him, kneeling among the obscene harvest of the dead, his body smeared with blood, his face streaked with tears, a pain, piercing and deep, made her cry out. It was worse than any that had befallen her that day. Her hand went to her chest. She bent double, her breath rapid and shallow, willing it to pass.

Inside her, the wolf, denied his rightful work, bared his sharp teeth and tore into her heart.

## – EIGHTY-ONE –

The jagged scream tore apart the placid afternoon.

It was followed by a loud, heavy smash, and the sound of running feet.

Fate, peeling apples at the kitchen table, looked up, alarmed. Avara, stirring a soup at the hearth, dropped her ladle into the ashes.

232

"What the devil is going on out there?" she shouted. "Hugo! Huuuugo!"

Fate and Avara reached the door together and saw an earthenware bowl lying in pieces on the stone steps. Bright green peas were scattered around it. Two hens had rushed over and were greedily pecking at them.

Fate soon saw that it was Maman who had screamed and Tavi who'd dropped the bowl. They were running down the drive. Two figures were walking up it. Felix was shirtless. His long brown hair, damp and lank, hung down his back. His trousers were stained with blood. His gaze was inward, as if focused on something only he could see. His arm was around Isabelle's neck, possessively, protectively, as if he was afraid she would be snatched away from him. The skirts of Isabelle's dress were smeared with crimson. Sweat and dirt streaked her face. Her hair, flecked with ash, had tumbled loose from its carefully pinned coil.

"God in Heaven, what happened?" Avara shouted. She skirted the broken mess on the steps and joined the others. Hugo walked out of the stables, wiping his hands on a rag. He dropped it and broke into a run when he saw Isabelle and Felix.

Fate remained in the doorway. "It *can't* be," she hissed. "How is she still alive?"

Realizing that it would look callous for her to remain where she was, Fate hurried down the drive, too. Maman was in tears, pressing Isabelle's face between her hands one minute, asking the name of the brave knight who was with her the next. Tavi was shushing her.

Felix apologized for being bare-chested and filthy. He'd left his blood-soaked shirt in Malleval and had tried to douse himself clean under the village's pump, he said, but the water had only washed away so much. Then he told what had happened to them. How they'd ended up in Malleval after Volkmar had slaughtered its people. How Isabelle had somehow found a sword and shield and had faced him down. How they'd abandoned their plans to go to Paris and had made the long walk home.

It was quiet when they finished. No one spoke.

Then Tavi, her voice quavering with anger, said, "You could've been *killed*, Isabelle. What were you *thinking*?"

"That I wanted to kill Volkmar," Isabelle said in a flat, grim voice. "That I wanted to cut into his black heart and watch him bleed to death at my feet. That's what I was thinking." Silent and hollow-eyed, she led Nero into the stables to untack him.

They all watched her go, then Hugo turned to Felix and said, "Come inside. Sit down. Have something to drink."

Felix shook his head. "I'm going to the camp. To warn Colonel Cafard. The sooner I get there, the better."

Hugo insisted on driving him. He'd been just about to leave for the camp, he explained. The cook had sent for milk. Men had left for the front that morning. Every wagon in the camp had been needed to carry tents, arms, and ammunition. Not one was left to fetch food for those remaining.

Felix thanked him and asked to borrow a shirt. Usually, Avara would have balked over such a request, badgering Felix not to stain it or wear out the elbows, but she didn't utter one word of protest. Worry crinkled the skin around her eyes. Her gaze drifted over her fields, her orchards, her cattle, her son.

Fate knew what she was thinking, what they were all thinking: Malleval was only ten miles away. "Volkmar won't come here," she soothed, the lie rolling smoothly off her tongue. "He wouldn't dare, not with Colonel Cafard camped right outside the village."

Avara nodded, but the furrows remained. "You're right, Tantine. Of course you are," she said. Then she took a deep breath. "Octavia, you broke my bowl! Do you have any idea what bowls like that cost? Clean up the mess and get the rest of the peas shelled!" But her voice lacked its usual vinegar.

Tavi bent over the pottery shards. She made a sling of her apron and put them in it. Maman helped her. Avara returned to her soup.

And Fate remained outside, watching as Felix shrugged into Hugo's shirt, then climbed up on the wagon seat next to him. As the two boys headed down the drive, her bright eyes searched the farmyard for Isabelle. They spotted her by the pond. She'd led Nero to the water; he'd waded in up to his shoulders and was drinking his fill.

Isabelle followed him in, fully clothed except for her boots and stockings. As Fate watched, she submerged herself. When she came back up, she sat down on the bank and rubbed at the bloodstains on her dress, then scrubbed at her hands, roughly, furiously, as if whatever was on them would never come off.

When she was finished, she lowered her head and wept. Even at a distance, Fate could see her shoulders shaking, her body shuddering.

*How on earth did Volkmar fail to kill her?* she wondered. *She's just a girl. Crumpling under the bloodshed she witnessed.*

Fate meant to get an answer to her question. Pleading tiredness after all the upset, she abandoned the bowl of apples she'd been peeling, closed herself in her room, and took Isabelle's map out of her trunk. She moved quietly. Losca was asleep in a trundle bed, her head tucked under her arm.

Fate smoothed the map out on her table, sat down, and looked it over.

She had tried to shorten Isabelle's path to her death, and it hadn't worked. Was it her inks? Maybe the ingredients hadn't been the best quality. The light was bad in this room; perhaps her artistry had suffered as a result.

But no, it was neither of these things. Fate's expert eyes found the problem. She had drawn a new path for Isabelle, a shortcut through Malleval to Volkmar, and Isabelle had followed it—most of the way. Just shy of the end, however, she'd turned off the shortcut and made her way back to her old path.

Fate sat back in her chair. She drummed her fingers on its arm. *Have I underestimated her?* she wondered.

Isabelle had refused to abandon her mother in a burning house. She'd saved three horses at the expense of her own freedom. She'd taken on Volkmar. This wasn't the same girl who'd stood by as Maman turned Ella into a servant, or who'd locked her stepsister in her room when the prince had come to call. Why, she was even walking taller these days, more confidently.

*At least she failed to see Ella*, Fate thought with some relief. That was the day's one bright spot.

But the boy—the first piece—he was worrisome. He'd had an arm around Isabelle as they'd walked up the drive. They seemed to have grown closer. Fate consulted Isabelle's map again, poring closely over the detour she'd made, then she pounded her fist on the table. The noise startled Losca awake. She sat up, bright-eyed and blinking.

"They reconciled!" Fate fumed. He made a slipper for her. *That's* why she's walking taller. "He even asked her to go with him to Italy!" She peered at the map again. "She told him she could not . . . That's good. But he promised to find a way." She shook her head in disgust. "What if he does? What if Isabelle *leaves*?"

Fate rose; she paced back and forth. "That cannot happen," she said. She knew she had to find a way of keeping Isabelle in Saint-Michel, but her bag of tricks was rapidly emptying. Warm from her pacing, she moved across the room to open her window. It was a casement frame with metal hinges, one of which had developed an unpleasant squeak.

"I must get after Hugo to fix that," she muttered.

236

*Hugo.*

Fate whirled around. She rushed to her desk and scrawled a hasty letter on a piece of parchment.

"Up, girl!" she barked at Losca when she'd finished.

Losca rose. She smoothed her dress.

"Take this to Monsieur Albert, head of the bank in Saint-Michel. He'll be at home, eating his Sunday dinner. I need a good sum of money. More than he has in his vault. It'll take him a day or two to get it, no doubt, and we must move quickly. Hurry now! Go!" Fate said.

She walked Losca out of their room, through the house, past Tavi shelling peas, and down the drive, giving her directions to Monsieur Albert's. The girl set off running, the letter clutched in her hand.

Fate watched her until she disappeared down the road, then started back to the house. A movement caught her eye. It was Isabelle. She was in the pasture, riding Nero. She'd rigged up a scarecrow. His body was made out of branches; he had a cabbage for a head. He was propped up on a fence post she'd sunk into a soft patch of ground. She was brandishing something in her right hand. Fate squinted and saw that it was an old sword that had belonged to Monsieur LeBenêt and had hung in the stables.

As she watched, Isabelle charged the scarecrow, sword raised high, and lopped his head off. She turned Nero sharply and charged again. The scarecrow lost an arm. Then his torso was hacked in two. Fate did not like what she was seeing.

Her expression darkened further as she passed by Tavi again and saw that she was using the peas she'd shelled to form equations. Her eyes lingered on the girl.

A few weeks ago, after the incident with the cheese, Hugo had come to her complaining bitterly about Tavi, asking Fate to get her married off.

Back then, Fate had thought the idea unnecessary, but perhaps it was time to act on Hugo's suggestion now. With a few slight modifications.

A wedding would be such a joyous affair.

"For everyone," Fate whispered darkly. "Except the bride and groom."

## – EIGHTY-TWO –

"Once again from the top. With feeling, please!" Chance shouted.

He was standing in front of his stage, a glass in one hand, watching his players rehearse. They were doing a terrible job. Missing cues. Mangling lines. Torchlight, playing over his face, revealed new creases engraved around his eyes.

"Louder, please!" he yelled, raising his hand, palm up. "I can barely hear you!"

The fortune-teller shouted her lines. The actress and diva joined her onstage and ran through theirs. Chance clapped out a quick tempo to speed them up.

One of the footlights, lacking a glass chimney, had been placed too far upstage. The fortune-teller's skirt brushed it. The fabric caught. The sword-swallower shouted at her, waving his hands. He hurried to stamp the flames out. Frightened by the fire, the fortune-teller ran, but not before the sword-swallower's foot came down on her hem. There was sound of cloth tearing, and then the fortune-teller found herself standing center stage in her petticoat.

The fire-breather, up in the rigging, peered down to see what was going on, lost his balance, and fell. His foot got tangled in a rope that was attached to a painted backdrop. The backdrop shot up and smashed in the rigging. Splintered pieces rained down, knocking off the diva's wig and the actress's crown. The fire-breather dangled, his head only inches from the stage floor.

Chance closed his eyes. He pinched the bridge of his nose. Isabelle's map was gone. Fate was undoubtedly redrawing it to speed the girl to her doom. And what was he doing? Presiding over a disaster of a play.

Chance opened his eyes. "Someone cut him free, please," he said, gesturing to the fire-breather, who was still hanging upside down, spinning in slow circles like a human plumb bob.

"You tell him," hissed a voice from behind Chance.

"No, *you* tell him."

"Where's the cognac? Let's refill his glass. Bad news always goes down better with a glass of cognac."

"I really think *you* should tell him."

Chance turned around. "Tell me what?" he asked.

The cook and the magician were standing there, solemn-faced.

"Isabelle never made it to Paris," said the magician. "She didn't see Ella."

Chance swore. He turned and threw his glass against a tree. All the actors stopped what they were doing. A hush fell over the company.

Chance tilted his head back. He covered his eyes with his hands. He felt he was only one teetering step away from defeat.

"This play is it," he said, lowering his hands. "My last move. It's all I have left to convince Isabelle that she can make her own path. If it fails, then I've failed. And Isabelle is doomed."

The actors all started talking at once. Then yelling. Pointing fingers. Shaking fists. The noise grew louder and louder.

Until the fortune-teller, still in her petticoat, took charge. "Quiet, everyone!" she shouted, stamping her foot. "Places! Start again from the top . . ."

"Good girl. Put your heart into it," the magician urged her, walking to Chance's side.

"Deliver those lines like Isabelle's life depends on it," said the cook, joining them.

Chance nodded gravely. "Because it does."

## – EIGHTY-THREE –

"Octavia! Isabelle! Wake up!"

Isabelle sat up groggily. She'd been fast asleep. *Did someone call my name?* she wondered.

"Wake *up*, girls! I need to speak to you!"

It was Madame LeBenêt. Isabelle reached for her dress, pulled it over her head, and hurried to the edge of the hayloft, fumbling with the buttons.

Madame was standing by the ladder, hands on her hips. "Come to the house," she said brusquely. "Bring your mother."

Isabelle remained where she was, staring over the ledge, blinking stupidly.

"What are you waiting for? Get the hay out of your hair and get a move on!" Madame barked.

She turned on her heel and strode from the barn, and Isabelle felt as if she was walking right over her heart. Panic rose inside her. She wondered what they had done. Was it the horses she'd saved? The bowl Tavi had broken? *Madame is going to turn us out*, she thought. *We've angered her once too often.*

"Tavi, Maman, get up. Get dressed. Madame wants us," Isabelle said, trying to keep her voice from trembling.

When they'd finished dressing, the three women made their way down the ladder and across the yard to the house. Isabelle smoothed her hair when they reached the door, then knocked.

"Come in!" Madame yelled.

With her heart in her mouth, Isabelle stepped inside. Tavi and Maman followed her.

Tantine was at the table, setting out cups. Madame was pulling a large copper frying pan off a trivet in the hearth. She carried the pan to the table, then gave it a knock with the heel of her hand. A fluffy yellow omelet flipped out onto a platter.

"Ten eggs in that!" she grumbled. "That's ten I can't sell."

"Now, now, Avara," Fate chided.

There was a pot of hot black coffee on the table with a jug of rich cream to pour in it, sliced bread, a dish of fresh butter and another of strawberry jam. Isabelle, who—along with Tavi and Maman—had been subsisting on stale bread and thin soup, felt her stomach twist painfully. She desperately hoped that Madame would give them something to eat before she sent them packing. Gazing at so much delicious food was torture to the hungry girl; she turned away and distracted herself by looking around the room.

Isabelle had only been inside Madame LeBenêt's house a handful of times and had never lingered. Now she had time to take it in. The room where they were standing—both kitchen and dining room—was small and low-ceilinged. There were no pictures on the gray stone walls, no flowers in a vase, no rugs on the floor, nothing warm or welcoming anywhere. She felt a rush of sympathy for Hugo, living in a cold, loveless house, with a mother who rarely, if ever, spoke a kind word.

"Sit down, girls," Madame said impatiently, waving them toward the table with the wooden spoon she was holding.

Isabelle and Tavi exchanged confused glances.

241

"Sit down? There at the table?" Isabelle asked.

"You mean us?" Tavi said.

"I said *you*, didn't I?" Madame replied.

"No, you said *girls*," Tavi pointed out.

Madame gripped her wooden spoon as if she wanted to throttle it. Tantine, who'd finished setting cups out, ushered the three women to the table.

Isabelle had no idea what was happening. Was Madame going to let them stay? Or was she giving them a good breakfast before she threw them out to ease her conscience? She didn't have to wait long to find out.

As everyone settled around the table, Madame counted the pieces of bread that had been sliced from the large wheaten round. "That's two pieces per person. *Two!*" she said, glowering. "Tantine, you will ruin us."

"Avara, serve the breakfast, please," Tantine said, her teeth gritted.

Madame, lips pursed, dished out the omelet.

"I should explain why we invited you here," Tantine said as she passed the bread. "This breakfast is a bit of a celebration. As you know, my late husband left a small legacy to Monsieur LeBenêt. Since monsieur passed away, it was left to my discretion whether to bestow it upon a member of his family. I'm pleased to say that I've come to a decision—the money will go to the next LeBenêt male—Hugo."

Hugo was speechless. He sat there like a trout, mouth open, unblinking, until his mother kicked him under the table. "Thank you, Tantine!" he finally said. He puffed his chest out and leaned so far back in his chair, he almost fell out of it. At a dirty look from his mother, he sat forward again, bringing the front legs of the chair down with a crash.

"This is *great!*" he crowed, slapping his hands down on the table. "This means I can . . ."

Isabelle had never seen him so animated. Neither had his mother, apparently, for her look changed from one of disapproval to one of suspicion.

"You can do what?" she asked.

Hugo hunkered down in his chair, a furtive look on his face.

*Marry Odette*, Isabelle thought. *But he's too scared to say so.*

"I...um...I can..." he stammered. Then he brightened. "I can have some money!"

"Use it to buy a brain!" Tavi said under her breath.

Tantine continued. "The legacy is enough to secure the future of this farm and continue the LeBenêt line, which is what my dear husband wished. But..." She held up a finger. "Fortune is only *good* fortune if it is shared, and I mean to see that you are *all* well taken care of. Not just my family, but also you, Isabelle, and your family. You are three women alone in the world. You cannot go on living in a hayloft. What kind of life is that for you? What will happen to you come winter? And so I have taken steps. I have made arrangements."

Tantine picked up her coffee cup and took a sip. Isabelle's hands tightened on her napkin. Hope leapt inside her. What had Tantine done? Was she giving them some money, too? She'd mentioned the hayloft—had she found them something better? Isabelle was afraid to ask, lest she'd gotten her hopes too high, but she had to know. "You found us a new place to stay, Tantine?" she ventured. "A room somewhere? A tiny house?"

"Yes, child. A house and something more," Tantine said, lowering her cup.

Isabelle glanced excitedly at Tavi and then Maman. "What is it?" she asked.

Tantine settled her cup into its saucer. Beaming at Isabelle, she said, "A husband!"

## EIGHTY-FOUR

Isabelle's blood froze in her veins. Her body went rigid in her chair; she was unable to move. "What do you mean a—a *husband*, Tantine?" she asked in a small voice.

"Why, just what I said, child—a man! A tall, strapping man in britches and boots! Just what every girl wants."

"*Isabelle?*" Hugo said, looking surprised. "But I thought . . . I thought Tavi would marry first. She's the oldest."

Tavi said nothing at all; she was shocked speechless.

Maman, however, was overjoyed. "This is *wonderful* news!" she exclaimed. "Who is he? A baron? A viscount?" She looked from Tantine to Avara and back again, but they gave her no answer. "No? Well, no matter. A squire is acceptable, too. After all, these are difficult times."

"Will the wedding be soon?" Hugo asked.

"Within a matter of days," Tantine replied.

"*Yes!*" Hugo crowed. "Tell us, Tantine," he urged, rocking back in his chair again. "Who is it? Who will Isabelle marry?"

Tantine leaned across the table and covered one of Hugo's hands with her own. "Why, dear boy, haven't you guessed?" she asked. "It's *you!*"

## EIGHTY-FIVE

Everything happened at once.

Hugo fell over backward with an earth-shaking crash, hitting his head so hard he knocked himself out. Maman slumped into a faint. Tavi jumped up to revive her at the same time that Madame jumped up to tend to Hugo. They smacked heads, then staggered back, dazed.

And Isabelle squeezed her coffee cup so hard it broke, splashing hot coffee all over her hands. She didn't even feel it. She could hardly breathe. Her heart was pounding; it was beating out the name *Hu*-go, *Hu*-go, *Hu*-go over and over, like a funeral march.

Isabelle could not believe Tantine had done this. Moments ago, she'd been hopeful, believing that the old woman would help them find a new place to live. Now she felt like an animal in a trap. *Why* had she done this? Isabelle had never shown the slightest interest in Hugo, nor he in her.

"Tantine, I can't . . . Hugo and I, we don't . . . we never . . ." she said, struggling for the right words.

Tavi, who was chafing her mother's wrists, came to her aid. "But Hugo and Isabelle can't stand each other! It's a terrible idea, Tantine. This is the eighteenth century, not the tenth. She doesn't have to do it!"

"Girls, girls, calm down! Of course, Isabelle doesn't *have* to marry Hugo. She doesn't have to marry *anyone*," Tantine soothed. "But how unfortunate it would be if she didn't. You see, there are one or two things I may have neglected to mention. Hugo's legacy? It only goes to him if he marries. How can he continue the family line without a wife? And really, what girl wouldn't want to marry such a fine boy, especially one with a farm and fifty acres?" She paused. Her eyes caught Isabelle's and held them. Isabelle felt as if she was being pulled helplessly, hopelessly, into a cold gray abyss. "Isabelle is certainly free to refuse the proposal," Tantine continued. "She is also free to leave the farm and find herself, and her family, another place to live."

Isabelle felt the gray depths close over her and pull her down. She fought her way back up. She had to find a way to navigate between the two impossibilities Tantine had presented.

"Madame," she said, turning to Hugo's mother. "I am nowhere near good enough for your son."

"True enough," Madame allowed, through a mouthful of omelet. "But as your own mother said, these are difficult times and one cannot be choosy. You are not a pretty girl, but cows don't care about looks and neither do cabbages. You're a hard worker, I'll give you that, and that's what counts on a farm. Plus, you're strong and sturdy, with a good pair of hips to carry sons and a fine bosom to suckle them. You'll breed well, I think."

Isabelle flushed a deep red, unaccustomed to hearing herself talked about as if she were a broodmare.

"There! We're all settled, then, aren't we?" Tantine said cheerfully, shoveling more omelet onto Isabelle's plate. "Now, eat your breakfast, child," she admonished. "You'll need your strength. You have a wedding to prepare for. I'm thinking next Saturday. A week from today. That's time enough to make the necessary preparations. What do you think, Avara?"

Isabelle didn't care what anyone thought. She looked at the cold wobbly omelet on her plate. Nausea gripped her. She got to her feet. "Pardon me, please," she said, hurrying toward the door.

"She probably needs to collect herself. Shed a tear of joy or two in private," Tantine said knowingly. "Brides-to-be are *such* emotional creatures."

Isabelle wrenched the door open, ran outside, and vomited her breakfast into the grass.

- EIGHTY-SIX -

"A week," Isabelle said hollowly, leaning against the barn wall. "That's all I've got."

"We'll think of something," Tavi said. She was sitting on the same bench as Isabelle. "There has to be a way out of this."

Hugo, who had regained consciousness, was sitting between them, his head in his hands, his elbows on his knees, groaning.

Breakfast was over. The dishes had been cleared away. Maman, inconsolable that Isabelle was marrying a farm boy, not an aristocrat, had taken to the hayloft. Madame was tending a sick hen. Tantine had retired to her room. Isabelle, Tavi, and Hugo were busy veering between panic and despair.

"There's no way out," Isabelle said miserably. "Either I go through with it or we starve to death."

Hugo picked up his head. "I can't do it. I just can't. Why did you two ever have to come here? *Why?*" He groaned again.

"Stop it. You sound like a calf with colic," Tavi said irritably.

Hugo turned and looked at her. "You're kind of a bitch, you know that?"

"Old news, Hugo."

"You could at least show some sympathy. I'm in a terrible spot," Hugo huffed. "It wasn't supposed to happen this way."

Tavi's eyes narrowed. "What do you mean, *happen this way?*" she asked.

Hugo looked alarmed. And guilty. "Nothing," he quickly said.

But Tavi didn't buy it. "You know something about this. Tell us."

Hugo looked trapped. "I—I told Tantine that you had to go. I asked her to matchmake. To find a husband for *you*, Tavi," he admitted. "I thought if you got married, you'd leave and take Isabelle and your mother with you. I wanted you to leave because I can't stand you, but also because I thought I might have a better chance of convincing my mother to let me marry Odette if you were gone. She'd be more agreeable if there were fewer mouths to feed." Hugo glanced from Tavi to Isabelle. "That's, um . . . that's what I thought."

"So this is *your* fault!" Isabelle said angrily. "You were going to ruin Tavi's life, but you ruined mine instead!"

Tavi rubbed her temples. "Do us a favor, Hugo, don't think anymore. Just don't," she said.

"I won't," Hugo said fervently. "I promise. Just get me out of this mess, Tavi. *Please.* I can't marry Isabelle. I want Odette. I can't stop dreaming about her. I have that feeling."

"What feeling is that?" Tavi asked.

"The feeling that you want to own someone body and soul, spirit them away from everyone else, have them all to yourself forever and ever and ever," Hugo said dreamily. "It's called love."

"No, it's called *kidnapping*," said Tavi.

A pit of hopelessness opened in Isabelle's chest as she listened to Hugo. She lowered her head into her hands.

Tavi saw her. "I'll do it, Iz," she said impetuously. "I'll marry him."

"Oh, Tav," Isabelle said, leaning her head on her sister's shoulder.

"I'd do it. I would. I'd sacrifice myself for you," Tavi bravely offered.

Hugo turned to look at her, offended. "*Sacrifice?*" he said.

Isabelle was deeply touched. She knew her serious, sober sister didn't talk just for the sake of talking. If she said something, she meant it. "You *would* do it, wouldn't you? You'd take on a fate worse than death for me."

"Worse than *death*?" said Hugo.

"It is. Just picture the two of us married," Isabelle said to him. "Milking cows and making cheese for the rest of our lives."

Hugo paled. "Together. In the same house. In the same kitchen," he said grimly.

"In the same bed," Tavi added.

"God, Tavi, shut up!" Isabelle said, mortified.

"I'm just adding that aspect of things into the equation."

248

"Well, don't!"

"I bet you snore, Isabelle. You look like the type," said Hugo.

"Oh, do I, Hugo? Well, I bet you fart all night long."

"I bet you drool on the pillow."

"I bet your breath stinks."

"I bet your feet stink."

"Not as much as yours do. Only three-quarters as much, in fact."

"Eating breakfast together. Dinner. Supper. Staring at you across the table for the next twenty years. Thirty. Fifty, if we're really unlucky," said Hugo.

"Fifty *years*," Isabelle groaned. "My God, can you *imagine* it?"

Hugo, his face as white as lard, said, "There *must* be a way out of this."

Isabelle expected him to say something awful here, to deliver some stinging insult. But he didn't. Instead, he gazed down at his hands and said, "You terrify me, Isabelle. I've never met a girl like you. You're a fighter, fierce as hell. You never quit. You don't know how. I've never seen anyone cut cabbages so fast just to get a bowl of my mother's horrible soup. You don't need anyone. You certainly don't need me." He looked up. "I don't want to marry you, either, Tavi. You're not scary. You're just weird."

"Thanks," Tavi said.

"I don't want a fierce girl. Or a weird girl. I want a sweet girl. A girl who makes me her whole world, not one whose only ambition is to turn the world upside down." He slumped against the barn wall. "Tavi, can't you figure this out?"

"I'm trying. Hard as I can."

Hugo sighed. "Where's Leo Newdanardo when you need him?" he asked.

Tavi laughed humorlessly. "Where, indeed?"

## EIGHTY-SEVEN

"I just want you to know, that no matter what you might've heard, it's not true. I swear to God it's not."

Felix was in his master's workshop carving a regimental insignia on the lid of a fancy coffin, a lieutenant's coffin. He slowly turned around.

"What have you done now, Isabelle?" he said, a smile twitching at the corners of his mouth.

Isabelle, fretting the hem of her jacket, looked down at the sawdust-covered floor. "I got engaged to Hugo."

Felix's chisel hit the coffin lid with a loud thud. *"What?"*

Isabelle's head snapped up. "But it's not my fault!"

Two other men working in the shop lifted their heads, casting curious glances in Isabelle's direction.

Felix, his cheeks coloring, grabbed Isabelle's hand and pulled her after him. Through the long workshop, past coffins on trestles, and workbenches littered with tools, out a door at the rear of the building and into the adjoining stables, where the master kept his delivery wagon and the team of workhorses that pulled it.

As soon as he closed the door behind them, Isabelle, talking a million miles a minute, told Felix what had happened, and how Tantine was pressuring both her and Hugo to marry within the week.

"We're going to come up with a way out of this, Felix. Me, Hugo, Tavi ... we're all trying to figure out a solution," she said. Glancing at the open stable doors, she added, "I—I have to get back to the market. I left Hugo alone with the wagon and it's busy this morning ..."

Ever since the breakfast at Madame's, two days ago, Isabelle had been desperate to see Felix, tell him what had happened, and that she had no intention of going through with betrothal, before he heard it from someone else. Tantine had been telling anyone who would listen about the wedding. She'd ordered a fancy cake from the baker, informed the priest that his services would shortly be required, and had even offered to pay for a wedding dress.

All while Isabelle had been talking, Felix had been silent, his arms tight to his sides, his gaze slanted down. He didn't move, or speak, even after she'd finished.

"Felix? Felix, say something," she begged now, worried that he was hurt or angry.

"He'd make a decent husband."

Isabelle blinked, speechless.

"He's not so bad."

"Then *you* marry him!"

"All I'm saying is that maybe you should think about it."

Isabelle took a step back, devastated. She felt betrayed by his words, confused by the strange, sad look on his face. Only a moment ago, he'd appeared shocked to hear that she and Hugo were betrothed. Now he was telling her she should consider going through with the marriage.

"Felix, why would you *say* that?" she asked. "Hugo doesn't love me. He loves Odette. And I don't love him. I—I love you."

Her words were a knife to his heart. She could see they were and it killed her.

"Should I not have said that? Is the boy supposed to say it first? Is that the rule?" she asked, utterly bewildered. "I never seem to be able to follow the rules. Maybe if I knew what they were I could, but I thought you . . . I thought we . . ."

"Sit down," Felix said, motioning to a wooden bench.

"I'm not marrying Hugo!" she said angrily, tears smarting behind her eyes.

"All right, Isabelle. You don't have to. You *won't* have to."

*What does he mean by that? Why is he being so strange?* she wondered.

251

Felix soon answered her questions.

As she sat, he reached into his vest and pulled out a small leather purse, tightly cinched across the top. He knelt down by her legs, opened the purse, and poured its contents into her lap.

Six shiny gold coins glinted up at her like a promise.

"Take them," he said. "It's enough to get yourself to Rome. To get your sister and mother there, too. You can find a small room. Live cheaply. You'll be safe there, Isabelle. Far away from this war."

"What do you mean *Take them*? Why would I take your money? And why did you say *I'd* be safe? What about you?"

"I'm not going to Italy."

Isabelle's head started to spin. "I—I don't understand, Felix. Just a few days ago, you said you *were* going. You said you wanted me to come with you . . ."

Felix looked down. "Yes, I did. But things have changed."

"You're regretting it. You don't want me. You don't love—"

Felix cut her off. "I do love you. I always have and I always will," he said fiercely. "More than my life."

"Then *why*?"

Felix took her hands in his. His blue eyes found hers.

"Isabelle," he said. "I enlisted."

## – EIGHTY-EIGHT –

It was suicide.

Felix was a dreamer, an artist, not a fighter.

Isabelle tried to pull away. She tried to reason with him, but he tightened his grip on her hands and would not let her speak.

"I had no choice," he said. "Not after Malleval. I can barely work. I can't sleep. I see the dead in my dreams."

Isabelle remembered the smell of smoke in the air, the bodies in the field. "Can you blame me?" he asked her.

Her anger, her arguments—they all fell away. "No," she said. "I can't."

"Remember your book? *An Illustrated History of the World's Greatest Military Commanders*? In all the stories we read, the best warriors went to war reluctantly. Volkmar is a different creature."

"He's not a warrior, he's a murderer," Isabelle said, her voice hardening.

"What if he raids Saint-Michel? How could I live with myself if I did nothing to stop him?"

"When do you leave?" she asked.

"In four days."

Isabelle felt the breath go out of her. "So soon?" she said when she could speak again.

"The recruiting sergeant wanted me right away, but I told him I needed a little time. I have a coffin to finish. A hand, too. And a general for my army of wooden soldiers."

Isabelle looked down so that Felix wouldn't see her eyes welling. The gold coins were still in her lap. She scooped them up, dropped them into the purse and cinched it shut. "I'll wait for you. You'll come back. You *will*," she said, handing it back to him.

But he wouldn't take it.

"You've seen the wagonloads of wounded coming back to camp just like I have," he said. "And the wooden crosses blooming in the fields next to it. We both know I'm not much good with a rifle."

"Felix, no, don't say these things," she pleaded, leaning her head against his.

His words hollowed her out. She had just found him, and now she was losing him again. Could the fates be so cruel?

"Go, Isabelle. Go for both of us. Leave Saint-Michel. And cows and cabbages. Leave Hugo and a life you don't want. There's nothing here for you. There never was."

"There was you."

Felix let go of her hands. He stood. His eyes were shiny, and he didn't want her to see. He was a soldier now. And soldiers didn't cry.

"Will I see you again? Before you go?" she asked.

"It's hard, Isabelle," he said.

She nodded. She understood. It *was* hard to say good-bye to the person you loved. It was excruciating.

"I'll write," he said. "If I can."

*While you can, you mean*, Isabelle thought. *Before a bullet finds you.*

He turned to go, but she snatched at his arm and stopped him. Then she took his face in her hands and kissed him. Kissed him until she'd filled her heart with him. And her soul. Kissed him enough to last her a lifetime.

When she finally stepped away from him, her cheeks were wet, but not from her own tears. Felix shook his head; he pulled her back. Crushed her to him. And then he was gone. And Isabelle was all alone.

She pictured Felix on a battlefield. Running through mud and smoke. She heard the sound of cannons firing, the thunder of charging horses, battle cries and death screams. She saw Volkmar, crazed by bloodlust, swinging his fearsome sword.

Wrenching emotions took hold of her. Heartbreak. Anger. Terror. Grief.

And one more. One that had appeared in a haze of green, like a bad fairy furious that she hadn't been invited to the party. One that Isabelle was quite familiar with, though she didn't understand why she felt it now.

Jealousy.

## EIGHTY-NINE

"There used to be so many spiders in here. Now I never see one. Don't you think that's weird? No spiders? In a *stable*?"

"Incredibly weird, Hugo," said Isabelle distractedly as she hung up Martin's harness.

She and Hugo had just returned from the market. They'd driven the empty wagon out to the fields, ready to be loaded again in the morning; then they'd walked Martin back to the stables. After putting him in his stall with oats and fresh water, they cleaned his tack and put it away.

Hugo frowned. "You've been very quiet. You barely said a word the whole way home from the market. Is something wrong?"

*Yes, whatever was left of my heart was just ripped out, Hugo*, she thought. *That's what's wrong.*

All she could think about was Felix and the gold coins he'd given her. She hadn't decided what to do with them. At first, she thought she would hide them and hold on to them, as if by not spending them she could make sure he returned from the war.

She would marry Hugo and sacrifice her happiness if it meant Felix survived. But as she thought about it, she saw that holding on to a bag of coins couldn't guarantee his life, and that she would be sacrificing Hugo's happiness, too. And Odette's. Maybe Tavi's and Maman's. And she realized she didn't have the right to do that.

By the time Martin turned up the drive to the LeBenêts', she'd made a decision—she would tell Hugo and Tavi about the money and they would figure out what to do with it together.

"Hugo, stay here for a minute, will you?" she said now.

"Why? Where are you going?"

"To get Tavi. I'll be right back."

Isabelle found her sister in the dairy house. She made her come with her back to the stables, then she led them both into an empty horse stall and told them to sit down in the hay.

"Why are we hiding in a horse stall?" Hugo asked.

"So no one sees us. Or hears us."

Tavi gave her a questioning look. "This is all very mysterious, Iz."

Isabelle waited until they'd settled, then said, "Felix gave us a way out of the wedding. If we want to take it."

"Yes!" Hugo shouted, leaping to his feet. "We do! We absolutely do!"

"Be quiet!" Isabelle hissed, grabbing his arm and pulling him back down.

When he was seated again, Isabelle told them what had happened. Both reassured her that Felix would come back, and both felt that using the money to leave Saint-Michel was the only way to stop the wedding.

Isabelle listened to them but still felt uneasy with the decision. "There might be one other way out," she said.

"Go on," Tavi urged.

"I could use the money to rent rooms for us right here, in Saint-Michel," Isabelle offered. "If we do that, Hugo and I still wouldn't have to marry, but you and I and Maman would have shelter."

Tavi crossed her arms. "Yes, let's rent rooms. Smack in the middle of the village, if possible," she said. "It will make it so much easier for Cecile and the baker's wife and whoever it was that burned our house down to call us ugly and throw things at us. Why, we can have our windows broken every day!"

Isabelle, stung by the sarcasm, tossed her a dirty look.

"Tavi's right. The people here won't forget. And they'll never let *you* forget," said Hugo. "Start over, Isabelle. Somewhere new. That's what Felix wants for you. It's why he gave you the money. Can't you see that?"

Isabelle knew Hugo was right. And so was Tavi; the abuse would never end if they stayed here.

"It will be hard getting to Italy, Tavi. And once we're there, we'll have to live frugally to make the money last. One room for all of us. Few pleasures or luxuries," Isabelle cautioned.

Tavi shrugged. "It might be hard, but it won't be bad. For me, at least," she said. "In fact, it will be wonderful. Every bit as wonderful as life here, on the farm, has been. Maybe even more so."

*"Wonderful?"* Isabelle repeated, incredulous. "In case you haven't noticed, you've been living in a hayloft. Milking cows and cutting cabbages and digging potatoes all day long. What is wonderful about any of that?"

Tavi examined her work-roughened hands. "My gowns are burned, my satin shoes and silk corsets destroyed. Parties and balls are a thing of the past. Suitors no longer come to my door. The world calls me ugly and stays away."

Isabelle's heart ached at her sister's words, but then Tavi raised her head and Isabelle saw that she wasn't sad; she was smiling.

"And so the world sets me free," Tavi said, her smile deepening. "The days are hard, yes. But at night I have a candle and quiet and my books. Which is all I've ever wanted. So, yes. *Wonderful.* Don't you see? A pretty girl must please the world. But an ugly girl? She's free to please herself."

"All right, then," Isabelle said, swallowing the lump in her throat. "We'll go."

Tavi grinned. Hugo threw his arms around her. And then the three of them immediately set about making a plan.

Isabelle would not hear of leaving Nero behind, so she, Tavi, and

Maman would ride to Italy. She'd managed to salvage two saddles from the stables when the Maison Douleur burned; Hugo said she could take an old one of theirs, too. They would sleep at inns along the way but would need to buy food, canteens for water, and oilskins, in case it rained. New dresses, too, as theirs were little more than rags, and warm things for the cooler weather. It was September now but would be well into autumn by the time they arrived at their destination.

Isabelle had moved the other two horses she'd rescued from the slaughter yard to the pasture at the Maison Douleur to make Madame happier. They had filled out on the sweet grass there and had built up a bit of muscle. Tavi could ride one, Maman the other. Martin would have to stay behind. Isabelle choked up at the thought, but he was too old to make the trip.

"I'm not going unless you swear on your life to take good care of Martin," she said to Hugo.

"I will."

"*Swear*, Hugo, or I'll stay here and marry you!"

Hugo swore, quickly and vehemently.

Tavi estimated it would take them four days to assemble their supplies, which meant they could leave on Friday—one day before the wedding. The girls would take turns going to market with Hugo and shop for provisions while they were there. They decided to say nothing of their plans to Maman—who could not be trusted to keep secrets—Tantine, or Hugo's mother. Avara and Tantine would likely be furious when they learned that the wedding was off and might make Isabelle and her family leave the farm before they were ready.

They rose and left the horse stall, and the stables, together. They were resolute, determined to go about their chores and keep to their routines in order to raise no suspicions.

They had no idea as they walked out into the bright afternoon that someone else had been with them in the stables. Had they once looked up, they would have seen her, a black-haired girl sitting in the rafters, her thin legs dangling.

Watching. Listening.

Eating spiders.

## – NINETY –

Isabelle stared up at the ceiling beams of the hayloft.

Maman and Tavi were asleep, she could hear their steady breathing, but she couldn't sleep, no matter how hard she tried. Even though she was only wearing a thin chemise, she was sweating. It was hot. The air was still. She'd tossed and turned for the last several hours, unable to get comfortable.

Sighing, she got up, crossed the room, and sat down on the floor by the hayloft's open doors, hoping a breeze might blow in to provide some relief.

The moon was nearly full. Its rays fell over the farm, illuminating the fields and orchards. The pond and pastures. The chicken coop. The dairy house. The woodpile.

And, to Isabelle's surprise, a fox. She was sitting on the chopping block, next to the ax, her tail wrapped neatly around her feet.

"Your Grace," Isabelle said, nodding to her.

With a sinking feeling, she realized why Tanaquill had come.

"You've heard, haven't you? You know I'm leaving."

The fox nodded. The gesture was small, quick, yet in it Isabelle read the fairy queen's displeasure and disappointment.

Isabelle bent her head, ashamed. "I found two of the pieces," she said. "I found Nero. And I'll never let anyone take him from me again. I found Felix . . . just in time to lose him again." Her voice caught. The tears she held back all day came, and this time she couldn't stop them. "He's not coming back, Tanaquill. No matter what Tavi and Hugo say. He's too gentle to drive a bayonet through another human being." She wiped her eyes with the back of her hand. "Ella is the third piece, isn't she? I tried to see her, tried to tell her that I'm sorry. But I didn't. And now I'll never get the chance."

She raised her head; her eyes found the fox's again.

"I failed, I'm afraid. I didn't get all the pieces. Is that why my heart hurts so?" She pressed her palm to her heart, anguished. "Something inside it gnaws and gnaws, and sometimes I think it will never stop, that it will torment me until I'm in my grave. What is it, this pain? Do you know?"

The fox made no reply.

"Ah, well," Isabelle said with a broken laugh. "I guess I was never meant to be pretty, and ugly girls don't get happily ever afters, do they?" She went silent for a moment, then said, "Thank you for your gifts. The sword and shield saved my life. It looks like I'm not going to find out what the seedpod does, but I'd like to keep all three if I may. To remember you. And the linden tree. And home."

The fox nodded. And then, in the blink of an eye, she was gone.

Isabelle knew she would never see the fairy queen again, and the knowledge was heavy inside her. She would never see the Wildwood again, or Saint-Michel. The uneasiness she felt about leaving deepened into a certainty that leaving was wrong. But she knew what Hugo and Tavi wanted. Felix, too. And the decision was made now; she would have to go through with it.

"What else can I do?" she asked the darkness.

That's when a face, small and furry, appeared in the open doorway.

## – NINETY-ONE –

Isabelle scrambled backward, frightened.

Then she saw it was only Nelson, dressed in his customary pearls.

"You gave me such a scare!" she scolded in a whisper, so as not to wake anyone. "What are you doing here? And how did you get those pearls back? I gave them to the diva!"

Nelson thrust out his paw. He was clutching a small piece of paper, folded over several times.

Isabelle took it from him and unfolded it. Swirls and curlicues of gold ink decorated the border. In the center was an invitation, written in a swooping script.

*His Excellency the Marquis de la Chance requests your presence at the Château Rigolade for the premiere of his new theatrical extravaganza, An Illustrated History of the World's Greatest Military Commanders.*

"How strange," she said slowly. "That's the title of a book. One I owned a long time ago." She looked up at the monkey, perplexed. "How can that be?"

Nelson looked away. He fingered his pearls.

"When is this happening? Tomorrow?"

Nelson grabbed the piece of paper back and shook it in Isabelle's face. She looked at it again, more closely this time. At the very bottom was one word: *Now.*

Isabelle squeezed her eyes shut. "This is a dream. I'm dreaming. I *must* be," she said.

She opened her eyes. Nelson was still there. He grabbed a lock of her hair and pulled it so hard that she yelped.

"Fine. I'm *not* dreaming," she said, extricating her hair from his grasp. "But it's the middle of the night. And the château is miles away. And it's a *château* and the marquis is a marquis and he'll have invited other people. And they'll all be very important and beautifully attired. I have one dress, and it's full of holes. I can't go. I'd only be an embarrassment."

Nelson regarded Isabelle; then he regarded his pearls. He heaved an anxious sigh, unhooked his necklace, and handed it to her. Isabelle was deeply touched. She had a feeling those pearls meant the world to the little creature.

"You'd let me borrow them? Really?"

Nelson looked longingly at his treasure, now clutched in her hand. Isabelle could see he was struggling with his decision, but he nodded.

"All right, then," she said, hooking the pearls around her own neck. "Let's go."

She was off to see a play. At a marquis's estate, with a monkey, in the middle of the night.

"I *am* still dreaming," she said as she pulled her dress on over her head. "At least I hope I am, because if I'm not, I've lost my mind."

- NINETY-TWO -

The moon lit the way as Nero carried Isabelle and Nelson over meadows and hills to the grounds of the Château Rigolade.

They'd taken a shortcut and emerged through the woods at the back of the château. Isabelle was surprised to find that the building was completely dark.

An eerie yellow light was emanating from another part of the property, though—the clearing behind the château. Isabelle remembered that that was where Felix had built the marquis's stage. She turned Nero toward it.

As they drew close to the structure, Isabelle saw that it was footlights that were casting the glow. They illuminated the stage, with its red velvet curtains and its garlands of fresh roses twining across the arch.

Strangely, the stage itself, and the grounds around it, were deserted. Isabelle had expected dozens of dazzling people talking and laughing. Jewels bobbing on swells of cleavage. Hair rising like swirled meringue. The rustle of silk. Gilded chairs set out in rows.

But only a single chair stood in front of the stage. A chill shuddered through her. *It's as if the marquis was expecting me, and only me*, she thought uneasily.

Nelson jumped down from her shoulder to Nero's rump to the ground and scampered off. Isabelle got down, too, then walked past the chair to the foot of the stage.

"Marquis de la Chance?" she called out.

He didn't answer. No one did. Isabelle realized that she was in a strange place, in the dead of night, alone.

"I think we'd better go back," she said to Nero.

That's when a man in a mask stepped out from behind the curtains.

## – NINETY-THREE –

Isabelle backed away from the stage warily. Her hand tightened on Nero's reins.

The man bowed to her. Isabelle relaxed as she realized it was the marquis. Though he was masked and in costume, she recognized his long braids. He straightened, then began to speak, in a deep, resonant voice.

Greetings to you, honored guest.
We're here at Chance's own behest.
Tarry now.
We beg you, stay.
Indulge us as we give our play.

These are not the tales you've heard
In spoken verse, or written word.
Of kings and emperors,
Warlords, knights,
Slaughtering enemies in their sights.

These are tales little told,
Of generals mighty, rulers bold,
Whose courage, cunning,
Wit and skill,
Were partnered with an iron will.

Heroes all, but most unknown.
Reduced by time to dust and bone.
Yet on this stage,
They live again.
Such power has our playwright's pen.

Hear their stories, all but lost.
Watch them rise and bear the cost.
Some will lose
and some will win.
Sit now. Watch our play begin.

As the last words left Chance's lips, the footlights blazed high, startling Isabelle so badly that she stumbled backward and fell into the chair. The curtain rose. Trumpets blared. Drums pounded. Cymbals clashed. Isabelle clutched the arms of the chair, her heart thumping. She looked around for Nero. In her fright, she'd dropped his reins. She soon saw that he was only a few yards away, unperturbed by the noise, happily munching the marquis's lawn. His calmness calmed her. She turned back to the stage.

The curtains had opened to reveal a book. It was standing upright and was at least eight feet tall. *An Illustrated History of the World's Greatest Military Commanders* was written in huge letters on the cover.

Did the marquis know she'd owned a copy of that book, and that it had meant the world to her? Or was this all just a coincidence?

As she watched, entranced, the cover slowly swung open. Pages turned, as if flipped by an invisible finger, then stopped. The book stood open to the chapter on ancient Rome's most esteemed generals. And then a door, cut into the page, opened and a man dressed in a leather breastplate and short cloth skirt stepped out of it. On his head he wore a steel helmet with a red plume. In his hand was a fearsome sword.

Isabelle recognized him. He was Scipio Africanus. She'd looked at his portrait and pored over his story, a thousand times.

The pages turned again, and Scipio was joined by Achilles. Then Genghis Khan. Peter the Great. And Sun Tzu. All were dressed and armed for battle. Together they strode to the front of the stage, weapons raised, shields aloft.

The Roman spoke first, delivering his words in a booming stage voice.

> I, Scipio, brave and strong,
> Waged a battle bloody and long,

Against my foes on Carthage's plains.
Their defeat was proud Rome's gain.

Next came Achilles.

In war's own furnace I was forged,
And on my enemies' blood I've gorged.
A son of Ares, made for glory,
All quake to hear Achilles's story.

Then it was Genghis Khan's turn.

A Mongol conqueror without equal
A warrior king, a god to his people—

"Oh, *enough!*" declared a voice from offstage.

Isabelle looked for its source. She saw the curtain at the right ripple, then heard sharp, indignant footsteps. A few seconds later, a woman emerged from the wings.

She was slender and straight-backed, with vivid red hair styled high on her head. A stiff lace collar framed her face. She wore a white gown embroidered with pearls, emeralds, and rubies. In one jeweled hand, she carried a bucket of a paint; in the other, a brush.

Peter the Great stepped forward. He puffed out his chest. "Who are *you*, madam?" he demanded.

"Elizabeth the first. Move," she said, waving him and the others aside with her paintbrush.

Flabbergasted and sputtering, they did as she bade, half shuffling to the right side of the stage, half to the left.

Elizabeth walked through the path they'd cleared and up to the towering book. She kicked the cover with a well-shod foot. It slammed shut. Then she dipped her brush into the bucket, crossed out the word *History*, dipped the brush again, and wrote *HER STORY* in its place.

## – NINETY-FOUR –

Isabelle sat forward in her chair, mesmerized.

"This wasn't in the book," she whispered.

As she watched, Elizabeth walked to the front of the stage and addressed her.

"I am the daughter of England's Henry the eighth," she said. "I was a disappointment to him because I was not the son he wished for. I survived his neglect, my half sister's hatred, attacks on my country and attempts on my life to become the best monarch England has ever seen." She smiled smugly, then added, "Or ever will."

The book receded. The footlights blazed again. The actors playing Scipio and his fellows crouched low, using their hands to cast shadows of horses and knights on the walls.

A din rose of shouted commands, shrill whinnies, a fanfare. There was a cannon blast, a flash of light, and then the theater's left wall fell flat to the ground with a boom, followed by its right. The back wall fell next, carrying the arch with it. And then, before Isabelle's astonished eyes, the shadows came to life. Warhorses in chain mail stomped and snorted. Officers sat astride them. Soldiers massed next to them, carrying bows, pikes, swords, and halberds. The oak-sheltered clearing became an army camp on the banks of the river Thames.

And Elizabeth, standing in a gown only a moment ago, now rode in on a white charger, wearing a steel breastplate. She held her reins in one hand, a sword in the other. Her red hair streamed down her back.

"Tilbury camp, 1588!" she shouted at Isabelle. "The Spanish king sends his armada, the most powerful naval force in the world, to invade my country. His nephew the Duke of Parma joins him. They have fearsome warships, troops, and weapons." She grinned. "But England has *me*!"

She spurred her horse on and rode to her troops.

"My loving people!" she addressed them. "I am come amongst you . . . being resolved, in the midst and heat of the battle, to live and die amongst you all; to lay down for God, and for my kingdom, and my people, my honor, and my blood, even in the dust!"

As Isabelle watched, spellbound, the Thames swelled into a roiling blue sea and a naval battle commenced. Swift English warships fired broadsides at the Spanish vessels. Cannons boomed. Ships burned. Smoke billowed. When it finally cleared, the armada had been routed. England was victorious.

The scene changed. Bells pealed as Elizabeth rode through the streets of London. Roses were strewn in her path. She reached Isabelle and dismounted. A groom led her horse away; the cheers died down. "The victory was England's greatest, and mine," Elizabeth said. "But there are more battles. More wars. More victories. Not told in any book."

She waved her hand. Trumpets blared. And then a woman walked out of the trees toward her. And then another. And another. Until there were dozens. Scores. Hundreds. When they had all assembled, Elizabeth introduced them one by one.

"Yennenga, a Dagomba princess," she announced, and a young

Ghanaian woman, wearing a tunic and pants of woven red, black, and white cloth, stepped forward. She was carrying a javelin. London gave way to lush plains. Two lions walked out of the tall grass and sat at either side of her.

"I commanded my own battalion and fought against my country's enemies," she said. "No one could match me on a horse."

She threw her javelin high. It pierced the night sky and exploded into a silvery fountain of shooting stars.

Isabelle could hardly breathe, she was so excited. All her life, she'd been told that women rulers were only figureheads, that women did not fight or lead soldiers in war. She stood on her chair, the better to see these remarkable creatures.

"Abbakka Chowta," Elizabeth said as a young woman from India wearing a pink silk sari walked to the center of the stage. "A woman who shot flaming arrows from her saddle, a woman so brave she was named Abhaya Rani, the fearless queen."

Abhaya Rani nocked an arrow into the bow she was carrying, aimed for the sky, and released it. It burst into brilliant blue flames. She smiled at Isabelle. "I fought my country's invaders for forty years. I was captured but died as I lived, fighting for freedom."

Isabelle thought her heart might burst. One by one, queens, pirates, empresses, and generals from all the corners of the world told their stories, bowed their heads, and left the stage.

They were not pretty, these women. Pretty did not begin to describe them.

They were shrewd. Powerful. Wily. Proud. Dangerous.

They were strong.

They were brave.

They were beautiful.

Finally, after what felt to Isabelle like only minutes, but was actually hours, only Elizabeth was left on the stage.

"Strange, isn't it, how stories that are never told are the ones we most need to hear," she said, then she bowed, too, and walked off into the darkness.

Isabelle realized the play was ending. "No," she whispered hungrily. "Don't go."

The marquis, still wearing his mask, reappeared. In one hand, he held a heavy silver candlestick with a flaming taper in it. He stepped forward and began to speak.

> Now our queens have told their stories,
> Of battles won, of conquests, glories.
> But power is a treacherous thing,
> Its bite is sweet, its kiss can sting,
> And, unless I'm much mistaken,
> It's never given, always taken.
>
> Each queen was once a girl like you.
> Told who to be and what to do.
> Not pretty, not pleasing, far too rough.
> Lacking, less than, not enough.
>
> Till wounded subjects, anguished dead,
> Mattered more than things that others said.
> Then, like a flag, her will unfurled.
> Go now, girl. Remake the world.

The marquis bowed. He raised his candle to his lips and blew it out.

Most of the footlights had burned out, a few still glowed faintly. In their light, Isabelle could see that the marquis and his players were gone.

270

The stage was empty and silent. All Isabelle could hear was the sound of her heart beating.

The spell of the play was broken. Isabelle looked around and realized she was still standing on the chair. She stepped down, her hands clenched. The excitement and wonder and sheer joy she'd felt only moments ago ebbed away. Grief, agonizing and deep, filled the void it left.

"Why show me this?" she shouted wretchedly to the darkness. "Why show me something I can never have? Something I can never be?"

No one was there. Isabelle was talking to herself.

She unhooked Nelson's pearls from around her neck and placed them on the seat of the velvet chair where he would be sure to find them.

A moment later, she and Nero were galloping back over the marquis's grounds. Just before she disappeared into the woods, Isabelle looked back. At the ruined stage. The dark château.

"Damn you," she whispered. *"Damn you."*

## – NINETY-FIVE –

Tavi stretched tall, then bent to unknot her skirts.

"When I leave here, I never want to see another cabbage as long as I live," she said.

Isabelle agreed with her. The day in the field, harvesting under the hot sun, had been long and exhausting. Isabelle's dress was soaked with sweat. Her boots were filthy from treading in the black dirt. She was looking forward to dunking herself in the duck pond, and later, falling into her hayloft bed.

She'd been tired all day. Last night had been unrestful. She'd had such a strange dream. Nelson had appeared in the hayloft. Then she'd taken a midnight ride to the Château Rigolade, where the marquis and his friends had presented a play.

The dream had felt so real, but it wasn't. It couldn't be. All those women . . . leading armies into battle, fighting for their realms . . . they were merely a fantasy cooked up by her vivid imagination, that's all. A fond childhood wish.

"You need a pistol. We didn't think of that. You're three women traveling alone."

Hugo, who had been working one field over, digging potatoes, had joined Isabelle and Tavi. His words dispelled the lingering images of Isabelle's dream.

"If there are three of us, then we're not alone," Tavi said.

Hugo looked at her as if she were an idiot. "You don't have a man with you. Of course you're alone. You can buy a secondhand pistol in the village while we're at the market tomorrow. Use some of Felix's money. You'll need gunpowder and bullets, too."

Tavi picked up her knife and the basket she used to carry cabbages to the wagon. Isabelle did the same. Hugo rested his spade on his shoulder, and together the three walked to the barn, talking about their secret plan the whole way. Isabelle and Tavi would leave in three days, and there was still a good deal to do.

As they rounded the side of the farmhouse, Isabelle's head was bent toward Tavi; she was concentrating on what her sister was saying. Her gaze was on the ground.

Had she been paying more attention, she might've seen the signs of trouble up ahead.

The many hoofprints in the dirt.

The blur of blue uniforms by the stables.

The tall, imperious Colonel Cafard eyeing the horse that had been brought from the pasture on his command.

A black horse. Her horse.

Nero.

## NINETY-SIX

It was only when Isabelle rounded the corner of the barn that she real-ized something was very wrong.

Nero was in the yard in front of it, wearing his bridle. He was wild-eyed and rearing. A young soldier was struggling to hold on to his lead.

"Let go of him!" Isabelle shouted. She ran to the man and snatched the lead from his hands.

The soldier hadn't seen her coming. He stumbled backward, star-tled, and fell on his rear end. There were others with him. They hooted and laughed. Tantine, Avara, and Maman were standing together nearby, worried expressions on their faces.

"Looks like the girl's even feistier than the horse!" one of the soldiers shouted. "Maybe she needs a good crack across the backside, too!"

Isabelle whirled on him. "*Too?* Did you hit my horse, you jackass?"

The soldier stopped laughing. His eyes turned mean. "Maybe she needs a good crack across the mouth," he said. "And maybe I'm just the one to give it to her."

"Isabelle!" Tavi called out, alarmed. She'd caught up with her. Hugo was close on her heels.

But Isabelle didn't hear her. She was focused on her adversary. Still gripping Nero's lead, she took a step toward the man.

"Maybe you are. Get a crop. I'll get one, too. We'll find out." When the soldier made no move, she cocked her head. "Scared? I'll make it a fair fight. I'll tie one hand behind my back."

A ripple of laughter rose from the others.

"Hey, isn't she one of the ugly stepsisters?" the one who'd fallen on his backside called out.

"It's her. She's ugly all right," said the one Isabelle had challenged.

The familiar shame seared Isabelle, but this time she didn't blush. She didn't lower her head. She looked him in the eye and said, "Every bit as ugly as a man who beats a defenseless animal."

"Isabelle, *please!*" Tavi hissed.

Isabelle ignored her. "Why are you here? What were you doing with my horse?" she asked her antagonist.

Another man, one wearing a bicorne hat and black boots that were so shiny, he could see his own reflection in the toes when he looked down at them—which he did quite often—stepped forward. "I'm afraid he's my horse now, mademoiselle," he said.

Isabelle looked him up and down. "Who the devil are you?" she asked, tightening her grip on Nero's lead.

Tantine was immediately at her side. "This is Colonel Cafard, Isabelle, the officer in charge of the army camp near the village."

"That doesn't give him the right to take my horse," Isabelle said.

"Actually, it does," the colonel said. "The army is short of mounts. They're the first thing the enemy shoots at. We're commandeering any sound animal we can find."

"By whose orders?" Isabelle asked, panic rising inside her.

"The king's," the colonel replied, clearly growing tired of the exchange. "Will that do?"

"Enough, Isabelle!" Tantine hissed. "Give the creature up before we're all hauled off to jail!" She pried the lead from Isabelle's fist and handed it to a soldier. Then she pulled her away. "We're at war, you foolish girl!" she scolded.

Isabelle twisted free of her grasp. She ran to Cafard, ready to plead, ready to drop down on her knees and beg him not to take her horse. Let his soldiers laugh and jeer. She didn't care. All she could see in her mind's eye was her beloved horse falling on a battlefield, his side ripped open by a bullet.

"Please, Colonel," she said, pressing her hands together. "Please don't—"

And then Tantine was beside her again, sinking her fingers into Isabelle's arm, her grip as strong as iron. "Please don't let Volkmar win," she said, drowning her out. "Use the horse to defeat him. We are honored to help our king."

Cafard gave her a curt nod. Then he strode off toward his own mount, a cowed-looking chestnut mare. The horse shied slightly as he swung himself into his saddle. Isabelle's expert eyes swept over the animal, looking for a reason. She soon found it. There was blood on the mare's sides, behind the stirrups. She looked at Cafard; he was wearing sharp silver spurs. Isabelle's heart lurched.

"Colonel!" she cried, running after him.

Cafard turned. His brittle smile couldn't hide his irritation. "Yes?"

"Please don't use spurs on him. He listens if you're kind to him. And he'll do anything for an apple. He loves them."

Cafard's smile thinned. "My men love apples, too. They rarely get them these days, yet they still do what I tell them." He nodded at Nero. "That creature is a horse, mademoiselle, and he will be treated like one. Intractable animals must be made tractable."

Nero whinnied loudly; he tossed his head, trying yet again to tear the lead away from the soldier holding it. When that didn't work, he spun around and kicked at him.

An image flashed into Isabelle's head. Of Elizabeth on her white charger. Of Abhaya Rani, shooting flaming arrows from astride her mount. Neither woman would have let *anyone* take her horse.

"He's hungry, sir," she said. "He usually gets his supper now. If you let me feed him, he'll be manageable for the trip to your camp."

Cafard looked at the unruly horse and at his men stumbling over themselves as they tried to get him under control.

"You have ten minutes," Cafard said. Then he barked at his men to hand the horse over to her.

Isabelle whispered to Nero to calm him. Head down, she led him to the stables.

Had the soldiers seen the determined set of her mouth and the fire in her eyes, they never would have let her.

## - NINETY-SEVEN -

Isabelle walked to the barn at a normal pace. To do anything else would raise suspicion.

The barn had two large doorways—the one *she* and Nero had just passed through, and one directly across from it that led out to the pasture. A large open area spanned the space between the two doors. To the right of it were horse stalls; to the left, stanchions for the cows.

Isabelle walked slowly, veering a little to the right, as if she were going to lead Nero into a stall. As she did, she cast a casual glance over her shoulder. Three of the soldiers were talking to the colonel. A few were milling about. One was watching her. She caught his gaze; he held it. She wiped her eyes, hoping to appear as if she were crying. It worked. The soldier, embarrassed, turned back to his companions.

Within seconds, she and Nero were through the far door. She tensed as they walked out of the barn, expecting to hear shouts or the sound of footsteps. But it was quiet. No one had seen them.

An old milk can stood under the eaves of the barn. Isabelle used it as a mounting block. Once on Nero's back, she knotted the loose end of his lead into his halter. It would serve as reins. There was no time to get proper ones, or his bridle and saddle. When she was finished with the knot, she quietly urged Nero forward. He was across the hardpan that separated the barn from the pasture in a few strides.

Isabelle knew that as long as she kept the barn between herself and the soldiers, they could not see her ride off. Anger, blind and beyond reason, drove her. Nero was *hers*; she would not allow Cafard to take him.

She gripped his improvised reins and clucked her tongue. As if he understood her purpose, Nero jumped the wooden fence that enclosed the pasture and landed almost noiselessly in the grass.

Isabelle touched her heels to his sides, and he was off. Within seconds, he reached the far side of the pasture. He sailed over the fence again, and then they were streaking across a wide meadow to the forest. She looked back, just for an instant, as they reached the tree line. No one was after her. Not yet. She probably had another minute or two before Cafard told one of his men to see what was taking her so long, but it was already too late; they'd never find her. They didn't know the Wildwood like she did.

Isabelle faced forward now. The woods were dense and navigating them commanded all her attention. Her hands were shaking, her heart pounding.

She was headed to the Devil's Hollow.

## - NINETY-EIGHT -

Some people are afraid of the forest; others only feel truly safe under its sheltering canopy.

Isabelle was among the latter. The sights and scents of the forest were familiar and comforting to her. She had spent the happiest days of her life in the Wildwood.

After she and Nero had escaped, they'd ridden hard through the trees for a good half hour to put distance between themselves and Colonel Cafard; then Isabelle had dismounted, unknotted the makeshift reins, and walked the horse. Dusk was falling as they reached the path that would take them into the Devil's Hollow. Isabelle wanted to be down in the Hollow before dark. The path was treacherous when you could see it, suicide when you couldn't.

The Wildwood covered the gently sloping south side of a small mountain and abruptly gave way to the mountain's craggy, cliff-laden north side. The narrow path to the Hollow zigzagged down the north face, obscured in parts by thorny, scrubby shrubs. It snaked through rocks and boulders at the bottom, and ended at a river. It had once been used by travelers to Saint-Michel, but as the village had grown, and the roads leading to it had improved, the path through the Devil's Hollow had fallen out of use.

Isabelle and Nero picked their way carefully down the path and through the rocks. When they finally reached the river, Isabelle's stomach growled loudly. She realized that she hadn't eaten anything since noon, and it had to be nearly eight by now. Nero hadn't eaten his nightly ration of oats. Nor would he, for she hadn't packed any. She had no food and no money with which to buy some. Felix's money was back in the hayloft. So were all the provisions she and Tavi had managed to assemble. She reached into her pocket, hoping against hope that she'd stuffed a crust of bread in it. Instead, her hand found Tanaquill's gifts. The seedpod pricked her fingers.

Something else pricked her, too—her conscience. She was walking slowly to make sure Nero could find his footing, but now she stopped, racked by an agonizing uncertainty.

"What have I done?" she said aloud.

She'd been so determined to save Nero's life that never for a second had she considered what impact her rash actions might have on anyone else's. She'd tricked a colonel of the French army. What if he took his wrath out on her family? Or the LeBenêts and Tantine?

Isabelle saw that she'd let her anger drive her actions, once again. Just as she had with Ella. The baker's wife. The orphans. She'd been selfish. She didn't want Nero to die, but there were mothers, wives, and children who didn't want their sons, husbands, and fathers to die, either. Men were giving their lives to the fight; Felix might well give his.

Groaning, she buried her face in Nero's neck. She wanted to be a better person. She wanted to change, yet here she was, endangering people who needed her, running away from her responsibilities.

"I have to go back," she said, her heart heavy. It was the right thing, the only thing, to do.

It was just as those words left her lips that she heard the voices, drifting toward her across the river, from deep within the trees.

She stood perfectly still, listening. Fear plucked at her nerves. Were the old ones right? Was the Hollow haunted? Or could it be a band of outlaws or deserters?

Or maybe the voices belonged to Cafard's men, out hunting for her? No, that wasn't possible. There was another way to get to the Hollow, but it involved a long ride around the mountain on a narrow, rutted road. It was unlikely his soldiers could've gotten down it so quickly.

Isabelle waited for the voices to speak again, but Nero's breathing was the only sound she could hear.

"Stay here, boy," she said, looping his lead over his neck.

She ventured closer to the water and looked across it. In the dying light, she could make out the far riverbank, and the dense line of trees along it, but nothing else. Here and there leaves rustled, but that could be the breeze. Just when she'd convinced herself she'd imagined the voices, she heard them again. And then the strong smell of tobacco wafted to her.

Isabelle had never seen a ghost. She did not know much about them, but she was certain of one thing: Ghosts did not smoke cigars.

## – NINETY-NINE –

Nelson crept quietly through the partly open window.

He dropped down to the bench underneath it, then cast an anxious glance back at Chance.

"Go!" Chance mouthed at him from outside the window. "Fetch the map!"

He could see it, open on Fate's table, from where he stood; the skull at the bottom was as black as ebony.

Fate, busy digging in her trunk, her back turned to the window, didn't see the little creature scamper across the floor.

But Losca, roosting on top of the wardrobe, did.

With an ugly shriek, she launched herself at him. The monkey jumped from the floor to the bed. The raven wheeled about and flew at him again. Nelson rolled across the bed, dodging her, then threw himself on her back.

Fate whirled around. Her eyes went to the tangled animals.

"What on *earth*—" she started to say, but a high, rusty screech cut her off. It was the hinge on the casement window. Chance had just climbed through it. He rushed to the table and the map laying rolled up upon it. But Fate got there first. She stood in front of it, blocking him, a long silver stiletto in her hand.

"Step aside. I don't want to fight you," Chance warned.

A vicious smile twisted Fate's lips. She snapped her wrist and a split second later, the stiletto was flying straight at his heart.

Chance pivoted to the right. The stiletto sank with a *thuk* into the wall behind him. He was about to advance again, but at that instant, a fox leapt through the window. She lunged at the fighting animals. The monkey, terrified, catapulted himself into Chance's arms. The raven flew high, circled the room, then landed back on top of the wardrobe.

Growling and snapping, the fox jumped onto Fate's table. With a sweep of her tail, she sent Fate's inks flying. Bottles smashed on the floor; lurid colors seeped into the cracks between the boards. She dropped to the floor again, and a few seconds later, a woman stood where the fox had been, clutching the map in her hand.

"*Enough,*" Tanaquill said, tucking the parchment deep within the folds of her cloak.

"That map is mine," Fate said, starting toward her. "Give it to me."

Tanaquill bared her teeth, snarling. "Come, crone. Take it," she dared her.

Chance stepped forward. "Keep the map, Tanaquill. But help Isabelle. Save her."

"The girl will make her next move herself. Neither of you will make it for her. There is only one person who can save Isabelle now . . . Isabelle."

With a swirl of red, she was through the open window and gone. Fate and Chance were left standing by themselves.

Chance pulled the stiletto out of the wall. He handed it back to Fate. She put it down on the table, then looked around the room, at the havoc Tanaquill had wreaked. Losca was already down off the wardrobe, in her human form, cleaning up the broken glass.

"I have a bottle of port," Fate said with a sigh. "At least the fairy queen did not break that."

"A good vintage?"

"I am too old to drink bad ones."

281

Chance rocked back on his heels, weighing her offer. "I *do* enjoy a good port."

Fate crossed the room and dug in her trunk once more. A pair of hand-blown goblets emerged. A porcelain platter. The port. A box of dried figs dipped in dark chocolate. Roasted almonds flecked with salt. A hunk of crumbly Parmesan wrapped in waxed cloth.

"Do something useful," Fate said. "Pull the chairs up to the fire."

One chair, squat, with soft cushions was already near the fireplace. Chance pushed it closer; then he carried over the wooden chair that stood by the table. He spied a stool and positioned it between them. Fate arranged the treats on the platter and set it on the stool. She poured two glasses of port and handed one to Chance.

"This changes nothing," she cautioned. "No quarter asked—"

"None given," Chance finished.

"The skull is jet black. I doubt she will survive the night."

"As long as she still breathes, there is hope," said Chance defiantly.

Fate shook her head, muttering about fools and dreamers, but the two ancient adversaries sat down by the fire and enjoyed a brief truce in their eternal war. They drank a toast to foolish humans, who stumbled and fell, made more wrong choices than right ones, who broke their own hearts again and again but somehow managed to do one or two things right, fine port and good Parmesan among them.

And out in the darkness, the fox ran, carrying the map in her mouth. Across the fields and over the stone walls she loped, through the tall grass and the brambles, until she came to a burned-out ruin and the linden tree that stood by it.

She dropped the map down into the hollow at the tree's base, then turned and sat, watching and waiting. Her thoughts were silent, known only to herself. But she sent them Isabelle's way.

Stop burdening the gods. Stop cursing the devil. They will make no path for you. They gave you their dark gifts: reason and will. Now you must make your own way.

What's done is done. Whether to you, or by you, and you cannot change it.

But what's not done is not done.

And there, both hope and hazard lie.

Believe that you can make your way. Or don't. Either way, you are right.

Every war is different, yet each battle is the same. The enemy is only a distraction. The thing you are fighting against, always, is yourself.

## – ONE HUNDRED –

"I'll be right back, Nero. Stay here and don't budge," Isabelle whispered.

She wanted to know who was in the Hollow. It was close to Saint-Michel and her family, and outlaws and deserters were dangerous. One had stolen from her and almost killed her.

Isabelle knotted her skirts up and waded into the water. Luckily it wasn't too high, only up to her knees. Her boots were getting soaked, and the slipper Felix had made for her, too, but she didn't dare remove them and leave them on the bank. Without them, she moved slowly, and she might need to run. When she reached the other side, she scrambled up the bank, which was steep and loamy. She grabbed gnarled tree roots to pull herself up it. She was careful to be quiet as she climbed, not wanting to alert anyone to her presence. As she reached the top of the bank and peered over it, she sucked in a sharp breath. Before her were tents, hundreds of them. Not in neat rows but dotted over the ground. They were made of dark cloth and blended in perfectly with the trees.

Then she saw men. They were wearing uniforms. Talking in low voices. Cleaning rifles. Sharpening bayonets.

*There must be a thousand of them. Are they the king's army? What are they doing here?* she wondered.

Snatches of conversations drifted over to her, but they were so broken, they made no sense.

After a few minutes, though, she was able to piece the fragments together, and they did. And then terror squeezed the breath out of her.

The men were an army, yes, but not the king's army.

They were Volkmar's.

## – ONE HUNDRED ONE –

Isabelle dashed for cover behind a large tree, her heart thumping.

After a few seconds, she peered out from it and bit back a cry. One of the soldiers was heading right for her, a glowing cigar clamped in his teeth. Had he seen her? She ducked behind the tree again, trying to make herself as small as possible.

The man stopped just short of her hiding place. Then he planted his feet in the dirt and relieved himself. Isabelle didn't move; she didn't breathe.

While he was still hosing down the other side of the tree, several of his fellow soldiers called to him. Isabelle heard the name Volkmar over and over. The men's voices were low but excited.

Finally, the soldier buttoned his trousers and rejoined his friends. Isabelle's entire body sagged with relief. She risked another peek at the enemy's camp. Every soldier was hurrying from his tent to the center of the camp.

*Why?* she wondered. *What's happening?*

Isabelle knew she should run. She should get away while she had the chance. What could she possibly do? She was alone. Defenseless. Just a girl.

*Like Elizabeth*, a voice inside her said. *Like Yennenga. Abhaya Rhani. They were just girls once, too.*

She stepped out from behind the tree and, crouching low, made her way between the tents into the heart of the enemy encampment.

Inside her, the wolf stopped gnawing. He became still. Tensed. Ready.

## – ONE HUNDRED TWO –

They were gathered in a large circle, several rows deep.

A man was standing in the center, speaking. Isabelle couldn't see him—the soldiers blocked her view—but she could hear him.

*If someone sees me . . . If I'm caught . . .*, fear yammered at her.

She silenced it and tried to figure out how to get closer.

There was a boulder up ahead. She would be able to see over the men if she climbed it, but if one of them turned around, he would see her, too. Then she spotted a pine tree. Its lower branches were bare, but the upper ones were thickly needled. If she got up high enough, she could see without being seen. A tent, wood-framed, larger than the others, stood near the tree. It would block her from view as she made her way up the trunk.

It had been years since Isabelle had scaled a tree, but it came right back to her. She made her way up through the branches easily and silently, just as she had when she and Felix were pretending to climb the mast of Blackbeard's ship. Higher and higher she climbed. When she was certain no one could see her, she slowly pressed down on a branch, lowering it slightly to give herself an unobstructed view.

Several lanterns had been placed in the center of the circle. The light they gave illuminated a man wearing a tricorne hat. His dark hair, shot through with gray, was tied in a ponytail underneath it. A traveling cloak swirled about him as he moved. He was tall and broad-shouldered with a commanding stride. A scar ran down one cheek. Lantern light glittered in his violent eyes.

*Volkmar*, she said silently, her heart nearly shuddering to a stop.

*He's here.*

## – ONE HUNDRED THREE –

Isabelle sat motionless, watching as Volkmar talked.

He was telling his men to attack Saint-Michel. They were going to slaughter every last person in the village, like they'd done in Malleval. That's why there were so many of them.

Volkmar finished talking and swept his arm out before him. As he did, another man appeared. He stood at the edge of the lantern's light, flanked by half a dozen of Volkmar's soldiers.

Isabelle's hand came up to her mouth. *No*, she thought. *God help us, no.*

It was the grand duke.

Dread bloomed in her belly; its dark vines twined around her heart. Volkmar's forces had taken him. They must've ambushed him as he was coming or going from Paris to Cafard's camp. How else would they have captured him? What were they going to do with him? Torture him? Execute him? He was one of the most powerful men in the realm. Only the king outranked him.

As Isabelle watched, breathless, Volkmar von Bruch strode up to the grand duke.

And embraced him.

Isabelle felt as if she were made of ice. Her heart had frozen. The blood was solid in her veins. Her breath was frost. If she moved a muscle, she would shatter.

The grand duke, who was sworn to protect king and country, was in league with Volkmar von Bruch. Volkmar, who had slaughtered thousands of French soldiers. Who had burned towns, killed fleeing people.

Isabelle thought of her family. Felix. Her village. She thought of Remy, and the silver cross he'd given her, and his friend Claude, and all the other young soldiers who might never go home again.

She watched, stone-faced, as Volkmar's soldiers raised their fists in a noiseless salute to their leader and to the grand duke. She watched as the soldiers walked back to their tents, the fire of war glowing in their faces, as Volkmar and the grand duke made their way to Volkmar's tent—the tent at the base of the very tree she was in—and sat down in the two canvas chairs in front of it. She watched as a young private appeared with lanterns, a box of cigars, a decanter of brandy, and two crystal glasses.

The fear was gone. Isabelle felt only one emotion now—a cold, lethal fury. It didn't control her now, though; she controlled it. She let it help her instead of hurt her.

Slowly, she climbed down the tree, as silent as a shadow, lowering one bare foot to a branch, then another, without disturbing so much as a single pine needle.

Lower and lower she climbed, until she was only a yard above their heads. And then she listened.

"To France's new Lord Protector," Volkmar said, touching his glass to the grand duke's. "As soon as I defeat the king, the country will be mine and you will rule it for me."

Smiling, the grand duke bowed his head. Then he handed Volkmar a rolled parchment. "A gift."

Volkmar took it, broke the red wax seal—the king of France's seal—and unrolled it.

"A map . . ." he said, his eyes roving over the document.

"Showing the size and location of every battalion the king has left."

"Well done!" Volkmar exclaimed. "This will make hunting them all down much easier." He took a deep swallow of his brandy. "Is everything in order for tomorrow?"

"It is. You will attack Cafard's camp at dusk. He just sent four regiments to Paris and has only one left. After you kill his remaining troops, go to the field hospital and kill the wounded. I've no use for them. Leave Cafard alive, of course, and take him prisoner for appearance's sake. We'll reward him when the war is over. He's been a loyal ally."

Volkmar looked at the map again. "The civilians of Saint-Michel . . . will they put up a fight?"

The grand duke chuckled. "With what? Wooden spoons? I've been riding up and down the countryside, asking them to donate any weapons they had to the war effort. They're completely defenseless."

The young private, Volkmar's manservant, appeared again. Volkmar handed him the map and asked him to take it inside his tent, then bring them some food.

"I want to move swiftly on the king's other garrisons as soon as we're finished in Saint-Michel. Take them one by one until we get to the king himself," said Volkmar.

"I say take the king first. He'll surrender and that will break the spirit of any surviving troops."

"What if he doesn't?"

"He will. I'm certain of it. Don't forget that we have a very valuable bargaining chip."

Volkmar arched an eyebrow. "You're not terribly fond of your young sovereign, are you?"

The grand duke's expression soured. "The king is a fool. He had his pick of princesses from esteemed royal houses and he married a kitchen girl. He allows her to persist in her idiotic missions—caring for the wounded, housing orphans in the homes of the nobility—when it would be so much less of a burden on the crown's coffers to simply let them die. My own château is swarming with peasant brats." He shook his head disgustedly. "The king has demeaned the crown. While he fights in the field, a lowborn girl sits on the throne of France. Worse yet, the heir to the throne will have the blood of a commoner running in his veins."

"That's not a worry," Volkmar said. "The king's days are numbered. He will not live long enough to sire a child."

The grand duke drained his glass. "Unless he already has."

Volkmar was silent as he leaned forward to pour more brandy for his guest. Then he sat back in his chair and said, "I can have no heirs to challenge my claim to the throne. You know what that means."

The grand duke took a sip of his drink, then lifted his eyes to Volkmar's. "It means the queen must die, too."

## – ONE HUNDRED FIVE –

Isabelle climbed up to a higher branch and sat down, her back against the trunk, her hands wrapped around smaller branches, her feet dangling.

It is said of great commanders that their blood runs cold in the fiery hell of battle. That the cannons' roar, the screams of the dying, the smoke and sweat and blood, only serve to sharpen their perception, the better to see where advantage lies.

Isabelle felt that clarity now.

She was in a tree, only yards above two bloodthirsty men who would kill her without a second thought if they were to discover her, yet she sat quietly, calmly considered her options, and determined the way forward.

Volkmar wanted to kill the king, and the queen, too; she had to find a way to stop him. She could try again to get to Paris and see Ella, or to get to the king and tell him what she'd learned, but she had no idea how she would do that, or if either of them would believe her if she did somehow manage to gain access to them.

A memory surfaced in Isabelle's mind now, like a fish jumping in a lake. She was back at the Maison Douleur. Blood dripped into the dirt from her maimed foot. The grand duke was walking toward Ella, carrying the glass slipper on a velvet cushion when he suddenly stumbled and dropped it. Isabelle remembered the sound of it shattering. It was an accident, he said. Except it wasn't. He tripped on purpose; she'd seen it.

Because he didn't want Ella to marry the prince. Because she wasn't highborn. She wasn't good enough. Ella, who was kind and good. Ella, who was more beautiful than the sun. With a few cold words, the grand duke had defined her and dismissed her.

Then Isabelle heard another voice: the old merchant's voice. He had done the same thing to *her*. He'd called her ugly. Defined her before she ever had a chance to define herself. In the space of a moment, he'd decided everything she was and ever would be.

But now Isabelle saw something she'd never seen before—that the merchant hadn't acted alone. He'd had an accomplice—she, herself.

She'd listened to him. She'd believed him. She'd let him tell her who she was. And after him, Maman, suitors, the grand duke, Cecile, the baker's wife, the villagers of Saint-Michel.

"They cut away pieces of me," she whispered in the darkness. "But I handed them the knife."

The merchant's voice still echoed in her head. Others joined it.

. . . *just a girl . . . ugly little monkey . . . ugly stepsister . . . strong . . . unruly . . . mean . . .*

Isabelle sat, listening to the voices, trying so hard to hear her own.

And then she did. *The map,* it said. *You have to get the map.*

The voice was not shrill or fearful. It was clear and calm and seemed to come from the very core of her being. Isabelle recognized it. When she was a child, it was the only voice she'd ever heard. It had never led her astray then, and it didn't now.

If she got the map, she could stop Volkmar's attack. She would read it, then ride like the wind to the closest loyal army encampment. The camp's commander would certainly want to know how she'd come into the possession of a secret map with the king's seal on it. She would tell him, and he would send his troops to Saint-Michel's rescue. She had until tomorrow, at dusk. That's when Volkmar was going to attack.

Volkmar's servant had put the map inside his tent. Isabelle knew she had to get into the tent, snatch it, and get out again. Looking down, she saw that Volkmar and the grand duke were still deep in conversation. Volkmar's servant had set up a table for them outside the tent and had brought them supper. They weren't even halfway through it.

*It's now or never*, she thought, then she climbed the rest of the way down the tree. Crouching low, she crept to the back of the tent. She listened for a moment, to make sure no one was inside it, then lifted the canvas flap and ducked under it. A large campaign table stood in the middle of the space. Spread across it were quills, an inkpot, letters, a telescope . . . and the map.

Her heart leapt. *You can do this*, she told herself. *Just take it and go.*

She'd been so focused on finding the map that her eyes had gone straight to the table instead of sweeping around. As she dashed toward it, a movement to her right caught her eye. She stopped dead, her heart in her mouth.

There, sitting on a canvas cot, her wrists bound, her mouth cruelly gagged, was a girl. Isabelle's eyes widened. She took a step toward her.

Then she whispered one word.

*"Ella?"*

## - ONE HUNDRED SIX -

Isabelle half dropped, half skidded to her knees by the cot. She fumbled the knot out of Ella's gag.

"Isabelle!" Ella whispered, choking back a sob.

"What happened? How did you get here?" Isabelle whispered back, horrified to see her stepsister tied up like an animal.

"The grand duke," Ella said. "He and his guards were supposed to be escorting me to a manor east of Saint-Michel. I was going to see if it could house war orphans. Halfway there, we turned off the road. He ordered his men to bind me and bring me here. Volkmar—"

"I know," Isabelle said grimly. "I heard him and the grand duke talking. I'm going to get the king's map. Then we're going to leave."

"How, Isabelle?" Ella asked. "There are hundreds of soldiers in this camp!"

"I got in. I can get out."

"But my restraints . . ." Ella lifted her hands. She tried to say more but dissolved into sobs again.

Isabelle took her face in her hands. "Listen to me, Ella," she said sternly. "You need to trust me. You have no reason to, I know, but I'll get you out of here. I promise. I—"

"Where is that blasted boy? No matter, I'll fetch it myself . . ." a voice bellowed.

It was coming from right outside the tent. And belonged to Volkmar.

## - ONE HUNDRED SEVEN -

*Simple is the opposite of hard*, Isabelle thought. *Easy is also the opposite of hard. But simple is not the same as easy. Not at all. I bet Tavi has a theorem for that.*

Isabelle was babbling to herself. Silently. To calm her crashing heart. To force her lungs to pull air in. To distract herself from the fact that Volkmar von Bruch's big black boots were only inches from her face.

What she had to do was simple—get Ella and herself out of here— but it was far from easy. And Volkmar coming into the tent had just made it ten times harder.

The instant she'd heard his voice, she'd put the gag back on Ella. Then she'd dived under the cot and pulled her skirts in after herself. She'd frozen, barely breathing, as he'd opened the tent flap and walked in.

"Ah, Your Highness. Comfortable, are we? No? Well, you won't have to endure it for much longer. Tomorrow the grand duke and I attack your husband's encampment and barter your life for his surrender. Of course, I have no intention of upholding my end of the deal. But don't worry. Neither of you will suffer. The men on my firing squad have excellent aim."

*A very valuable bargaining chip*, the grand duke had said. That chip was Ella.

Isabelle's hands knotted into fists. She could smell Volkmar—alcohol, sweat, and the greasy mutton he'd just eaten.

"Now, where is that brandy?" Isabelle heard him say. Then, "Ah! There it is!"

Volkmar left the tent. In a flash, Isabelle was out from under the cot and on her feet. She unknotted Ella's gag again, then found a dagger on the table and used it to slice through the ropes binding her wrists and ankles. Ella stood unsteadily.

"Walk!" Isabelle whispered. "Get the feeling back in your feet! Hurry!"

While Ella took a few steps, Isabelle snatched the map off the table and rolled it up. As she did, a document that had been lying underneath it caught her eye. It was another map—one that showed the locations of Volkmar's troops. Isabelle's pulse raced as she saw it. This would turn the tables on Volkmar and that viper of a grand duke.

She rolled the second map around the first one, then silently beckoned to Ella. The two girls slipped out of the tent the way Isabelle had come in. Once outside, Isabelle held a finger to her lips and listened. The camp was quiet. The gathering for Volkmar and the grand duke had broken up. Most of the soldiers were in their tents—most, but not all. Some still moved between the rows. Isabelle could hear them talking.

When she was certain no one was nearby, she took Ella's hand and started off. Staying low, they hurried, ducking behind the tents, careful to avoid any twigs, eyes peeled for movement. They had to double back and find a new route when a tent flap opened and a soldier put his boots outside, and again when they nearly ran out in front of a group of men smoking under a tree.

Scared, disoriented in the deepening darkness, Isabelle nonetheless managed to work her way toward the outskirts of the camp. Just as they reached the edge of it, though, an alarm was raised. Terse voices quickly spread the message that the queen had escaped and must be found. Crouched behind the same tree that had hidden Isabelle when she first discovered the camp, they watched as soldiers hurried out of their tents, clutching swords or rifles. Then Isabelle grabbed Ella's hand and blindly ran to the riverbank. Half skidding, half stumbling, they made their way down it.

When they reached the water, Isabelle hiked her skirts with one hand, held the maps up high above the water with the other, and waded in. Ella, who was wearing delicate silk shoes, took them off, gathered her skirts, and followed. The river rocks were treacherous. After taking only a few steps, she slipped on one and fell. As she went down, she lost her grip on her dainty shoes and the fast-flowing water carried them away. Drenched, weighed down by her wet clothing, she struggled to her feet, lurched after her shoes, and fell again.

"Leave them!" Isabelle hissed.

Ella's falls had made loud splashes. Had anyone in the camp heard them? Isabelle anxiously wondered. She stuffed the maps down the front of her dress to keep them dry, nervously glancing back at the bank. Then she walked to Ella and held out her hand. Ella took it. Isabelle pulled her up, and together the girls carefully picked their way over the stones.

They were halfway across the river when a harsh voice rang out.

"Stay right there! Hands in the air! Don't move or I'll shoot!"

## - ONE HUNDRED EIGHT -

Isabelle couldn't see the man shouting the orders. She couldn't see anything. Soldiers were shining lanterns in her direction, blinding her. She tried to shade her eyes with her raised hands. She could hear dogs barking and snarling. Rifles being shouldered, triggers cocked. Her stomach tightened with fear.

And then a voice said, "Ah, there you are, Your Highness. I was wondering where you'd gotten to. And who have we here?"

"Lower the lanterns, you fools!" the grand duke ordered.

His soldiers did so. Isabelle lifted her hands above her eyes.

"It's the queen's stepsister. The girl who cut off her toes." That was the grand duke. "I recognize her."

"I recognize her, too," said Volkmar. "We met in Malleval." His eyes glittered darkly. "Now we can finish what we started there." He made his way down the riverbank.

*He can't kill us both, not at the same time*, Isabelle thought. *And it's dark. The soldiers aiming at us might miss.*

"Run, Ella, *run*!" she whispered. "Nero's on the path to the Wildwood. You can make it."

Ella began to weep. "I won't leave you," she said.

"No need for tears, Your Highness," Volkmar taunted. "I'm not going to kill *you*. Not yet. Just your ugly stepsister. You should thank me for that."

He pulled his sword from its scabbard. The sight of it shocked Isabelle into remembering that she had a sword, too. And a shield. Instinctively, she reached toward her pocket, where she kept the fairy queen's gifts.

"Keep your hands up!" a soldier shouted. "Or I'll shoot you dead!"

Volkmar reached the bottom of the bank and stepped into the river. Isabelle's insides turned to water. Fear threatened to overwhelm her, but before it could, she felt a sharp pain on her thigh. She looked down. Her pocket was bulging. Curved black thorns were sticking through the fabric of her dress.

*The seedpod!* she thought, hope leaping inside her. *Tanaquill's last gift!*

But Volkmar saw it, too. "What do you have there?" he barked.

The seedpod grew bigger. It pushed through the fabric, shredding it. The bone and walnut shell fell into the river. "No!" Isabelle cried. Desperation gripped her. All she had left was the seedpod. Maybe it would turn into a weapon, too. If only she could get it.

But as she watched, the pod burst open. The seeds, which were red and shiny and as big as marbles, all fell into the water and sank. Then the husk fell in and was swiftly carried away. Her last hope disappeared with it.

Volkmar was close now. Isabelle knew that he would kill her here and let the river take her body. Then he would use Ella to carry out his ruthless plan. Their lives were lost. Saint-Michel was lost. Everything was lost.

He raised his sword, ready to swing it. Ella screamed. Isabelle braced for her death.

But the blow never came. Because an instant later, Volkmar's sword went flying through the air.

And then Volkmar did.

## - ONE HUNDRED NINE -

"Isabelle, what's happening?" Ella asked, her voice shaking with fear.

"I—I don't know, Ella," Isabelle said, reaching for her hand again.

A vine, as thick as a man's thigh, had risen up out of the water, thrashing violently. It had caught the blade of Volkmar's sword and launched it into the treetops; then it had slammed Volkmar against the riverbank. Thorns, some a foot long, sprouted from the vine. They'd carved red stripes in his chest.

"Blackbriar," Isabelle whispered. Just like the vines that grew on the trunk of the linden tree, the vines from which Tanaquill had plucked the seedpod.

As Isabelle watched, another vine rose out of the water, and then another and another, dizzyingly quick. Until there were dozens of them. Reaching, spiraling, they cracked like whips, catching rifles, launching snarling dogs, knocking soldier after soldier to the ground, forcing the grand duke back. As they writhed, their thorns caught, tangling them.

Some of the vines had shot up in front of the girls, other were rising behind them.

"We're going to be trapped!" Isabelle shouted. "Come on, Ella, run!"

She pulled her stepsister after her. Ella stumbled over the slick rocks, tripping, stubbing her toes, falling to her knees. Each time she fell, Isabelle hauled her up again until finally they made it to the other side.

As they staggered out of the water, panting, Isabelle looked back. The blackbriar vines had twisted together to form an impenetrable wall, twenty feet high. She heard commands being shouted behind it, guns firing, dogs barking, but nothing could get through. She and Ella were safe. For the moment.

"We have to go," Isabelle said, still gripping Ella's hand.

"What is that thing, Isabelle?" Ella asked, staring at the blackbriar wall.

"Tanaquill's magic."

Ella turned to her, smiling. "You found the fairy queen?" she asked excitedly.

"She found me. I'll tell you all about it later. We can't stay here."

"Isabelle, how did you find me?" Ella asked as they hurried through the brush. "What were you doing in Volkmar's camp?"

Isabelle didn't know where to start. "I was running away. On Nero," she began.

"*Nero?* But Maman sold him."

"I got him back. But Madame LeBenêt—our neighbor, remember her? The house burned down—"

"*What?*"

"We were living in her hayloft, and she wanted me to marry Hugo—"

"*Hugo?*"

"So that Tantine would give him an inheritance. But I don't love Hugo. And he certainly doesn't love me."

Ella stopped dead. She made Isabelle stop, too. "How did this all *happen*?" she asked, upset.

"There's no time, Ella," Isabelle protested, glancing back the way they'd come. "I'll tell you later. I'll . . ."

Her words trailed away. She'd been so focused on getting Ella out of the camp, she'd had no time to think of anything else. Now the enormity of the danger they were facing hit her. The grand duke was a traitor, in league with Volkmar, and Volkmar's troops were hidden in the Devil's Hollow, and Ella knew everything. Volkmar and the grand duke would try to stop her at all costs. She and Ella might not make it to safety. They might not make it out of the Wildwood, or even up the path. This might be her only chance to tell Ella what she needed to tell her.

So she did. She told her everything that had occurred since the day Ella had left with the prince. About Tanaquill. The fire. The marquis. The LeBenêts. Tantine's ultimatum. And lastly, Felix and his note, and how Maman had destroyed it and caused them both so much pain.

"Things would have been so different, Ella. If we'd run away like we'd planned. If Maman hadn't found his note and destroyed it. *I* would have been different. Better. Kinder."

"Isabelle . . ."

"No, let me finish. I need to. I'm sorry. I'm sorry for being cruel. For hurting you. You were beautiful. I was not. You had everything, and I'd lost everything. And it made me so jealous." Shame burned under her skin. She felt helpless and exposed saying these things, like a small

299

desert creature, tumbled from its den and left to die in the sun. "You wouldn't know what that's like."

"I might know more than you think," Ella said softly.

"Can you ever forgive me?"

Ella smiled, but it wasn't the sweet smile Isabelle was used to. It was bitter and sad. "Isabelle, you don't know what you're asking."

Isabelle nodded. She lowered her head. The fragile hope she'd felt when she'd told Ella that she was sorry had just been shattered. She had found her stepsister, found another piece of herself that had been cut away, but it didn't matter. There would be no forgiveness, not for her. The wounds she'd inflicted were too deep. Tears spilled down her cheeks. She had not known that remorse could feel so much like grief.

"Isabelle, don't cry. Please, please don't cry. I—"

Ella's words were cut off by the sound of barking.

Isabelle's head snapped up. "We need to get going," she said, wiping her eyes. "We need to find a safe place for you."

"Where?"

"I don't know. I'll think of something. The important thing is that we get you there without getting shot. All right?"

Ella nodded. "All right," she said.

Isabelle gave Ella her hand. Ella took it and held it tightly. The two girls started running again.

For their lives.

- ONE HUNDRED TEN -

Isabelle threw a pebble at the window.

It hit a pane of glass and fell back to the street.

She was standing in front of an old stone building at the edge of Saint-Michel. Looking nervously up and down the dark street, she picked the pebble up and threw it again. And once more. And finally, the window opened.

Felix leaned out in a linen shirt that was open at the neck, holding a candle and blinking into the darkness.

"Felix, it's *you!*" Isabelle said breathlessly. He'd told her he lived over the carpenter's workshop, but she wasn't sure she'd had the right window.

"What are you doing here, Isabelle?" he asked, bleary-eyed with sleep.

"Can we come in? We're in trouble. We need to hide."

"We?"

"Felix, *please!*"

Felix pulled his head inside. A moment later, he was at the workshop's gate with his candle. Isabelle met him there. She pointed across the street. Ella was standing in the wide, arched gateway of a stonemason's yard, holding Nero's reins. She hurried toward them.

"That's Ella," Felix said to Isabelle. "As in your stepsister. As in the queen of France."

"Yes."

"I forgot my trousers. The queen of France is standing at my door, and I'm in my nightshirt." He looked down at himself. "With my knees showing."

"I like your knees," Isabelle said.

Felix blushed.

"I do, too," Ella said.

"Your Royal Highness," he said.

"Ella will do."

"Your Royal Ella-ness," he amended. "I'd bow, but . . . uh, this nightshirt's a little on the short side."

Ella laughed.

Felix ushered them into the work yard. Then quickly took Nero around the side of the shop to the stables at the back. After giving him a drink and putting him in an empty stall, he returned to the work yard and locked the gate. Moving quickly and quietly, he led the two girls through the workshop and up a narrow flight of stairs to his room. After he'd put his candle down on the small wooden table in the center of it, he snatched his britches from the footboard of his bed and awkwardly stepped into them.

"Sit down," he said, motioning to the pair of rickety chairs on either side of the table. Ella did so, gratefully, but Isabelle couldn't. She was too agitated; she paced instead.

"You're bleeding," Felix said, pointing at Ella's bare foot.

A cut snaked across the top of it. He got her a rag and some water to wash it, then handed her a pair of battered boots.

"My old ones," he said. "They're too big for you, but they're better than nothing." He turned to Isabelle. "So what did you do?"

"What makes you think *I* did something?"

"Because you always got into trouble and Ella never did," Felix said, taking an oil lamp down from a shelf.

As Ella, exhausted, closed her eyes for a few minutes, and Felix removed the glass chimney from the lamp, Isabelle told him what had happened. Anger hardened his expression as he listened.

"After we escaped from Volkmar, we made it up the path and rode through the Wildwood," she said, finishing her tale. "I didn't know where else to go. I can't go back to the LeBenêts'. Cafard's men may be waiting there for me. I'm sorry, Felix. I didn't mean to drag you into this."

"Don't be," Felix said. "I'm glad to help you and Ella. I just don't know how." As he spoke, he tipped his candle to the lamp's wick.

"I don't know what to do, either," Isabelle said, sitting down across

302

from Ella. She moved things aside—chisels, knives, wooden teeth— leaned her elbows on the table, and rested her forehead in her hands.

"We've got to get the maps I stole, and Ella, to the king's encampment," she said. "We have to prevent Volkmar from attacking Saint-Michel. But how? Soldiers will be out looking for us."

"Volkmar's men?" Felix asked.

"I don't think so," Isabelle said. "He won't risk showing himself. Not yet. Not until he wipes out Cafard's troops. It's the grand duke we have to worry about. No one knows that he and Cafard are in league with Volkmar. No one but Ella and me. He may have ridden out of the Devil's Hollow back to Cafard's camp to send out search parties. If he finds Ella, she's done for."

Felix trimmed the lamp's wick, now burning brightly, then replaced the chimney. As the light illuminated the large attic room, Ella gave a little cry. Not one of fright or horror, but wonder.

"What is it?" Isabelle asked, lifting her head.

And then she saw them.

Standing on the narrow shelves that lined the walls, on the mantel, on a dresser, in rows under the narrow bed, and jumbled into several crates and a large harvest basket, were carved wooden soldiers.

"My goodness, Felix. There must be *hundreds* of them," Ella said, standing up to admire them.

"Just over two thousand," said Felix.

Isabelle walked to a shelf and picked one up. He was a fusilier, complete with a torch. He looked war-weary and haggard, as if he knew he was going to die.

"These are beautiful," said Ella.

Felix, who was now heating up a pot of cold coffee over some glowing coals in the small fireplace, shyly thanked her.

"You must've been working on them for years," said Ella.

303

"Ever since I left the Maison Douleur."

"You put a lot of emotion into them. I can see it," Ella said. "Love, fear, triumph, sorrow, it's all there."

"It had to go somewhere," Felix said, glancing at Isabelle.

Ella winced, as if his words had cut her. She abruptly rose from her chair, cupped her elbows, and walked to the window. Then she whirled and walked back again, as if she was trying to get away from something.

"Ella? Are you all right?" Isabelle asked.

Ella started to reply, but her words were cut off by the sound of hooves clopping over the cobblestones. It carried up from the street and in through the open window. Felix, Isabelle, and Ella traded anxious glances.

"Soldiers," Isabelle said tersely. "What if they're going door to door?"

Felix risked a glance out the window. The tension in his face softened. He smiled. "Not soldiers, no," he said. "But maybe saviors."

## – ONE HUNDRED ELEVEN –

Isabelle was out of the door and down the stairs in no time.

She'd rushed to the window to see what Felix was talking about and had spotted Martin. He was pulling a wagonload of potatoes. Hugo was in the driver's seat. Tavi was sitting next to him.

Isabelle ran in front of the them, waving her arms. "Why are you in the village so early?" she asked. It wasn't even dawn yet.

Tavi explained they had to go to the army camp first, deliver the potatoes, return to the farm, milk the cows, and then bring another load to the market.

"Colonel Cafard was so furious when you took off that Tantine made him a gift of the potatoes. To help the war effort. And to keep him from throwing us all in jail. My mother was up fuming about it half the night. Thanks a lot, Isabelle," Hugo said.

Isabelle ignored his grousing. "You've come in the nick of time," she said. "We need you."

"Who needs us?" Tavi said, looking around.

"The village of Saint-Michel. The king. All of France. And Ella."

*"Ella?"* Tavi echoed.

"Enemy soldiers are trying to kill her. And me."

She quickly explained what had happened since she'd left them. Tavi and Hugo listened; then Tavi, eyes sparking with anger, said, "We have to stop them. They can't do this. They *won't* do this."

"Come upstairs. Hurry," said Isabelle.

Tavi climbed down out of the wagon and rushed to Felix's room. Hugo quickly tied Martin to a hitching post and followed her.

"Ella, is that *you*?" Tavi said as she entered the room.

Ella nodded. Tavi's habitually acerbic expression, the one she used to keep the world away, softened. Her eyes glistened. "I never thought I'd see you again," she whispered. "I never thought I'd get the chance to . . . Oh, Ella. I'm sorry, I'm so sorry."

"It's all right, Tavi," Ella said, reaching for her hand.

"Hey, Ella. Nice boots," Hugo said shyly, staring at the huge, battered cast-offs she was wearing. "Should I bow or something?"

"Maybe later, Hugo," Ella said.

"We need to get Ella and Isabelle out of here before the whole village wakes up," Felix explained, handing out cups of hot coffee. "What if we hid them in the wagon, under the potatoes, and headed to a camp that's loyal to the king?"

"According to the map I stole, the nearest one is fifty miles away," said Isabelle. "Martin wouldn't make it."

Ella had released Tavi's hand; she was sitting at the table again, looking out of the window, a troubled expression on her face.

Hugo said, "Could we use Nero?"

305

Isabelle shook her head. "He's never pulled a wagon. He'd kick it to pieces."

Ella covered her face with her hands.

For the second time, Isabelle noticed her distress. "Ella? What's wrong?" she asked, putting her coffee down.

"You are all so kind to me. So good," Ella replied, lowering her hands. "Isabelle, you saved my life. But I . . . I don't deserve your kindness."

"Don't be ridiculous," Isabelle said. "You deserve that and more. You—"

"No, *listen* to me!" Ella cried. "You apologized to me, Isabelle, back in the Devil's Hollow, and now you have, Tavi. And that was brave of you both. Very brave. And now it's my turn to be brave. As I should've been years ago." The words came out of her mouth as if they were studded with nails. "Isabelle, earlier you asked me to forgive you and I said you didn't know what you were asking. I said that because *I'm* the one who needs to be forgiven."

"I don't understand . . ." Isabelle said.

"The note," Ella said, her voice heavy with remorse. "The one Felix left for you in the linden tree. You said Maman found it and destroyed it, but you're wrong. *I'm* the one who found it. I took it and burned it and ruined your life. Oh, Isabelle, don't you see? I'm the ugliest stepsister of all."

## - ONE HUNDRED TWELVE -

Isabelle sat down on Felix's bed. She felt as if Ella had kicked her legs out from under her.

Ella had destroyed the note. Not Maman. *Ella.* No matter how many times Isabelle repeated this to herself, it still made no sense.

"*Why?*" she asked.

"Because I was jealous, too."

"Jealous? Of whom?" Isabelle asked.

"Of *you*, Isabelle. You were so fearless, so strong. You laughed like a pirate. Rode like a robber. And Felix loved you. He loved you from the day my father brought you, Tavi, and Maman to the Maison Douleur. He was my friend and you took him away."

"I was still your friend, Ella. I was always your friend," Felix said, wounded.

Ella turned to him. "It wasn't the same. I didn't jump over stone walls on stallions. I didn't race you to the tops of tall trees." She looked at Isabelle again. "You and Felix were always having adventures. They sounded so wonderful and I couldn't bear it. Couldn't bear that he liked you better than me. Couldn't bear to be left behind. So I made sure I wasn't."

Isabelle remembered how upset Ella would get when she and Felix rode off to the Wildwood and how relieved she always was when they returned. *I should be angry. I should be furious*, she thought. But she wasn't—just deeply, achingly sad.

"I was so sorry afterward," Ella continued. "When I saw how miserable you were. But I was too afraid to tell you what I'd done. I thought you would hate me for it. But then everything changed between us and you hated me anyway."

Ella got up, crossed the room, and sat down next to Isabelle. "Say something. Anything," she pleaded. "Say you hate me. Tell me you wish I were dead."

Isabelle exhaled loudly. Raggedly. As if she'd been holding her breath not for seconds, or minutes, but years.

"It's like a fire, Ella," she said.

"What is?"

"Jealousy. It burns so hot, so bright. It devours you, until you're just a smoking ruin with nothing left inside."

"Nothing but ashes," Ella said.

Isabelle closed her eyes now and sifted through those ashes.

Everything would have been different if Ella hadn't burned Felix's note. She wouldn't have lost Felix. Or Nero. She wouldn't have lost herself.

She thought about the day Felix left, and the years that had come after. The music tutors and dancing masters. The dress fittings. Sitting for hours at her needlework, when her heart longed for horses and hills. The excruciating dinners with suitors looking her up and down, their smiles forced, their eyes shuttered as they tried to hide their disappointment. The aching loneliness of finding that nothing fit. Not dainty slippers or stiff corsets. Not conversations or expectations, friendships or desires. Her entire life had seemed like a beautiful dress made for someone else.

"I'm sorry, Isabelle. I'm so sorry," Ella said.

Isabelle opened her eyes. Ella's hands were knotted into fists in her lap. Isabelle reached for one. She opened the fingers, smoothed them flat, then wove her own between them.

She was sorry for so many things. She was sorry for her mother, who had always looked to mirrors for the truth. She was sorry for Berthe, who cried when she was mean, and Cecile, who didn't. She was sorry for Tavi writing equations on cabbage leaves.

She was sorry for all the grim-tale girls locked in lonely towers. Trapped in sugar houses. Lost in the dark woods, with a huntsman coming to cut out their hearts.

She was sorry for three little girls who'd been handed a poisoned apple as they played under a linden tree on a bright summer day.

## - ONE HUNDRED THIRTEEN -

Ella stood.

She crossed the room and knelt by Tavi's chair.

"I'm so sorry, Tavi," she said. "What I did hurt you, too."

"It's all right, Ella," Tavi said, rising. She pulled Ella up and hugged her. Isabelle joined them. The three stood for a moment, locked in a fierce, tearful embrace.

Then Ella turned to Felix. "I need to apologize to you, too," she said, reaching for his hand. "Your life would also have been different if I hadn't stolen the note."

"Oh, Ella," Felix said, taking her hand. "I'm sorry you thought I wasn't your friend anymore."

Ella turned to Hugo next. "You wouldn't even be here now if it wasn't for me," she said to him. "In this room. In this mess . . ."

Hugo shrugged. "Actually, my life kind of got better. The last few weeks, with you two around"—he nodded at Isabelle and Tavi—"have been really awful but exciting, too. I mean, what did I have before you came? Cabbages, that's about it. Now I have friends."

Isabelle hooked her arm around Hugo's neck and pulled him into the embrace. He tried to smile, but it came out like a grimace. He hastily patted Isabelle on the back, then extricated himself. She knew he wasn't used to affection.

"We better get going. We have to find a way to get Ella to safety and the maps to the king," Hugo said. "And that's going to become a lot harder once the sun is up."

"We'll need an armed escort," Tavi said hopelessly. "Our own regiment. No, make that an entire army."

Isabelle was quiet. She was slowly walking around Felix's room, eyeing his shelves. His bureau. The mantel. Then she turned to the others and said, "We don't need to find an army. We already have one."

"We do? Where is it?" Tavi asked.

309

Isabelle picked up a carved wooden soldier from a shelf and held it out on her palm.

"Right here."

## – ONE HUNDRED FOURTEEN –

Hugo blinked at the little soldier on Isabelle's palm. He forced a smile.

"You can lie down, you know. On Felix's bed. If you're tired, you can rest," he said.

Isabelle shot him a look. "I'm not tired. Or crazy, which is what you really mean. I'm serious. There's a fairy queen. She comes and goes as a fox and lives in the hollow of the linden tree. She has strong magic."

"A fairy queen . . ." Hugo said, raising an eyebrow.

"It's true, Hugo," Ella said. "She came to me one night when my heart was broken and asked me what I wanted most. I told her, and she helped me get it. How else do you think I got to the ball?"

"I've seen that fox," Felix said. "When I was a boy. Her fur is red like autumn leaves. She has deep green eyes."

"She turned mice into horses and a pumpkin into a coach," said Ella.

"She could enchant these carved soldiers and turn them into real soldiers. I *know* she could," said Isabelle. "All we have to do is get them to the linden tree."

"But how?" Tavi asked, turning in a slow circle. "There are so many of them."

"Two thousand one hundred and fifty-eight, to be exact," Felix said.

"We would have to find cases or trunks to put them in. Do you have any?"

"No, but we have plenty of coffins," said Felix. "I bet two of them would get the job done."

"We could use Martin and the wagon to transport them," Isabelle said. "We'd just have to unload the potatoes."

"Then let's unload them," Ella said decisively. "We have an enemy to defeat. A king and a country to save. And traitors to capture." She smiled grimly. "And then hang, draw, and quarter."

Both of Hugo's eyebrows shot up. He scratched under his cap. "You're different, Ella. You're not the girl I remember. I guess it's true what they say. What doesn't kill you—"

"Makes you the queen of France," Ella finished. "Let's go," she added, glancing out Felix's window. "Hugo's right. It's going to be a lot harder to sneak two thousand soldiers to a fairy queen in broad daylight."

## – ONE HUNDRED FIFTEEN –

Felix opened the gates to the work yard, and Hugo backed the wagon into it as quickly as he could.

Working together, the five unloaded the potatoes, heaping them on the ground. It was decided that they would load the coffins into the wagon first, then carry the wooden soldiers down from Felix's room in crates, baskets, bedsheets—anything they could find.

The coffins were simple, slender pine boxes, not terribly heavy. Felix and Isabelle picked the first one up by its rope handles, carried it out of the shop, and set it down on the wagon's bed. Felix pushed it, trying to get it to slide in neatly under it seats, but it wouldn't go. It seemed to be blocked by something. He was about to push it again just as Hugo and Tavi appeared, carrying the second coffin.

"Wait! Felix, don't!" Hugo cried. "You'll let it out!"

"Let what out?" Felix asked, confused.

"The sweaty dead dog," Hugo said as he and Tavi slid the second coffin into the wagon.

"There's a dead dog in the wagon?" Ella asked, confused.

"No, it's a cheese. Tavi invented it. It's in a box under the seats," Isabelle explained.

"It smells so bad, I can't get rid of it," Hugo said. "Be careful, you really don't want to knock the lid off."

He climbed into the wagon, shoved the wooden box over to the left side of the bed, then slid the first coffin in next to it. Isabelle pushed the second one in. They just fit.

Everyone worked together to bring the soldiers downstairs. Soon, both coffins were full. As Felix was securing the lids, tapping a few nails into them to keep them from sliding during the trip, Isabelle went to the stables to see Nero. She would leave him there, hidden away, to keep him safe. If Cafard saw him, he would take him, and she did not want a traitor to have her horse.

She scratched Nero's ears, kissed his nose, and told him to be good. She didn't know if they would make it to the Maison Douleur, or if she would see her beloved horse again after tonight. As if sensing her distress, Nero nudged at her with his nose. She kissed him again, then hurried away without looking back. Nero watched her go, blinking his huge, dark eyes; then he gave the stall door a good hard kick.

The others, except for Felix, were already in the wagon by the time Isabelle rejoined them. She climbed in and settled herself on the back seat. Tavi and Ella were up front. Hugo, in the driver's seat, guided Martin out of the work yard. Felix closed the gates, then swung up beside Isabelle.

Hugo cracked the reins, and Martin trotted down the dark street. Isabelle looked up. The moon was still high, but the sky was beginning to lighten. Worry shriveled her insides.

"Volkmar's men are only a few miles away, and what are we doing?"

she said, turning to Felix. "Hauling tiny wooden soldiers off to a magical fox who lives in a hollow inside a tree. That sounds like the craziest thing yet in a night full of crazy things. Ella says she told Tanaquill what her heart wanted. And Tanaquill granted it to her. Do you think it will work?"

Felix looked at Ella, nestled in between Hugo and Tavi. Then he took Isabelle's hand and held it.

"Maybe it already has," he said.

## - ONE HUNDRED SIXTEEN -

The old farmer, bleary-eyed and grizzled, raised a hand in greeting.

Hugo did the same, and their two wagons passed in silence.

They'd made their way out of Saint-Michel without seeing another soul. Ever since they'd left the safety of Felix's room, Isabelle had felt as if iron bands were wrapped around her chest. As they started toward the gentle hills that lay beyond the village, she finally felt like she could take a breath, as if they might actually make it to the Maison Douleur.

Until Hugo swore and pointed up ahead of them. Isabelle could see the old church silhouetted on top of the hill in the thinning darkness. On the road next to it, riding fast, was a group of soldiers.

"If we stay calm, we can get out of this," Tavi said.

"How? They're going to recognize Ella right away," Hugo said.

*He's right*, Isabelle thought. "Ella, change places with Felix," she said. "They might not see you so well if you're sitting in the back. Tavi, you come back here, too. We'll put Ella between us."

They quickly rearranged themselves, but it wasn't enough, and they knew it. Ella still shined like a star.

Felix pulled a brightly printed handkerchief from his pocket. "Wrap your hair up," he said.

Hugo handed her his glasses. "Put these on, too."

Ella did as they bade her. The three girls were sitting on an old horse blanket that had been folded over to cushion the seat. Tavi pulled it out from under them and draped it around Ella's shoulders. Isabelle spotted a clod of dirt by her feet. She picked it up, crushed it, then rubbed it on Ella's soft hands, working it into her knuckles and nails so that they looked just like her and Tavi's rough ones.

"This might just work," Tavi said.

Felix, his eyes straight ahead, grimly said, "It better. They have rifles."

A few minutes later, the soldiers approached them, riding two abreast. Isabelle's nerves were as taut as a bowstring.

Hugo nodded solemnly at the first riders. The men looked him and his companions over but didn't stop. The two lines moved quickly by. Isabelle saw that they wore the uniforms of the French army. They were Cafard's men, they had to be. Thankfully, the grand duke was not among them. The riders' commander brought up the rear. He, too, peered closely at them as he trotted by.

*Keep going*, Isabelle silently urged him. *Nothing to see here.*

"Halt!" the commander suddenly bellowed to his men, turning his horse around.

Isabelle's heart dropped.

"Let me do the talking," Tavi said quietly. "I have an idea."

"*You* have an idea?" whispered Hugo, his hands tightening on the reins. "God help us all."

## – ONE HUNDRED SEVENTEEN –

"Why are you about at this hour? Where are you going?" the commander demanded, looking at Hugo.

But it was Tavi who answered him. "Where are we going? Where *would* we be going with two coffins in the back and the churchyard just up ahead?" she shrilled. "It's hardly a mystery, Sergeant!"

"It's *Lieutenant*. And it's very early in the day to be going to the cemetery."

Tavi gave him a contemptuous snort. "Death doesn't keep bankers' hours. My husband here"—she slapped Hugo's shoulder—"must be in the fields by sunup. My brother-in-law, too," she said, nodding at Felix. "My sister and I just lost two brothers to this blasted war. Their bodies came home yesterday. One was a married man. Now my sister-in-law here"—she gestured to Ella—"is a widow with three small children."

Ella lowered her head and sniffled into the horse blanket.

"They have no one to provide for them. My husband and I must take them in," Tavi continued. "Four more mouths to feed when we've barely got enough for ourselves. So, Lieutenant, if you are satisfied now, can we move on? Bodies don't keep in the heat."

"The queen is missing," said the lieutenant. "The grand duke fears she's been kidnapped. He's given orders to stop anyone who looks suspicious and to inspect all wagons."

Tavi laughed out loud. "The queen is a great beauty, lieutenant. Who is a beauty here? Me, in my old dress? My sister in hers? Or perhaps my four-eyed sister-in-law?"

Ella looked up. She squinted through Hugo's eyeglasses. The lieutenant's gaze passed right over her.

"Let me see your feet. Each of you ladies," he said. "It's well known that the queen has the daintiest feet in all the land."

One by one, the three girls showed the lieutenant their feet. Isabelle's were big, her boots filthy. Tavi's, too. Ella's were absolutely enormous in Felix's old, battered boots.

"Now, if you're finished harassing a grieving family . . ." Tavi said.

Hugo made ready to crack his reins, but the lieutenant held up a hand.

*Now what?* Isabelle wondered, panic rising in her.

"You could be smuggling the queen in those coffins," the lieutenant said. He directed two of his men to the back of the wagon. "Open them up!"

Isabelle was paralyzed by fear. She glanced at the others. Felix's shoulders were up around his ears. Hugo was saucer-eyed. Tavi had turned pale, but she hadn't given up.

"This is a desecration!" she shouted. "Have you no shame?"

The two soldiers selected for the task glanced uneasily at each other.

"That was an order!" the lieutenant barked at them.

The soldiers dismounted from their horses.

"The bodies are several days old!" Tavi protested. "Must our last memories of our loved ones be an ungodly smell?"

*An ungodly smell.*

With those words, Isabelle's paralysis broke. She knew exactly what to do. She turned around and faced backward, pretending to watch the soldiers. As she did, she snaked her right hand under the seat. Her fingers found the wooden box there. Slowly, carefully, she wedged them under the box's lid.

Anticipating that the coffin lids would be nailed down, as coffin lids always are, one of the soldiers pulled a dagger from his belt to pry them off. He shoved the blade in under one of the lids and levered the handle. A few nails screeched free of the wood. As they did, Isabelle made her move.

She slid the lid off the wooden box and unleashed the sweaty dead dog.

The carnage was magnificent.

The horses shrieked. Three of them threw their riders. Some of the soldiers lost their suppers. Even the lieutenant turned green.

Isabelle, Tavi, and Ella, sitting right over the rank abomination, felt their eyes burning from its fumes. Tears poured down their cheeks, making them look even more like the bereaved family they claimed to be.

Tavi saw her advantage and took it. Standing up in the wagon, she shook a finger at the lieutenant. "You should be *ashamed* of yourself, sir!" she shrilled. "Disturbing the dead! Upsetting mourners! Making a poor widow weep!"

"For God's sake, seal it up!" the lieutenant thundered, his hand over his nose.

The soldier who'd pried up a corner of the lid now frantically hammered it back down with the butt of his dagger.

"I've half a mind to tell the good Colonel Cafard what you've done," Tavi continued. "We are not kidnapping anyone. We are poor, grieving folk trying to bury our loved ones!"

"My apologies, madame. Drive on!" the lieutenant said, waving his hand.

Hugo nodded, then clucked his tongue. Martin trotted off. Isabelle, still facing backward, quickly slid the lid back over the dead dog. It lessened the stink, but Hugo urged Martin into a canter nonetheless, in an attempt to outrun the lingering fumes. A few minutes later, they crested the hill, leaving the soldiers behind them.

When they'd made it down the other side, Hugo stopped the wagon. He leaned forward, breathing heavily. His hands were shaking.

"That was very, very close," Felix said, a tremor in his voice.

"We don't know if that's the only patrol. We should keep going," Isabelle urged.

Hugo sat up, having caught his breath. "I need my glasses back. Before I drive us off the road."

Ella handed them to him. "Thank you, all of you. You saved my life," she said.

"It was Tavi," said Hugo. "She made that thing."

Tavi shook her head modestly. "It was Leeuwenhoek."

"Who?" Ella asked as Hugo started off again.

"It's a long story. I'll tell it to you one day. If we live long enough," Isabelle said grimly. Hugo coaxed Martin into a canter again. As he did, one of the wagon's wheels caught a pothole and jounced Tavi to the edge of her seat.

Ella grabbed hold of her, then took her hand to keep her safe. She took Isabelle's hand, too. As the wagon sped through what remained of the night, neither Isabelle, nor Tavi, nor Ella let go.

## – ONE HUNDRED NINETEEN –

The stars were fading as Martin trotted up the drive of the Maison Douleur to the linden tree. Before Hugo had even brought him to a halt, the others were out of the wagon.

An inquisitive whinny carried through the grounds. Isabelle knew it was one of the two rescued horses that now lived in the pasture. Martin whinnied back. Ella stared at what was left of the mansion.

"I'm sorry, Ella. It was your home. Long before it was ours," Isabelle said.

"I don't miss it," Ella said. "I hope all the ghosts escaped when the walls fell in."

Felix and Hugo had already carried one of the coffins to the base of the linden. Felix pried the lid off with a knife he'd tucked into his pocket.

Tavi and Isabelle carried the second coffin. Felix pried the lid off that one, too. Then they all turned to Ella.

"How do we do it?" Felix asked her. "How do we summon Tanaquill?"

"I—I don't actually know," Ella said. "Isabelle, do you?"

Isabelle felt a flutter of panic. "No," she said. "I can't remember exactly what I did."

Ella took a deep breath. "Let me think . . . I remember walking to the linden tree after everyone had left for the ball. I was so upset. I wanted to go more than I've ever wanted anything. With my whole heart. And then suddenly, she just appeared."

"A tall woman . . ." Felix said, with a shiver in his voice.

"Yes," said Ella.

"With red hair and green eyes and sharp teeth."

"How do you know that?"

"Because," Felix said, pointing past them to the ruins, "she's already here."

- ONE HUNDRED TWENTY -

Tanaquill walked out of the shadows.

She wore a gown made of black beetle shells that gleamed darkly in the moon's waning light. Her crown was a circlet of bats. Three young adders curled around her neck; their heads rested like jewels on her collarbone.

Tanaquill addressed Ella. "I did not expect to see you back here. And certainly not in the company of your stepsisters. All you wanted when last we spoke was to get away from this place. Now you return?"

"I would not be here, standing in front of you, if Isabelle had not rescued me from a traitor's plot. If Octavia had not thrown my enemies off my scent. I owe them my life. Now Isabelle needs your help, Your Grace."

Tanaquill circled Isabelle. She placed a sharp black talon under her chin and lifted it.

"Have you found all the pieces, girl?"

"Yes, Your Grace. I—I think so. I hope so," Isabelle said.

"And now that your heart is whole, what does it tell you?"

Isabelle looked down at her clenched hands. She thought of Malleval and tears of anger welled in her eyes. She thought of the grand duke coolly arranging the deaths of his young king and queen. She remembered the sweet weight of a sword in her hand.

"It tells me impossible things," she whispered.

"Do you still desire to be pretty? Say the word and I will make it so."

Isabelle looked up at the sky for some time, blinking her tears away. "No," she finally said.

"What is it that you wish for, then?" Tanaquill asked.

"An army," Isabelle replied, meeting the fairy queen's eyes. "I wish to raise an army against Volkmar and the grand duke. I wish to save my family, my friends, my country."

"You ask a great deal," Tanaquill said. "Nothing comes from nothing. Magic must come from something. Coaches can come from pumpkins; that is child's play. But an army? That is far more difficult. Even I cannot make a private out of a pebble, a major out of a mushroom."

"We brought you these," Isabelle said, hurrying to the coffins. She picked up a figure—an officer holding a saber across his chest—and put it in Tanaquill's hand.

Tanaquill regarded it. She cocked her head.

"Please, Your Grace" Isabelle said. "Please help us."

Tanaquill's deep green eyes caught Isabelle's. Held by their gaze, Isabelle felt as if the fairy queen could see deep inside her. Tanaquill stepped back, raised one hand high, and swirled it through the air.

A breeze rose. It turned into a wind. And the wind curled in on itself, spinning in a widening gyre.

Isabelle's pulse quickened as the wind whirled the figurines out of the coffins and spread them across the lawns, the gardens, the paddocks and fields.

When the coffins were empty, the wind stopped.

And a new sound rose.

## – ONE HUNDRED TWENTY-ONE –

Isabelle felt the ground under her feet rumble and shudder.

Creaks and groans and sharp, shattering cracks were heard—the sounds trees make in a violent storm. Isabelle looked out over the hills and fields, illuminated now by the dawn's first light.

Felix's tiny carved figures were growing.

Isabelle's heart beat madly as she watched them. Wooden bodies drew breath. They stretched tall, heads back, arms open wide to the sky. Wooden cheeks flushed with color. Blank eyes ignited with the fire of war.

Shouts carried across the fields as sergeants ordered men into formation. Isabelle heard the heavy metallic clunks of rounds being chambered and rifles being shouldered. A sea of blue uniforms flowed around her.

Two horses jumped the paddock fence and galloped to Tanaquill. As the fairy queen stroked them and spoke to them, Isabelle realized that they were the two she had rescued. They looked nothing like their former selves. Their coats gleamed; their manes rippled. They huffed and blew and raked at the ground, impatient for their riders.

Tanaquill stepped back as two men—lieutenants, Isabelle reasoned, judging from their uniforms—claimed the horses. They swung up into their saddles easily, lengthened their reins, then turned to Isabelle.

"Our general, mademoiselle. Where is he?" one of them asked her. "We await our orders."

Isabelle craned her neck. She looked past the lieutenants. Out over the garden. The paddocks. Searching for their general. He would be tall and powerful. Scarred from his many battles. An intimidating man with a fierce bearing.

But she didn't see him.

"Where is he?" she asked, turning to Felix. "Where's the general?"

"Isabelle . . ." Felix said, shaking his head. "I—I didn't carve one."

## – ONE HUNDRED TWENTY-TWO –

"Felix, what do you mean, you didn't carve one?" Isabelle asked, panicking.

"I was going to carve him at the end. I'd finished the soldiers and all the other officers—I just didn't get to the general."

"What are we going to do?" Isabelle said.

"What about the marquis?" Tavi asked. "He would make a good general."

"Yes! The marquis!" Isabelle said, turning to Tanaquill. "I'll go fetch him. It won't take long. It—"

"There's no time," Tanaquill said, cutting her off. She pointed at the enchanted army. "Look at them."

The soldiers' movements were becoming stiff and jerky. Their color was fading. Their eyes were dulling.

"What's happening to them?" Isabelle asked, distraught.

322

"They are warriors. They exist only to fight. If they have no general to lead them into battle, their fire fades. The magic dies."

Isabelle's panic bloomed into terror. She couldn't lose this army. It was the only chance Ella had. The only chance their country had.

"What about Felix? Or Hugo? Can you transform one of them into a general?" Isabelle asked.

She turned to the boys, expecting to see Felix wearing a uniform, to see Hugo with a sword, but they remained exactly as they were.

"What's wrong? Why didn't anything happen?" she asked.

"That is your wish, not theirs," Tanaquill replied.

Isabelle turned to the two boys. *"Please,"* she begged them.

"Isabelle, I'm a *carpenter*. I haven't even reported for training yet. I'd get these men killed," Felix said.

Hugo shook his head; he stepped back.

Isabelle pressed the heels of her hands to her head. "What can we do?"

Tanaquill circled her again. "What is your heart's wish, Isabelle? Its truest wish?" she asked.

"To save my queen, my king, my country," Isabelle babbled madly. "To save innocents from being slaughtered."

But again, nothing happened.

"To give these fighters a general who is brave. Who's a true warrior. Who will give everything to the fight—his blood and tears. His body and soul. His life."

Tanaquill stopped in front of Isabelle. She pressed a taloned hand to her chest.

Isabelle could hear her heart beating, louder and louder. The sound was crashing in her ears. Filling her head.

Tanaquill's voice cut through it like thunder. "I will ask you one last time, Isabelle—what is your heart's desire?"

Isabelle tried to speak, to form words, but her heart was pounding so loudly, the sound filled her throat and they wouldn't come.

She closed her eyes and a thousand images swirled through her head. She saw herself as a child, happy and free. Before she was told that she was less than, that all the things she loved were the wrong things.

She saw herself flying over fences on Nero. Galloping over fields, the mud flying from his hooves. She saw herself climbing to the top of the linden tree with Felix, imagining the branches were the rigging of a pirate ship. Fighting duels with a mop handle. Fighting off a hungry wolf from the chicken coop with nothing but a broomstick.

Those childhood images vanished and others came. She saw herself fighting against Maman. Against dull boys she wouldn't have willingly spent ten minutes with, never mind a lifetime. Fighting against the endless dreary days of teacups and cakes, fake smiles and small talk.

Isabelle saw now that she'd been fighting her entire life to be who she was.

With anguish, and hope, and yearning, she asked her heart how to win that fight.

And her heart answered.

She covered Tanaquill's hand with her own.

And Tanaquill, smiling, said, "Yes."

Isabelle opened her eyes and looked around.

Tanaquill had stepped away, into the shadows under the linden tree.

But Tavi, Ella, Felix, and Hugo were frozen in place. They were staring at her. Tavi was smiling. Ella was wide-eyed. Hugo was openmouthed. Tears were spilling down Felix's cheeks.

Isabelle looked down at herself and caught her breath.

Her worn dress was gone. She was wearing leather britches, a tunic of chain mail, and a gleaming silver breastplate. In her hands she held a finely made helmet. The weight of her armor, and the drag of her sword at her hip, were sweet to her. She felt taller, stronger, as if she were no longer made of blood, bones, and tender flesh, but iron and steel.

A high, fierce whinny echoed across the gray morning.

Isabelle turned and saw a black stallion cantering up the drive. He was wearing a blanket of mail and a silver faceplate. He looked fierce and majestic, a horse fit for a warrior.

He slowed to a trot, then stopped in front of Isabelle and snorted. Isabelle laughed. She patted his neck.

"He was shut in a stall. In a stable in the village," she said, turning to the fairy queen. "How did he get out?"

Tanaquill shrugged. "Kicked the door down, I imagine. You know what he's like."

Isabelle walked around to Nero's left side. Hugo held her helmet while Felix boosted her up into the saddle. Tavi and Ella gathered close.

The lieutenants sat up tall in their saddles, awaiting orders. All across the grounds of the Maison Douleur, in its fields and meadows, soldiers stood at attention.

It was dead silent as they waited, their eyes on Isabelle.

"I'm afraid," she whispered, squeezing Felix's hand. "I don't know how to do this. I've never been a general."

"You know the most important thing," Felix said. "You know how to be brave. You've always known that."

"You know how to outmaneuver the enemy," Ella said. "You got us here."

"You know how to fight," Tavi said.

"You're the worst girl I've ever met, Isabelle," Hugo added, with touching sincerity. "You're so tough and stubborn, you give me nightmares."

Isabelle gave him a tremulous smile. "Thank you, Hugo. I know there's a compliment in there somewhere."

"Go now," Felix told her, releasing her hand. "And then come back."

Hugo handed Isabelle her helmet. She took it, then bowed her head to the fairy queen. "Thank you," she said, with a catch in her voice.

Tanaquill nodded. "What was cut away is whole again," she said. "The pieces of your heart are restored. The boy is love—constant and true. The horse, courage—wild and untamed. Your stepsister is your conscience—kind and compassionate. Know that you are a warrior, Isabelle, and that a true warrior carries love, courage, and her conscience into battle, as surely as she carries her sword."

Isabelle put on her helmet. She drew her sword from its scabbard and raised it high. Nero stamped at the ground. He turned in a circle and pulled at the reins, eager to be off. The muscles in Isabelle's arms rippled. The sword's silver blade gleamed.

A cheer rose, a war cry from two thousand throats. It rang out over the land and echoed through the hills. Isabelle smiled, reveling in the thunderous sound.

"Soldiers!" she shouted as it died down. "We march on a fearsome enemy this morning! He murders our people, he plunders our villages and towns, lays waste to our fields. He has no claim to our lands. Greed and bloodlust are all that drive him. He and his fighters are without mercy. Their hearts burn with the flames of conquest, but ours shine with the light of justice. We will surround the Devil's Hollow. We will fight him there, and we will vanquish him!"

The roar that rose then was the sound of a hurricane, a tidal wave, an earthquake. It rolled on, an awesome force that nothing could stop. The soldiers were mesmerized by Isabelle. They would have marched into the depths of hell and fought the devil himself had she asked them to.

"For king, and queen, and country!" Isabelle shouted.

She touched her heels to Nero. He reared, hooves battering the sky, then lunged forward, bolting for the stone wall and the field beyond. Her lieutenants rode after her. Her soldiers followed.

Isabelle rode tall in her saddle. Her color was high, her eyes were flashing.

She was fearsome.

She was strong.

She was beautiful.

## – ONE HUNDRED TWENTY-FIVE –

The moon had faded. The stars had all winked out.

Tanaquill's work was done.

She watched, a half smile on her lips, as Felix, with his dagger, and Hugo, with an ax he pulled from a chopping block, followed the troops, determined to fight with them.

Ella and Tavi clambered back into the cart and started down the drive to what was left of their stables. Tavi planned to stow the cart there, put Martin in the pasture, and hide in the chicken coop with Ella until it was safe to come out.

As the wagon trundled off, two figures emerged from behind the ruins of the mansion. One was an elderly woman, dressed all in black, the other a young man in a blue frock coat and suede britches.

"She did it. I had my doubts," Tanaquill said as the two figures approached her. "The girl is brave. Far braver than she knows."

"I've come for the map. It's mine," said Fate. "You must return it to me."

"You should give it to me. I won the wager," said Chance.

Tanaquill faced the crone. "Isabelle's life will no longer be mapped out by you." She turned her green eyes on Chance. "Nor will it be altered by you," she said. "Her life is a wide-open landscape now, and if she survives the day, she will make her own path through it."

As Tanaquill spoke these words, she pulled Isabelle's map from the folds of her cloak. She tossed it high into the air and whispered a spell. The map dissolved into a fine, shimmering dust and was carried away on the breeze.

Fate and Chance watched it disappear, then turned to the fairy queen, full of protests. But she was gone. They saw a flash of red as a fox leapt over a stone wall. Their gaze followed her as she loped through the fields and over the hills. She stopped at the edge of the Wildwood to glance back at them once, then vanished into the trees.

There *is* magic in this sad, hard world. A magic stronger than fate, stronger than chance. And it is seen in the unlikeliest of places.

By a hearth at night, as a girl leaves a bit of cheese for a hungry mouse.

In a slaughter yard, as the old and infirm, the weak and discarded, are made to matter more than money.

In a poor carpenter's small attic room, where three sisters learned that the price of forgiveness is forgiving.

And now, on a battlefield, as a mere girl tries to turn the red tide of war.

It is the magic of a frail and fallible creature, one capable of both unspeakable cruelty and immense kindness. It lives inside every human being ready to redeem us. To transform us. To save us. If we can only find the courage to listen to it.

It is the magic of the human heart.

## – ONE HUNDRED TWENTY-SIX –

The scout brought good news.

The wall of blackbriar rising up from the river, thick and impenetrable, was still there.

"Good," Isabelle said quietly. "That walls off the southern edge of Volkmar's camp and blocks any chance of escape up the mountain into the Wildwood."

As she spoke, she sketched a diagram of the Hollow in the dirt with a stick. Her lieutenants stood clustered around her, watching as she drew the camp, hidden in the hollow's center.

"We need to surround the other three sides and block off *all* escape routes," she continued, drawing an arc from one edge of the blackbriar wall to the other and enclosing the camp within it. "Divide the troops in two. One half goes to the west, the other to the east. They meet here, where we are now," she said, tapping her stick at the diagram's northernmost point. "Be quick. Be silent. Send the signal as soon as you're in place. Go."

Isabelle had brought her troops out of Saint-Michel, around the Wildwood, and down a long, rutted road to the border of the Devil's Hollow. They had marched double time the whole way, but the sun was rising now, and they no longer had darkness as their ally. Isabelle had maintained what she hoped was about a two-mile distance between her troops and Volkmar's camp, to keep them from being seen or heard, but she knew the chances of their being spotted increased with every moment that passed.

If that happened, she would lose the asset of surprise. She believed that her troops outnumbered Volkmar's, but Malleval had shown her what the enemy was capable of. Isabelle knew she would need every advantage she could get. Until the signal came, she would be on tenterhooks.

The lieutenants rode to their troops and gave their orders in low, urgent voices. Immediately the soldiers disappeared among the trees. They were made of wood. They were creatures of the forest, and as they moved into place, they became one with it again, making no more noise than a branch creaking in the wind, or leaves whispering in the breeze.

Isabelle nodded to a young, wiry private. He saluted her, then climbed a tall pine tree behind her, a spyglass tucked inside his jacket.

Twenty minutes passed. Thirty. Isabelle had given orders that each company send a man up a tree with a piece of red cloth. The man was to wave it when all the members of his company were in place. Forty minutes went by.

She tightened her grip on her sword. *What is taking them so long?* she wondered tensely. Nero tossed his head but made no noise.

Just when she thought her taut nerves would snap, she heard it—a hawk's cry, made by the young private high in the tree above. That was the signal. The red flags had all been sighted. Everyone was in place.

Isabelle lowered her head. *Elizabeth, Yennenga, Abhaya Rani, be with me,* she prayed. *Give me cunning and strength. Make me fearless. Make me bold.*

Then she lifted her head, raised her sword, and shouted, *"Charge!"*

## – ONE HUNDRED TWENTY-SEVEN –

The grand duke never saw Isabelle coming.

After she and Ella had escaped, he'd ridden to Cafard's camp to order search parties out after them; then he'd returned to Volkmar's camp, where he'd spent the rest of the night. He'd been in his tent, shaving in front of his mirror, as Isabelle had been fanning her forces out along the edge of the Devil's Hollow.

He'd been buttoning his jacket as she took her place at the head of them.

He was sitting at a campaign table, slathering butter on a slice of toast, as she and her fighters descended.

Shouts and screams brought him to his feet. He heard gunshots. Horses whinnying. A jet of blood spattering across the wall of his tent. The wet *thuk* of a blade being driven home.

He grabbed his scabbard, buckled it around his waist, and ran out into the fray. The camp was in chaos. Isabelle's soldiers were swarming through it, savaging Volkmar's troops.

"My horse! Bring me my horse!" he bellowed, but no one answered his command. Men were falling all around him. The air was filled with the white smoke of gunpowder. The grand duke's hand went to the hilt of his sword, but he never got a chance to draw it. His last sight was of a girl on a black stallion, an avenging fury bearing down on him. And then Isabelle drove her blade into his chest, straight through his treacherous heart.

He fell to his knees, a crimson stain blooming across his jacket, an expression of surprise on his face. Then he toppled forward into the dirt.

Isabelle did not stop to exult, for she took no pleasure in killing, but rode on determined to do more of it. Soldier after soldier fell under her slashing sword. Her men swirled through the camp like a raging, flood-swollen river, some fighting with swords, others with bayoneted rifles. They set fire to tents, destroyed paddocks, freed horses, smashed wagons.

Though they'd been surprised, Volkmar's men quickly rallied. They were formidable soldiers who were fighting for their lives, and they put up a strong counterattack. But Isabelle was fighting for the lives of her countrymen and she fought like a lion, urging Nero on, deeper and deeper into the camp.

She'd just run her sword through an officer who'd been aiming his rifle at one of her lieutenants when she heard hooves behind her. Turning in her saddle, she saw a rider bearing down on her. He wore the uniform of the invaders. There was a sword in his hand and murder in his eyes.

*Someone's just walked over your grave*, whispered Adélie's voice.

Had he?

Here, in the Devil's Hollow, she would finally find out.

Isabelle whirled Nero around.

Came face-to-face with Volkmar.

And let the wolf run free.

## – ONE HUNDRED TWENTY-EIGHT –

Blue sparks flew into the air as the two swords clashed.

Volkmar was bigger, he was stronger, but Isabelle was nimble. She parried his blows with her blade, blocked them with her shield.

On and on they fought, their horses churning the dirt around them, their shouts and grunts and oaths mingling with those of their soldiers. Volkmar hammered against Isabelle's shield, making her left arm shudder. He had run out of his tent without armor. Isabelle deftly thrust her sword at his unprotected head, opening a gash in his cheek, but neither was able to deliver a killing blow.

Then Volkmar reversed direction and swung his sword at Isabelle's back, catching her with the flat of his blade. The force of the blow sent her sprawling out of her saddle to the ground. The impact knocked her helmet off, but she managed to hold on to her sword.

Volkmar jumped down from his mount and advanced on her. Dazed by her fall, Isabelle didn't see him coming. But as he raised his sword, one of Isabelle's soldiers, fighting only a few feet away, shouted a warning.

The blade slashed through the air. Isabelle rolled to her right, trying to get out of its way, but its tip bit into her left calf. She screamed and scrabbled backward across the ground with her good leg.

Volkmar ran at her and kicked her in the side, behind her chestplate. There was a crunch of bone. Blinding pain. She fell onto her other side, gasping, her sword underneath her.

"Get up, you little bitch. Stand up like the man you think you are and face your death."

Isabelle tried to get up. She struggled to her knees. Volkmar back-handed her savagely across the face, knocking her to the ground again.

Isabelle's entire body was made of pain. She struggled to see through its red fog. Volkmar was nearby, circling, playing with her before he killed her.

"Pick up your sword! Come at me!" Volkmar shouted at her.

Spitting out a mouthful of blood, Isabelle raised her eyes to his. He was holding his own sword across his body to protect his gut. She knew that her only chance was to somehow get to her feet, then get him to lower his blade.

*But how?* she wondered.

*Appear weak when you are strong, and strong when you are weak*, came the answer.

"Thank you, Sun Tzu," she whispered.

"Please," she begged Volkmar. "Don't kill me."

Her enemy smiled at the fear in her eyes, at the pain in her voice. "Oh, I *will* kill you. But not just yet," he said.

His arm relaxed slightly; his blade dipped a little.

With effort, Isabelle pushed herself to her feet, then tried to hobble away, dragging her wounded leg behind her.

Volkmar circled, taunting her. He'd already counted her among his kills. He had no idea that she had fallen off horses a thousand times and knew how to bury her pain. He did not know about the duels she'd fought under the linden tree as a child. How she'd practiced with scarecrows at the LeBenêts'. How she'd learned to parry and thrust, to feint, fall back, then strike. He could not see that she was feinting now. Her wound was bleeding badly, but it was not deep. The kick he'd delivered to her rib cage hurt like hell, but she had not lost her breath, her will, or her courage.

Panting, grimacing, one hand pressed to her side for effect, Isabelle stood, her head bent in supplication. She was leaning on her sword, using it as a crutch. Making it look as if she was helpless, her weapon useless.

Though her gaze was down, she could see Volkmar's feet and his sword. The tip was only an inch or so above the ground now. He walked toward her.

*Closer*, she urged him. *Just a little bit closer . . .*

"You're a good fighter, I'll admit. For a girl," Volkmar said, only a few feet away now. "But you're too rash to be a great fighter. You have more courage than common sense."

*Closer . . . that's it . . .*

"The grand duke told me about you. And how you maimed yourself to marry the prince." He chuckled. "I'll bet you surprised *him*. I saw you kill him. It was a lucky thrust, of course. But still. I'm sure he never expected to see you back here, and at the head of an army, no less. He never expected much at all from a plain girl pathetic enough to cut off her own toes."

*Closer . . .*

Isabelle tightened her grip on her sword. She took a deep, steadying breath, then slowly raised her head.

"No, of course not. Why would he? Why would you?" she asked. "But I don't cut off toes anymore . . ."

And then, with an earsplitting cry, she swung her blade high and sliced cleanly through Volkmar's neck.

"I cut off heads."

The door to Isabelle's carriage opened.

She stepped out and strode purposefully up the sweeping marble stairs that led up to the palace's tall, gold-washed doors. Soldiers lined both sides of the stairs. They snapped her a salute; she returned it.

This was a special day. Isabelle could barely contain her excitement.

Two footmen opened the doors for her, another ushered her inside. The grand foyer, all marble and mirrors, was illuminated by a thousand candles flickering in crystal chandeliers. As she walked through it, she thought about the first time she had come to the palace—with Tavi and Maman for the prince's ball.

Her heart clenched as she recalled how they'd left Ella at home, sobbing in the kitchen. Isabelle had been wearing a stiff silk gown then—trimmed with glass beads, festooned with lace. Her hair had been piled up on her head in an absurd bird's nest of a style. As she'd entered the palace, she'd caught a glimpse of herself in a mirror—and had hated the girl who'd looked back at her.

She passed that same mirror now and stopped, just for a few seconds, to look at her reflection. A different girl gazed back now—one whose bearing was confident, who stood with her head high. This girl wore her hair in a simple braid. She was dressed in a close-cut high-necked jacket of navy twill, and a long, matching split skirt that allowed her to ride with ease. Shiny black leather boots peeked out from its hem.

Underneath her uniform, a white bandage was wound tightly around her torso to help with the pain from the ribs Volkmar had broken when he'd kicked her. A line of stitches ran down the outside of her left calf where he'd opened a jagged gash with his sword. The wound was healing nicely. A field surgeon had stitched it closed after the Battle of Devil's Hollow.

That fight had been bloody and long, but Isabelle had won it. She and her forces had descended on Saint-Michel next, where they'd removed Colonel Cafard as commander and locked him up. Then she'd headed for the king's encampment.

She'd had the map showing the whereabouts of the rest of Volkmar's troops. She'd attacked them one after the other, winning three more battles before she even reached the king. Once she'd arrived at the king's camp, she'd explained who she was and why she'd come, and then she'd given the king Volkmar's map, and his own—as proof of the grand duke's treachery. Together they'd routed the rest of the invaders.

Tanaquill's magic was strong. It hadn't ended at midnight like the enchantment she'd made for Ella but had faded slowly. After each battle, when it came time for the dead to be collected and buried, none could be found. None of Isabelle's soldiers, that is. Those whose task it was to comb the fields after the fighting found only the bodies of Volkmar's troops, and sometimes, strangely, a small carved wooden figure tangled in the grass.

The blackbriar wall had sunk back into the river after the Battle of Devil's Hollow. Isabelle had returned to the linden tree, knelt down, and tucked a medal that she'd been given for valor into the hollow.

"For you," she had said, bowing her head. "Thank you."

A footman, hovering at Isabelle's elbow, cleared his throat now, pulling her out of her memories. "General, the king and queen are waiting in the Grand Hall," he informed her.

Isabelle nodded and followed him. He led her down a long corridor, to a pair of gilded doors. Giving them a mighty push, he entered the palace's Grand Hall and announced Isabelle's name.

At the far end of the hall, seated on golden thrones, were King Charles and Queen Ella. Lining both sides of the room, three rows deep, were the noble heads of France, dozens of courtiers, ministers, officials, and friends.

As Isabelle proceeded down the center of the room toward the royal couple, she saw Hugo and his new wife, Odette. Tavi was there, in her scholar's robes. At the queen's urging, the king had decreed that all the universities and colleges in the land must admit female scholars. Maman stood next to her, beaming at this duke and that countess. She had apologized to Ella, they had reconciled, and she now spent her days in the palace gardens, talking to royal cabbage heads.

Felix was there, too, and Isabelle's heart danced when she saw him, dressed up in a new jacket. The man to whom he'd sold the wooden soldiers demanded that Felix return his money, but the king had been so grateful to Felix for making the army that had saved France, that he paid the man back himself and gave Felix a scholarship to Paris's finest art school. Felix was busy every day learning how to sculpt stone, but he made time to ride with Isabelle every evening in the king's own forest.

Isabelle had reached the king and queen now. She stopped a few feet away from them, bowed her head, and knelt.

The king rose. A gloved servant stood nearby holding a gleaming ebony box. He opened it, revealing a heavy golden chain of office nestled in black velvet. The king lifted the chain out of the box, walked to Isabelle, and put it over her head. He settled it on her shoulders, then bade her rise and turn to face his court.

"Lords and ladies, citizens of France, we are all here today because of the courage and strength of this young woman. I can never repay her for all that she's done. And I will never part with her. I have come to rely upon her wise counsel. Her bravery and strength inspire me with hope as we move from the destruction of war to the golden days of peace. I have made sure she will always be by my side. At meetings of my nobles and ministers, and, should it ever come to it again, on the battlefield." The king smiled at Isabelle, then said, "Good people, I give you France's bravest warrior . . . and my new grand duchess."

The applause was deafening. Shouts and cheers echoed off the high stone walls.

Isabelle's heart beat strongly—with joy, with gratitude, with pride—as she looked at the faces of all the ones she loved.

Ella joined Isabelle and the king, and together they walked down the steps to greet the court. Well-wishers mobbed Isabelle. Family and friends hugged and kissed her. Nobles wanted to hear her recount her battles. Ministers asked for her thoughts on the state of fortifications along the border.

The attention was dizzying. She stepped back for a moment to ask a servant for a drink. As she did, she saw another face in the crowd. And for an instant, it felt as if time had stopped and the king and queen, and everyone in their court, had been frozen in place.

The Marquis de la Chance smiled. He was tossing a gold coin in the air. He flipped it at her. She caught it. Then he doffed his hat and disappeared into the press of people.

Isabelle watched him go, clutching the coin tightly in her hand.

She never saw him again.

She never forgot the day she'd met him, or how his friends had told her to want to be more than pretty. She never forgot Elizabeth, Yennenga, Abhaya Rani. She wore his gold coin on a chain around her neck until the day she died. But the thing she treasured most was the memory of his smile, a smile that was a wink and a dare. A wild road on a windy night. A kiss in the dark.

A smile that had given her all she'd ever wanted—a chance.

A chance to be herself.

# EPILOGUE

The boom of the large brass knocker, so rarely used, echoed ominously throughout the ancient palazzo.

The mother looked up from her work. Candlelight played over her face. "Are we expecting visitors?" she asked.

"Who is it?" the crone barked at a servant.

The servant scuttled to the map room's huge double doors and opened them, then he hurried down several flights of stairs to the street doors.

A man was standing on the threshold, dressed in a brown velvet frock-coat. His long black braids hung down his back. A large satchel was slung over one shoulder. A monkey was perched on the other. The servant gave the man a dark look, but he ushered him inside and led him upstairs.

"You had to bring your blasted monkey," the crone said, as the man walked into the map room.

"Nelson's very well behaved," Chance said.

"You have an odd idea of good behavior," the crone commented. "What can I do for you?"

Chance pressed a hand to his chest, feigning offense. "*Do* for me? I've come only to enjoy the pleasure of your company, not to beg favors," he said.

The crone gave him a skeptical look. "Our contest ended in a draw. I do not have to give you any maps."

"And I am still allowed to visit my three favorite ladies in their beautiful palazzo," Chance said, flashing a charming smile.

"If I allow you to stay, you must promise that you will not steal any more maps."

Chance solemnly held up his right hand. "I promise," he said.

The crone waved him inside and bade him sit down at the long work-table. The servant was sent to fetch refreshments. Other servants, cloaked and hooded, moved silently down the long rows of shelves that contained the Fates' maps.

Chance put his satchel on the floor and sat. He turned to the little monkey and patted him. "Hop down, Nelson," he said. "Stretch your legs."

"Don't let him go far," the crone warned.

"He won't. He'll just play around my feet," Chance assured her.

The servant reappeared with a bottle of port, four glasses, and a tray of fine cheeses. When everyone had been served, the crone asked, "To what do we owe the honor of your visit?"

"Truth be told—"

"I doubt it will be," said the maiden.

"—I felt bad about my last visit. It was a bit rushed. I left so abruptly."

"Thieves usually do," the crone said.

"I wanted to make amends, so I brought some gifts," Chance finished.

"I believe that's what the Trojans said to the Greeks," the mother observed.

Chance bent down and opened his satchel. One by one, he pulled presents out of it. "Pearls from Japan," he said, handing a small suede sack to the maiden. "Silk from India." He gave a bolt of shimmering crimson cloth to the mother. "And for you"—he handed the crone a velvet-covered box—"black opals from Brazil."

"These are generous gifts, thank you," said the crone. Then she gave him a knowing smile. "I still say you want something in return."

"No. Nothing," Chance said innocently. He smiled, waited a few beats, then said, "Well, perhaps *one* small thing . . ."

He dipped into his bag again and placed three small bottles on the table.

"Here are some inks I made especially for you," he said. "Perhaps you could try them out. That's all I ask. Here's *Moxie* . . ." He pulled out a bottle containing an ink the shimmering teal blue of a peacock's tail. "This one's *Guts*." That one was a fleshy, intestinal pink. "And my favorite, *Defiance*." He held that up to the light. It flared red and orange in the bottle, like liquid fire.

The crone gave the inks a dismissive wave. The mother eyed them suspiciously. But the maiden picked up *Defiance*, swirled it in the bottle, and smiled.

As she did, a noise was heard from deep within the towering rows of shelves. A sound like an entire shelf of maps falling to the floor.

The crone's eyes narrowed. "Where's that monkey?" she demanded.

"He's right here," Chance said, bending down to the floor. He picked up the little capuchin, who'd been sitting by his satchel, and placed him on the table. The monkey looked at the crone. He blew her a kiss.

The crone's scowl deepened. A servant hurried to see what had caused the noise, then reported back that some maps had, indeed, fallen to the floor. He suggested that the shelf had been overloaded and assured the Fates that the problem was being fixed. The crone nodded; her scowl relaxed back into a frown.

Chance drained his glass, thanked the Fates for their hospitality, then he said he must be going. He cinched his bag and picked it up. Nelson jumped onto his shoulder.

The crone accompanied him to the map room's doors. As they said their good-byes, she suddenly took hold of his arm. With something almost like pity in her voice, she said, "The girl—Isabelle—she was an exception. Do not ask more of mortals than they can give."

"You are wrong. They have so much to give. Each and every one of them. More, sometimes, than they know."

Fate released his arm. "You are a fool, my friend."

Chance nodded. "Perhaps, but I am happy."

"In this world, only a fool could be."

A servant led him out of the map room and back down the stairs to the street. Chance stepped outside, then turned to thank the servant, but he was gone. The doors were already locked behind him.

Chance tilted his face to the dark sky, happy to see the stars and the moon, happy to be out of the gloomy palazzo. Nelson, still on his shoulder, pointed to a group of colorfully dressed people who were loitering nearby, in the glow of a street lantern. Chance hurried across to them.

"Well?" said the magician, raising an eyebrow.

"She made me promise I wouldn't steal anything," Chance said. "I honored it."

The magician's face fell. So did everyone else's.

Then Chance opened his satchel. Three monkeys jumped out, chattering gleefully. Nelson chattered back.

"She didn't make *them* promise, though," Chance said, cracking his rogue's smile.

He opened the bag wide so his friends could see inside it. Nestled on the bottom, slightly squashed by the monkeys, were a dozen rolled maps.

Laughing, Chance took the magician's arm; then they and their friends ran down the sidewalk into the ancient city, into the crowd, into the beautiful, sparkling, full-of-possibilities night.

# AUTHOR'S NOTE

When I was little, I had a Golden Book version of *Cinderella* that I loved.

But not because of Cinderella.

I liked Cinderella and felt sorry for her, but I didn't identify with her. She was nothing like me. She was always good. I wasn't. She had dainty feet. I didn't. No matter how bad her life got, she kept smiling. She smiled with a tray in each hand and one on her head. She smiled when she cooked and cleaned. She was still smiling on the last page of the book, when she married the prince—a guy who looked older than my dad. This I did not understand.

I did understand her ugly stepsisters, though. And they were the characters that fascinated me. Like me, they were gawky, awkward, and lacking in the self-control department. They were selfish and impatient. They wanted things they weren't supposed to want.

I remember my grandmother reading that story to me and knowing that Cinderella would prevail.

She had to. After all, the stepsisters were ugly.

And Cinderella was beautiful.

And even five-year-olds know that beauty *always* wins.

Decades have passed since I first learned that the way for girls to survive in this world is to be pretty, good, and compliant. But I've never stopped wondering how it had gone for the stepsisters, for two girls who weren't any of those things. I always hoped that one day, they might tell me.

Eventually, one of them did, and her story became the book you're holding. Isabelle isn't pretty, good, or compliant. Spending time with her got me thinking about the notion of beauty and who gets to define it. I saw how all too often, we believe what others tell us we are. We let their words define us. We take the poison apple they offer us and bite right into it.

Writing Isabelle's story reminded me that beauty is more than someone else's assessment of us. It's the passion that burns inside of us. It's our strength and courage.

Isabelle showed me that there's a way to refuse that poison apple. A way for us to fight the tyranny of Likes and Follows and Rates. A way to stop letting magazines, movies, and social media tell us who's beautiful, a way to start defining beauty for ourselves, and most important, a way to find beauty *in* ourselves.

I hope you enjoy getting to know Isabelle as much as I have.

# ACKNOWLEDGMENTS

*Stepsister* is a story I've wanted to tell for years. That I finally get to is because of many wonderful people and I can never thank them enough, but I'm going to try anyway.

Thank you to Mallory Kass, my awesome editor, for her intelligence, huge heart, sense of humor, and affection for ugly stepsisters, balky horses, high-strung authors, and other difficult creatures. Isabelle and I are so lucky to have our very own Tanaquill in you—minus the sharp teeth and talons!

A huge, heartfelt thank you to Dick Robinson, Ellie Berger, David Levithan, Tracy van Straaten, Lori Benton, Rachel Feld, Lizette Serrano, Lauren Donovan, Alan Smagler and his team, Melissa Schirmer, Amanda Maciel, Maeve Norton, Elizabeth Parisi, and the rest of my Scholastic family for your incredible enthusiasm for *Stepsister*, and for your lovely welcome to my new home. It means the world to me.

Thank you to Graham Taylor and Negeen Yazdi at Endeavor Content, Bruna Papandrea at Made Up Stories, and Lynette Howell Taylor at 51 Entertainment, for working to bring *Stepsister* to film. I am so proud to be partnering with all of you, and so excited for what's to come. A huge thank you to film agent Sylvie Rabineau at WME, and Ken Kleinberg and Alex Plitt at Kleinberg Lange Cuddy & Carlo LLP, for your excellent counsel and guidance.

Thank you to my wonderful agent, Steve Malk at Writers House, for believing in *Stepsister*, and all my stories, and me. "Wherever you go, go with all your heart," Confucius tells us. I get to tell stories, to follow my heart every day, because I have Steve as my traveling companion on the writer's journey. Thank you, too, to my foreign rights agent, the amazing Cecilia de la Campa, for bringing *Stepsister* to readers across the world.

Thank you to my lovely family—Doug, Daisy, Wilfriede, and Megan—for reading early versions of the story and giving me valuable feedback and encouragement. An extra thank you to Doug for the cool tagline. Thanks most of all for putting up with me, guys. You teach me every day what real beauty is all about.

Thank you to illustrator Retta Scott for the Big Golden Book's *Cinderella*. Thank you to my grandmother Mary for reading it to me five million times. Thank you to Pablo Picasso. His saying *I am always doing things I cannot do, that's how I get to do them*, inspired a similar remark from the Marquis de la Chance when he first meets Isabelle, and has always inspired me.

Thank you to the fairy godparents—the countless generations of storytellers who told the ancient tales to sleepy-eyed children gathered around the fire at night, and to the collectors like Jakob and Wilhelm Grimm who preserved them in writing. Because of these elders, the old stories endured, as vital and relevant today as they were centuries ago.

Fairy tales were so important to me as a child. They were entertaining, instructive, and inspiring, but more importantly, they were truthful.

The world conspires in a thousand ways to tell us that we're not enough, that we're less than, that life's one big, long party on the beach and we're not invited. Dark woods? What dark woods? Wolves? What wolves? Don't worry about them. Just buy this, eat that, wear those, and you'll be on the invite list. You'll be cool. Hot. Liked. Loved. Happy.

Fairy tales give it to us straight. They tell us something profound and essential—that the woods are real, and dark, and full of wolves. That we will, at times, find ourselves hopelessly lost in them. But these tales also tell us that we are all we need, that we have all we need—guts, smarts, and maybe a pocketful of breadcrumbs—to find our way home.

And last, but never least, a huge thank you to *you*, dear reader. You are everything I wished for.

Keep reading for a sneak peek at the
next stunning fairy-tale retelling by

# JENNIFER DONNELLY

Once upon long ago, always and ever more, a girl rode into the Darkwood.

Her lips were the color of ripe cherries, her skin as soft as new-fallen snow, her hair as dark as midnight.

The tall pines whispered and sighed as she passed under them, the queen's huntsman at her side. Crows, perched high in their branches, blinked their bright black eyes.

As the sky lightened, the huntsman pointed to a pond ahead and told the girl that they must dismount to let the horses drink. She did so, walking with him at the edge of the water. Lost in her thoughts, she did not hear the soft hiss of a dagger leaving its sheath. She did not see the huntsman lift his face to the dawn or glimpse the anguish in his eyes.

A gasp of shock escaped the girl as the huntsman pulled her close, his broad hand spanning her narrow back. Her eyes, wide and questioning, sought his. She was not afraid; not yet. She felt almost nothing as he slid the blade between her ribs, just a slight, soft push, and then a bloom of warmth, as if she'd spilled tea down her dress.

But then the pain came, red clawed and snarling.

The girl threw her head back and screamed. A stag bolted from the brush at the sound. The crows burst from their roost, their wings beating madly.

The huntsman was skilled. He was quick. He had gutted a thousand deer. A few expert cuts with a knife so sharp it could slice blue from the sky, and the delicate ribs were cleaved, the flesh and veins severed.

The girl's head lolled back. Her legs gave out. Gently, the huntsman lowered her to the ground, then knelt beside her.

"Forgive me, dear princess. Forgive me," he begged. "This foul deed was not my wish, but the queen's command."

*"Why?"* the girl cried, with her dying breath.

But the huntsman, tears in his eyes, could not speak. He finished his grim task and got to his feet. As he did, the girl got her answer. For the last thing she saw before her eyes closed was her heart, small and perfect, in the huntsman's trembling hands.

⟨⟨⟩⟩

In the forest, the birds have gone silent. The creatures are still. Gloom lingers under the trees. And on the cold ground, a girl lies dying, a ragged red hole where her heart used to be.

"Hang the huntsman!" you shout. "Burn the evil queen!" And who would fault you?

But you've missed the real villain.

It's easily done. He's stealthy and sly and comes when you're alone. He stands in the shadows and whispers his poison. His words drip, drip, drip into the small, secret chambers of your heart.

You think you know this tale, but you only know what you've been told.

"Who are you? How do you know these things?" you ask.

Fair questions, both.

I am the huntsman. Dead now, but that's no matter. The dead speak. With tongues blackened by time and regret. You can hear us if you listen.

You will say that I'm telling you tales. Fairy stories. That it's all make-believe. But there are more things afoot in the Darkwood than you can imagine, and only a fool would call them make-believe.

Keep to the path, the old wives say. Stay out of the forest.

But one day, you will have to walk deep into those dark woods and find what's waiting there.

For if you do not, it will surely find you.

## ONE

*The day before . . .*

"Tally ho!" shouted the queen, spurring her fierce courser on.

The hounds had flushed their quarry. A gray wolf broke from the cover of a blackbriar patch and ran for the deep woods. The pack swept after it, baying for blood.

The bravest members of the hunting party followed close on the queen's heels, but the princess, bolder than any of them, streaked ahead on a white palfrey. She galloped after the wolf, weaving in and out of trees at breakneck speed, her skirts billowing out behind her. She jumped a stone wall, a wide stream, a tangle of brush so high, there was no telling what lay beyond it. Her hat came off, and her black hair unfurled behind her like ribbons of night.

The queen couldn't catch her. Nor could the princes, Haakon and Rodrigo, expert riders both. I saw them flashing through the woods, the queen in white, her nobles in rich hues of russet, moss, ochre, and indigo. I saw a baron crouched low over his horse's neck, his weight in his stirrups, his hands high up in the animal's mane. He narrowed the distance between himself and the queen, but then his horse stumbled. The baron lost his balance; there was a sickening crack as he hit the ground.

"Leave him, huntsman!" the queen shouted. "Leave anyone who falls!"

The man lay crumpled under a tree, his eyes closed, his head bloodied. I thundered past him; the rest of the riders did, too. Only the princess cast a look back at him, but she did not stop.

We trailed the hounds, navigating by their cries, swerving through the woods as they changed direction. The queen outpaced me as we charged down into a hollow. I lost sight of her as she disappeared in a pocket of mist.

Some moments later, I found the pack. They'd surrounded the wolf. The creature was huge and fearsome. It had killed two of the dogs. Their broken bodies lay nearby. The princess was there already, as well as the queen.

And him? Oh, yes. He was there, too.

He was always close by. Watching. Waiting.

I heard him in the wolf's low growl. Felt him in the nervous stamping of the horses. I saw him rise from the depths of the princess's eyes, like a corpse in a river.

Without warning, the wolf charged, snarling. The princess's horse whinnied and reared, but the princess kept her seat.

The queen jumped down from her saddle. She circled the fray, shouting at the hounds, exhorting them to attack. Three did. The wolf rounded on them, driving them off, but it was one against many; the hounds knew it and grew bold. But one, small and slight, hung back from the pack.

The queen saw it; her eyes darkened. "Fight, you damned coward!" she shouted.

The hound tucked its tail between its legs and backed away. Furious, the queen snatched a whip out of a groom's hands, but the dog darted out of reach. The queen started after it.

"Your Grace! The wolf is escaping!"

It was Prince Haakon. He'd caught up to the pack. The queen threw the whip down and ran back to her horse, but by the time she'd swung up into her saddle, the pack, and the princess, were already gone, in hot pursuit once more. The queen and Haakon set off after them.

For a long and treacherous mile, the princess pursued the wolf, over rocky fields and crumbling shale hills, until a ravine brought them up short. She stopped her horse a few yards before the edge, but the wolf ran right up to it. The sides were sheer, the chasm deep. The wolf turned and tried to backtrack, but the hounds closed in from the left.

A wall of blackbriar a good ten feet high ran from the woods to the edge of the ravine, blocking any hope of escape on the right. The desperate animal paced back and forth, tensed itself to jump across the ravine, but saw that it was hopeless.

The princess was so close to the wolf now, she could see the creature's silvery eyes, the scruff of white at her throat, the ragged edge of one ear. As the hounds pressed in, the princess glanced over her shoulder, searching the woods for the other riders, but they were far behind her. In a heartbeat, she was out of her saddle, one hand holding her reins. Striding among the slavering hounds, she drove them back, using her horse as a barrier, yelling at them, stamping at them, until she'd created an opening for the wolf.

"Go! Get out of here!" she shouted at the creature.

The wolf bolted for the blackbriar. Its long thorns were curved and cruel; they carved stripes in her snout and tore at her ears, but she pushed through the dense vines and disappeared. The hounds rushed after her, but their snouts were tender, their hides thin, and they could not penetrate the dense canes.

The princess thought she was alone; she thought that no one saw this, but I did. I had caught up to her, but stayed hidden. I hunted many things for the queen, not all of them wolves.

I saw the princess lean her head into her horse's lathered neck. I saw a weariness, heavy and deep, settle on her slender shoulders like a long, dark cloak. I saw her press a hand to her chest, as if to soothe a fierce ache under her ribs.

How it cost her, this charade of strength. How it would cost us all.

Hoof beats sounded in the distance. Shouts echoed. By the time the queen drew up, with Haakon and a few other riders, the princess's back was straight again, her weariness buried, a rueful smile pasted on her lips.

"I'm afraid our sport is over, stepmother," she said regretfully, nodding at the ravine. "The wolf chose a quicker death."

The queen rode to the very edge of the ravine and looked over it, frowning. "What a pity," she said, "that we are robbed of our kill."

Her eyes traveled to the hounds, then over the blackbriar. Her gaze sharpened. The princess did not see what had caught the queen's attention—she was climbing back into her saddle—but I did. There was a tuft of fur caught on a thorn. Gray fur. Wolf's fur.

Anger, cold and lethal, hardened the queen's frown. "Blow for home, huntsman!" she commanded.

I sounded a call on my trumpet, and the hounds set off, noses skimming the ground. The small, frightened one, her tail still between her legs, skittered along at the edge of the pack. The riders followed, chatting and laughing.

As the hoof beats faded from the clearing, there was a dry, rustling sound, like the whispering of silk skirts. I looked up and saw a crow, blue black and shrewd, drop down from the high branch where he'd perched.

He let out a shrill caw, then flew off into the Darkwood.

I hear his call still, echoing down the centuries.

It sounded like a warning.

It sounded like a death knell.

It sounded, most of all, like laughter.

- T W O -

There was blood on the reins.

Sophie saw it in the split second before she handed her horse to a groom.

She turned her palms up. Four thin crimson crescents lay across each one, gouged by her own fingernails. The horse she'd ridden was fast, and so high-strung, it had taken all her strength to control him. Terror had flooded through her veins as she'd galloped through the woods, certain she would fall and break her neck at any second.

But that wasn't the reason for the cuts in her palm, and she knew it. Her legs were still trembling even now, even though the hunt was over.

"Stupid, stupid, girl," she hissed, furious with herself.

What if the queen had somehow seen her let the wolf go? Or if someone else had? Her stepmother had eyes and ears everywhere, and as Sophie well knew, it was unwise to risk her ire.

Quickly, she pulled her gloves from her jacket pocket and slipped them on. The bold, fearless girl who could outride the princes, the huntsman, even the queen herself—the heartless girl who was keen to chase an animal down just to watch a pack of hounds kill it—that girl was a lie. The cuts were the truth, written in blood, and no one must ever read it. Rulers were ruthless. They did not show weakness or fear. They did not cry. They made others cry. Hadn't her stepmother told her that a thousand times?

She glanced around for her stepmother and her retinue, but the queen had not yet ridden in. *Good*, Sophie thought. The hunt itself, the small talk made during the ride back, the constant pressure to be witty and arch—it had all exhausted her. She wanted nothing more than to slip away to her chambers unnoticed, get out of her sweaty clothing, and sink into a hot bath.

Servants had set out a long, linen-draped table in the cobbled courtyard that was shared by the stables and kennels. It was laden with pies of rabbit and venison. There were roasted chickens, braised pheasants, smoked hams, cheeses, nuts, and fruit.

Sophie made her way past the table, head down, hoping to go unnoticed.

"Hail, bold Artemis, goddess of the hunt!" a voice bellowed from across the courtyard.

She looked up. It was Rodrigo. He was making his way to her, with Haakon in tow. She would not get away now. Her heart sank to her boots, but she smiled brightly. At Rodrigo, his full lips curved into a seductive smile, his dark eyes full of promises. And at Haakon, golden haired and bronzed, with a face like a marble god.

She had no choice but to smile. One of them might well become her husband.

The morning's hunt was the first in a series of events over the next few days to celebrate her birthday. There would be a ball tonight as well, a glittering affair with members of her stepmother's court and rulers from all the foreign realms in attendance. She would turn seventeen tomorrow and become an adult in the eyes of the law. She could marry, and that was the real purpose of the celebrations—to find her a husband. Her stepmother was determined to make Sophie an advantageous match with a powerful man.

"The young prince of Skandinay, perhaps," the queen had said, when she'd first raised the topic with Sophie. "Or the emperor's son. Maybe even the emperor himself . . . Now, *that* would be a coup . . ."

"But stepmother, I don't even know these men. What if I don't fall in love with any of them?" Sophie had asked.

"*Love?*" the queen had said contemptuously. "Love is nothing but a fable, a dangerous one. Your suitors should recite to you the size of their armies, the strength of their fortresses, and the qualities of their warhorses, not silly poems about flowers and doves."

Sophie knew why her stepmother wanted a powerful husband for her; the queen thought her weak. And she was not the only one. Sophie had grown up hearing the whispers. She knew what everyone at court thought about her. She remembered how they'd mocked her for being a shy, softhearted child.

Over the years, their words had lodged in her heart like blackbriar thorns. She heard them still, echoing inside her head . . . *she's not smart enough . . . not tough enough . . . not bold enough . . .*

Haakon traipsed over to Sophie now, dispelling the hard memories. He lifted the tankard of ale he was holding. "Fair Artemis has won my heart, but oh, cruel, selfish deity! She will not give me hers!"

Rodrigo, trailing behind him, snorted. "Can you blame her?"

"I pine. I languish. I *starve* for love," Haakon said, pressing a hand to his heart. Then he leaned over the breakfast table and tore a leg off a chicken. "I endure unending torment. Give me your heart, cold goddess, and end my suffering!"

"It's impossible, sir," Sophie said, with such a breezy smile, that no one would ever have guessed how desperately she longed for the quiet of her own room, or that she held herself there through sheer force of will.

"Why the devil not?" Haakon asked, gnawing the chicken leg. "Good looking lad like me . . . Why, I'm probably a god myself. I must be." He frowned, then nodded. "In fact, I'm sure of it. I'm the god . . . mmm . . . *Apollo*! Yes, that's the fellow. What a pair we would make, the two of us."

"If you recall your classics, and I'm certain that you do—" Sophie began.

"Scholar that you are," Rodrigo cut in.

"—then you know that Artemis swore she would never marry. And were she to break that vow, I doubt it would be for Apollo. Since he was her brother."

Haakon wrinkled his nose. "Ew."

"Very," said Rodrigo.

More riders trotted into the courtyard in a blur of chatter and clatter. Grooms and hounds followed them. Sophie thought she heard the lord commander among them and the queen barking orders. Haakon and Rodrigo turned to the party and waved some of the riders over. As they did, Sophie heard a smaller, softer sound than clopping hooves or Haakon's booming voice. She heard footsteps behind her, quick and shambling.

"Tom?" she said, turning around.

A young boy was running toward her. He was undersized for his age, awkward and shy.

"Be careful, Tom. Slow down before—" Sophie started to say. But it was too late. Tom caught the toe of his boot between two cobbles, stumbled, and fell. Sophie bent down to help him up.

"Clumsy ox," a voice said.

"Should've drowned him at birth. Isn't that what one does with runts?"

Tom winced. Sophie could see that the cruel remarks hurt him more than the fall he'd taken. The women who'd made them, two of the queen's ladies-in-waiting, laughed as they hurried by.

"Don't listen to them," Sophie quickly said, trying to make him feel better. "If you want to see clumsy, you should see Lady von Arnim"— she nodded at the shorter of the two women—"dance a sarabande. She looks like a donkey on ice!"

Tom laughed and Sophie smiled, but her smile faded as she saw the boy's skinned knees. "You mustn't run," she scolded. He was like the puppies he cared for, all loose limbs and big feet, and it was only when he rushed that he fell.

Tom brushed his bangs out of his eyes. "But I couldn't help it, your grace! I had to tell you!"

"Tell me what?" Sophie asked.

"Duchess had her puppies!"

Duchess was Sophie's favorite spaniel.

"She didn't!" Sophie said, her eyes widening with excitement.

"She did! Seven healthy pups! And all of them just as fat as sausages, with snub noses and pink feet! Come see them!"

Tom grew so excited that he forgot himself and reached for Sophie's hand. Sophie forgot herself and took it.

"What are you doing? Have you gone mad, boy? Don't put your hands on the princess!"

It was the lord commander, the man in charge of the queen's military. He strode up to Tom, grabbed his shoulder, and gave him a tooth-rattling shake. As he did, Sophie brusquely pulled her hand away. As if it was all Tom's doing.

She knew she could come to his defense. She should explain that they had both been carried away. But she did not. Holding hands with kennel boys, playing with puppies—this was not how a strong ruler behaved. Strong rulers were distant and aloof. If the queen heard of her lapse, she would not be pleased.

"It won't happen again, your grace," the lord commander said to Sophie. He turned to Tom again. "You remember your place, boy," he growled, giving him another shake before he released him and walked away.

The look of hurt and confusion in the boy's eyes twisted Sophie's heart.

"I-I'm sorry," he stammered.

"I didn't . . . I didn't mean to—"

His words were cut off by a horrible sound. It was a high, keening wail.

And it was coming from behind them.

– THREE –

The wretched creature had been backed into a corner.

It was a hound, and it was crying and cowering, trying to make itself as small as possible. Its face was turned toward the wall. Sophie recognized it. It was the small, skittish dog that had refused to attack the wolf.

The queen was pointing at it with her riding crop.

"That animal's worthless," she spat. "I want it killed."

Sophie stood frozen to the spot, silent. It was Tom who tried to stop the queen.

"No!" he cried, lurching toward the hound. "Please don't! She's a good dog!"

The queen whirled around, incensed. Her eyes sought the one who had dared to censure her. "Am I to be shouted at by a kennel boy?" she hissed. Her hand tightened on the crop.

Alistair, the kennel master and Tom's father, had come running from the dog pens, alarmed by the hound's cries. He saw what was coming. His eyes widened in fear. He grabbed Tom by the back of his shirt and pulled the boy to him just as the crop came whistling through the air. The blow missed the child, but caught Alistair across his face. It split his cheek open.

Sophie saw Alistair, heedless of his pain, heedless of the blood dripping from his jaw, beg for his son. "He's very sorry, your grace. He'll never do it again. Please forgive him. Apologize, Tom . . ."

"But Papa . . ."

*"Apologize!"* Alistair yelled, shaking him. *"Now!"*

It wasn't anger that made him shout at his boy. Sophie knew that. It was fear. The queen had carved a gully in Alistair's face, and he was a grown man. What would a blow like that have done to Tom's small body?

"I-I'm sorry, your grace," Tom stammered, looking at the ground.

"Attend to the rest of the hounds," the queen ordered.

Alistair let go of Tom. He drew a cloth from his pocket, pressed it to his cheek, then called the pack to him. The small dog stayed in the corner, hopeless, helpless. As if it knew it had been condemned.

"Come and see my new brood mare!" the queen said to a group of nobles.

As they headed to the stables, Tom made his way to Sophie.

"Don't let her be killed. Please, my lady," he begged, his voice breaking. "Her name's Zara. She was the runt of her litter. How can you kill a wolf if you're so small?"

"You can't, Tom," Sophie said, watching the queen head into the stables.

She remained rooted to the spot, astonished by her stepmother's cruelty.

*Why am I surprised?* Sophie asked herself. *I've seen enough examples of her cruelty. I should be used to it by now.*

But she wasn't. Sorrow corseted her chest so tightly she could barely breathe, but another emotion simmered underneath it now—*anger.* Anger at the injustice of her stepmother's actions. Anger that no one cared, that every single person in the courtyard went on eating and drinking, laughing and chattering, as if nothing had happened.

*No, you can't kill the wolf,* she thought, as the queen disappeared through the stable doors in a sweep of skirts, *but maybe you can outwit her.*

Tom had not moved. He was still standing by Sophie's side, his hands clenched.

"Go help your father," Sophie said to him.

Tom's shoulders slumped. Hope drained from his small face. "But my lady—"

"*Go.*"

Fear made her voice harsh. Allowing the wolf to escape was foolish. What she was about to do now was insanity.

As he moved off, Sophie glanced around. No one was paying

attention to her. The lord commander was cutting into a meat pie. Haakon was picking up a thick slice of ham with his fingers. Rodrigo was biting into a ripe peach. She walked to the far end of the courtyard, where the hound, her eyes closed, had slumped to the ground.

Sophie took a deep breath to shore up her nerve. She thought again of the harsh words she'd overheard others say about her.

*. . . She's not smart enough . . . or tough enough . . .*

Then she thought of Tom, shouting at the queen to spare the dog. He did not wear his courage as she did, as a mask to be slipped on and off. If a small boy could be brave, so could she.

"Zara, is it? You're a beauty," she said softly, as she approached the dog.

At the sound of her name, the hound was on her feet. Her eyes were huge and pleading.

"Shh, girl," Sophie said. "I'm not going to hurt you. No one is. Not if we're quick, you and I."

She hooked two fingers under Zara's collar and gently coaxed her away from the wall.

"Come on, girl . . . just a bit further . . . hurry now . . ."

Sophie led her across the courtyard. They reached a wooden gate a moment later. Sophie quickly unlatched it. "Go!" she whispered, as she opened it. "Run from here and never come back!"

The dog was off in a flash. Sophie's heart swelled as she saw a cream-colored blur streak across the fields and disappear into the woods. She latched the gate, then turned and glanced around again. All the members of the hunting party were still occupied with breakfast. No one had seen her. Sophie allowed herself to exhale. As she walked back across the courtyard, she passed by Tom. He was standing in the center, near the oak tree, turning around in a slow circle.

"My father says I'm to find Zara and bring her to him," he said dully, his spirit crushed. "Did you see where she went, your grace?"

Sophie affected a regretful expression. "The little hound?" she said. "I'm afraid she ran off, Tom. I opened the gate and I shouldn't have. I wasn't paying attention."

Tom smiled then. With his mouth, his face, his whole body. Sophie winked at him, then walked on, eager to finally get to her chambers.

It was then that she saw her stepmother.

The queen was standing in the open doorway of the stables, watching her. Dread's long, cold fingers closed around Sophie. How long had she been standing there? How much had she seen?

The queen's silence, cold and forbidding, silenced the chattering court. After a moment, she spoke.

"Cowardice is like a disease; it spreads. One sick individual can infect an entire population. The hound—the one I ordered to be put down, the one who appears to have escaped—that hound should have attacked when it was ordered to. What will happen next time, should the other hounds decide to do as they wish, not as they're told? I shall tell you: The *wolf* will attack, and your queen will die."

Sophie's dread turned to fear. But not for herself. "It was my fault the dog got out, your grace. I opened the gate," she quickly said.

"You are a princess of the realm, not a kennel-hand," the queen retorted. "The boy was negligent. He should have leashed the dog immediately." She paused, allowing her gaze to settle on Tom. "I order that every hound in the kennel is to be slaughtered, lest any have been infected with the disease of cowardice . . . And I order that this boy here, who coddles cowards, who places more value on a dog's life than the life of his queen . . . I order that he be taken to the guards' barracks, where he will receive ten lashes."

"No," Tom whispered, shaking his head. "*No*. Please. I'm sorry . . . I'm *sorry*!"

Sophie gasped. She wanted to shout at her, to beg her not to do this, but she knew she could do no such thing. So she watched, impotent and mute, as Tom backed away, stumbled, and fell again. Two guards picked him up, and half-marched, half-dragged him out of the courtyard.

"Papa! *Papa!*" he cried, reaching back for his father.

Alistair took a step toward him, but a burly guard blocked his way. He turned toward the queen, ready to beg her to spare his child, but she was already gone. There was nothing he could do except watch as the guards carried his boy off.

Sophie knew what the queen was doing. She wished to teach lessons.

Not to the boy. That was only a ruse. She wished to teach the powerful nobles who had accompanied her on the hunt that cowardice was dangerous, and disobedience even more so.

And she wished to teach Sophie a lesson, too.

And that lesson was perfectly clear: There is nothing more dangerous than kindness.